Scooby-Doo!™ Team-Up

Volume 1

Sholly Fisch Writer **Dario Brizuela** Artist **Franco Riesco** **Heroic Age** Colorists
Saida Temofonte **Deron Bennett** Letterers **Dario Brizuela** Cover Artist

Special thanks to **Leandro Corral**

Batman created by **Bob Kane**
Wonder Woman created by **William Moulton Marston**
Superman Created by **Jerry Siegel** and **Joe Shuster**.
By special arrangement with the **Jerry Siegel family**.
Supergirl based on the characters created by
Jerry Siegel and **Joe Shuster**.
By special arrangement with the **Jerry Siegel family**.

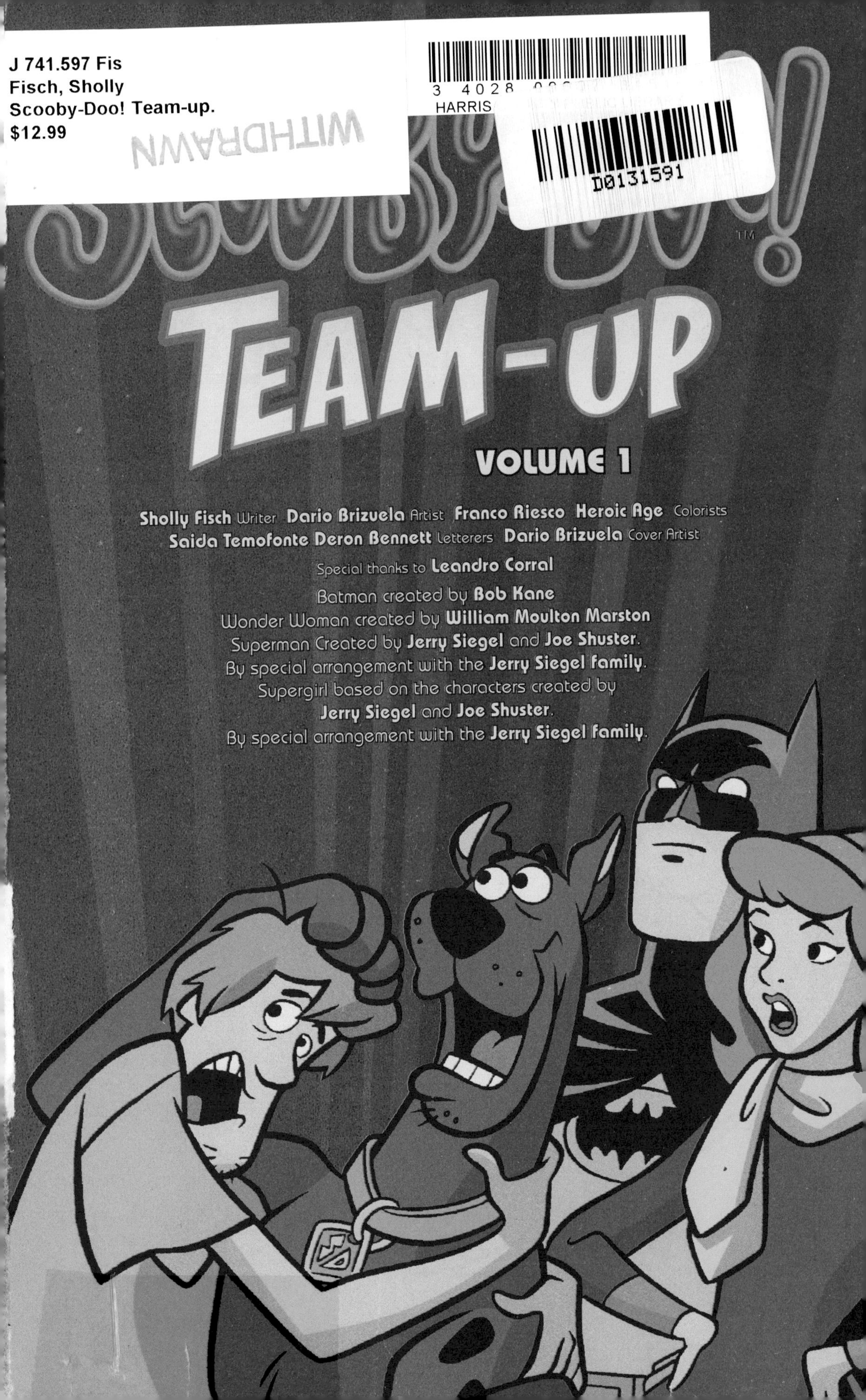

Kristy Quinn Editor – Original Series
Jessica Chen Assistant Editor – Original Series
Jeb Woodard Group Editor – Collected Editions
Liz Erickson Editor – Collected Edition
Robbin Brosterman Design Director – Books
Louis Prandi Publication Design

Bob Harras Senior VP – Editor-in-Chief, DC Comics

Diane Nelson President
Dan DiDio and **Jim Lee** Co-Publishers
Geoff Johns Chief Creative Officer
Amit Desai Senior VP – Marketing & Global Franchise
Management
Nairi Gardiner Senior VP – Finance
Sam Ades VP – Digital Marketing
Bobbie Chase VP – Talent Development
Mark Chiarello Senior VP – Art, Design & Collected Editions
John Cunningham VP – Content Strategy
Anne DePies VP – Strategy Planning & Reporting
Don Falletti VP – Manufacturing Operations
Lawrence Ganem VP – Editorial Administration & Talent
Relations
Alison Gill Senior VP – Manufacturing & Operations
Hank Kanalz Senior VP – Editorial Strategy & Administration
Jay Kogan VP – Legal Affairs
Derek Maddalena Senior VP – Sales & Business
Development
Dan Miron VP – Sales Planning & Trade Development
Nick Napolitano VP – Manufacturing Administration
Carol Roeder VP – Marketing
Eddie Scannell VP – Mass Account & Digital Sales
Susan Sheppard VP – Business Affairs
Courtney Simmons Senior VP – Publicity & Communications
Jim (Ski) Sokolowski VP – Comic Book Specialty &
Newsstand Sales

SCOOBY-DOO TEAM-UP VOLUME 1

Published by DC Comics. Compilation Copyright © 2015 Hanna-
Barbera and DC Comics. All Rights Reserved.

Originally published in single magazine form in SCOOBY-DOO
TEAM-UP 1-6 Copyright © 2014 Hanna-Barbera and DC Comics.
All Rights Reserved. Batman, Robin, Superman, Wonder Woman
and all related characters and elements are trademarks of
DC Comics. Scooby-Doo and all related characters and elements
are trademarks of and © Hanna-Barbera. The stories, characters
and incidents featured in this publication are entirely fictional.
DC Comics does not read or accept unsolicited ideas,
stories or artwork.

DC Comics, 4000 Warner Blvd., Burbank, CA 91522
A Warner Bros. Entertainment Company.
Printed by RR Donnelley, Owensville, MO. 8/12/15. Second
Printing.
ISBN: 978-1-4012-4946-5

Library of Congress Cataloging-in-Publication Data

Fisch, Sholly.
  Scooby-Doo team-up / Sholly Fisch, Dario Brizuela.
    pages cm
  ISBN 978-1-4012-4946-5 (paperback)
  1. Graphic novels. I. Brizuela, Dario, illustrator. II. Title.

PZ7.7.F57Sf 2014
741.5'973—dc23

2014027348

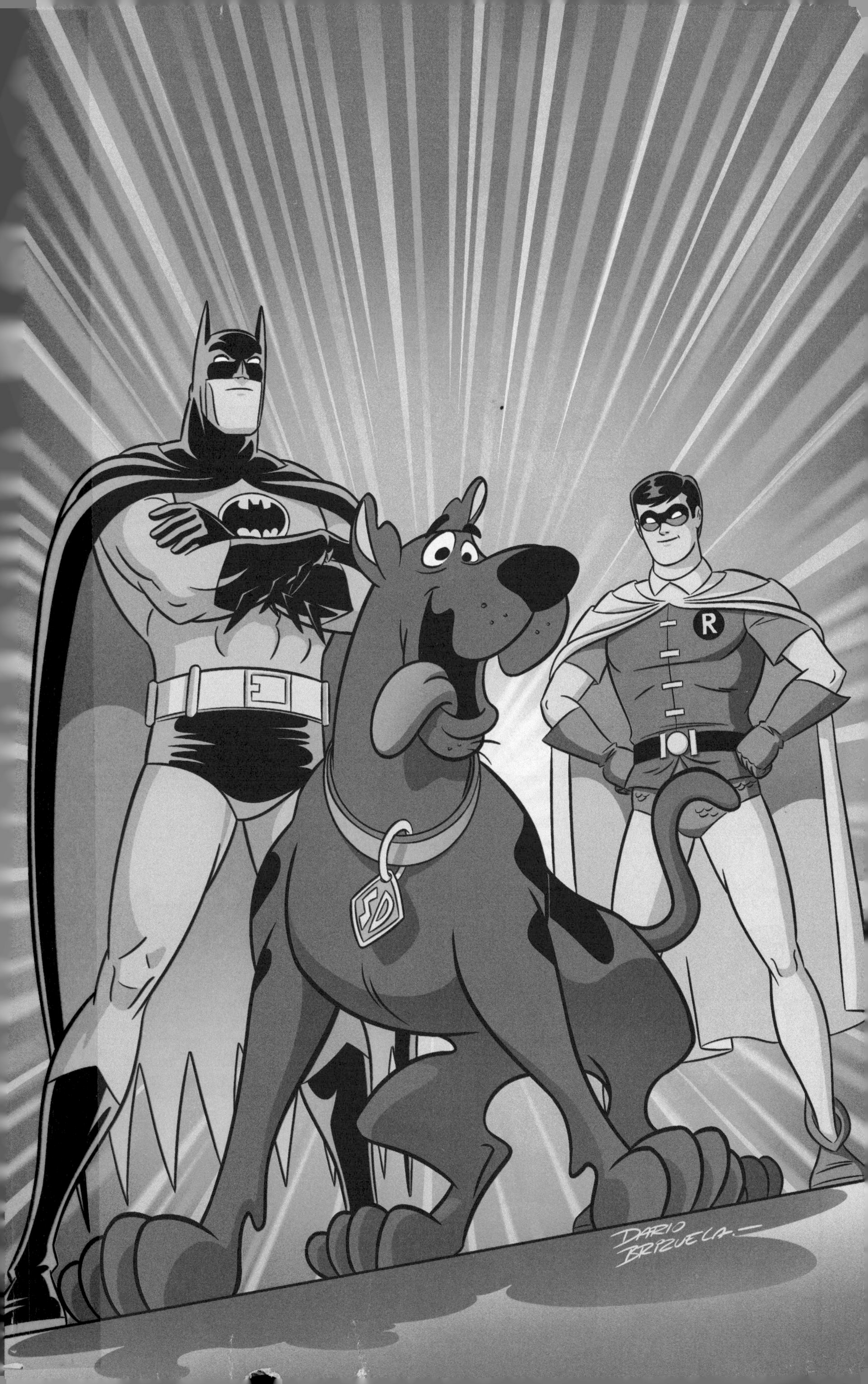
DARIO BRIZUELA

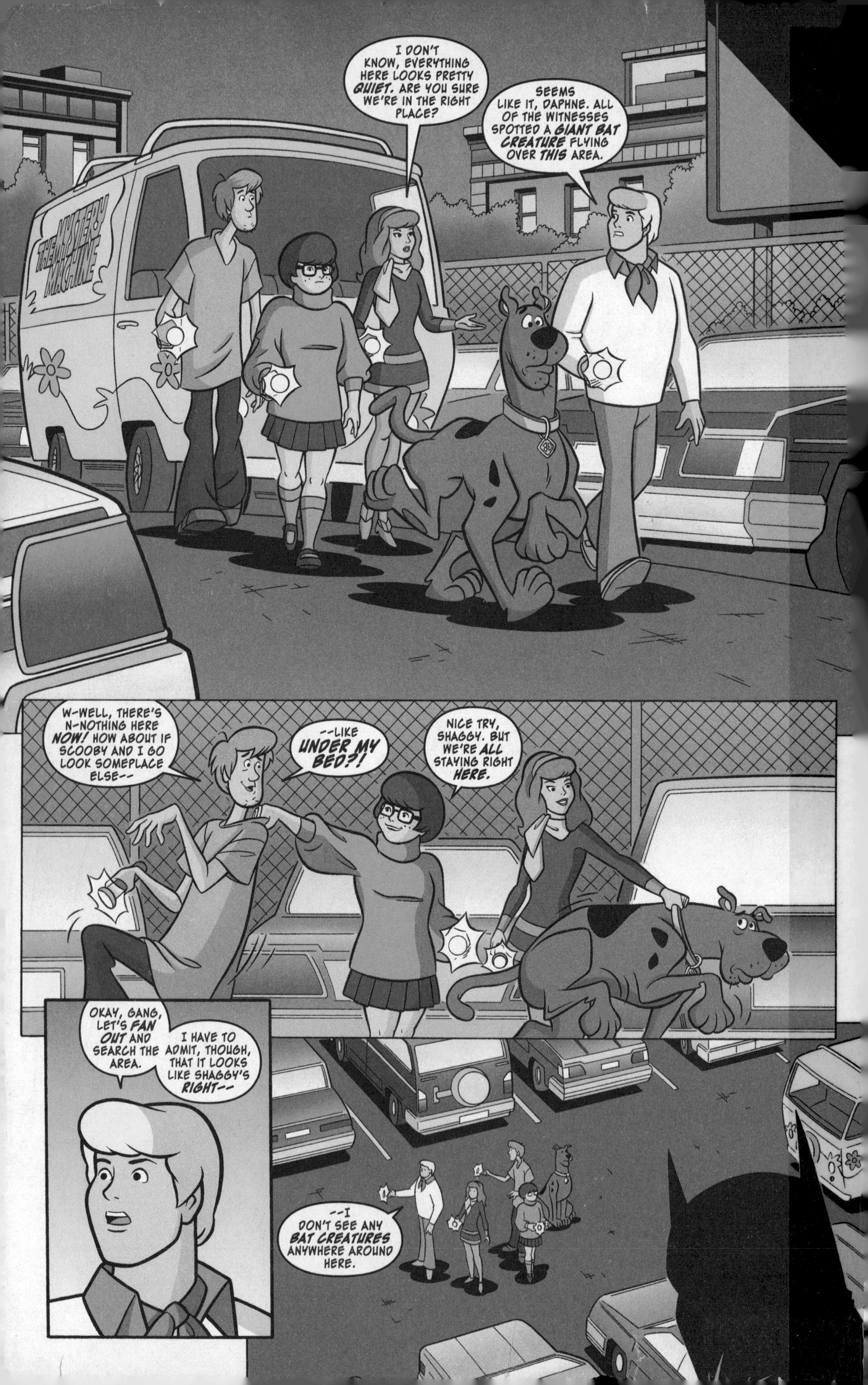

THE MYSTERY MACHINE
I DON'T KNOW, EVERYTHING HERE LOOKS PRETTY QUIET. ARE YOU SURE WE'RE IN THE RIGHT PLACE?
SEEMS LIKE IT, DAPHNE. ALL OF THE WITNESSES SPOTTED A GIANT BAT CREATURE FLYING OVER THIS AREA.
W-WELL, THERE'S N-NOTHING HERE NOW! HOW ABOUT IF SCOOBY AND I GO LOOK SOMEPLACE ELSE--
--LIKE UNDER MY BED?!
NICE TRY, SHAGGY. BUT WE'RE ALL STAYING RIGHT HERE.
OKAY, GANG, LET'S FAN OUT AND SEARCH THE AREA.
I HAVE TO ADMIT, THOUGH, THAT IT LOOKS LIKE SHAGGY'S RIGHT--
--I DON'T SEE ANY BAT CREATURES ANYWHERE AROUND HERE.

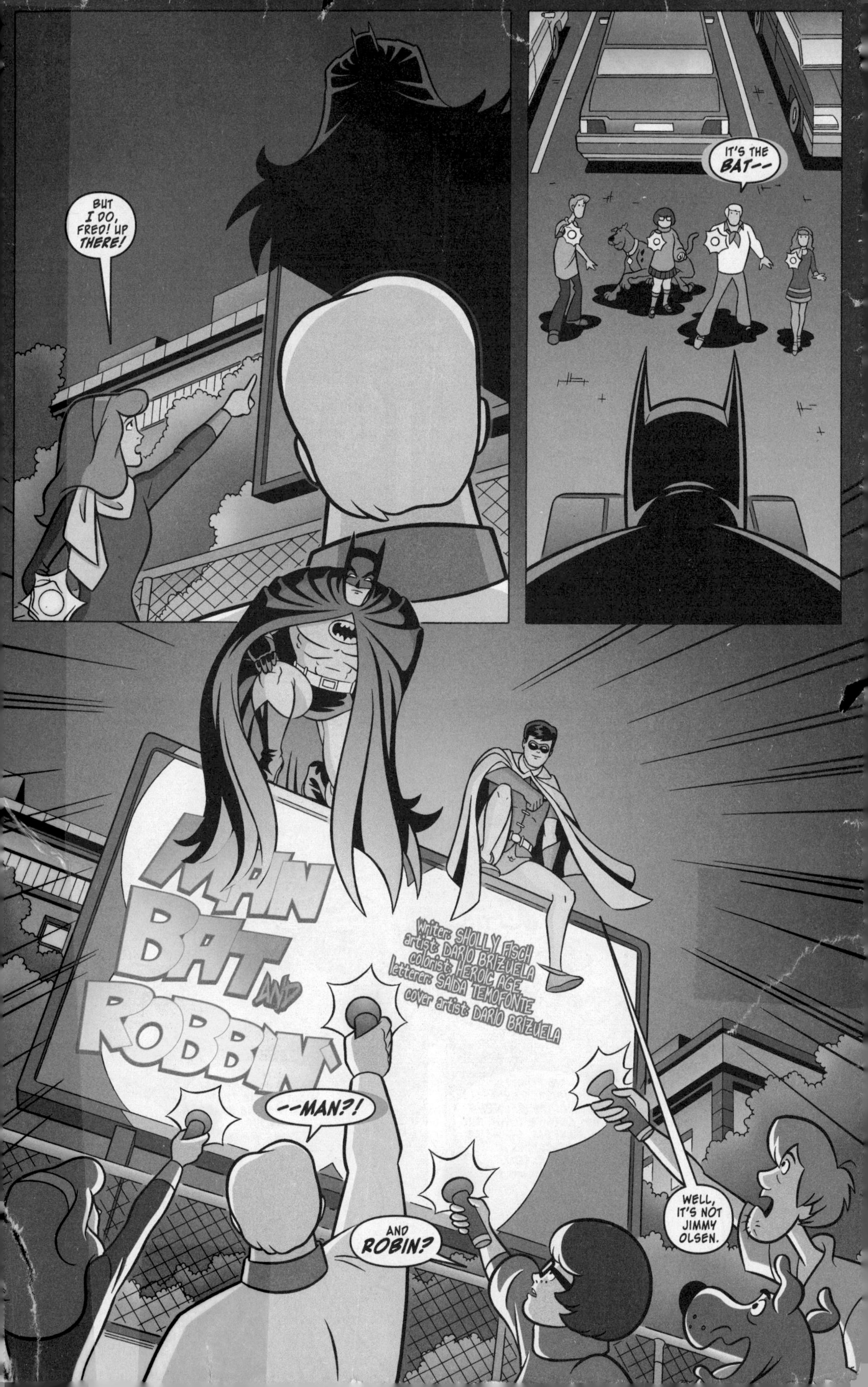

BUT I DO, FRED! UP THERE!
IT'S THE BAT--
MAN BAT AND ROBBIN'
Writer: SHOLLY FISCH
artist: DARIO BRIZUELA
colorist: HEROIC AGE
letterer: SAIDA TEMOFONTE
cover artist: DARIO BRIZUELA
--MAN?!
AND ROBIN?
WELL, IT'S NOT JIMMY OLSEN.

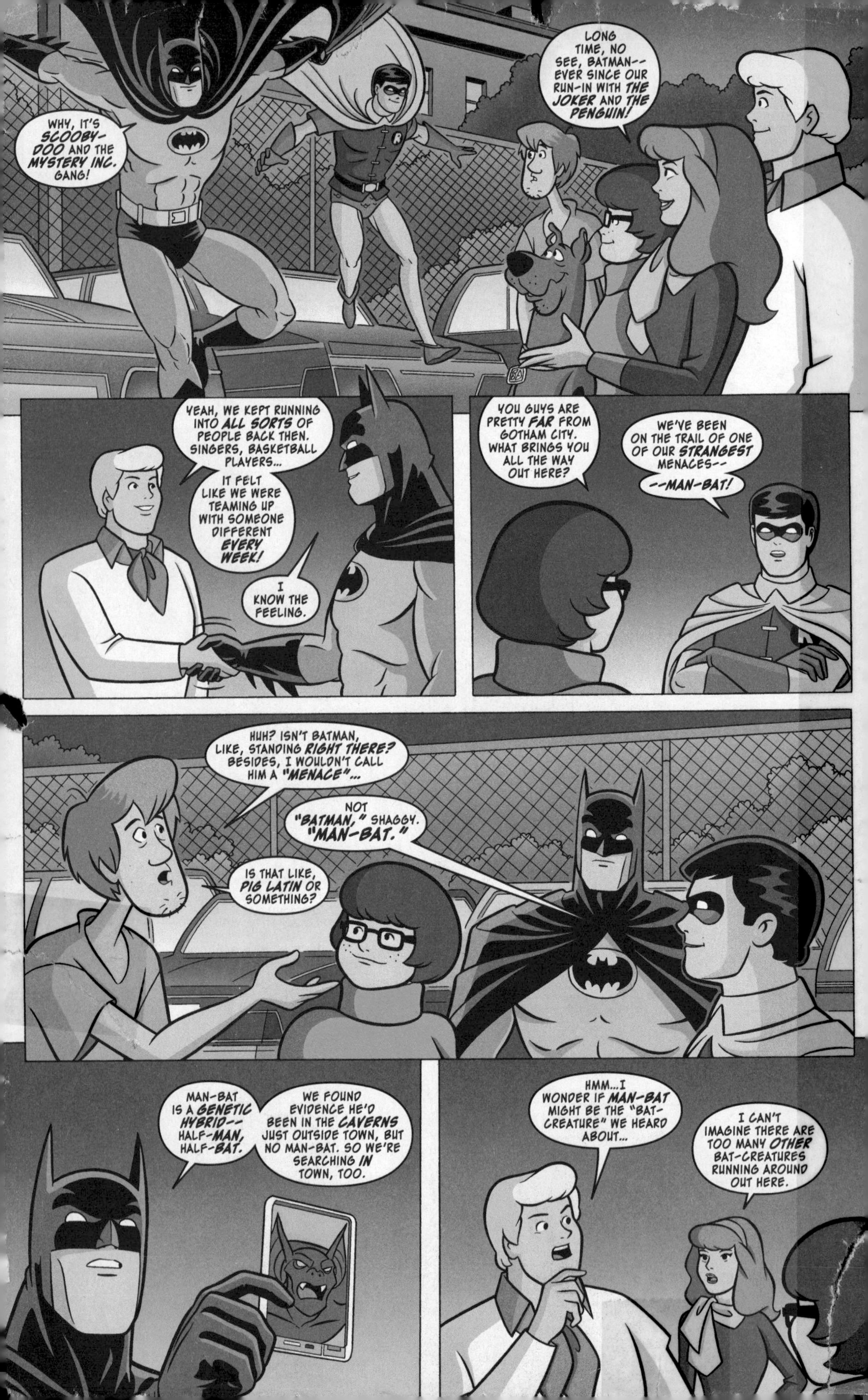
WHY, IT'S SCOOBY-DOO AND THE MYSTERY INC. GANG!
LONG TIME, NO SEE, BATMAN-- EVER SINCE OUR RUN-IN WITH THE JOKER AND THE PENGUIN!
YEAH, WE KEPT RUNNING INTO ALL SORTS OF PEOPLE BACK THEN. SINGERS, BASKETBALL PLAYERS...
IT FELT LIKE WE WERE TEAMING UP WITH SOMEONE DIFFERENT EVERY WEEK!
I KNOW THE FEELING.
YOU GUYS ARE PRETTY FAR FROM GOTHAM CITY. WHAT BRINGS YOU ALL THE WAY OUT HERE?
WE'VE BEEN ON THE TRAIL OF ONE OF OUR STRANGEST MENACES--
--MAN-BAT!
HUH? ISN'T BATMAN, LIKE, STANDING RIGHT THERE? BESIDES, I WOULDN'T CALL HIM A "MENACE"...
NOT "BATMAN," SHAGGY. "MAN-BAT."
IS THAT LIKE, PIG LATIN OR SOMETHING?
MAN-BAT IS A GENETIC HYBRID-- HALF-MAN, HALF-BAT.
WE FOUND EVIDENCE HE'D BEEN IN THE CAVERNS JUST OUTSIDE TOWN, BUT NO MAN-BAT. SO WE'RE SEARCHING IN TOWN, TOO.
HMM...I WONDER IF MAN-BAT MIGHT BE THE "BAT-CREATURE" WE HEARD ABOUT...
I CAN'T IMAGINE THERE ARE TOO MANY OTHER BAT-CREATURES RUNNING AROUND OUT HERE.

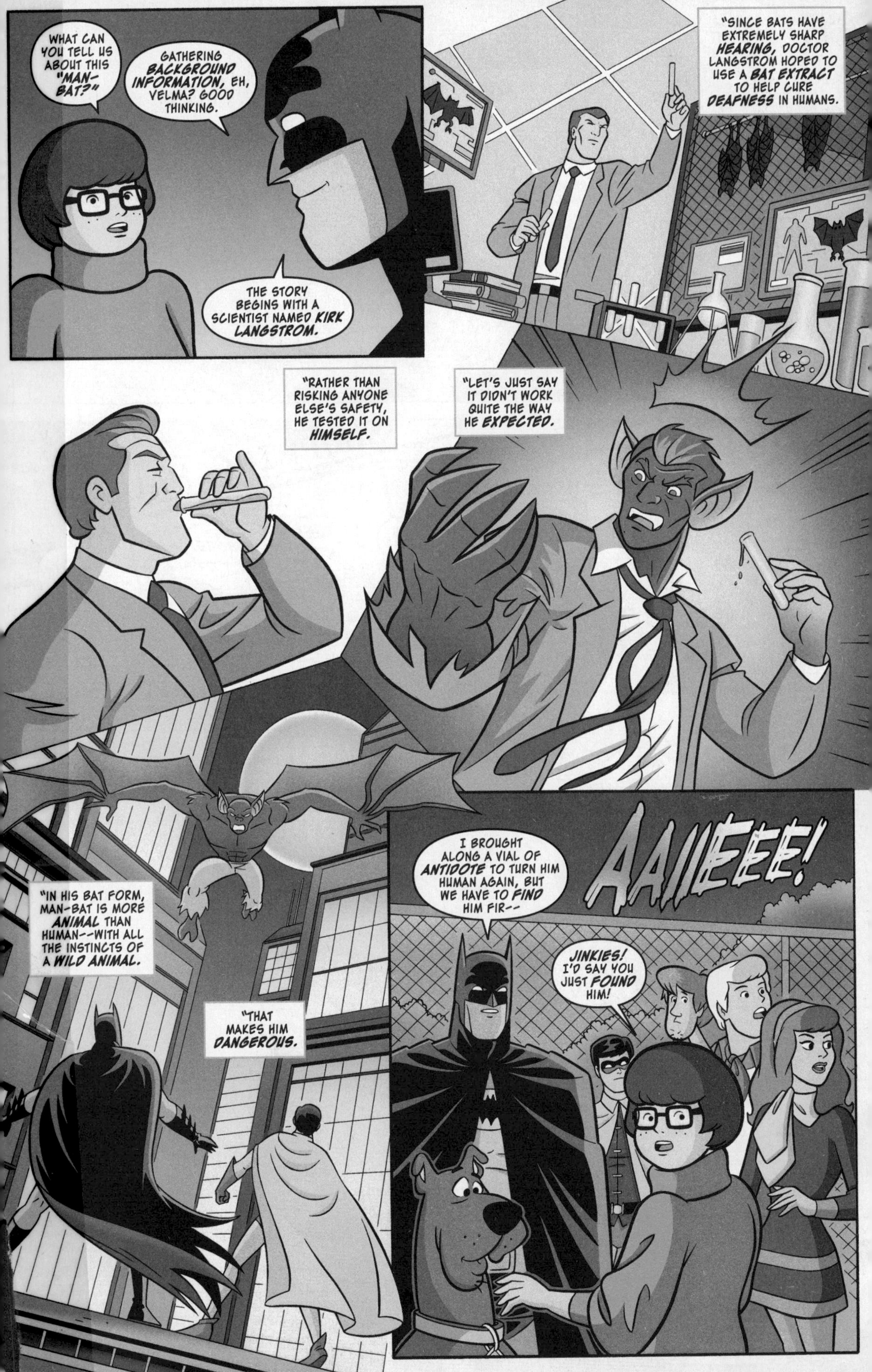
WHAT CAN YOU TELL US ABOUT THIS "MAN-BAT?"
GATHERING BACKGROUND INFORMATION, EH, VELMA? GOOD THINKING.
THE STORY BEGINS WITH A SCIENTIST NAMED KIRK LANGSTROM.
"SINCE BATS HAVE EXTREMELY SHARP HEARING, DOCTOR LANGSTROM HOPED TO USE A BAT EXTRACT TO HELP CURE DEAFNESS IN HUMANS.
"RATHER THAN RISKING ANYONE ELSE'S SAFETY, HE TESTED IT ON HIMSELF.
"LET'S JUST SAY IT DIDN'T WORK QUITE THE WAY HE EXPECTED.
"IN HIS BAT FORM, MAN-BAT IS MORE ANIMAL THAN HUMAN--WITH ALL THE INSTINCTS OF A WILD ANIMAL.
"THAT MAKES HIM DANGEROUS.
AAIIEEE!
I BROUGHT ALONG A VIAL OF ANTIDOTE TO TURN HIM HUMAN AGAIN, BUT WE HAVE TO FIND HIM FIR--
JINKIES! I'D SAY YOU JUST FOUND HIM!

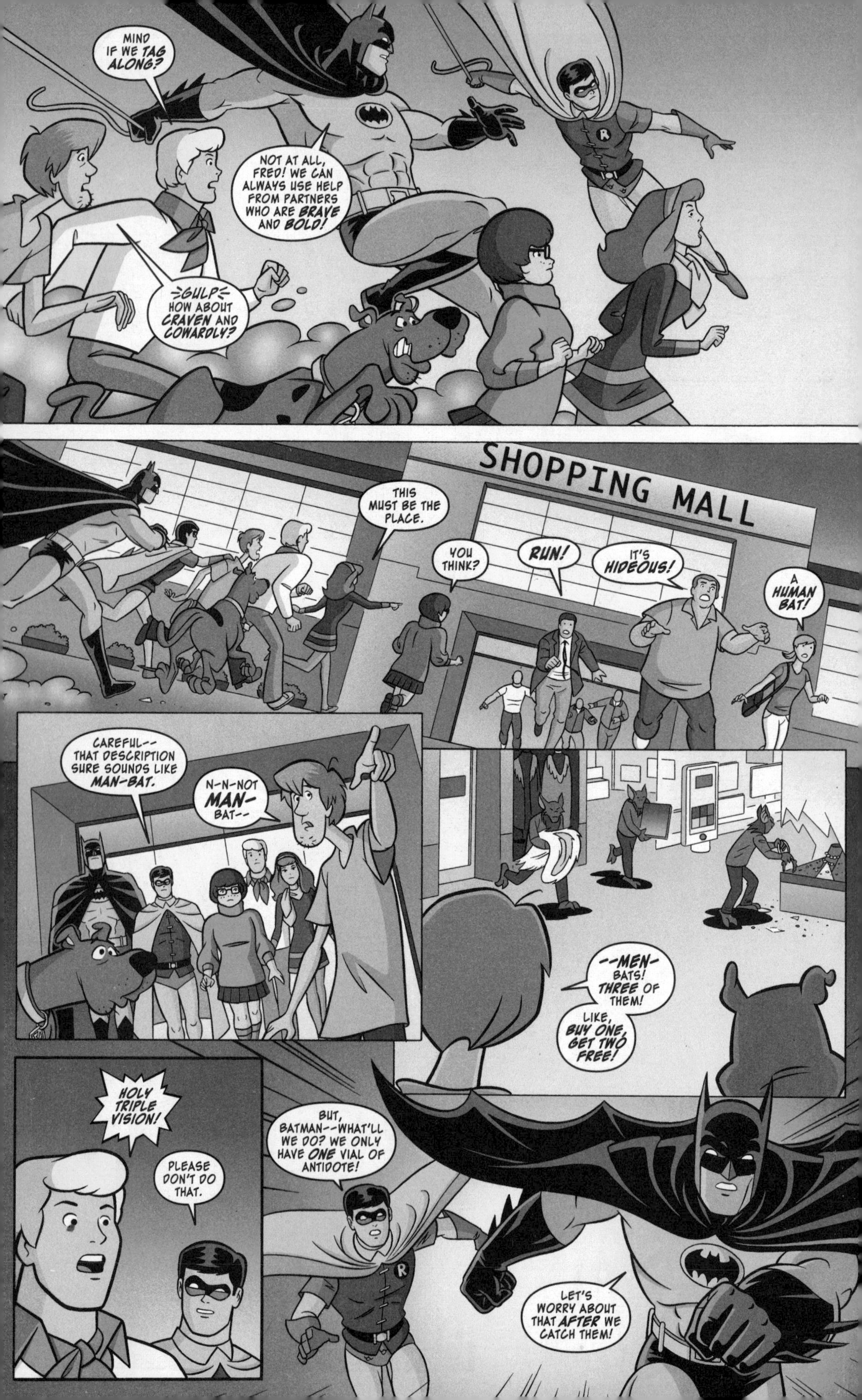
MIND IF WE TAG ALONG?
NOT AT ALL, FRED! WE CAN ALWAYS USE HELP FROM PARTNERS WHO ARE BRAVE AND BOLD!
=GULP= HOW ABOUT CRAVEN AND COWARDLY?
SHOPPING MALL
THIS MUST BE THE PLACE.
YOU THINK?
RUN!
IT'S HIDEOUS!
A HUMAN BAT!
CAREFUL-- THAT DESCRIPTION SURE SOUNDS LIKE MAN-BAT.
N-N-NOT MAN-BAT--
--MEN-BATS! THREE OF THEM!
LIKE, BUY ONE, GET TWO FREE!
HOLY TRIPLE VISION!
PLEASE DON'T DO THAT.
BUT, BATMAN--WHAT'LL WE DO? WE ONLY HAVE ONE VIAL OF ANTIDOTE!
LET'S WORRY ABOUT THAT AFTER WE CATCH THEM!

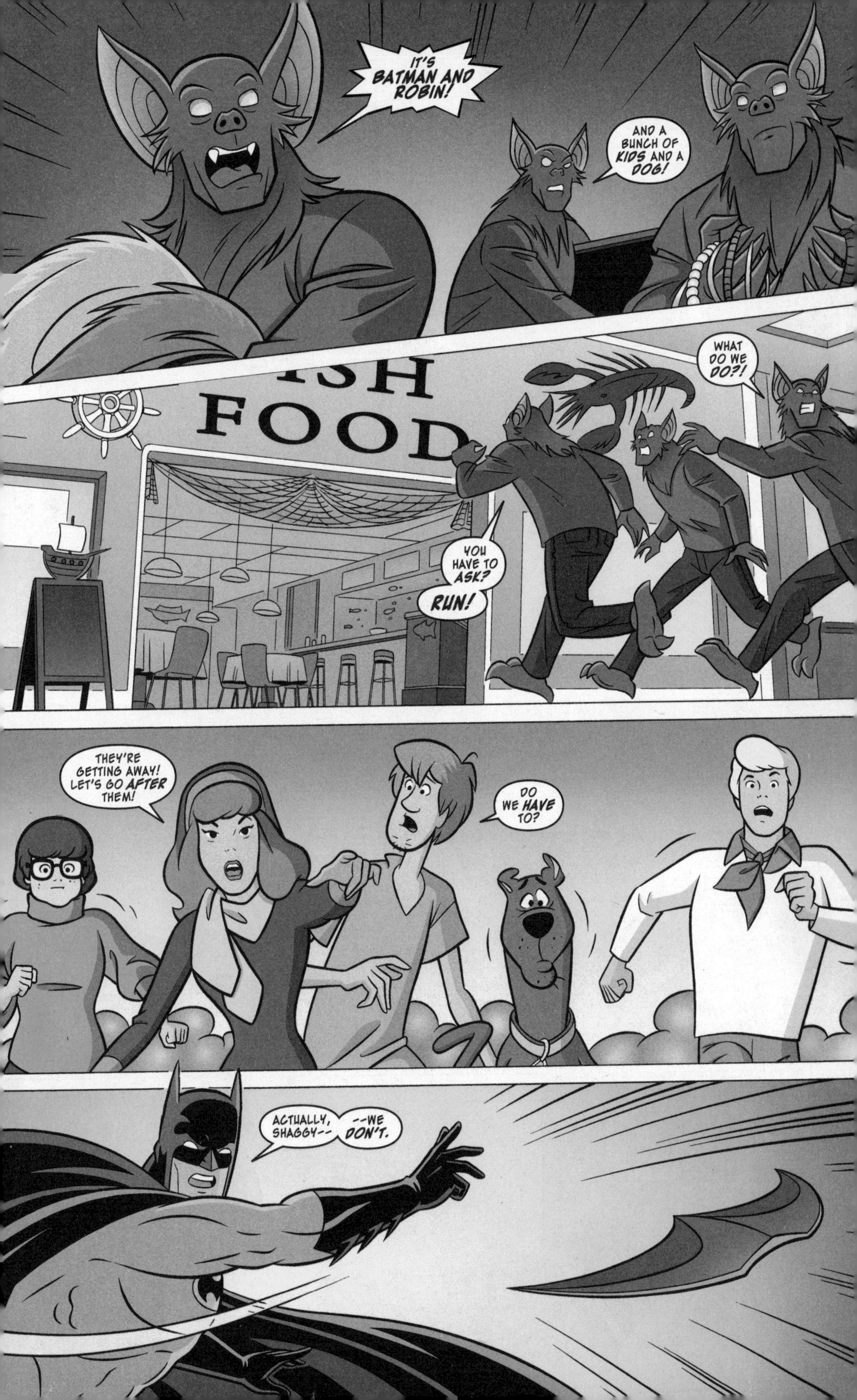
IT'S BATMAN AND ROBIN!
AND A BUNCH OF KIDS AND A DOG!
ISH
FOOD
WHAT DO WE DO?!
YOU HAVE TO ASK?
RUN!
THEY'RE GETTING AWAY! LET'S GO AFTER THEM!
DO WE HAVE TO?
ACTUALLY, SHAGGY--
--WE DON'T.

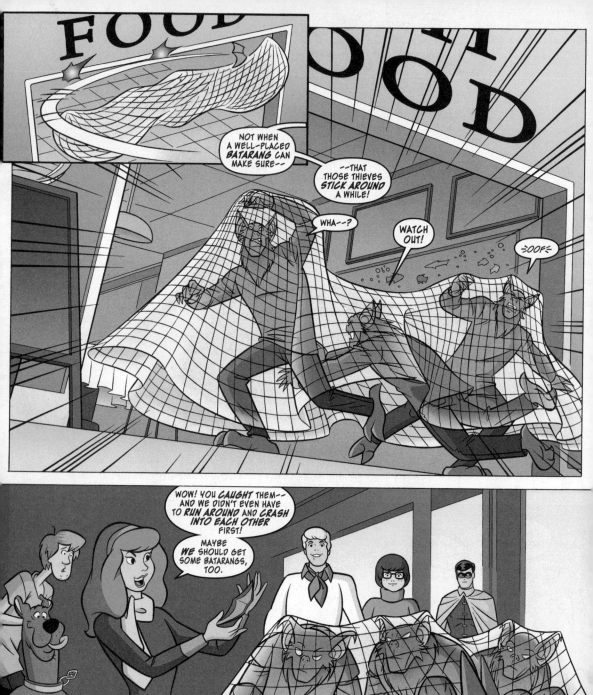

NOT WHEN A WELL-PLACED *BATARANG* CAN MAKE SURE--

--THAT THOSE THIEVES *STICK AROUND* A WHILE!

WHA--?

WATCH OUT!

≥OOF≤

WOW! YOU *CAUGHT* THEM-- AND WE DIDN'T EVEN HAVE TO *RUN AROUND* AND *CRASH INTO EACH OTHER* FIRST!

MAYBE *WE* SHOULD GET SOME *BATARANGS,* TOO.

SO WHICH ONE OF THESE THREE IS THE *ORIGINAL* MAN-BAT?

IT'S SIMPLE ENOUGH TO DEDUCE.

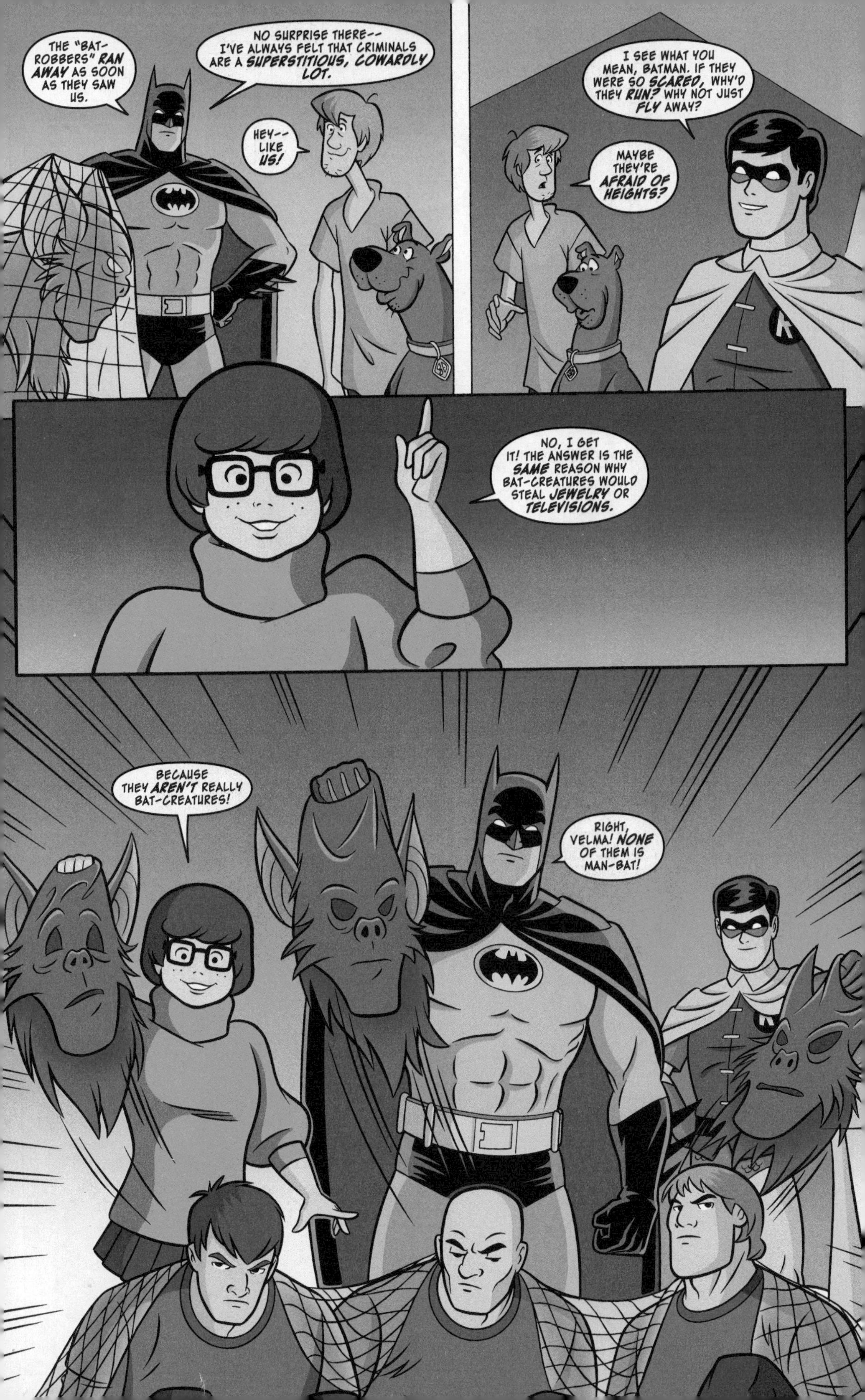
THE "BAT-ROBBERS" RAN AWAY AS SOON AS THEY SAW US.
NO SURPRISE THERE-- I'VE ALWAYS FELT THAT CRIMINALS ARE A SUPERSTITIOUS, COWARDLY LOT.
HEY-- LIKE US!
I SEE WHAT YOU MEAN, BATMAN. IF THEY WERE SO SCARED, WHY'D THEY RUN? WHY NOT JUST FLY AWAY?
MAYBE THEY'RE AFRAID OF HEIGHTS?
NO, I GET IT! THE ANSWER IS THE SAME REASON WHY BAT-CREATURES WOULD STEAL JEWELRY OR TELEVISIONS.
BECAUSE THEY AREN'T REALLY BAT-CREATURES!
RIGHT, VELMA! NONE OF THEM IS MAN-BAT!

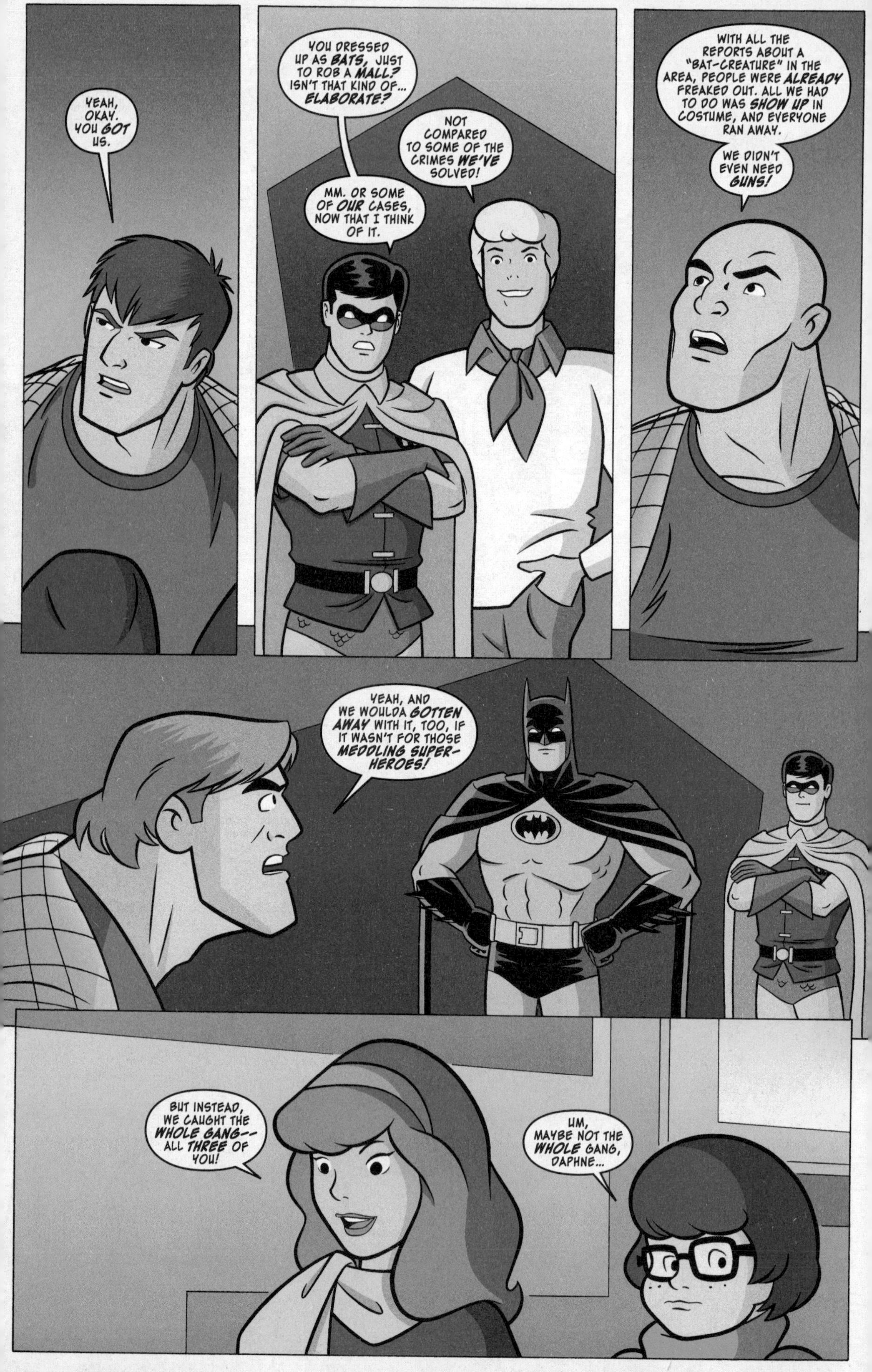
YEAH, OKAY. YOU GOT US.
YOU DRESSED UP AS BATS, JUST TO ROB A MALL? ISN'T THAT KIND OF... ELABORATE?
NOT COMPARED TO SOME OF THE CRIMES WE'VE SOLVED!
MM. OR SOME OF OUR CASES, NOW THAT I THINK OF IT.
WITH ALL THE REPORTS ABOUT A "BAT-CREATURE" IN THE AREA, PEOPLE WERE ALREADY FREAKED OUT. ALL WE HAD TO DO WAS SHOW UP IN COSTUME, AND EVERYONE RAN AWAY.
WE DIDN'T EVEN NEED GUNS!
YEAH, AND WE WOULDA GOTTEN AWAY WITH IT, TOO, IF IT WASN'T FOR THOSE MEDDLING SUPER-HEROES!
BUT INSTEAD, WE CAUGHT THE WHOLE GANG-- ALL THREE OF YOU!
UM, MAYBE NOT THE WHOLE GANG, DAPHNE...

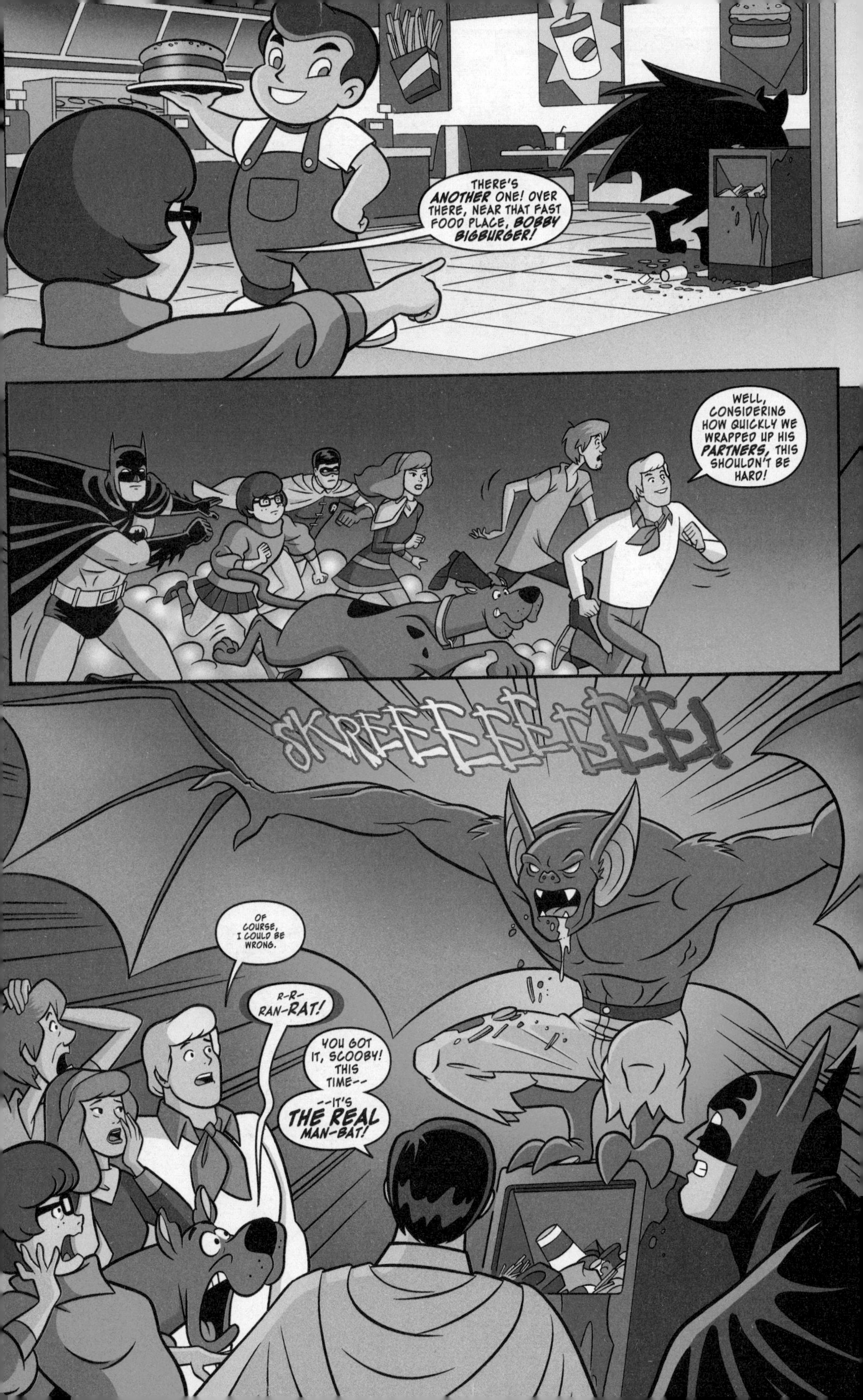
THERE'S ANOTHER ONE! OVER THERE, NEAR THAT FAST FOOD PLACE, BOBBY BIGBURGER!
WELL, CONSIDERING HOW QUICKLY WE WRAPPED UP HIS PARTNERS, THIS SHOULDN'T BE HARD!
SKREEEEEEEEEE!
OF COURSE, I COULD BE WRONG.
R-R-RAN-RAT!
YOU GOT IT, SCOOBY! THIS TIME--
--IT'S THE REAL MAN-BAT!

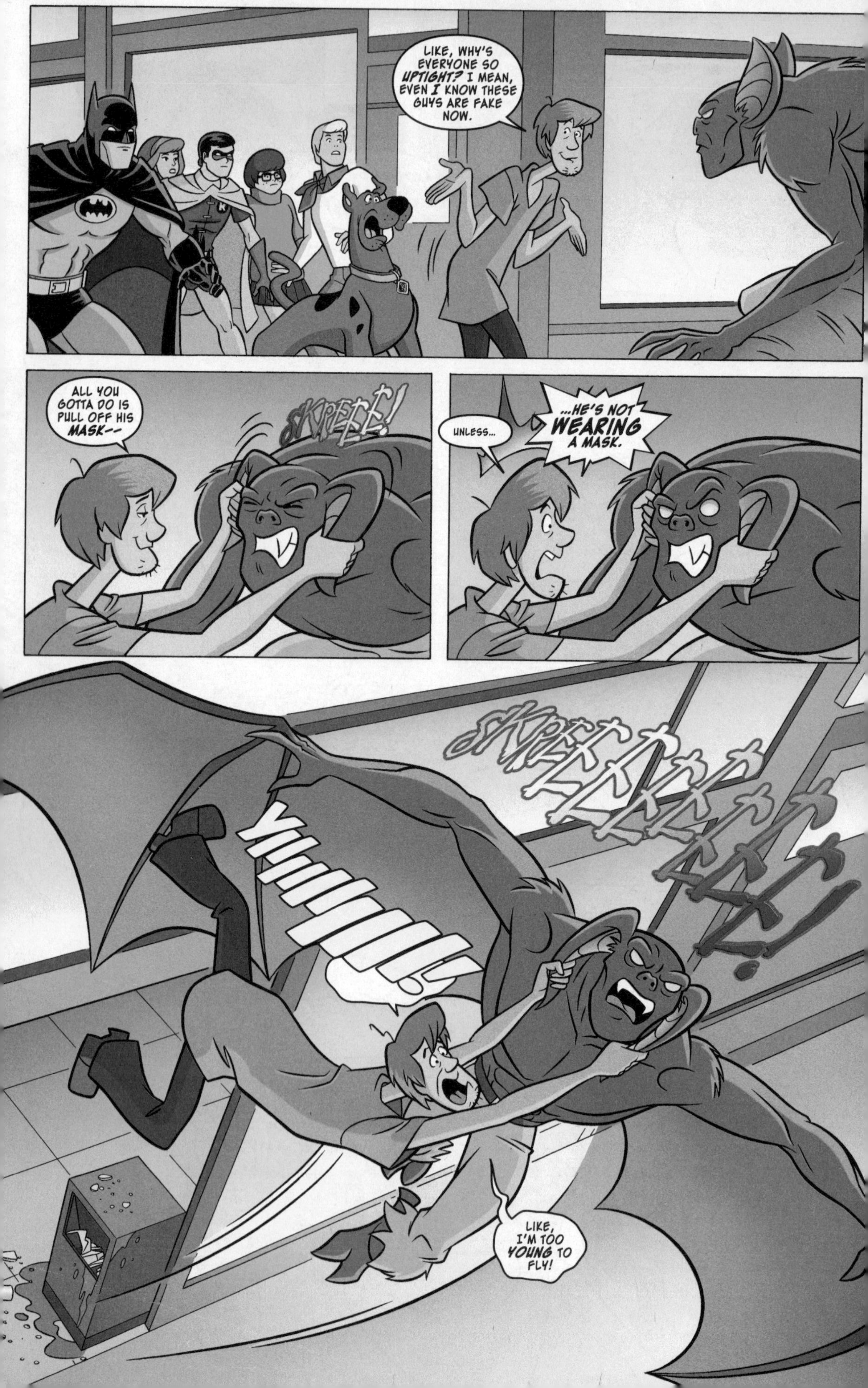
LIKE, WHY'S EVERYONE SO UPTIGHT? I MEAN, EVEN I KNOW THESE GUYS ARE FAKE NOW.
ALL YOU GOTTA DO IS PULL OFF HIS MASK--
SKREEE!
UNLESS...
...HE'S NOT WEARING A MASK.
YIIIIIIIIII!
LIKE, I'M TOO YOUNG TO FLY!

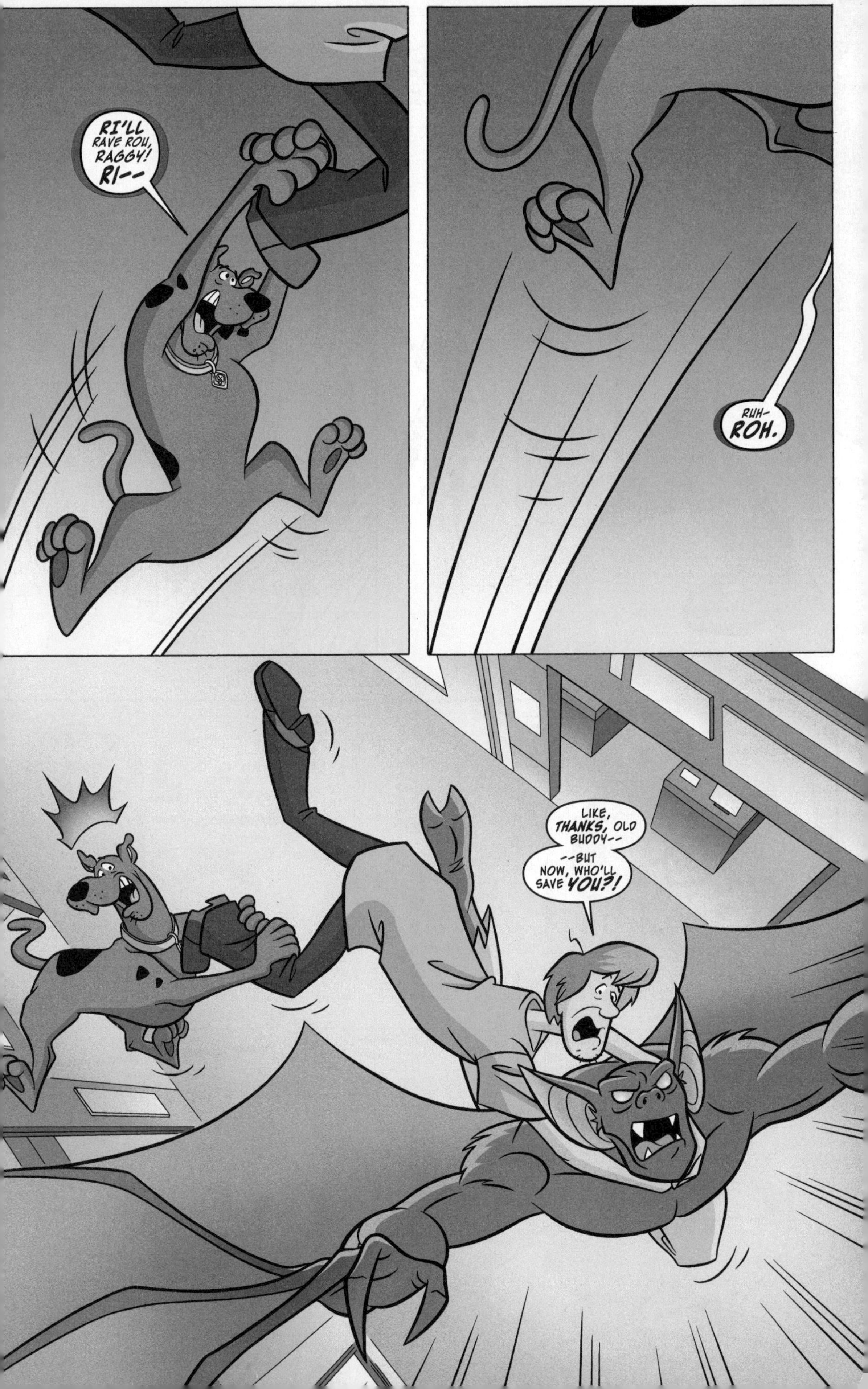
RI'LL RAVE ROU, RAGGY! RI--
RUH-ROH.
LIKE, THANKS, OLD BUDDY--
--BUT NOW, WHO'LL SAVE YOU?!

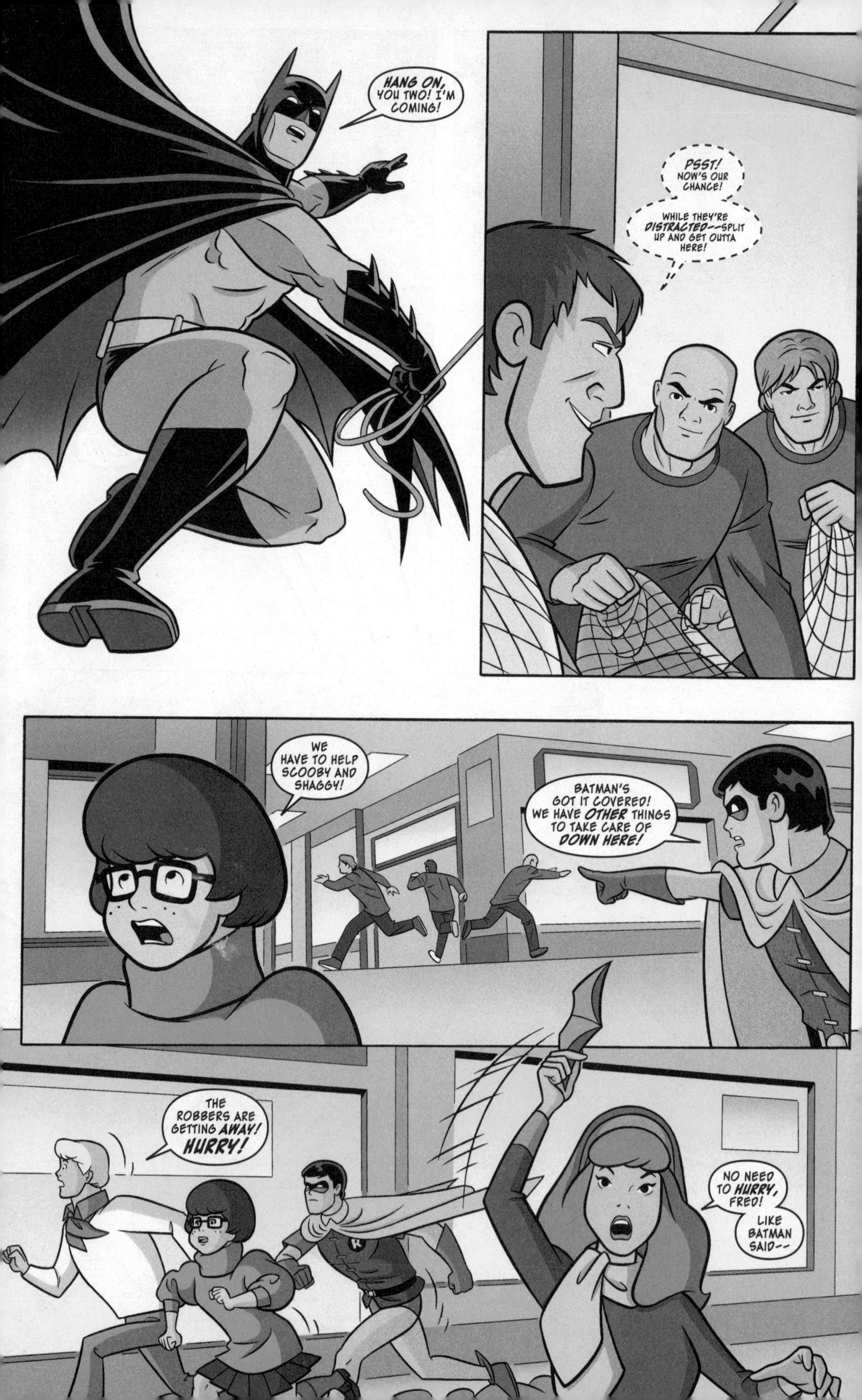
HANG ON, YOU TWO! I'M COMING!
PSST! NOW'S OUR CHANCE!
WHILE THEY'RE DISTRACTED--SPLIT UP AND GET OUTTA HERE!
WE HAVE TO HELP SCOOBY AND SHAGGY!
BATMAN'S GOT IT COVERED! WE HAVE OTHER THINGS TO TAKE CARE OF DOWN HERE!
THE ROBBERS ARE GETTING AWAY! HURRY!
NO NEED TO HURRY, FRED!
LIKE BATMAN SAID--

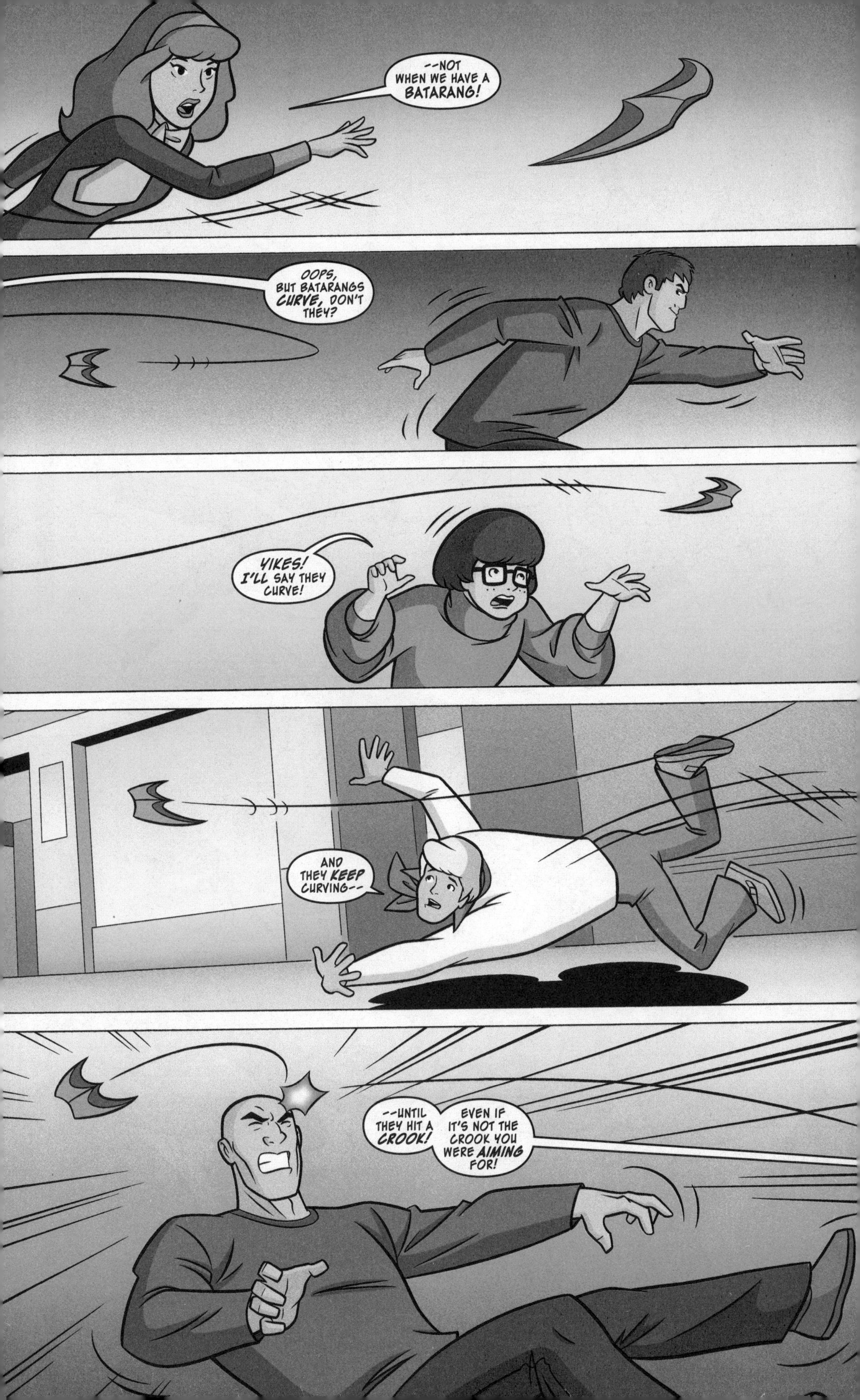
--NOT WHEN WE HAVE A BATARANG!
OOPS, BUT BATARANGS CURVE, DON'T THEY?
YIKES! I'LL SAY THEY CURVE!
AND THEY KEEP CURVING--
--UNTIL THEY HIT A CROOK!
EVEN IF IT'S NOT THE CROOK YOU WERE AIMING FOR!

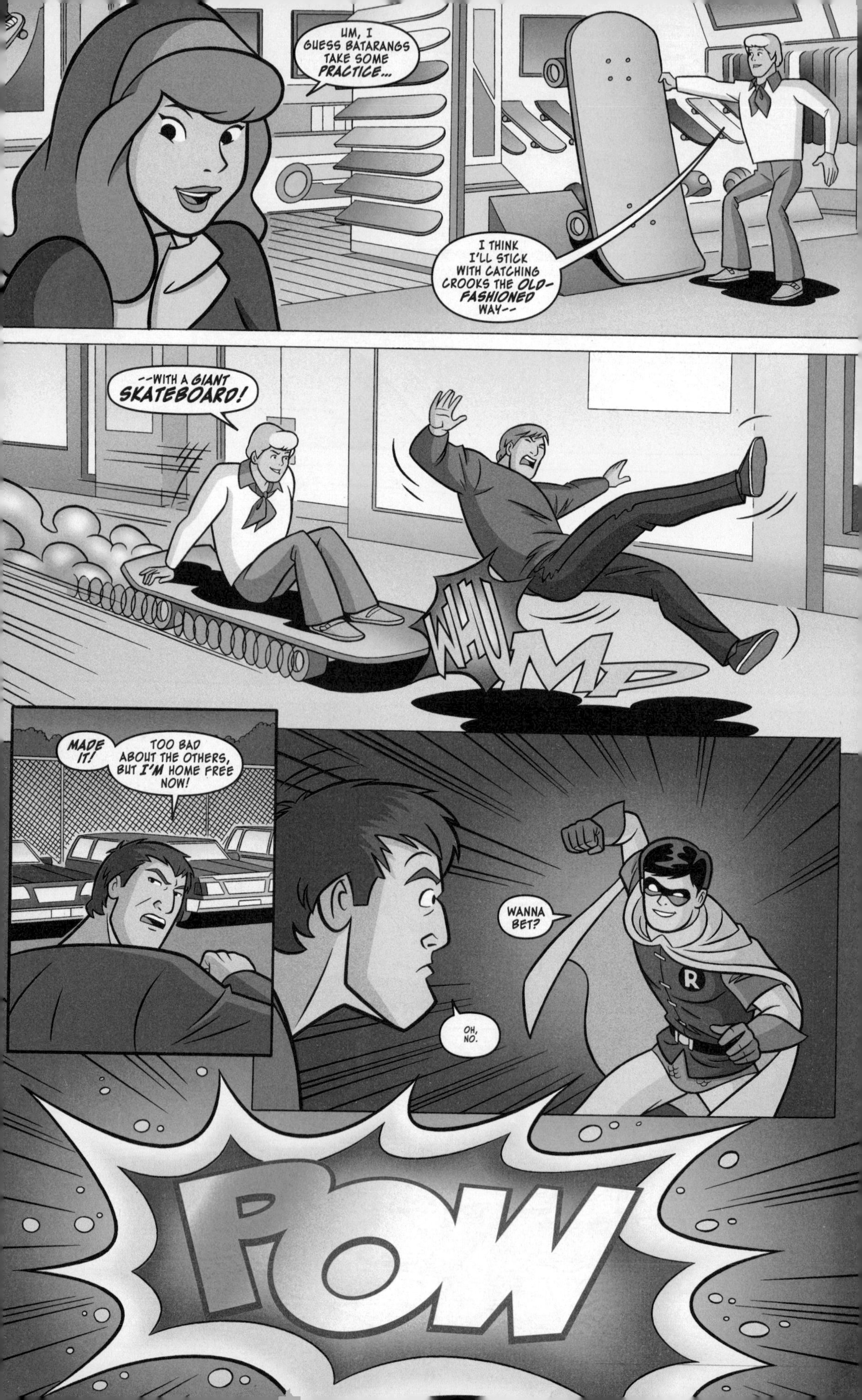
UM, I GUESS BATARANGS TAKE SOME PRACTICE...
I THINK I'LL STICK WITH CATCHING CROOKS THE OLD-FASHIONED WAY--
--WITH A GIANT SKATEBOARD!
WHUMP
MADE IT!
TOO BAD ABOUT THE OTHERS, BUT I'M HOME FREE NOW!
WANNA BET?
OH, NO.
POW

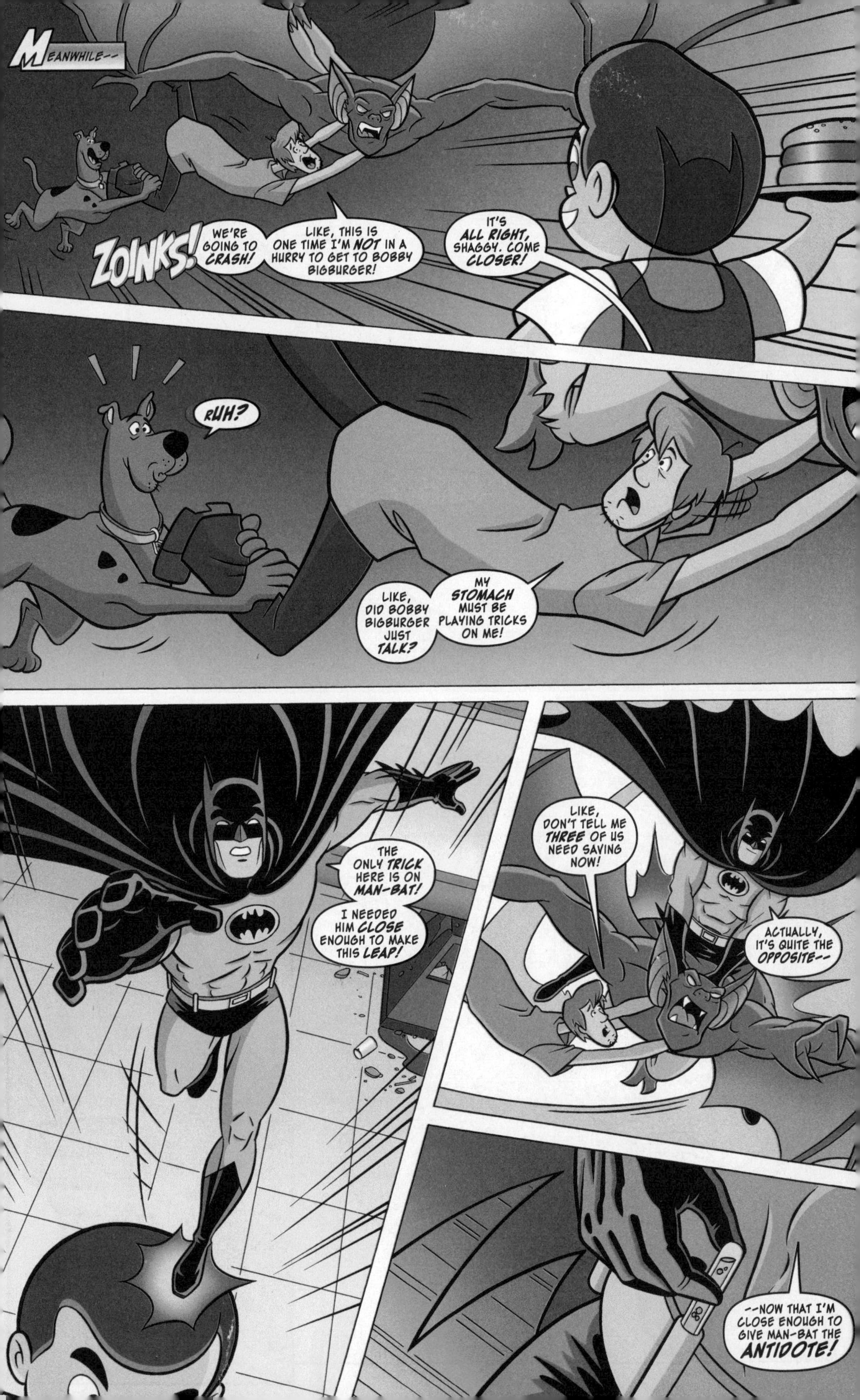
MEANWHILE--
ZOINKS!
WE'RE GOING TO CRASH!
LIKE, THIS IS ONE TIME I'M NOT IN A HURRY TO GET TO BOBBY BIGBURGER!
IT'S ALL RIGHT, SHAGGY. COME CLOSER!
RUH?
LIKE, DID BOBBY BIGBURGER JUST TALK?
MY STOMACH MUST BE PLAYING TRICKS ON ME!
THE ONLY TRICK HERE IS ON MAN-BAT!
I NEEDED HIM CLOSE ENOUGH TO MAKE THIS LEAP!
LIKE, DON'T TELL ME THREE OF US NEED SAVING NOW!
ACTUALLY, IT'S QUITE THE OPPOSITE--
--NOW THAT I'M CLOSE ENOUGH TO GIVE MAN-BAT THE ANTIDOTE!

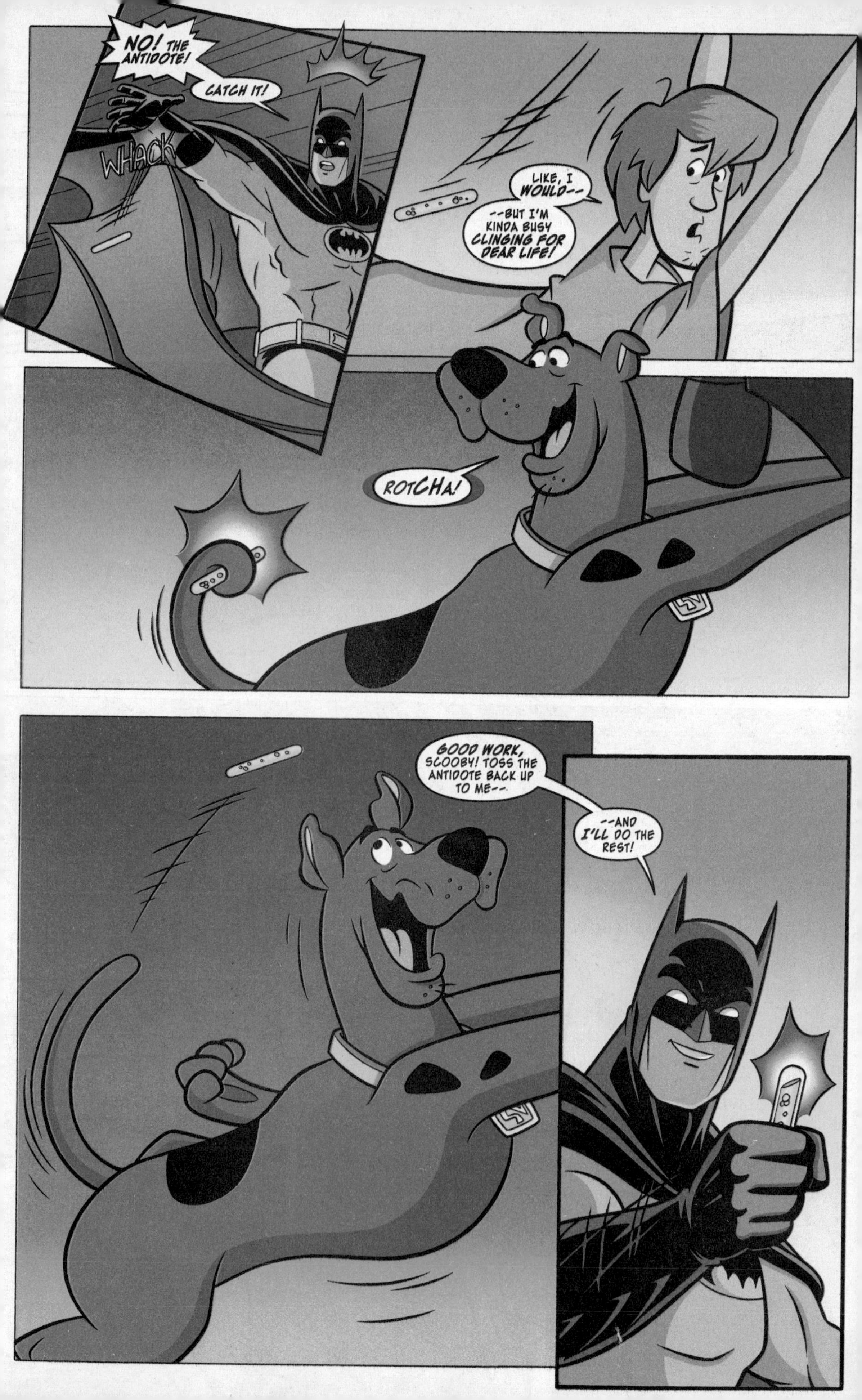
NO! THE ANTIDOTE!
CATCH IT!
WHACK
LIKE, I WOULD--
--BUT I'M KINDA BUSY CLINGING FOR DEAR LIFE!
ROTCHA!
GOOD WORK, SCOOBY! TOSS THE ANTIDOTE BACK UP TO ME--.
--AND I'LL DO THE REST!

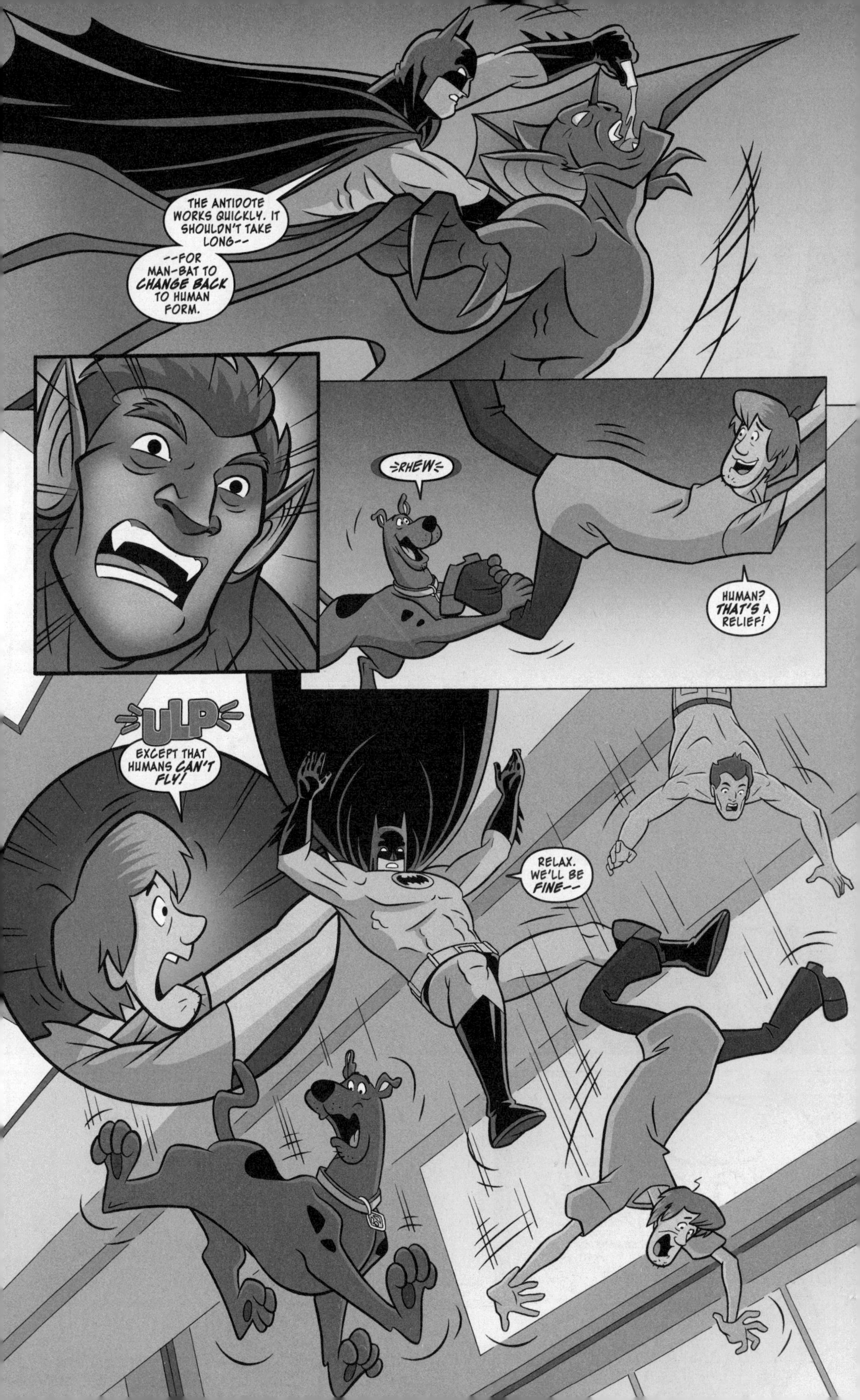
THE ANTIDOTE WORKS QUICKLY. IT SHOULDN'T TAKE LONG--
--FOR MAN-BAT TO CHANGE BACK TO HUMAN FORM.
RHEW
HUMAN? THAT'S A RELIEF!
ULP
EXCEPT THAT HUMANS CAN'T FLY!
RELAX. WE'LL BE FINE--

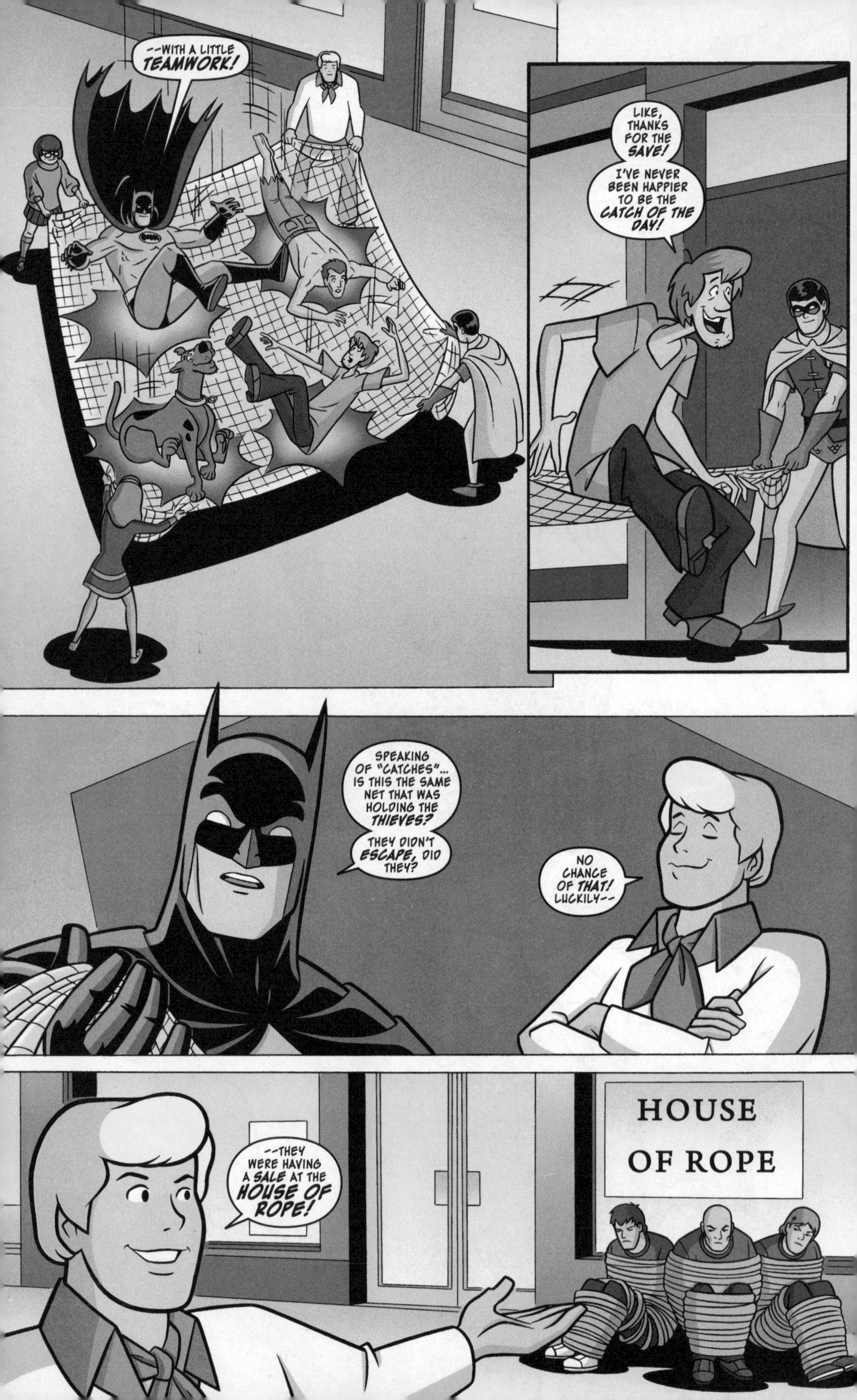

--WITH A LITTLE TEAMWORK!
LIKE, THANKS FOR THE SAVE!
I'VE NEVER BEEN HAPPIER TO BE THE CATCH OF THE DAY!
SPEAKING OF "CATCHES"... IS THIS THE SAME NET THAT WAS HOLDING THE THIEVES?
THEY DIDN'T ESCAPE, DID THEY?
NO CHANCE OF THAT! LUCKILY--
--THEY WERE HAVING A SALE AT THE HOUSE OF ROPE!
HOUSE OF ROPE

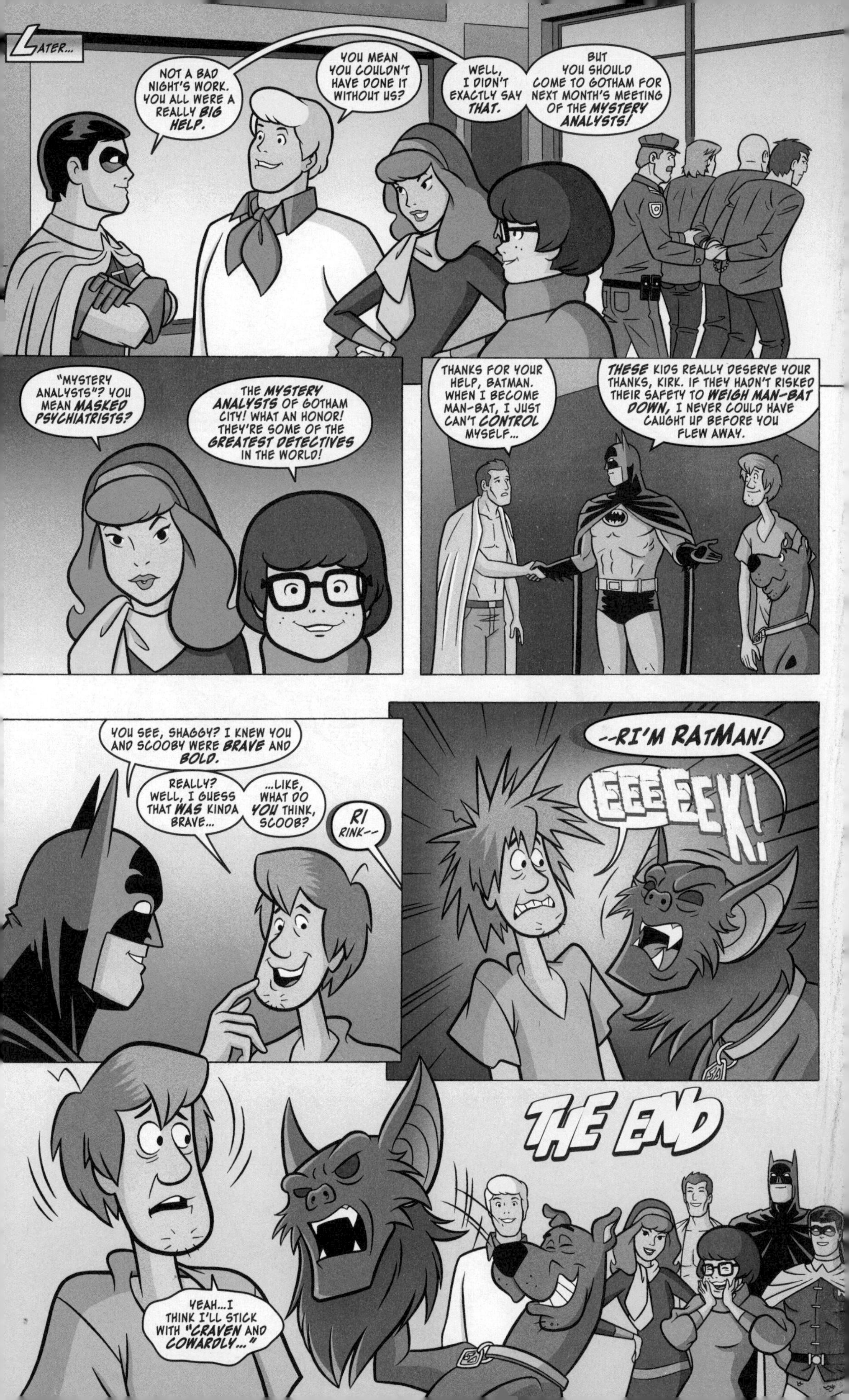
LATER...
NOT A BAD NIGHT'S WORK. YOU ALL WERE A REALLY BIG HELP.
YOU MEAN YOU COULDN'T HAVE DONE IT WITHOUT US?
WELL, I DIDN'T EXACTLY SAY THAT.
BUT YOU SHOULD COME TO GOTHAM FOR NEXT MONTH'S MEETING OF THE MYSTERY ANALYSTS!
"MYSTERY ANALYSTS"? YOU MEAN MASKED PSYCHIATRISTS?
THE MYSTERY ANALYSTS OF GOTHAM CITY! WHAT AN HONOR! THEY'RE SOME OF THE GREATEST DETECTIVES IN THE WORLD!
THANKS FOR YOUR HELP, BATMAN. WHEN I BECOME MAN-BAT, I JUST CAN'T CONTROL MYSELF...
THESE KIDS REALLY DESERVE YOUR THANKS, KIRK. IF THEY HADN'T RISKED THEIR SAFETY TO WEIGH MAN-BAT DOWN, I NEVER COULD HAVE CAUGHT UP BEFORE YOU FLEW AWAY.
YOU SEE, SHAGGY? I KNEW YOU AND SCOOBY WERE BRAVE AND BOLD.
REALLY? WELL, I GUESS THAT WAS KINDA BRAVE...
...LIKE, WHAT DO YOU THINK, SCOOB?
RI RINK--
--RI'M RATMAN!
EEEEEK!
YEAH...I THINK I'LL STICK WITH "CRAVEN AND COWARDLY..."
THE END

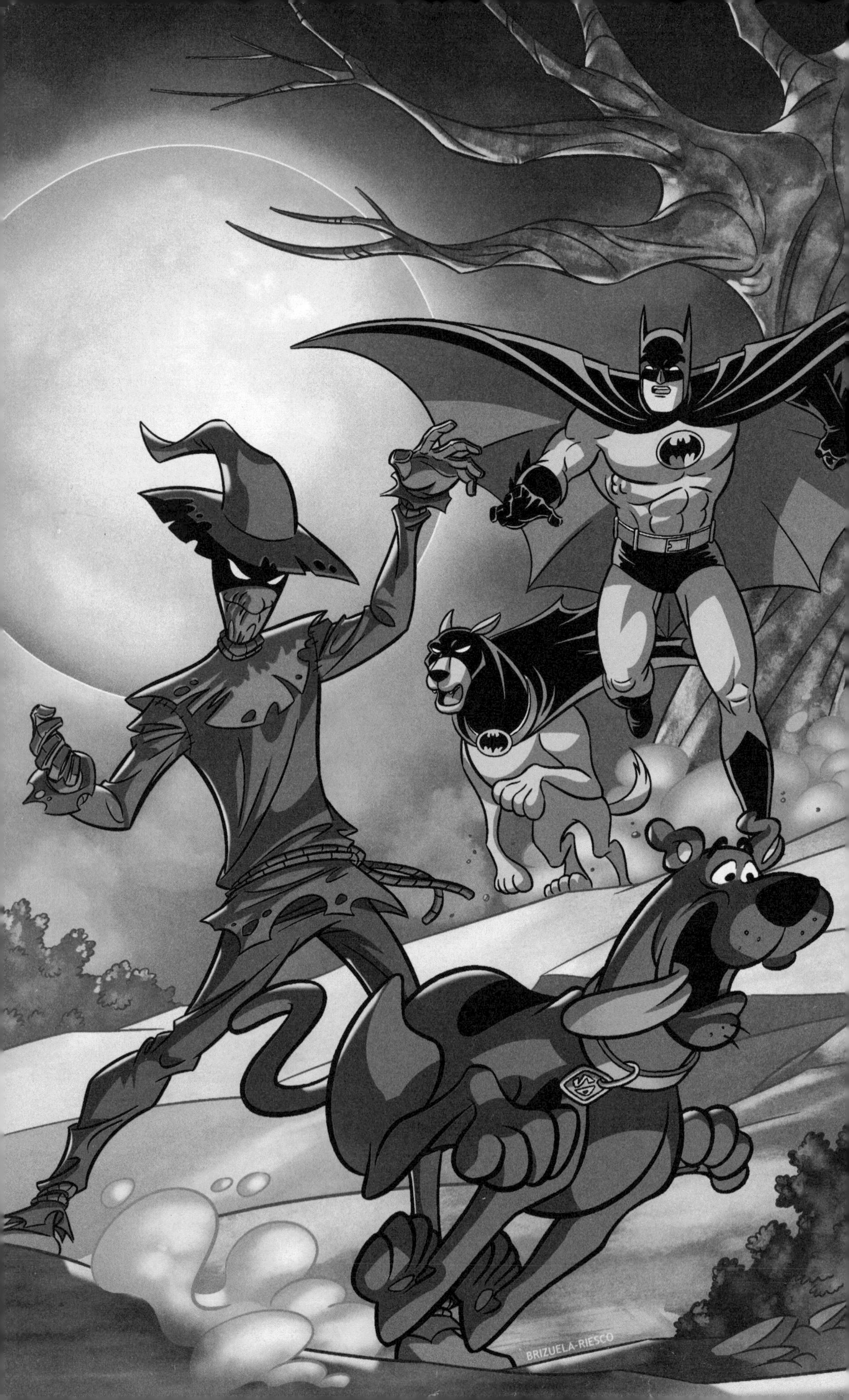
BRIZUELA-RIESCO

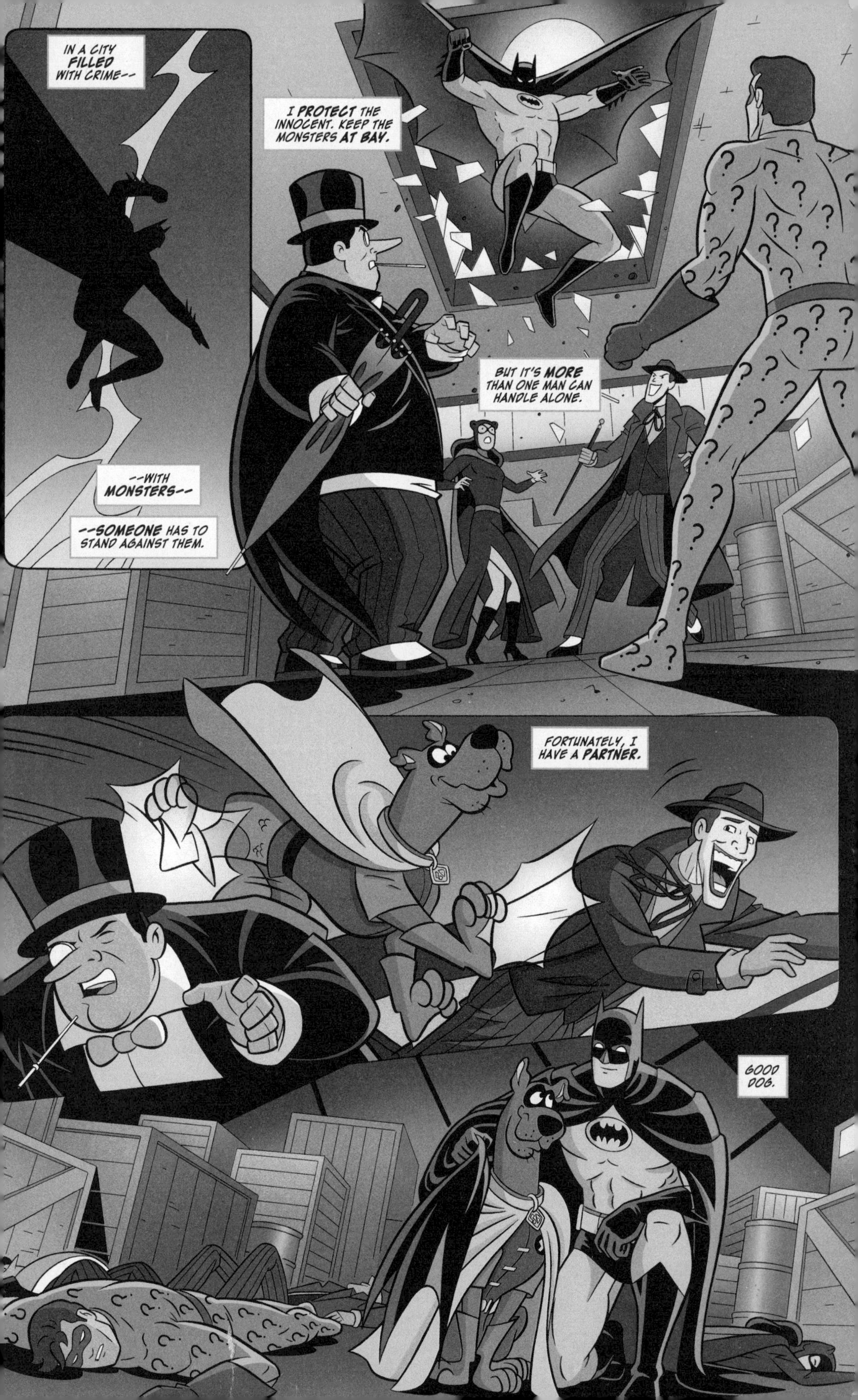
IN A CITY FILLED WITH CRIME--
I PROTECT THE INNOCENT. KEEP THE MONSTERS AT BAY.
--WITH MONSTERS--
--SOMEONE HAS TO STAND AGAINST THEM.
BUT IT'S MORE THAN ONE MAN CAN HANDLE ALONE.
FORTUNATELY, I HAVE A PARTNER.
GOOD DOG.

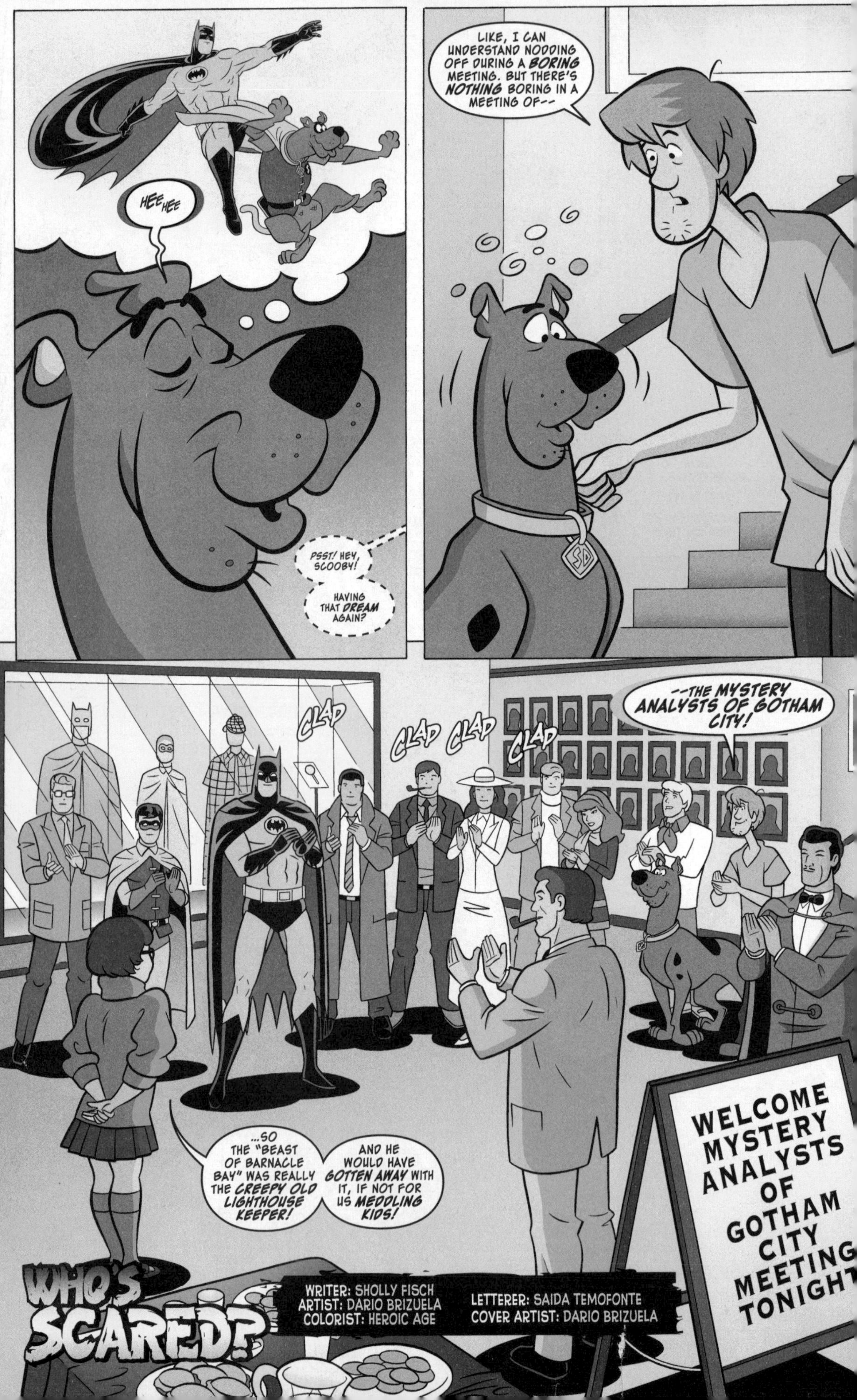
HEE HEE
PSST! HEY, SCOOBY!
HAVING THAT DREAM AGAIN?
LIKE, I CAN UNDERSTAND NODDING OFF DURING A BORING MEETING. BUT THERE'S NOTHING BORING IN A MEETING OF--
CLAP
CLAP CLAP
CLAP
--THE MYSTERY ANALYSTS OF GOTHAM CITY!
WELCOME MYSTERY ANALYSTS OF GOTHAM CITY MEETING TONIGHT
...SO THE "BEAST OF BARNACLE BAY" WAS REALLY THE CREEPY OLD LIGHTHOUSE KEEPER!
AND HE WOULD HAVE GOTTEN AWAY WITH IT, IF NOT FOR US MEDDLING KIDS!
WHO'S SCARED?
WRITER: SHOLLY FISCH
ARTIST: DARIO BRIZUELA
COLORIST: HEROIC AGE
LETTERER: SAIDA TEMOFONTE
COVER ARTIST: DARIO BRIZUELA

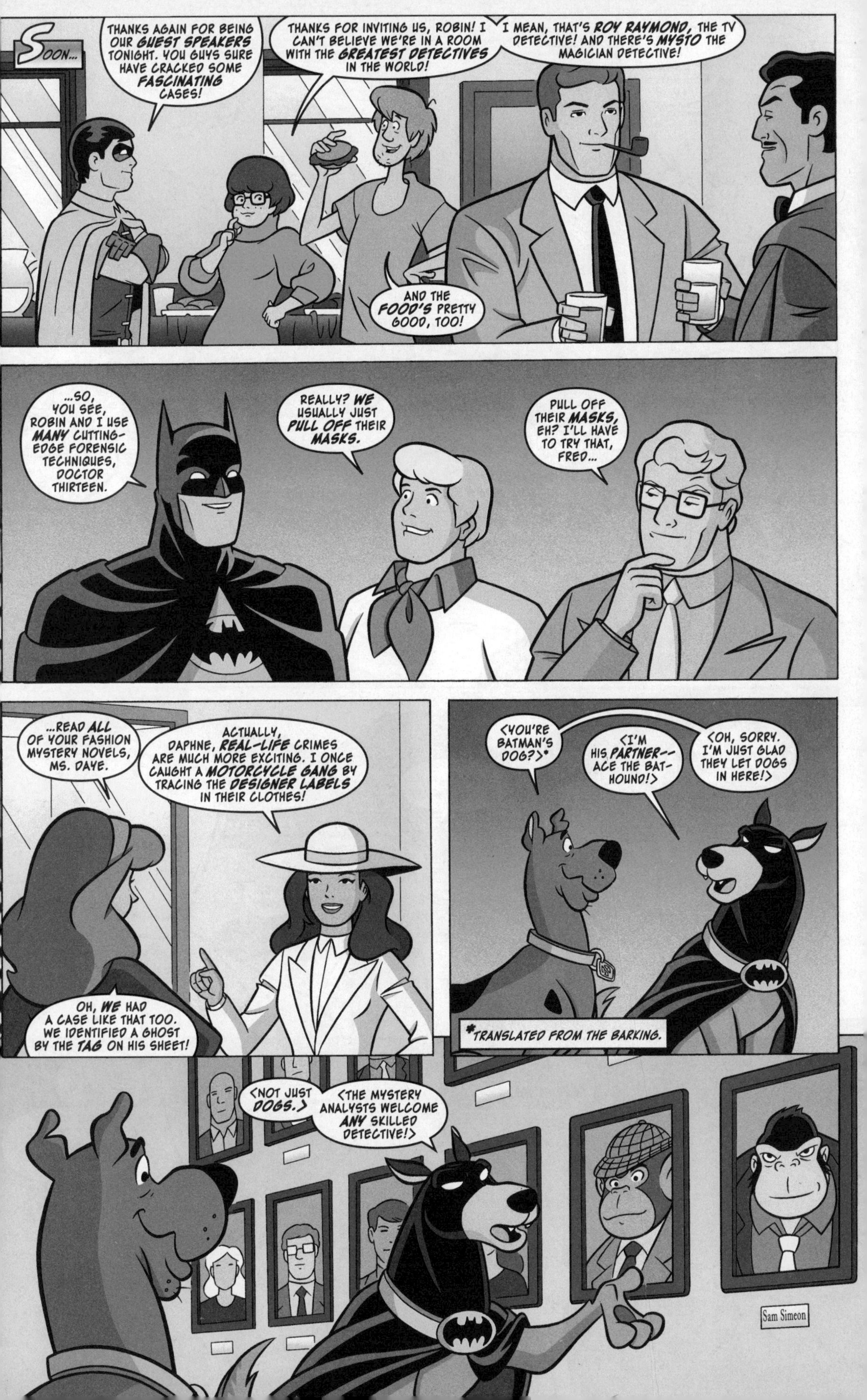
SOON...
THANKS AGAIN FOR BEING OUR GUEST SPEAKERS TONIGHT. YOU GUYS SURE HAVE CRACKED SOME FASCINATING CASES!
THANKS FOR INVITING US, ROBIN! I CAN'T BELIEVE WE'RE IN A ROOM WITH THE GREATEST DETECTIVES IN THE WORLD!
I MEAN, THAT'S ROY RAYMOND, THE TV DETECTIVE! AND THERE'S MYSTO THE MAGICIAN DETECTIVE!
AND THE FOOD'S PRETTY GOOD, TOO!
...SO, YOU SEE, ROBIN AND I USE MANY CUTTING-EDGE FORENSIC TECHNIQUES, DOCTOR THIRTEEN.
REALLY? WE USUALLY JUST PULL OFF THEIR MASKS.
PULL OFF THEIR MASKS, EH? I'LL HAVE TO TRY THAT, FRED...
...READ ALL OF YOUR FASHION MYSTERY NOVELS, MS. DAYE.
ACTUALLY, DAPHNE, REAL-LIFE CRIMES ARE MUCH MORE EXCITING. I ONCE CAUGHT A MOTORCYCLE GANG BY TRACING THE DESIGNER LABELS IN THEIR CLOTHES!
OH, WE HAD A CASE LIKE THAT TOO. WE IDENTIFIED A GHOST BY THE TAG ON HIS SHEET!
<YOU'RE BATMAN'S DOG?>*
<I'M HIS PARTNER--ACE THE BAT-HOUND!>
<OH, SORRY. I'M JUST GLAD THEY LET DOGS IN HERE!>
*TRANSLATED FROM THE BARKING.
<NOT JUST DOGS.>
<THE MYSTERY ANALYSTS WELCOME ANY SKILLED DETECTIVE!>
Sam Simeon

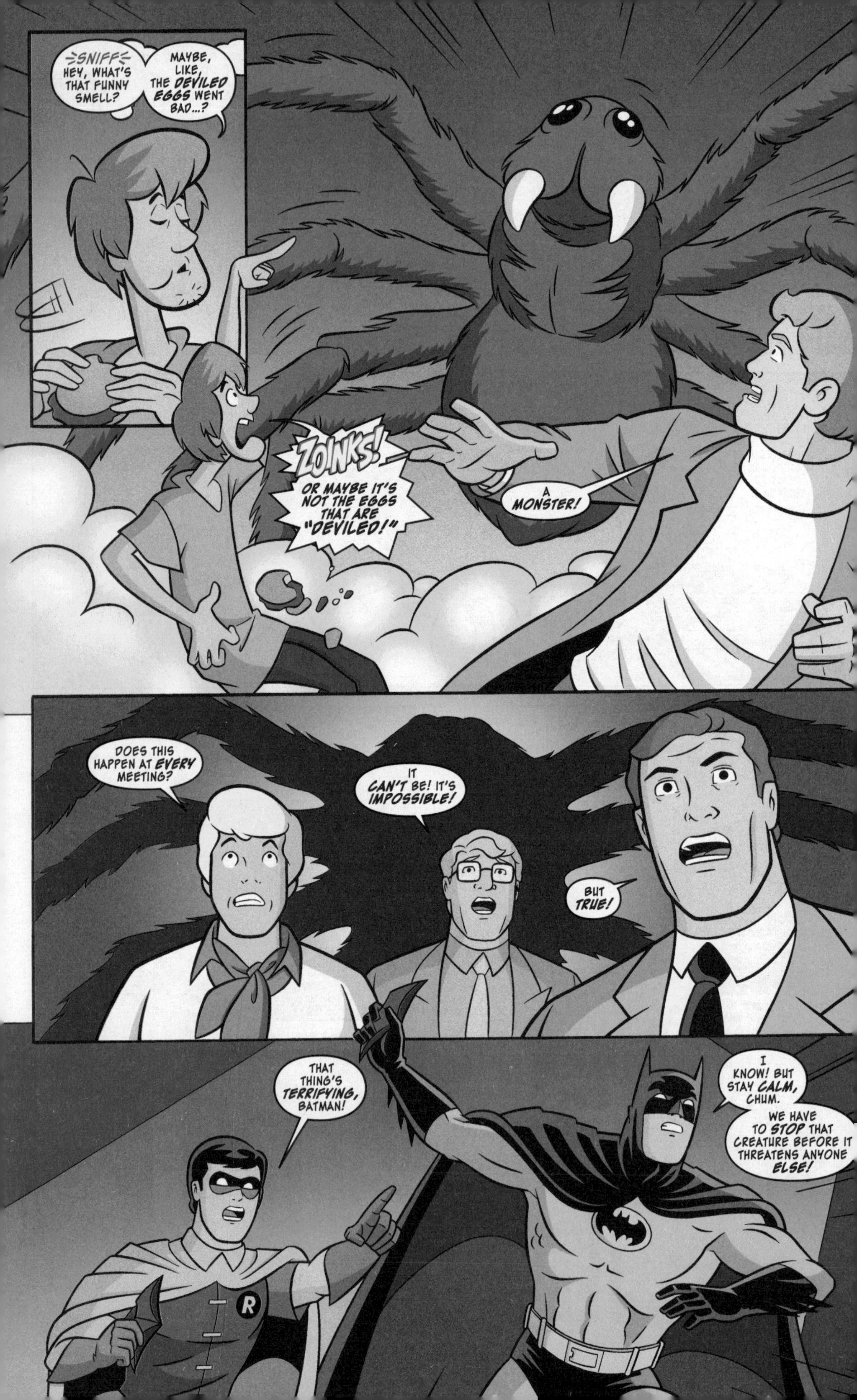

SNIFF HEY, WHAT'S THAT FUNNY SMELL?
MAYBE, LIKE, THE DEVILED EGGS WENT BAD...?
ZOINKS!
OR MAYBE IT'S NOT THE EGGS THAT ARE "DEVILED!"
A MONSTER!
DOES THIS HAPPEN AT EVERY MEETING?
IT CAN'T BE! IT'S IMPOSSIBLE!
BUT TRUE!
THAT THING'S TERRIFYING, BATMAN!
I KNOW! BUT STAY CALM, CHUM.
WE HAVE TO STOP THAT CREATURE BEFORE IT THREATENS ANYONE ELSE!

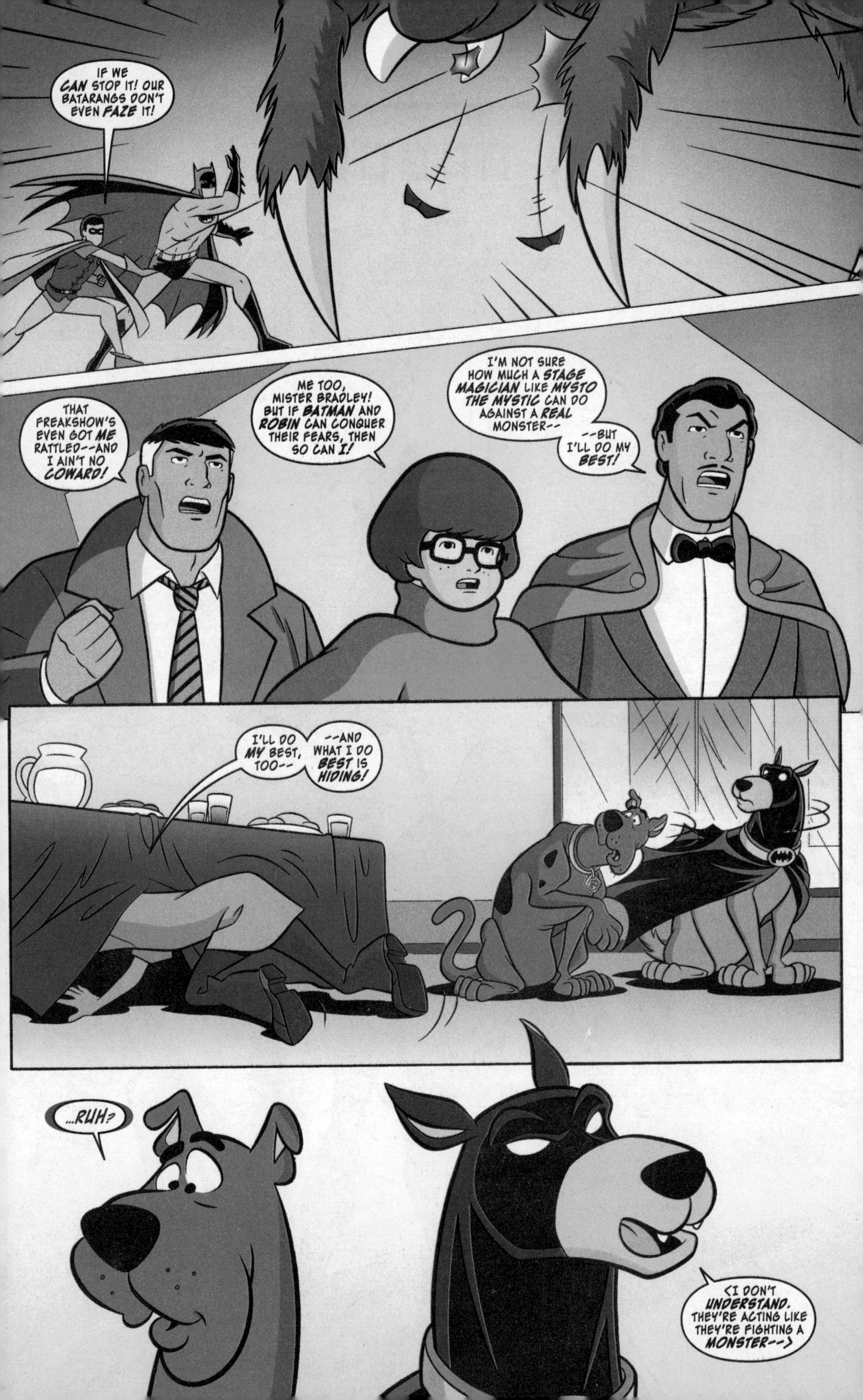
IF WE CAN STOP IT! OUR BATARANGS DON'T EVEN FAZE IT!
THAT FREAKSHOW'S EVEN GOT ME RATTLED--AND I AIN'T NO COWARD!
ME TOO, MISTER BRADLEY! BUT IF BATMAN AND ROBIN CAN CONQUER THEIR FEARS, THEN SO CAN I!
I'M NOT SURE HOW MUCH A STAGE MAGICIAN LIKE MYSTO THE MYSTIC CAN DO AGAINST A REAL MONSTER--
--BUT I'LL DO MY BEST!
I'LL DO MY BEST, TOO--
--AND WHAT I DO BEST IS HIDING!
...RUH?
<I DON'T UNDERSTAND. THEY'RE ACTING LIKE THEY'RE FIGHTING A MONSTER-->

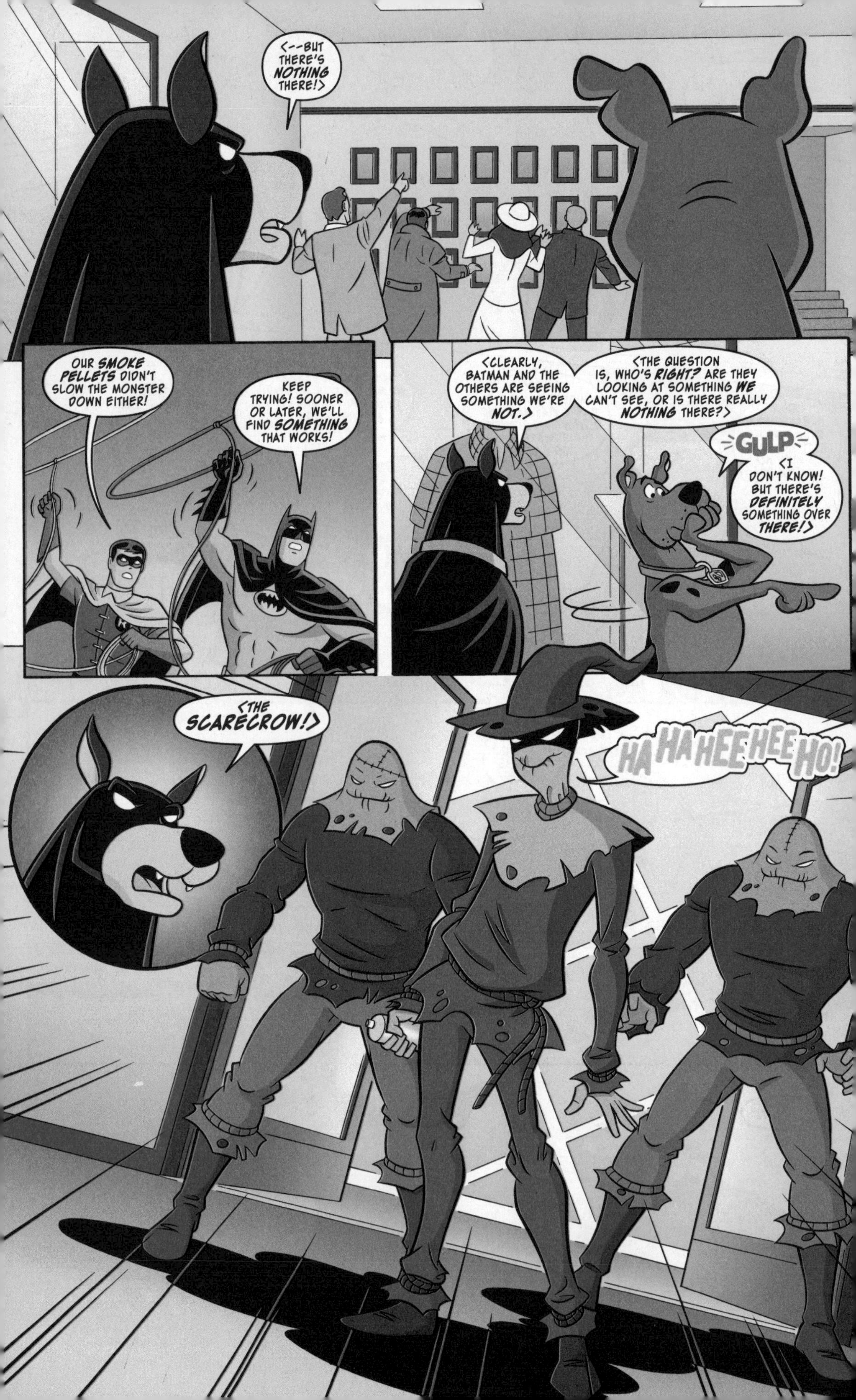
<--BUT THERE'S NOTHING THERE!>
OUR SMOKE PELLETS DIDN'T SLOW THE MONSTER DOWN EITHER!
KEEP TRYING! SOONER OR LATER, WE'LL FIND SOMETHING THAT WORKS!
<CLEARLY, BATMAN AND THE OTHERS ARE SEEING SOMETHING WE'RE NOT.>
<THE QUESTION IS, WHO'S RIGHT? ARE THEY LOOKING AT SOMETHING WE CAN'T SEE, OR IS THERE REALLY NOTHING THERE?>
GULP
<I DON'T KNOW! BUT THERE'S DEFINITELY SOMETHING OVER THERE!>
<THE SCARECROW!>
HA HA HEE HEE HO!

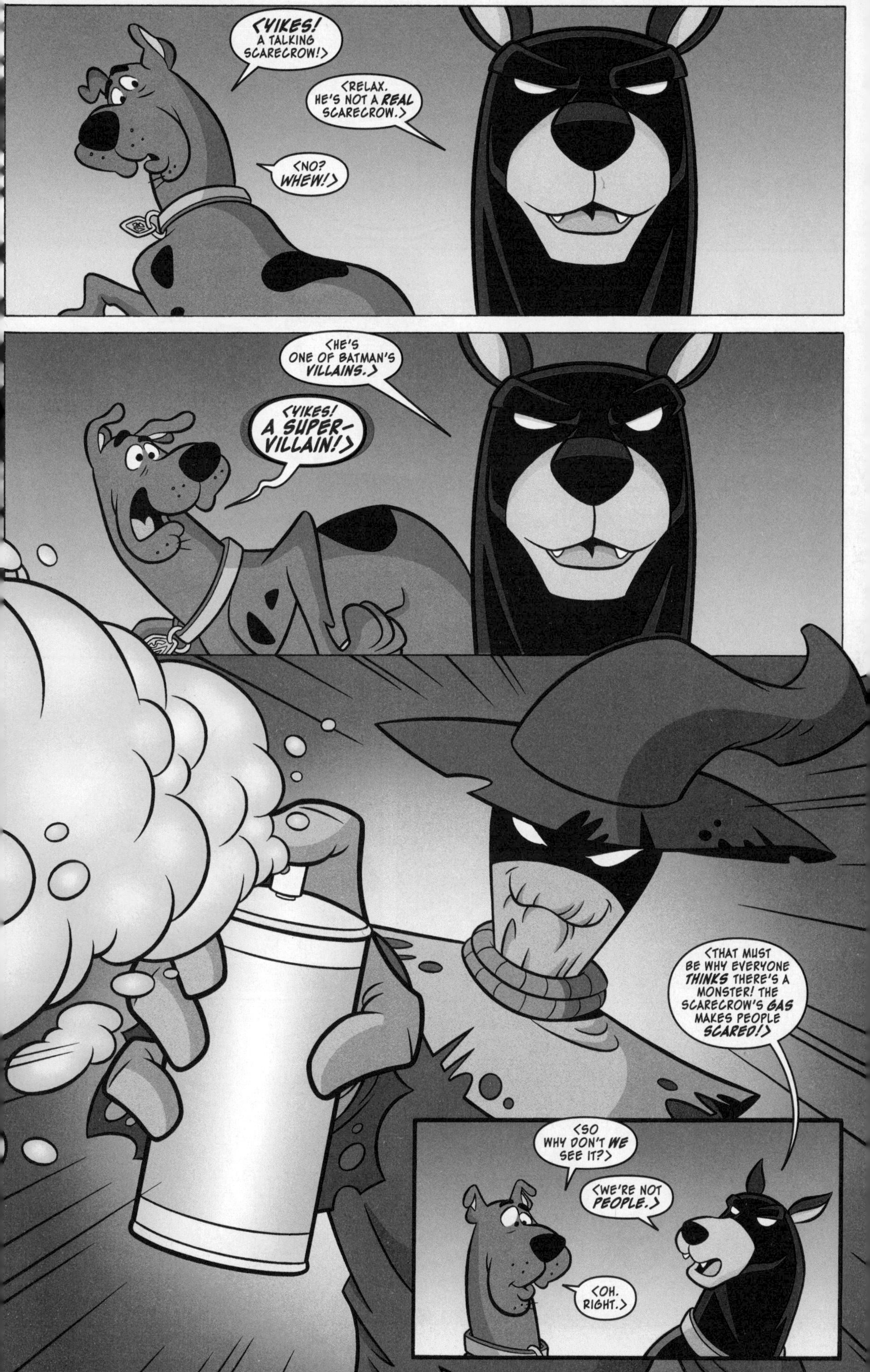

<YIKES! A TALKING SCARECROW!>
<RELAX. HE'S NOT A REAL SCARECROW.>
<NO? WHEW!>
<HE'S ONE OF BATMAN'S VILLAINS.>
<YIKES! A SUPER-VILLAIN!>
<THAT MUST BE WHY EVERYONE THINKS THERE'S A MONSTER! THE SCARECROW'S GAS MAKES PEOPLE SCARED!>
<SO WHY DON'T WE SEE IT?>
<WE'RE NOT PEOPLE.>
<OH. RIGHT.>

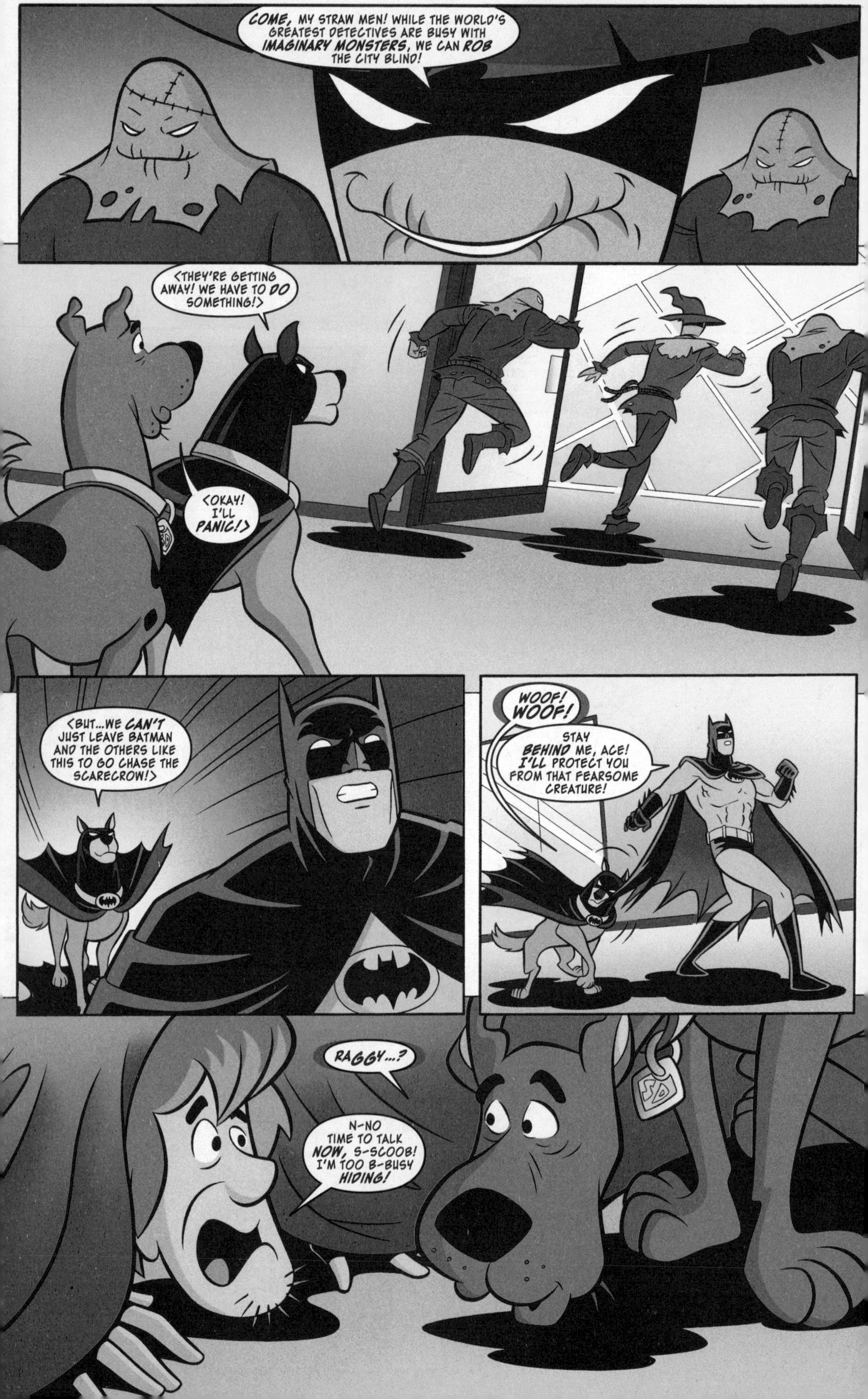
COME, MY STRAW MEN! WHILE THE WORLD'S GREATEST DETECTIVES ARE BUSY WITH IMAGINARY MONSTERS, WE CAN ROB THE CITY BLIND!
<THEY'RE GETTING AWAY! WE HAVE TO DO SOMETHING!>
<OKAY! I'LL PANIC!>
<BUT...WE CAN'T JUST LEAVE BATMAN AND THE OTHERS LIKE THIS TO GO CHASE THE SCARECROW!>
WOOF! WOOF!
STAY BEHIND ME, ACE! I'LL PROTECT YOU FROM THAT FEARSOME CREATURE!
RAGGY...?
N-NO TIME TO TALK NOW, S-SCOOB! I'M TOO B-BUSY HIDING!

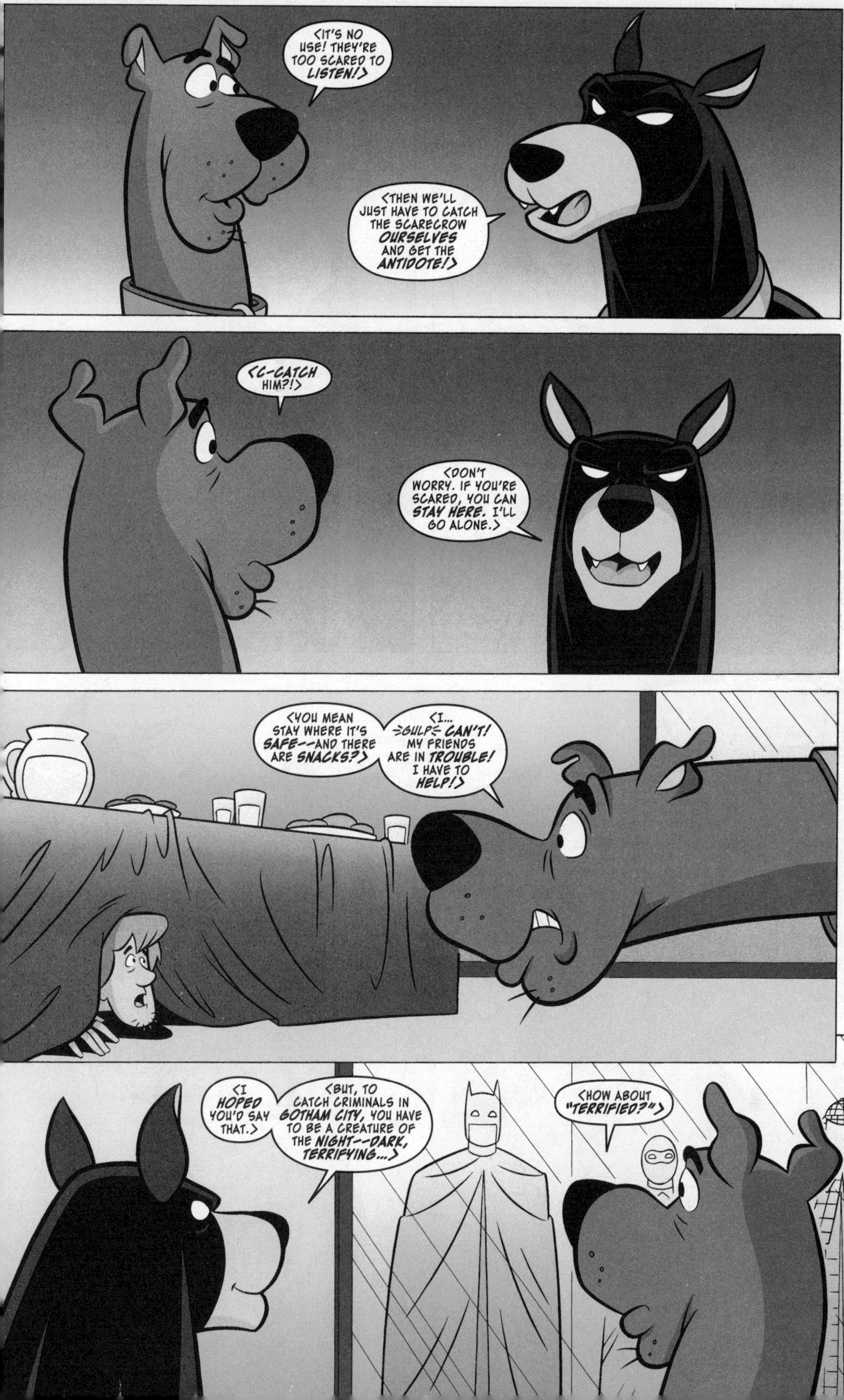

<IT'S NO USE! THEY'RE TOO SCARED TO LISTEN!>
<THEN WE'LL JUST HAVE TO CATCH THE SCARECROW OURSELVES AND GET THE ANTIDOTE!>
<C-CATCH HIM?!>
<DON'T WORRY. IF YOU'RE SCARED, YOU CAN STAY HERE. I'LL GO ALONE.>
<YOU MEAN STAY WHERE IT'S SAFE--AND THERE ARE SNACKS?>
<I... =GULP= CAN'T! MY FRIENDS ARE IN TROUBLE! I HAVE TO HELP!>
<I HOPED YOU'D SAY THAT.>
<BUT, TO CATCH CRIMINALS IN GOTHAM CITY, YOU HAVE TO BE A CREATURE OF THE NIGHT--DARK, TERRIFYING...>
<HOW ABOUT "TERRIFIED?">

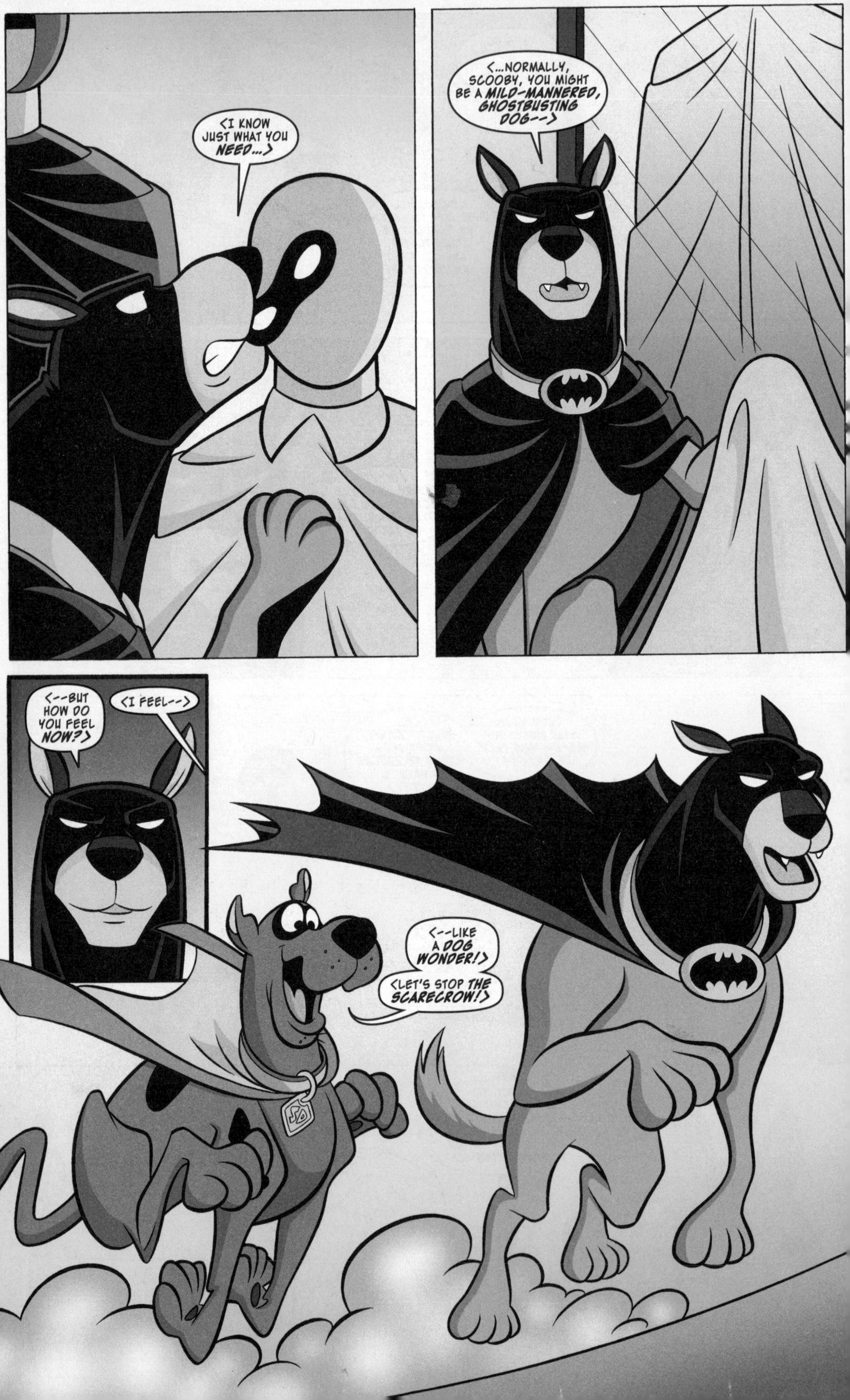

<I KNOW JUST WHAT YOU NEED...>
<...NORMALLY, SCOOBY, YOU MIGHT BE A MILD-MANNERED, GHOSTBUSTING DOG-->
<--BUT HOW DO YOU FEEL NOW?>
<I FEEL-->
<--LIKE A DOG WONDER!>
<LET'S STOP THE SCARECROW!>

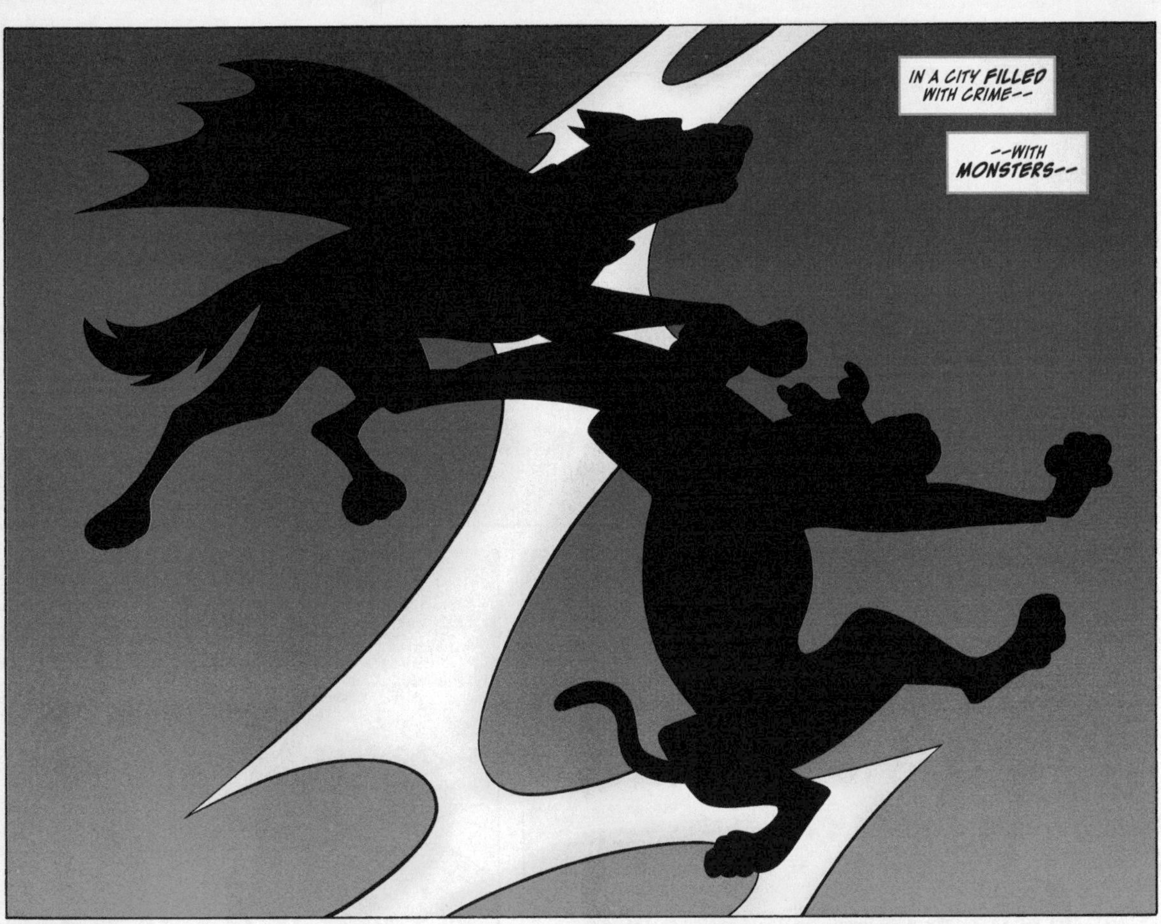
IN A CITY FILLED WITH CRIME--
--WITH MONSTERS--

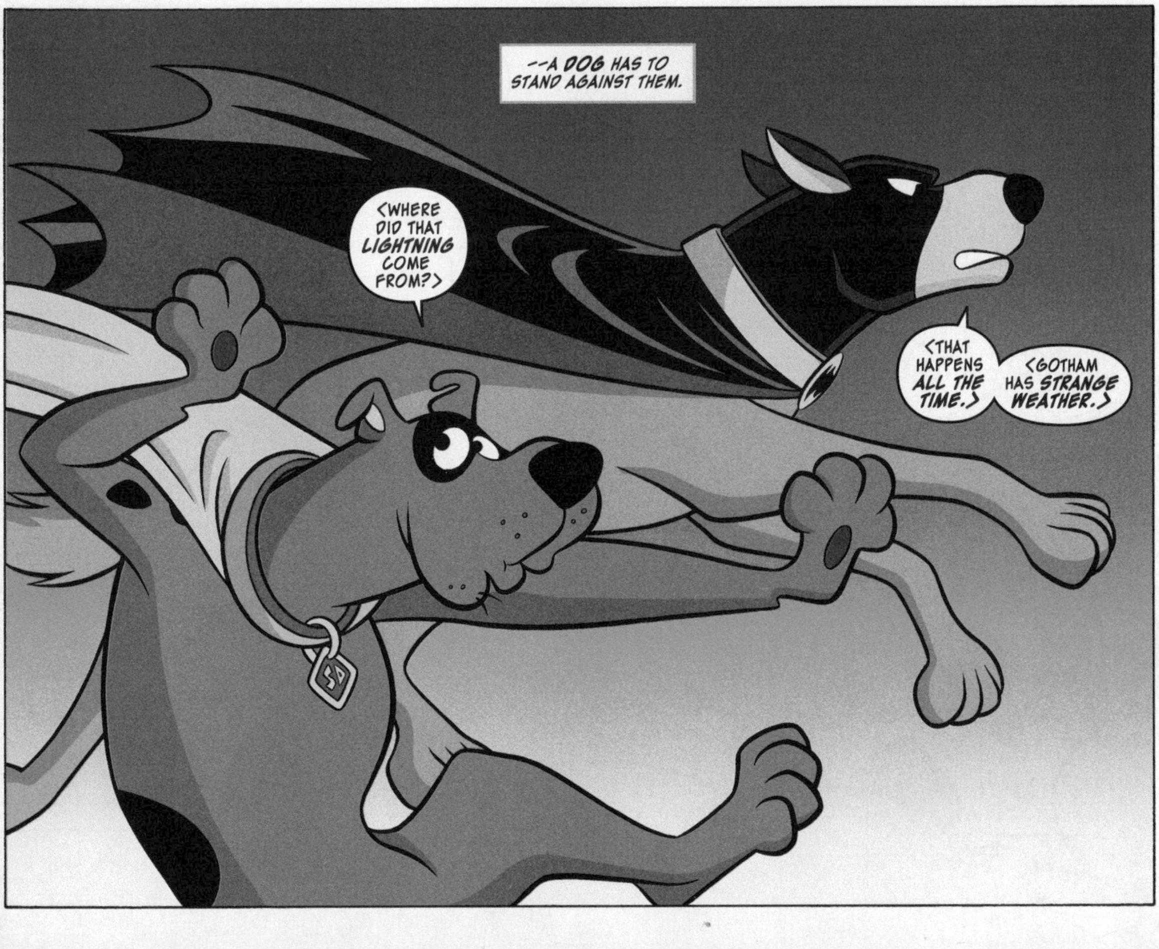
--A DOG HAS TO STAND AGAINST THEM.
<WHERE DID THAT LIGHTNING COME FROM?>
<THAT HAPPENS ALL THE TIME.>
<GOTHAM HAS STRANGE WEATHER.>

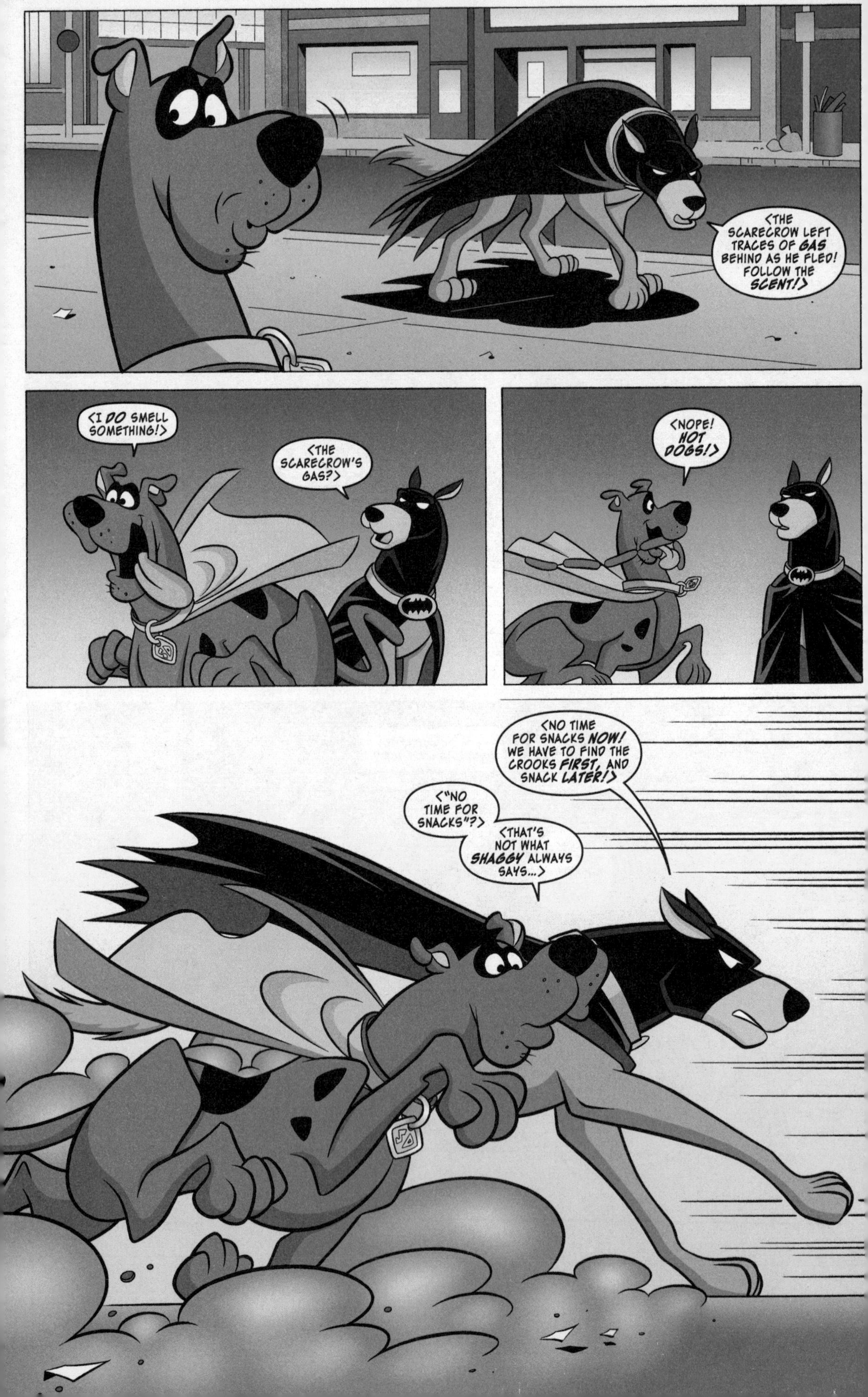
<THE SCARECROW LEFT TRACES OF GAS BEHIND AS HE FLED! FOLLOW THE SCENT!>
<I DO SMELL SOMETHING!>
<THE SCARECROW'S GAS?>
<NOPE! HOT DOGS!>
<NO TIME FOR SNACKS NOW! WE HAVE TO FIND THE CROOKS FIRST, AND SNACK LATER!>
<"NO TIME FOR SNACKS"?>
<THAT'S NOT WHAT SHAGGY ALWAYS SAYS...>

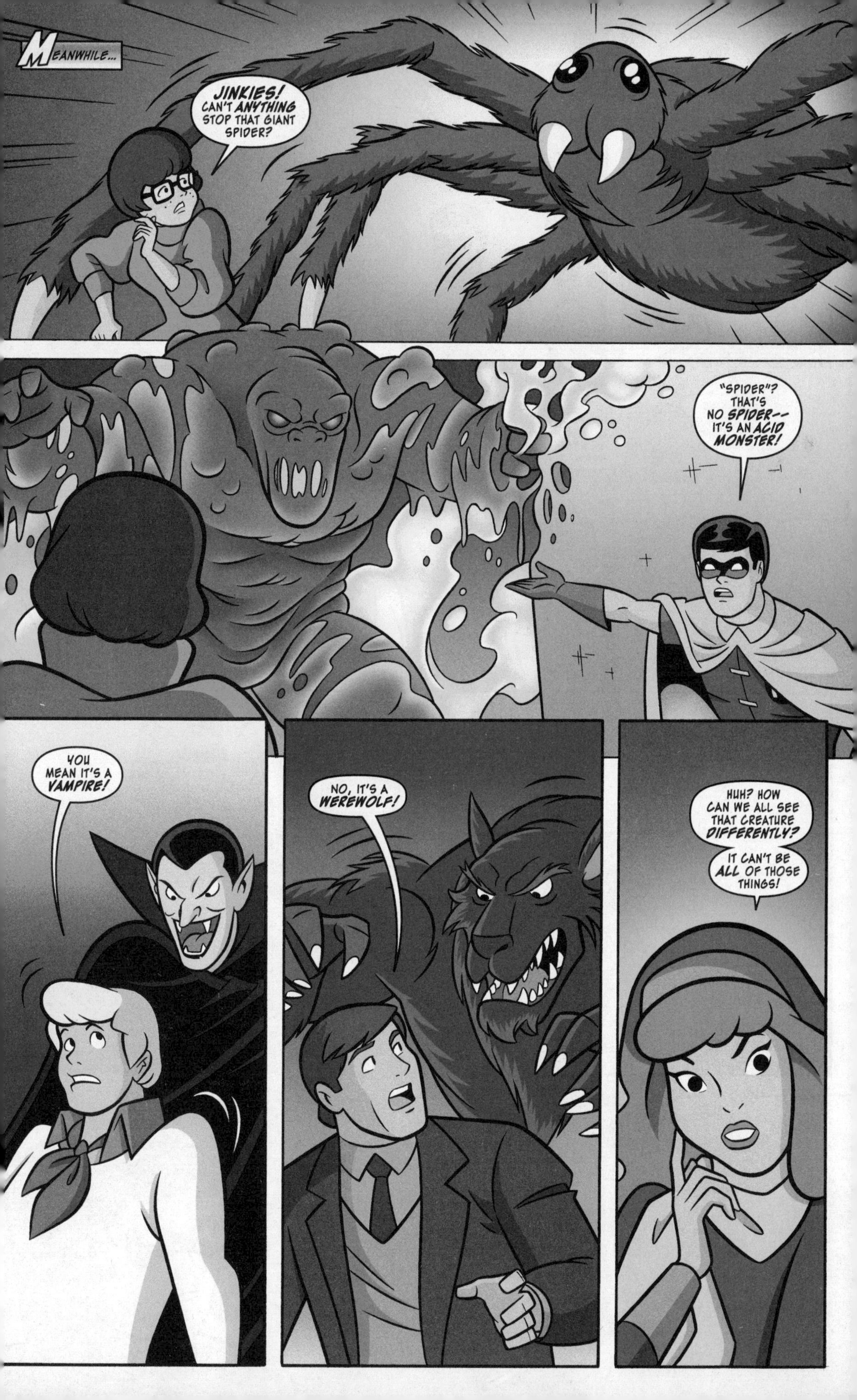
MEANWHILE...
JINKIES! CAN'T ANYTHING STOP THAT GIANT SPIDER?
"SPIDER"? THAT'S NO SPIDER-- IT'S AN ACID MONSTER!
YOU MEAN IT'S A VAMPIRE!
NO, IT'S A WEREWOLF!
HUH? HOW CAN WE ALL SEE THAT CREATURE DIFFERENTLY?
IT CAN'T BE ALL OF THOSE THINGS!

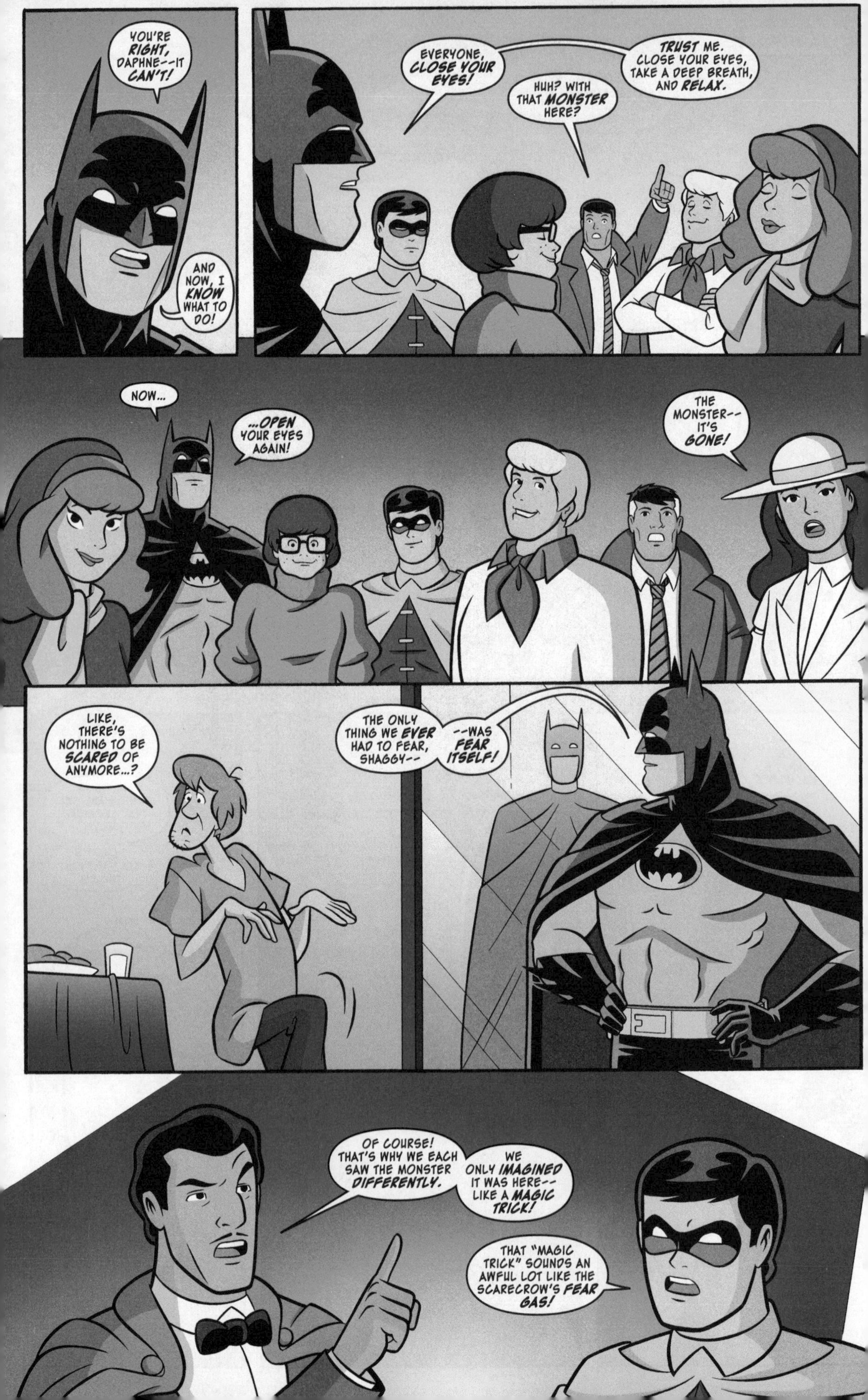

YOU'RE RIGHT, DAPHNE--IT CAN'T!
AND NOW, I KNOW WHAT TO DO!
EVERYONE, CLOSE YOUR EYES!
HUH? WITH THAT MONSTER HERE?
TRUST ME. CLOSE YOUR EYES, TAKE A DEEP BREATH, AND RELAX.
NOW...
...OPEN YOUR EYES AGAIN!
THE MONSTER--IT'S GONE!
LIKE, THERE'S NOTHING TO BE SCARED OF ANYMORE...?
THE ONLY THING WE EVER HAD TO FEAR, SHAGGY--
--WAS FEAR ITSELF!
OF COURSE! THAT'S WHY WE EACH SAW THE MONSTER DIFFERENTLY.
WE ONLY IMAGINED IT WAS HERE--LIKE A MAGIC TRICK!
THAT "MAGIC TRICK" SOUNDS AN AWFUL LOT LIKE THE SCARECROW'S FEAR GAS!

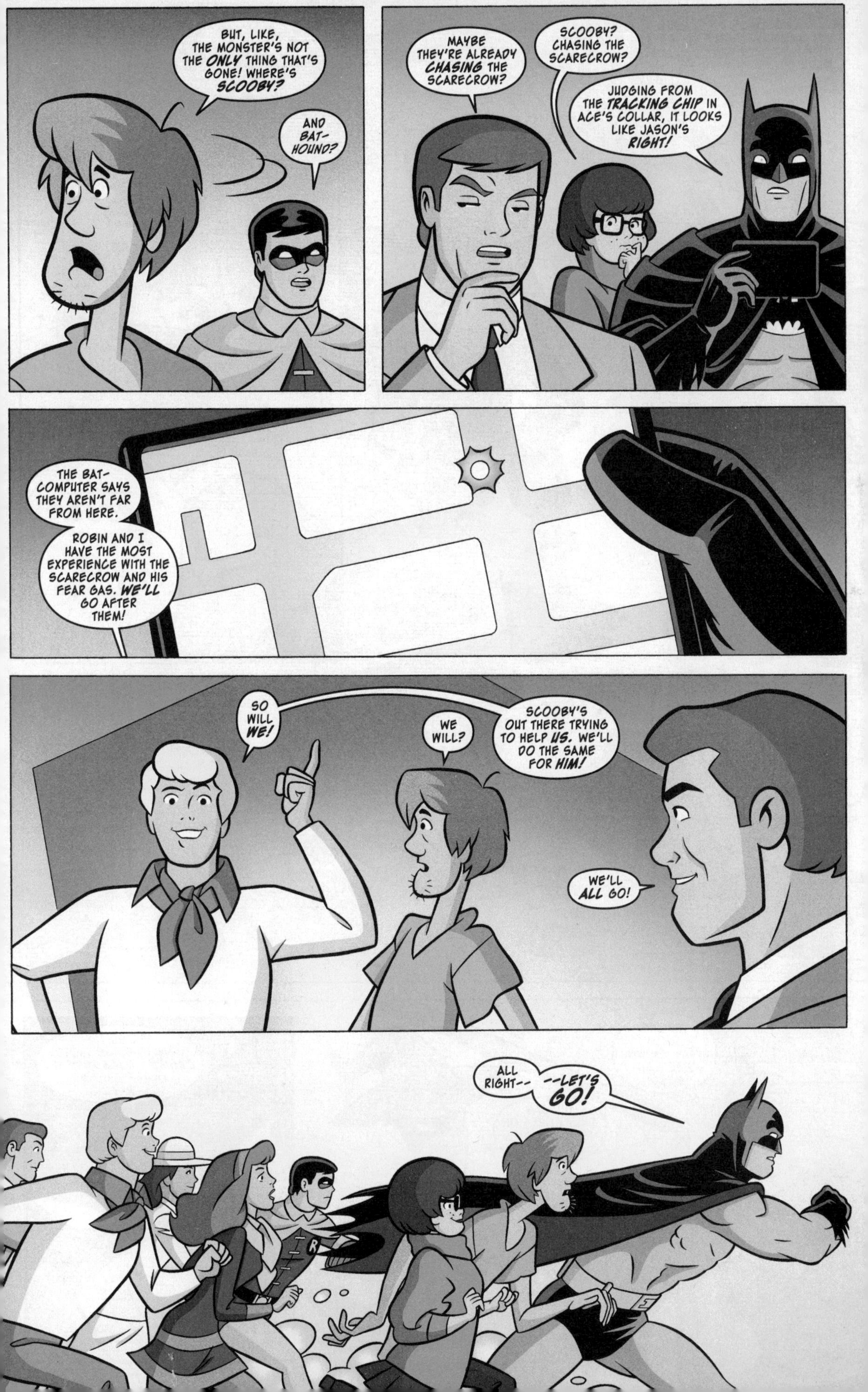
BUT, LIKE, THE MONSTER'S NOT THE ONLY THING THAT'S GONE! WHERE'S SCOOBY?
AND BAT-HOUND?
MAYBE THEY'RE ALREADY CHASING THE SCARECROW?
SCOOBY? CHASING THE SCARECROW?
JUDGING FROM THE TRACKING CHIP IN ACE'S COLLAR, IT LOOKS LIKE JASON'S RIGHT!
THE BAT-COMPUTER SAYS THEY AREN'T FAR FROM HERE.
ROBIN AND I HAVE THE MOST EXPERIENCE WITH THE SCARECROW AND HIS FEAR GAS. WE'LL GO AFTER THEM!
SO WILL WE!
WE WILL?
SCOOBY'S OUT THERE TRYING TO HELP US. WE'LL DO THE SAME FOR HIM!
WE'LL ALL GO!
ALL RIGHT--
--LET'S GO!

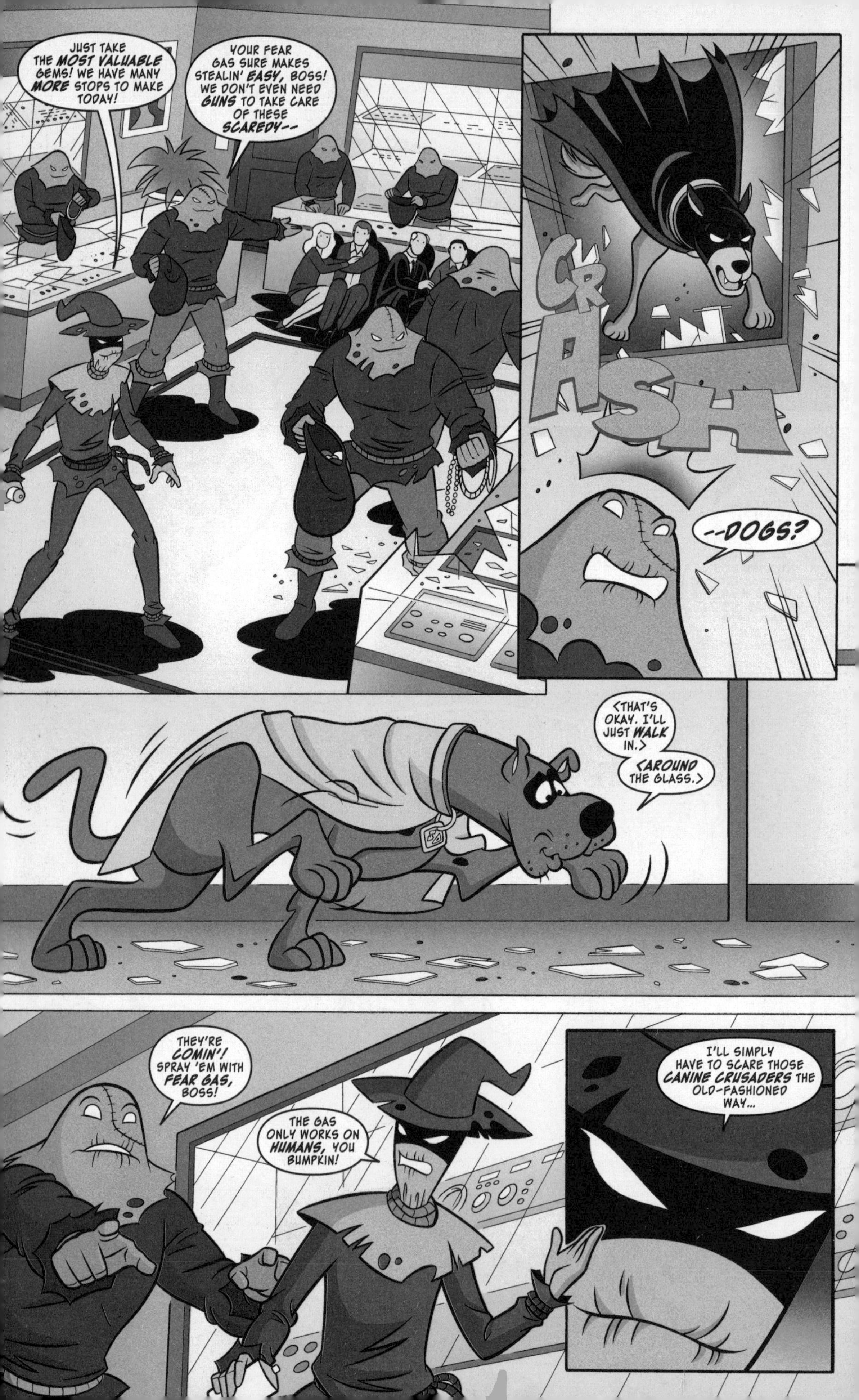
JUST TAKE THE MOST VALUABLE GEMS! WE HAVE MANY MORE STOPS TO MAKE TODAY!
YOUR FEAR GAS SURE MAKES STEALIN' EASY, BOSS! WE DON'T EVEN NEED GUNS TO TAKE CARE OF THESE SCAREDY--
CRASH
--DOGS?
<THAT'S OKAY. I'LL JUST WALK IN.>
<AROUND THE GLASS.>
THEY'RE COMIN'! SPRAY 'EM WITH FEAR GAS, BOSS!
THE GAS ONLY WORKS ON HUMANS, YOU BUMPKIN!
I'LL SIMPLY HAVE TO SCARE THOSE CANINE CRUSADERS THE OLD-FASHIONED WAY...

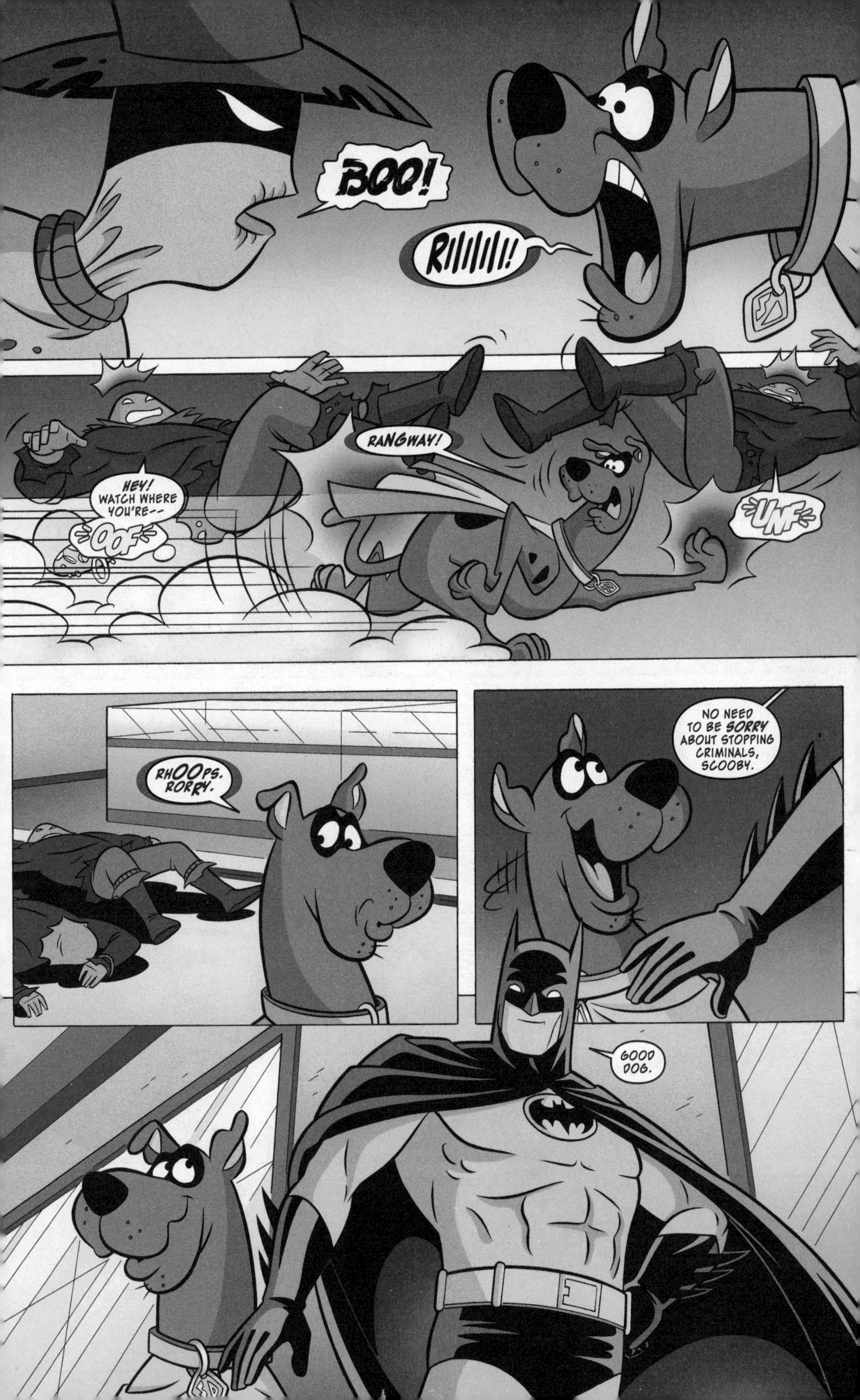
BOO!
RIIIIIII!
RANGWAY!
HEY! WATCH WHERE YOU'RE--
OOF
UNF
RHOOPS. RORRY.
NO NEED TO BE SORRY ABOUT STOPPING CRIMINALS, SCOOBY.
GOOD DOG.

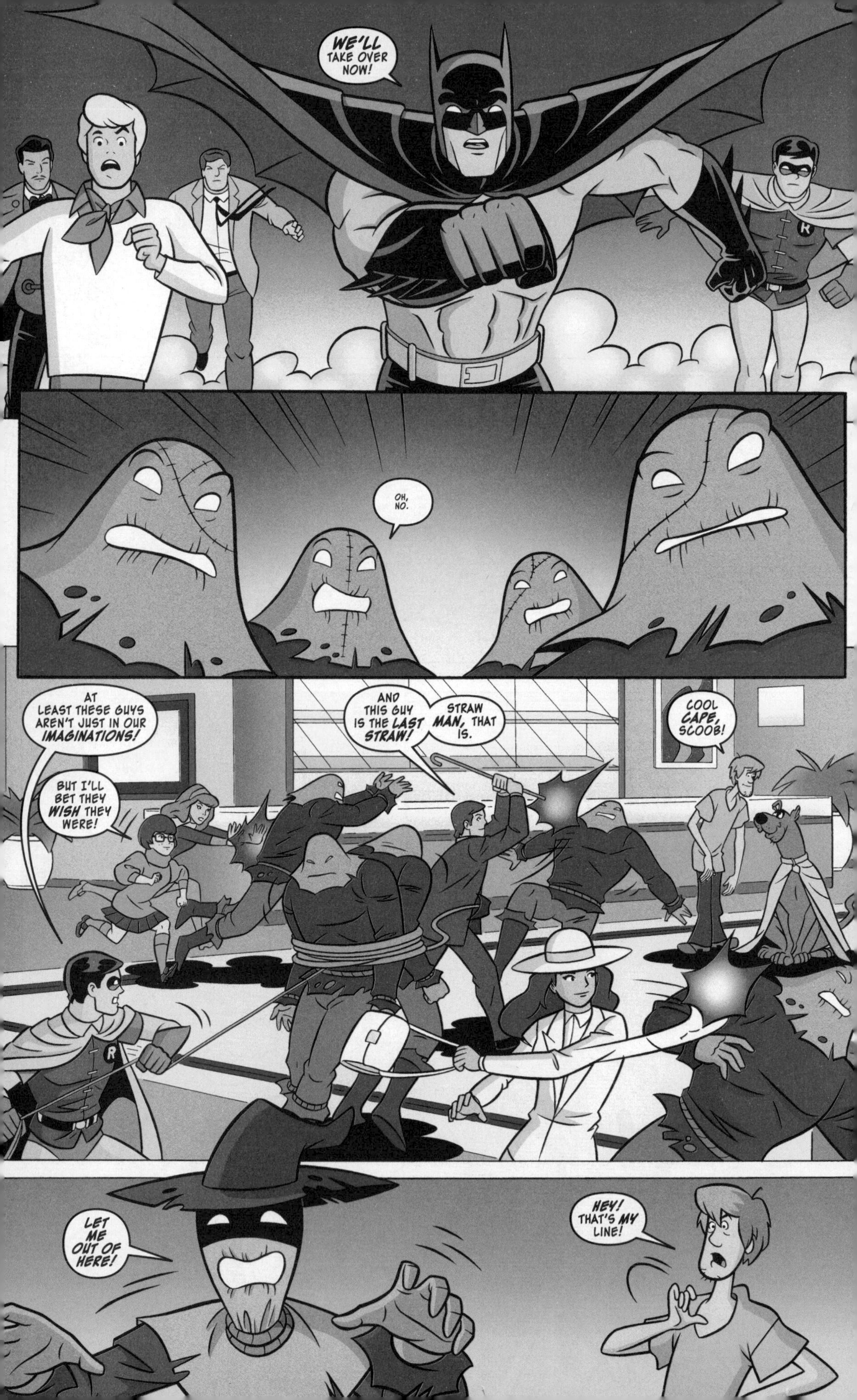
WE'LL TAKE OVER NOW!
OH, NO.
AT LEAST THESE GUYS AREN'T JUST IN OUR IMAGINATIONS!
BUT I'LL BET THEY WISH THEY WERE!
AND THIS GUY IS THE LAST STRAW!
STRAW MAN, THAT IS.
COOL CAPE, SCOOB!
LET ME OUT OF HERE!
HEY! THAT'S MY LINE!

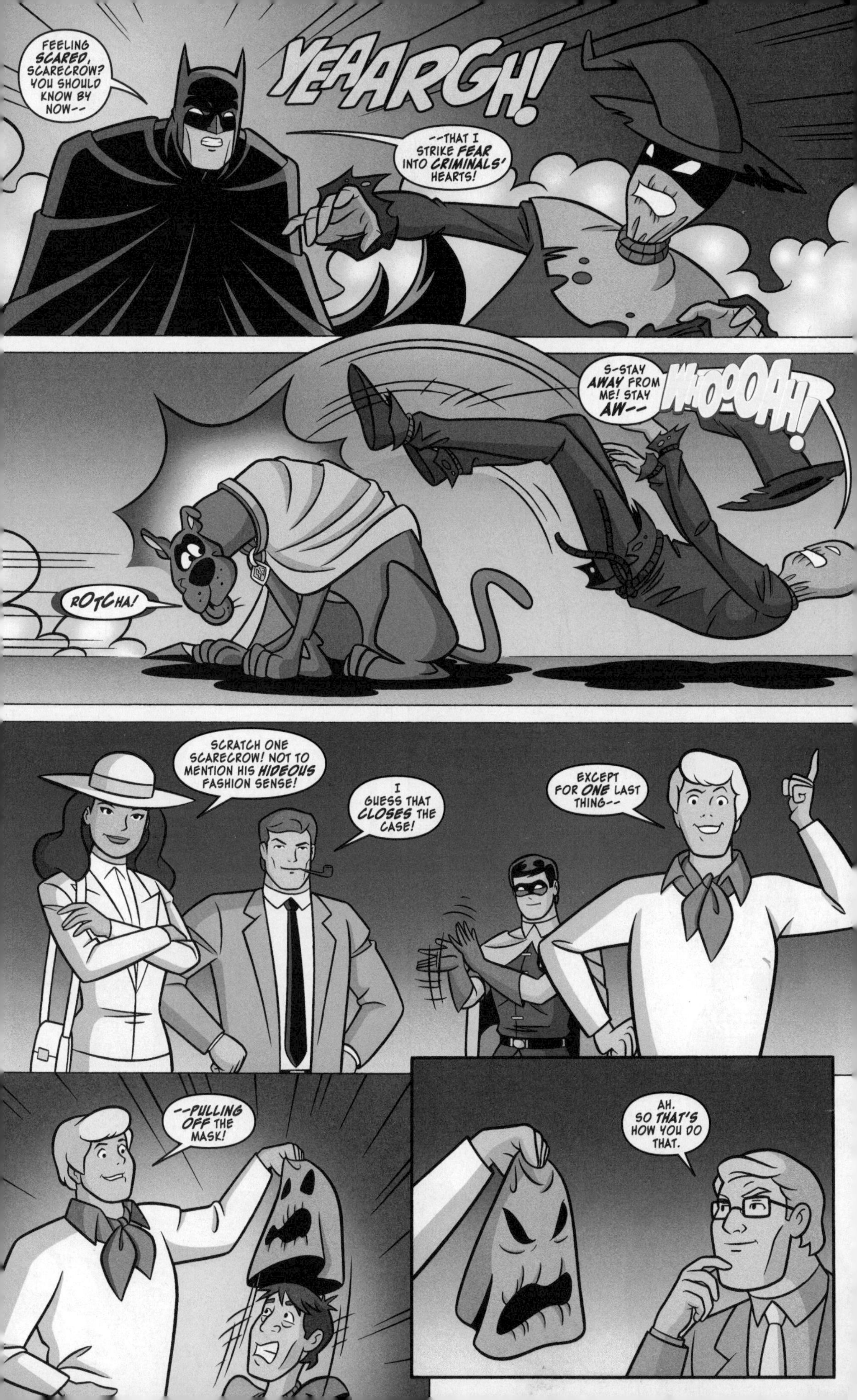
FEELING SCARED, SCARECROW? YOU SHOULD KNOW BY NOW--
YEAARGH!
--THAT I STRIKE FEAR INTO CRIMINALS' HEARTS!
S-STAY AWAY FROM ME! STAY AW--
WHOOOAH!
ROTCHA!
SCRATCH ONE SCARECROW! NOT TO MENTION HIS HIDEOUS FASHION SENSE!
I GUESS THAT CLOSES THE CASE!
EXCEPT FOR ONE LAST THING--
--PULLING OFF THE MASK!
AH. SO THAT'S HOW YOU DO THAT.

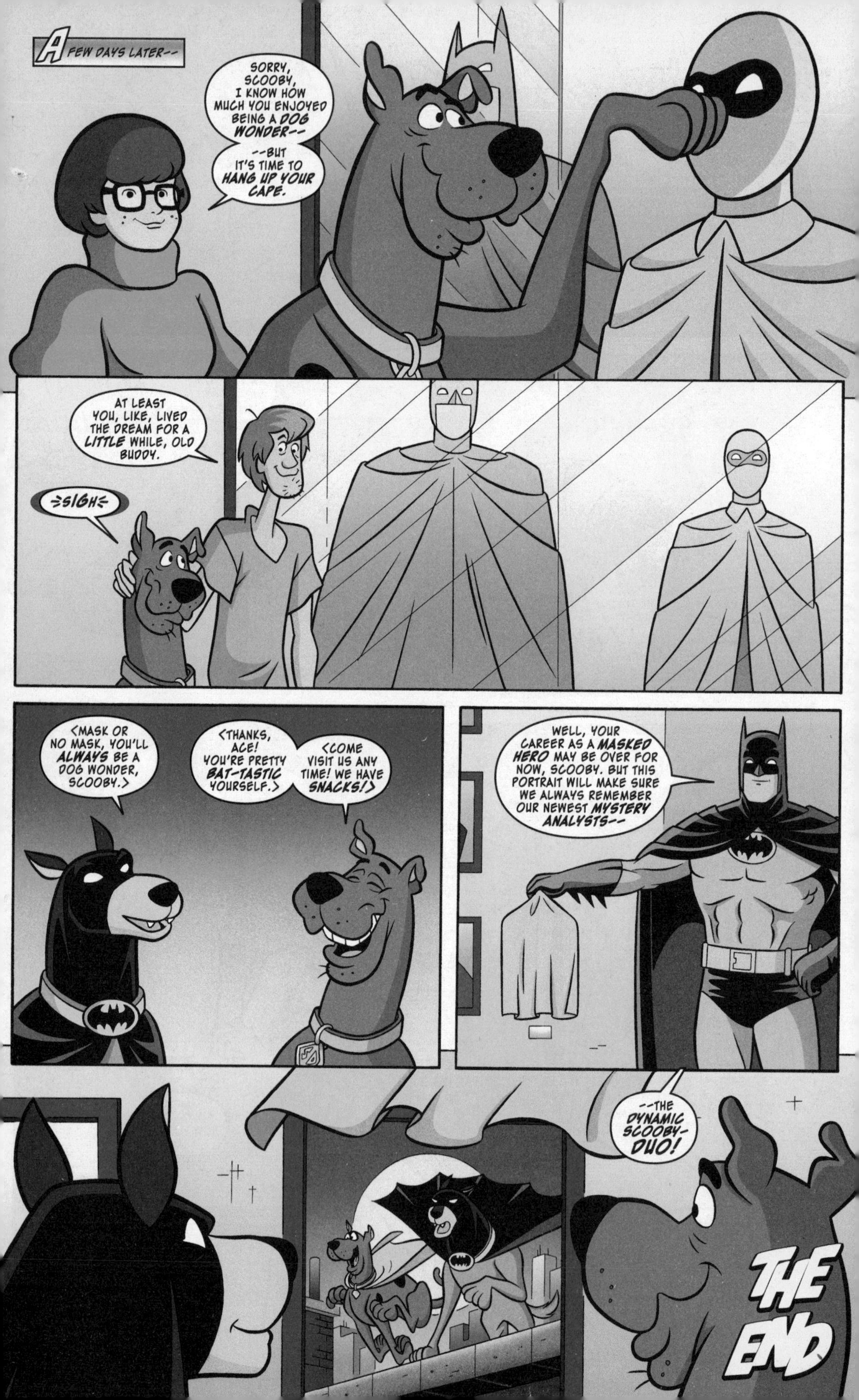
A FEW DAYS LATER--
SORRY, SCOOBY, I KNOW HOW MUCH YOU ENJOYED BEING A DOG WONDER--
--BUT IT'S TIME TO HANG UP YOUR CAPE.
AT LEAST YOU, LIKE, LIVED THE DREAM FOR A LITTLE WHILE, OLD BUDDY.
≥SIGH≤
<MASK OR NO MASK, YOU'LL ALWAYS BE A DOG WONDER, SCOOBY.>
<THANKS, ACE! YOU'RE PRETTY BAT-TASTIC YOURSELF.>
<COME VISIT US ANY TIME! WE HAVE SNACKS!>
WELL, YOUR CAREER AS A MASKED HERO MAY BE OVER FOR NOW, SCOOBY. BUT THIS PORTRAIT WILL MAKE SURE WE ALWAYS REMEMBER OUR NEWEST MYSTERY ANALYSTS--
--THE DYNAMIC SCOOBY-DUO!
THE END

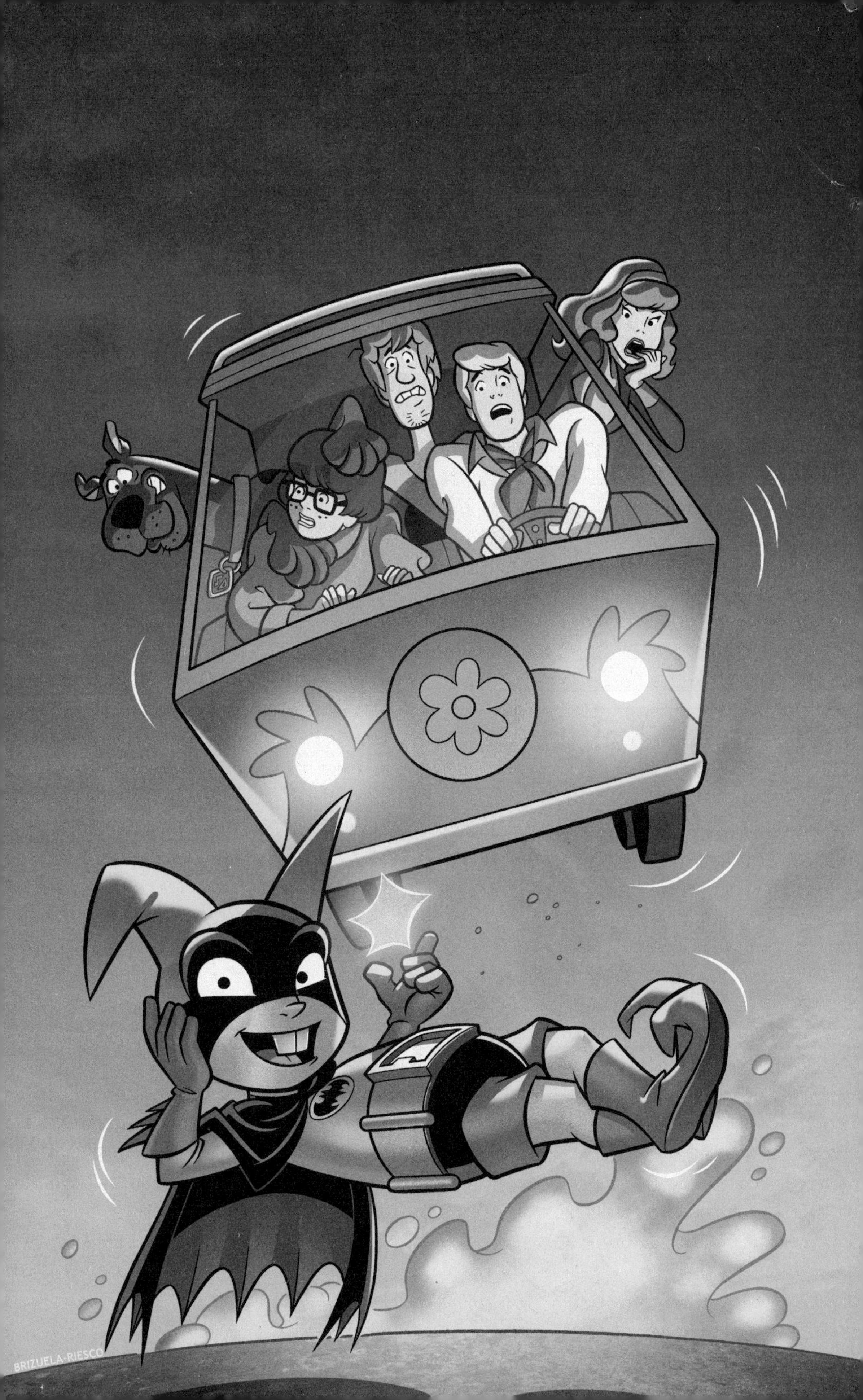
BRIZUELA-RIESCO

JINKIES, FRED. I ALWAYS *WONDERED* WHERE THE CROOKS WE CATCH GET ALL THE *COSTUMES* AND *GADGETS* THEY NEED TO POSE AS GHOSTS!

WITH BATMAN AND ROBIN'S HELP, WE'LL SOLVE THAT MYSTERY IN A MINUTE, VELMA--

--BECAUSE THE TRAIL LEADS RIGHT *HERE!*

GO AWAY!

CLOSED

NOBODY HOME

KRRRAAASSHHH!

JUST AS I SUSPECTED! THE COSTUMES AND EQUIPMENT ARE BEING SUPPLIED BY TWO OF OUR OLD VILLAINS--*THE SPOOK* AND *FALSE FACE!*

BATMAN AND ROBIN!

OF COURSE! FALSE FACE IS A *MASTER OF DISGUISE!* AND THE SPOOK IS A HUMAN CROOK WHO USES *TRICKS* TO MAKE HIMSELF *SEEM* LIKE A GHOST!

JUST THE THING FOR THE KINDS OF CROOKS *WE* FACE!

YOU WON'T CAPTURE US! NOT WHEN THE MISTS OF THE NETHERWORLD ARE AT MY COMMAND!

"MISTS OF THE NETHERWORLD"? YOU MEAN A SMOKE BOMB!

≥OOOF!≤

≥KOFF KOFF≤ RERE IS REVERYBOO--?

RHOOOOPS!

RORRY.

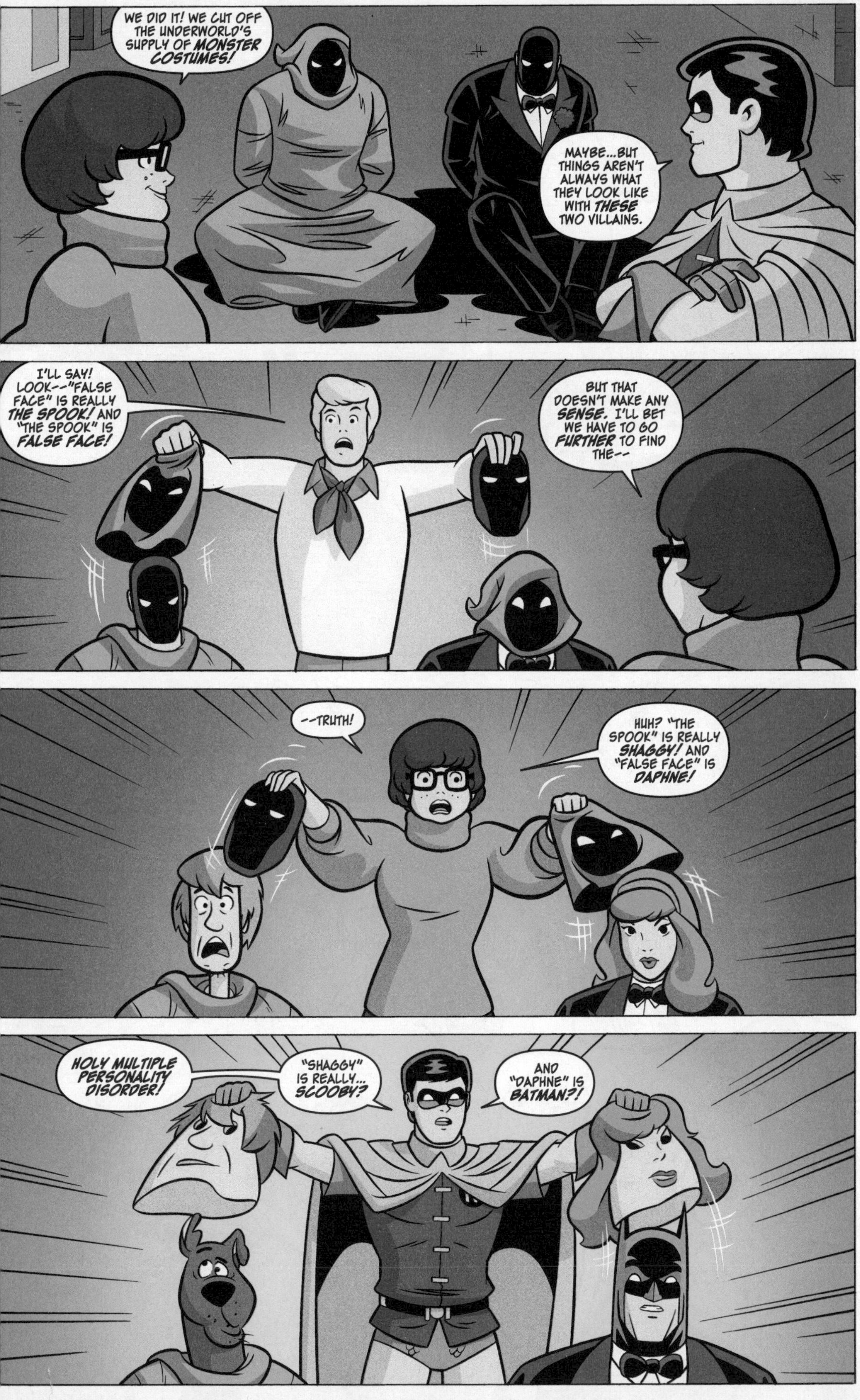
WE DID IT! WE CUT OFF THE UNDERWORLD'S SUPPLY OF MONSTER COSTUMES!
MAYBE...BUT THINGS AREN'T ALWAYS WHAT THEY LOOK LIKE WITH THESE TWO VILLAINS.
I'LL SAY! LOOK--"FALSE FACE" IS REALLY THE SPOOK! AND "THE SPOOK" IS FALSE FACE!
BUT THAT DOESN'T MAKE ANY SENSE. I'LL BET WE HAVE TO GO FURTHER TO FIND THE--
--TRUTH!
HUH? "THE SPOOK" IS REALLY SHAGGY! AND "FALSE FACE" IS DAPHNE!
HOLY MULTIPLE PERSONALITY DISORDER!
"SHAGGY" IS REALLY... SCOOBY?
AND "DAPHNE" IS BATMAN?!

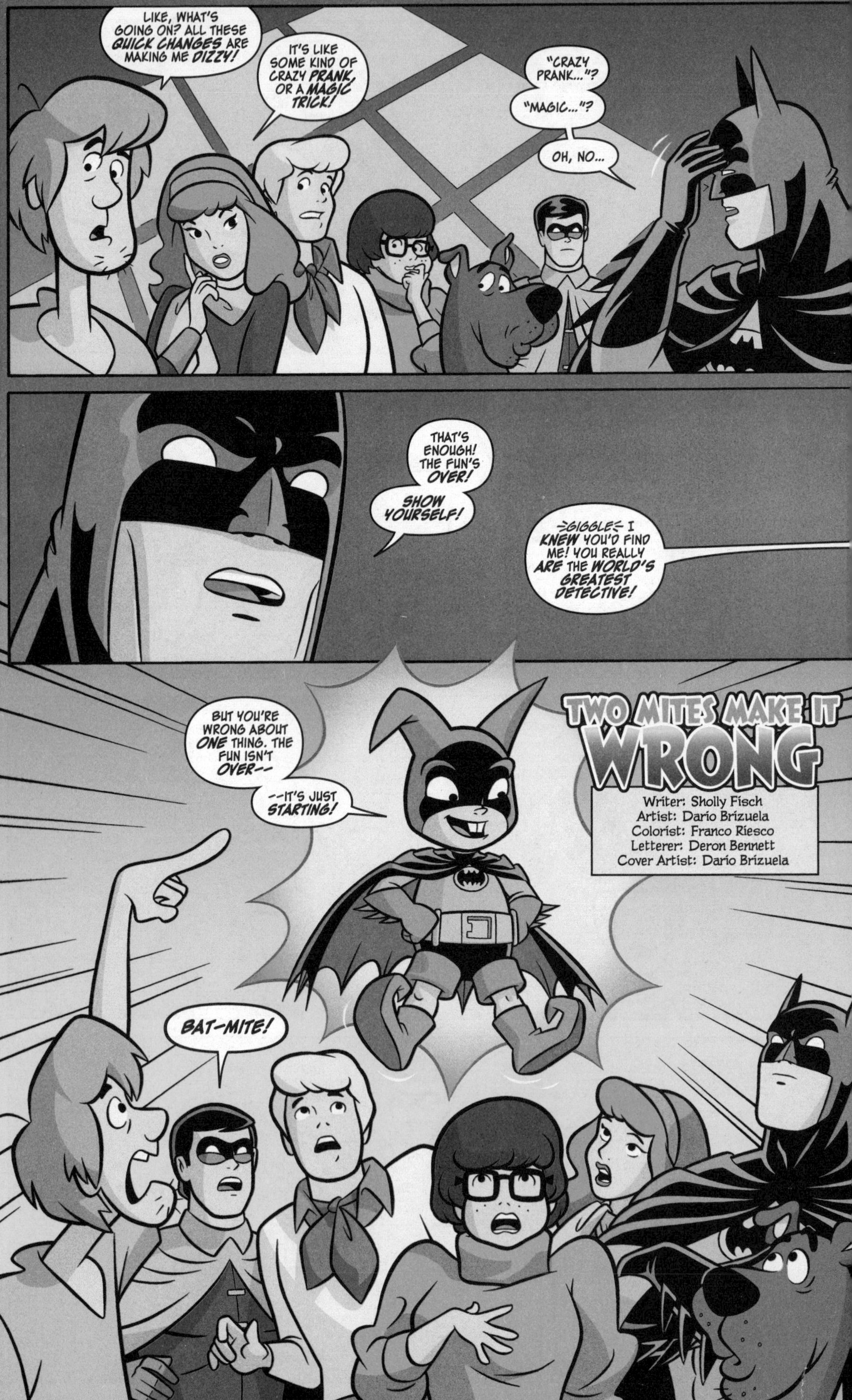
LIKE, WHAT'S GOING ON? ALL THESE QUICK CHANGES ARE MAKING ME DIZZY!
IT'S LIKE SOME KIND OF CRAZY PRANK, OR A MAGIC TRICK!
"CRAZY PRANK..."?
"MAGIC..."?
OH, NO...
THAT'S ENOUGH! THE FUN'S OVER!
SHOW YOURSELF!
=GIGGLE= I KNEW YOU'D FIND ME! YOU REALLY ARE THE WORLD'S GREATEST DETECTIVE!
BUT YOU'RE WRONG ABOUT ONE THING. THE FUN ISN'T OVER--
--IT'S JUST STARTING!
TWO MITES MAKE IT WRONG
Writer: Sholly Fisch
Artist: Dario Brizuela
Colorist: Franco Riesco
Letterer: Deron Bennett
Cover Artist: Dario Brizuela
BAT-MITE!

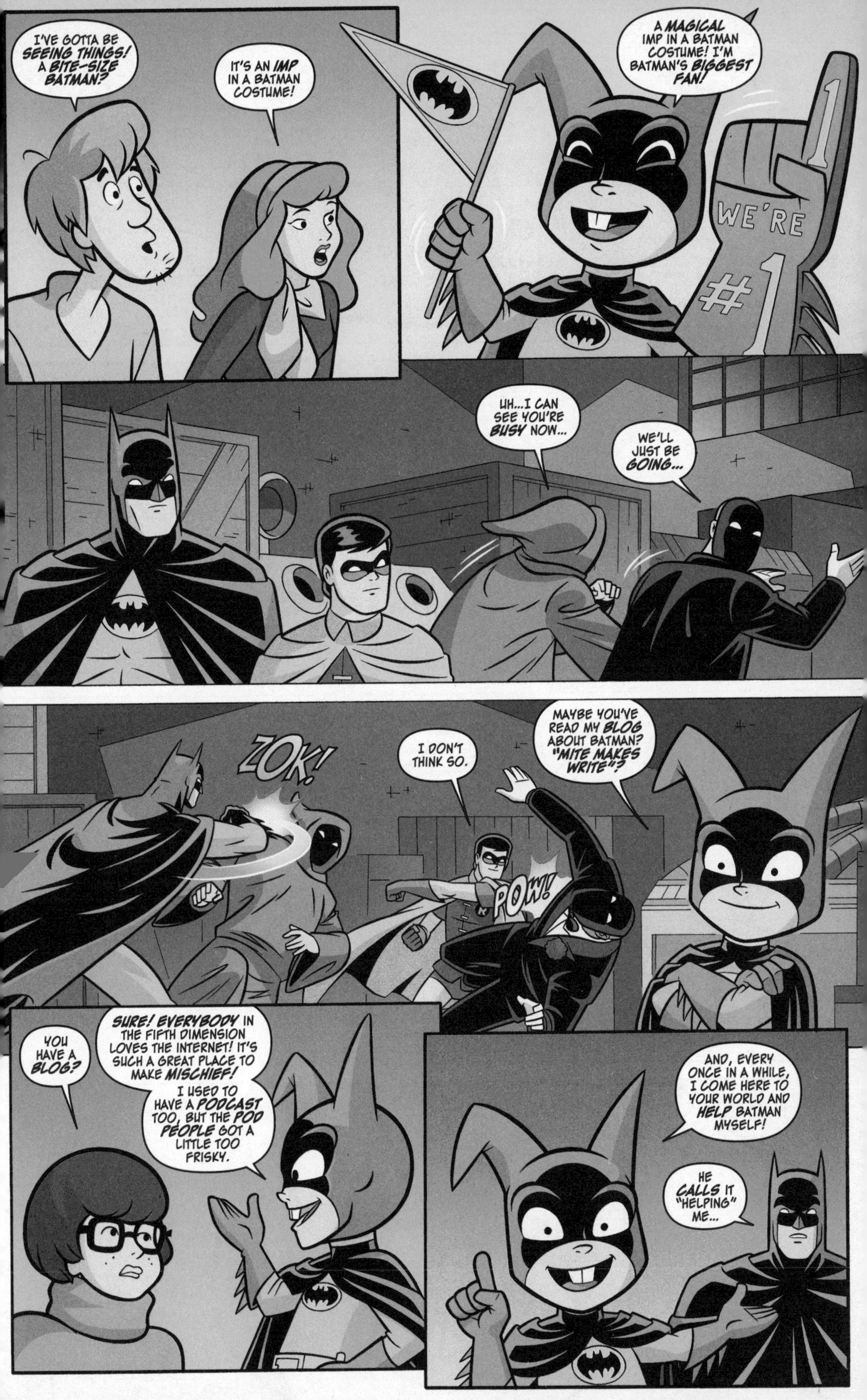

I'VE GOTTA BE SEEING THINGS! A BITE-SIZE BATMAN?
IT'S AN IMP IN A BATMAN COSTUME!
A MAGICAL IMP IN A BATMAN COSTUME! I'M BATMAN'S BIGGEST FAN!
1
WE'RE #1
UH...I CAN SEE YOU'RE BUSY NOW...
WE'LL JUST BE GOING...
ZOK!
I DON'T THINK SO.
MAYBE YOU'VE READ MY BLOG ABOUT BATMAN? "MITE MAKES WRITE"?
POW!
YOU HAVE A BLOG?
SURE! EVERYBODY IN THE FIFTH DIMENSION LOVES THE INTERNET! IT'S SUCH A GREAT PLACE TO MAKE MISCHIEF!
I USED TO HAVE A PODCAST TOO, BUT THE POD PEOPLE GOT A LITTLE TOO FRISKY.
AND, EVERY ONCE IN A WHILE, I COME HERE TO YOUR WORLD AND HELP BATMAN MYSELF!
HE CALLS IT "HELPING" ME...

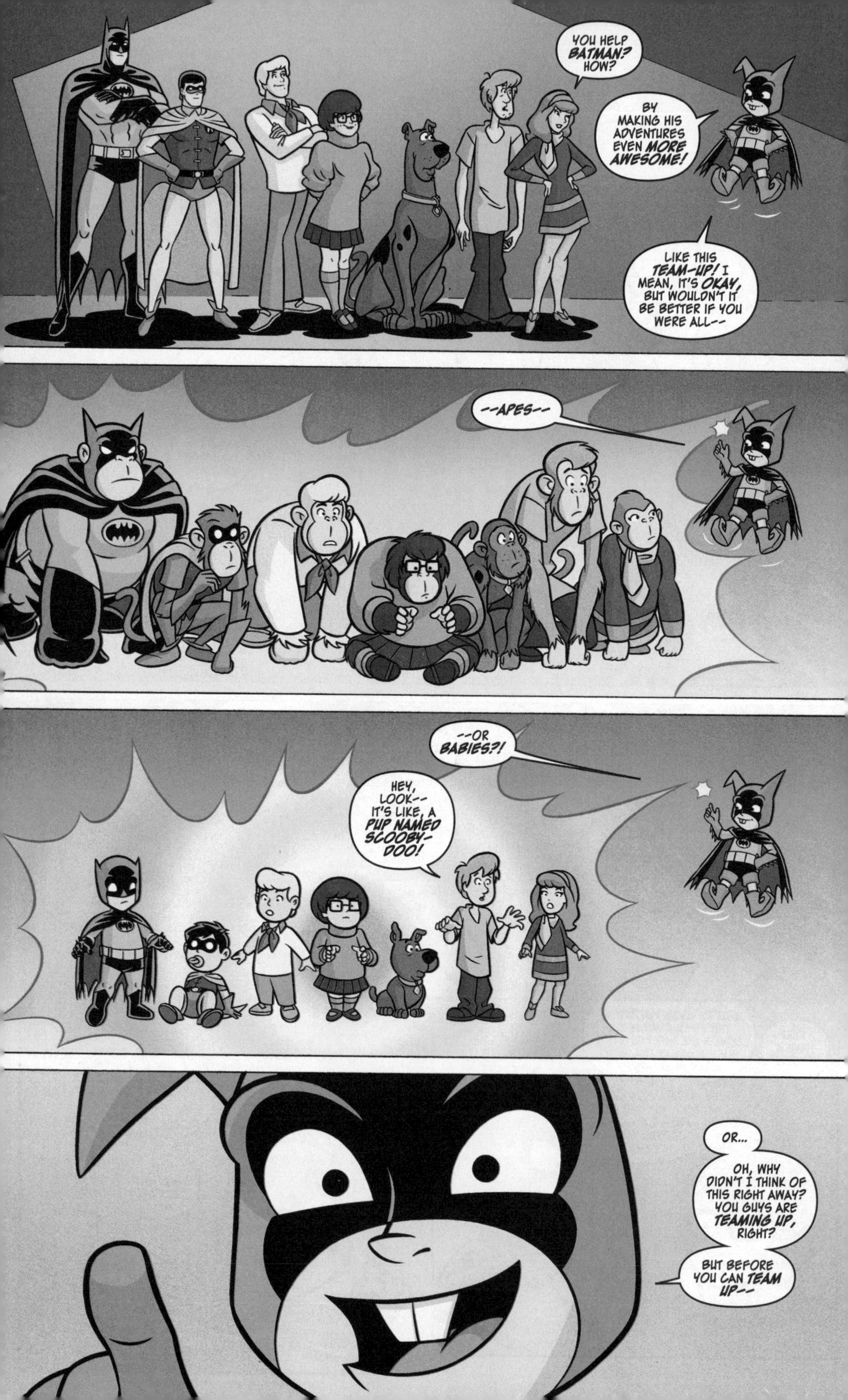
YOU HELP BATMAN? HOW?
BY MAKING HIS ADVENTURES EVEN MORE AWESOME!
LIKE THIS TEAM-UP! I MEAN, IT'S OKAY, BUT WOULDN'T IT BE BETTER IF YOU WERE ALL--
--APES--
--OR BABIES?!
HEY, LOOK-- IT'S LIKE, A PUP NAMED SCOOBY-DOO!
OR...
OH, WHY DIDN'T I THINK OF THIS RIGHT AWAY? YOU GUYS ARE TEAMING UP, RIGHT?
BUT BEFORE YOU CAN TEAM UP--

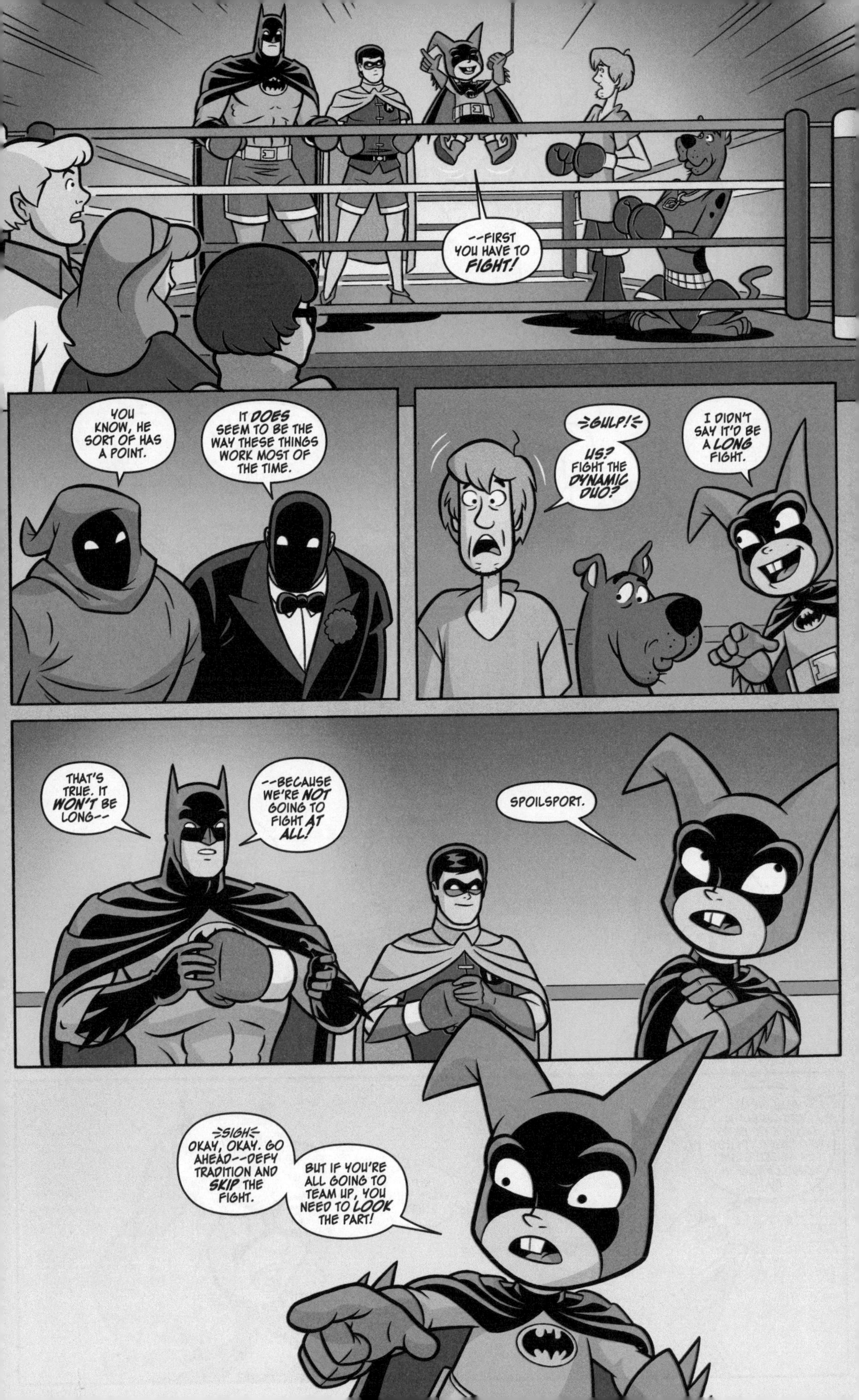
--FIRST YOU HAVE TO FIGHT!
YOU KNOW, HE SORT OF HAS A POINT.
IT DOES SEEM TO BE THE WAY THESE THINGS WORK MOST OF THE TIME.
=GULP!=
US? FIGHT THE DYNAMIC DUO?
I DIDN'T SAY IT'D BE A LONG FIGHT.
THAT'S TRUE. IT WON'T BE LONG--
--BECAUSE WE'RE NOT GOING TO FIGHT AT ALL!
SPOILSPORT.
=SIGH= OKAY, OKAY. GO AHEAD--DEFY TRADITION AND SKIP THE FIGHT.
BUT IF YOU'RE ALL GOING TO TEAM UP, YOU NEED TO LOOK THE PART!

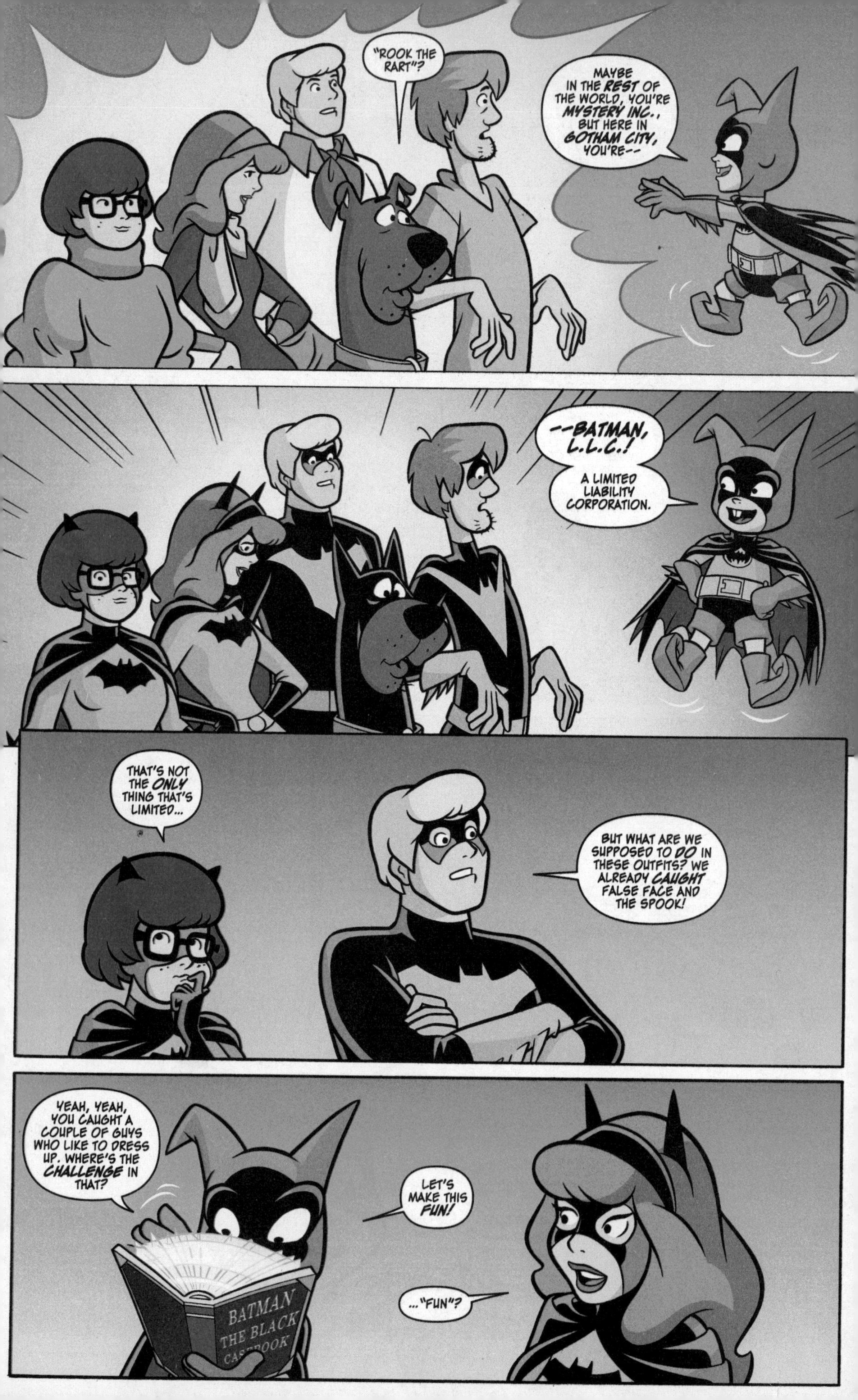
"ROOK THE RART"?
MAYBE IN THE REST OF THE WORLD, YOU'RE MYSTERY INC., BUT HERE IN GOTHAM CITY, YOU'RE--
--BATMAN, L.L.C.!
A LIMITED LIABILITY CORPORATION.
THAT'S NOT THE ONLY THING THAT'S LIMITED...
BUT WHAT ARE WE SUPPOSED TO DO IN THESE OUTFITS? WE ALREADY CAUGHT FALSE FACE AND THE SPOOK!
YEAH, YEAH, YOU CAUGHT A COUPLE OF GUYS WHO LIKE TO DRESS UP. WHERE'S THE CHALLENGE IN THAT?
LET'S MAKE THIS FUN!
..."FUN"?
BATMAN THE BLACK CASEBOOK

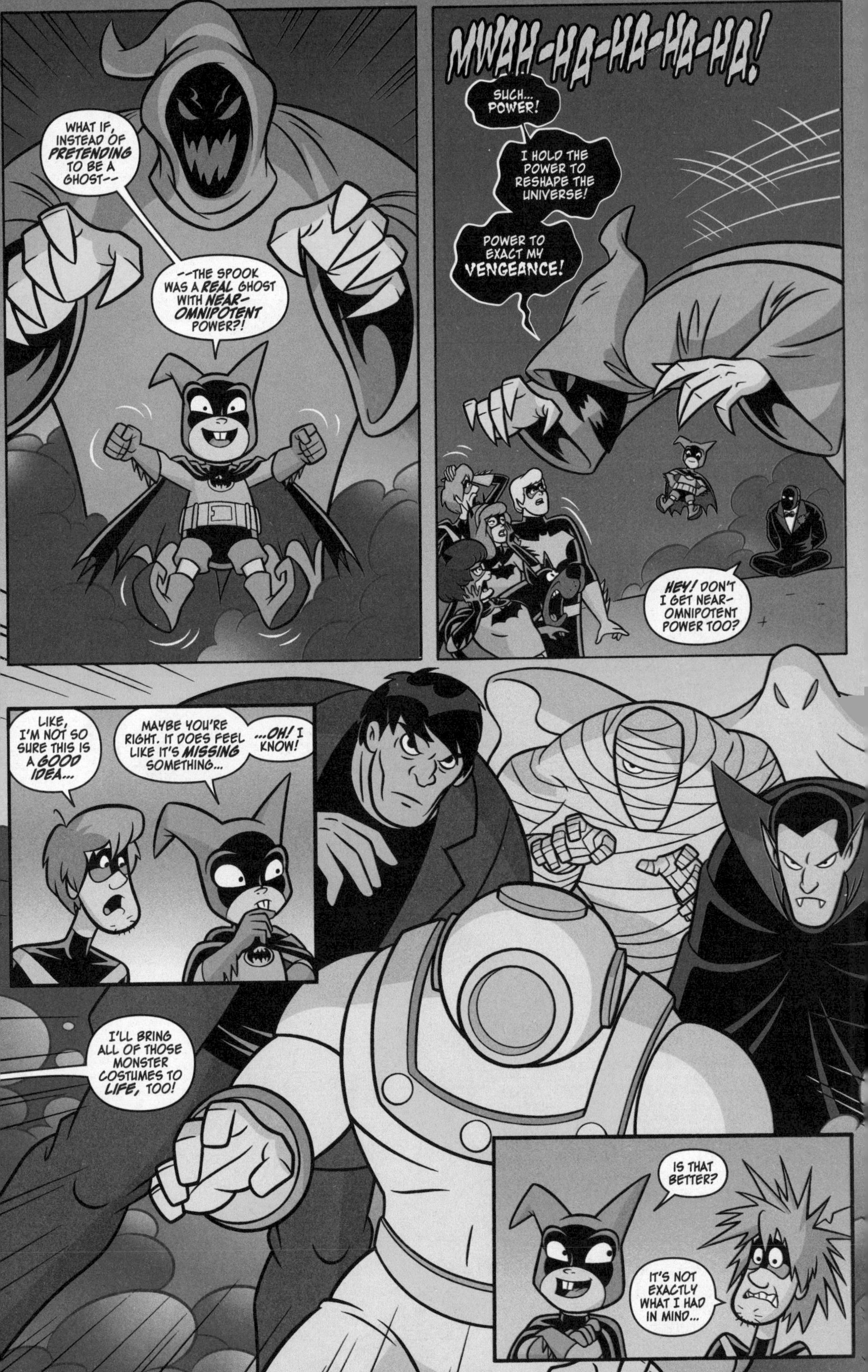
WHAT IF, INSTEAD OF PRETENDING TO BE A GHOST--
--THE SPOOK WAS A REAL GHOST WITH NEAR-OMNIPOTENT POWER?!
MWAH-HA-HA-HA-HA!
SUCH... POWER!
I HOLD THE POWER TO RESHAPE THE UNIVERSE!
POWER TO EXACT MY VENGEANCE!
HEY! DON'T I GET NEAR-OMNIPOTENT POWER TOO?
LIKE, I'M NOT SO SURE THIS IS A GOOD IDEA...
MAYBE YOU'RE RIGHT. IT DOES FEEL LIKE IT'S MISSING SOMETHING...
...OH! I KNOW!
I'LL BRING ALL OF THOSE MONSTER COSTUMES TO LIFE, TOO!
IS THAT BETTER?
IT'S NOT EXACTLY WHAT I HAD IN MIND...

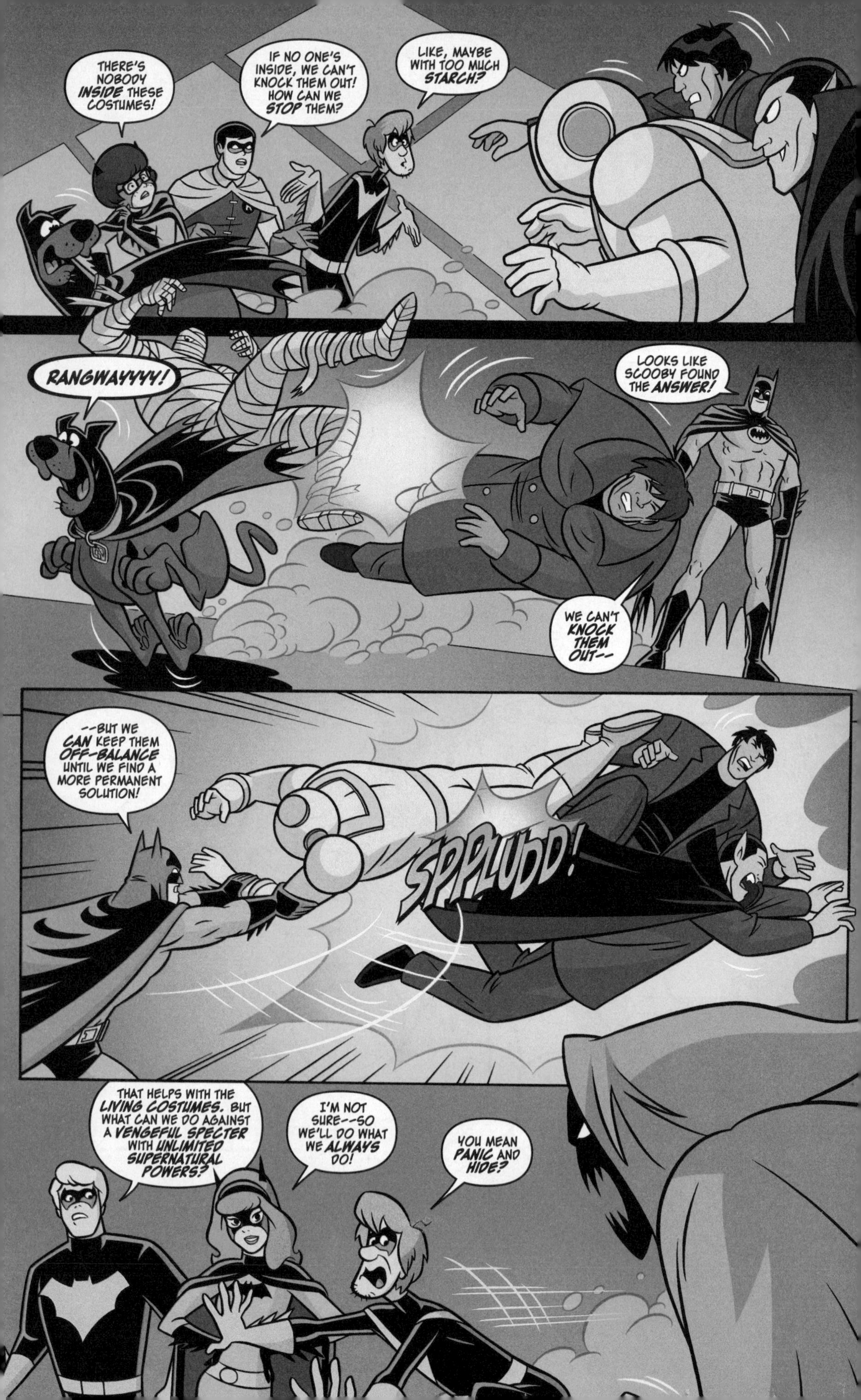
THERE'S NOBODY INSIDE THESE COSTUMES!
IF NO ONE'S INSIDE, WE CAN'T KNOCK THEM OUT! HOW CAN WE STOP THEM?
LIKE, MAYBE WITH TOO MUCH STARCH?
RANGWAYYYY!
LOOKS LIKE SCOOBY FOUND THE ANSWER!
WE CAN'T KNOCK THEM OUT--
--BUT WE CAN KEEP THEM OFF-BALANCE UNTIL WE FIND A MORE PERMANENT SOLUTION!
SPPLUDD!
THAT HELPS WITH THE LIVING COSTUMES. BUT WHAT CAN WE DO AGAINST A VENGEFUL SPECTER WITH UNLIMITED SUPERNATURAL POWERS?
I'M NOT SURE--SO WE'LL DO WHAT WE ALWAYS DO!
YOU MEAN PANIC AND HIDE?

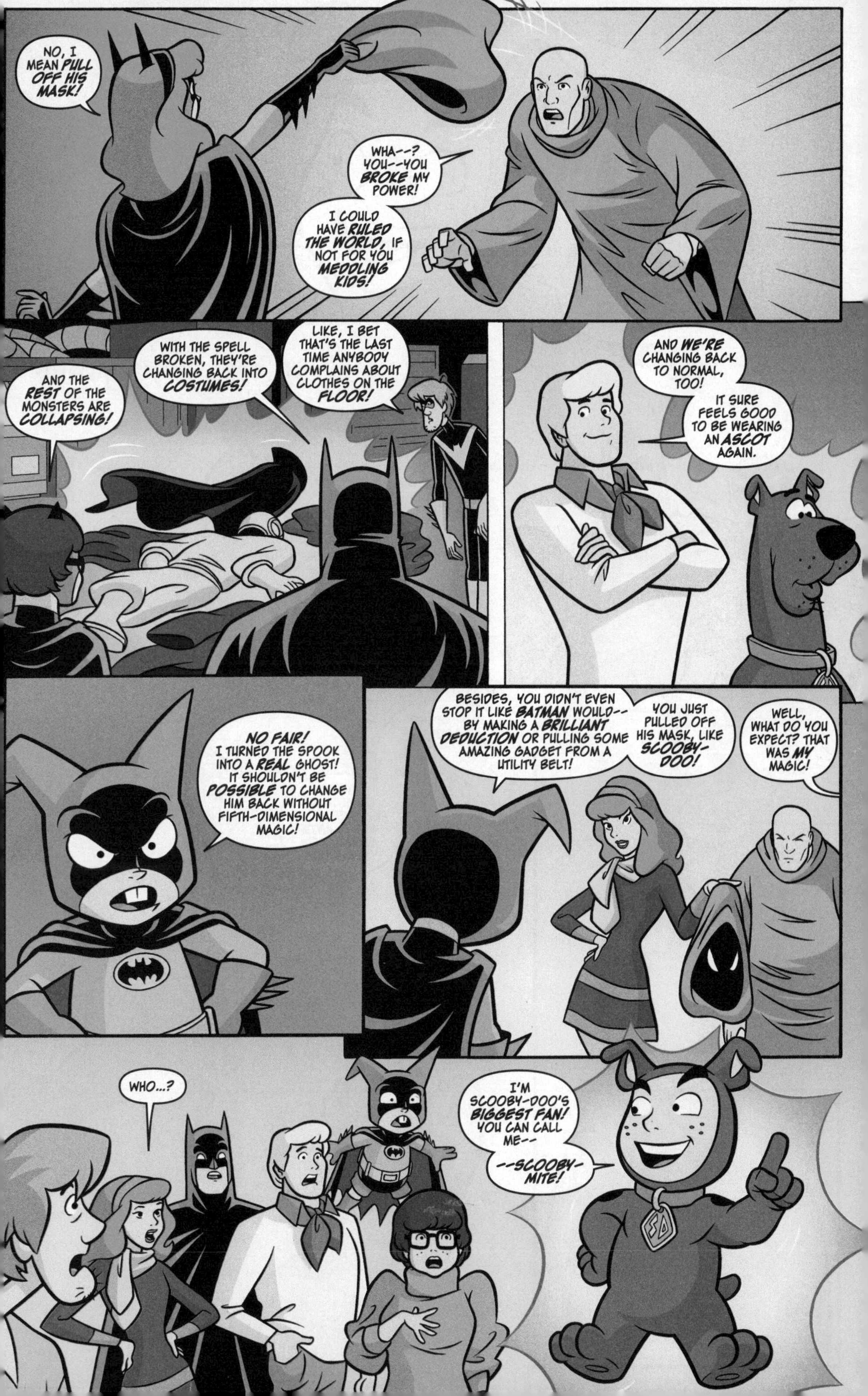
NO, I MEAN PULL OFF HIS MASK!
WHA--? YOU--YOU BROKE MY POWER!
I COULD HAVE RULED THE WORLD, IF NOT FOR YOU MEDDLING KIDS!
AND THE REST OF THE MONSTERS ARE COLLAPSING!
WITH THE SPELL BROKEN, THEY'RE CHANGING BACK INTO COSTUMES!
LIKE, I BET THAT'S THE LAST TIME ANYBODY COMPLAINS ABOUT CLOTHES ON THE FLOOR!
AND WE'RE CHANGING BACK TO NORMAL, TOO!
IT SURE FEELS GOOD TO BE WEARING AN ASCOT AGAIN.
NO FAIR! I TURNED THE SPOOK INTO A REAL GHOST! IT SHOULDN'T BE POSSIBLE TO CHANGE HIM BACK WITHOUT FIFTH-DIMENSIONAL MAGIC!
BESIDES, YOU DIDN'T EVEN STOP IT LIKE BATMAN WOULD-- BY MAKING A BRILLIANT DEDUCTION OR PULLING SOME AMAZING GADGET FROM A UTILITY BELT!
YOU JUST PULLED OFF HIS MASK, LIKE SCOOBY-DOO!
WELL, WHAT DO YOU EXPECT? THAT WAS MY MAGIC!
WHO...?
I'M SCOOBY-DOO'S BIGGEST FAN! YOU CAN CALL ME--
--SCOOBY-MITE!

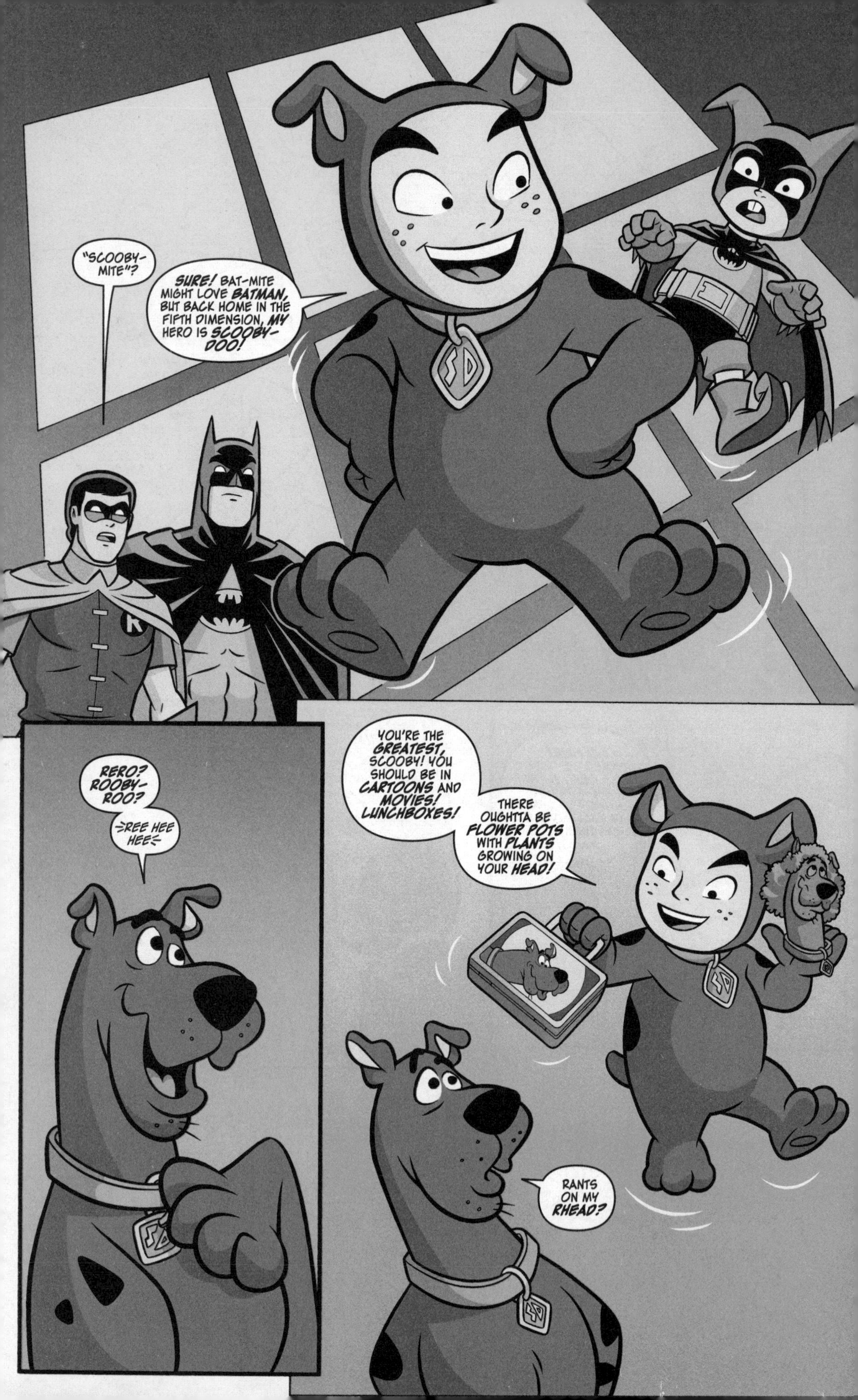
"SCOOBY-MITE"?
SURE! BAT-MITE MIGHT LOVE BATMAN, BUT BACK HOME IN THE FIFTH DIMENSION, MY HERO IS SCOOBY-DOO!
RERO? ROOBY-ROO?
REE HEE HEE
YOU'RE THE GREATEST, SCOOBY! YOU SHOULD BE IN CARTOONS AND MOVIES! LUNCHBOXES!
THERE OUGHTTA BE FLOWER POTS WITH PLANTS GROWING ON YOUR HEAD!
RANTS ON MY RHEAD?

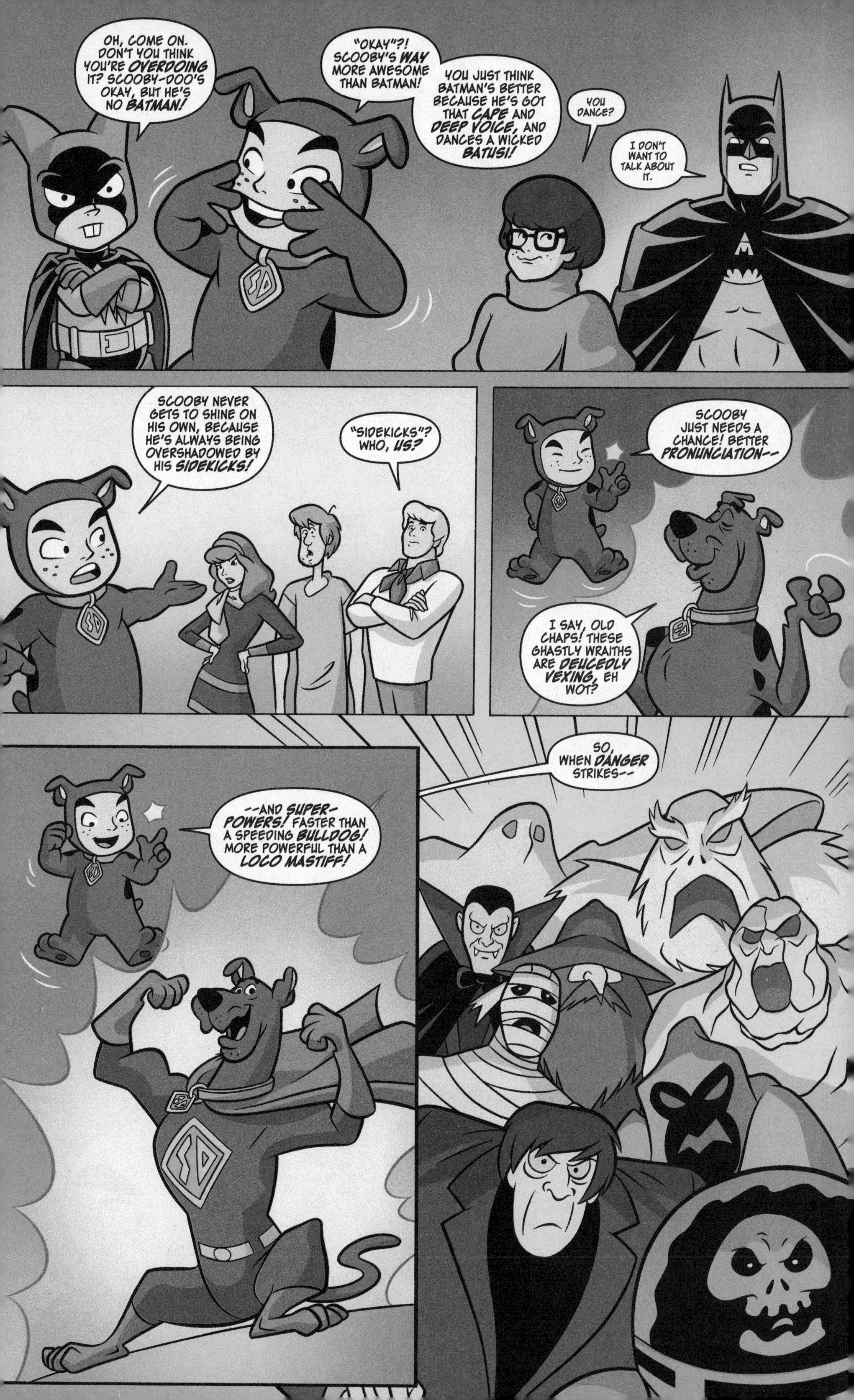
OH, COME ON. DON'T YOU THINK YOU'RE OVERDOING IT? SCOOBY-DOO'S OKAY, BUT HE'S NO BATMAN!
"OKAY"?! SCOOBY'S WAY MORE AWESOME THAN BATMAN!
YOU JUST THINK BATMAN'S BETTER BECAUSE HE'S GOT THAT CAPE AND DEEP VOICE, AND DANCES A WICKED BATUSI!
YOU DANCE?
I DON'T WANT TO TALK ABOUT IT.
SCOOBY NEVER GETS TO SHINE ON HIS OWN, BECAUSE HE'S ALWAYS BEING OVERSHADOWED BY HIS SIDEKICKS!
"SIDEKICKS"? WHO, US?
SCOOBY JUST NEEDS A CHANCE! BETTER PRONUNCIATION--
I SAY, OLD CHAPS! THESE GHASTLY WRAITHS ARE DEUCEDLY VEXING, EH WOT?
--AND SUPER-POWERS! FASTER THAN A SPEEDING BULLDOG! MORE POWERFUL THAN A LOCO MASTIFF!
SO, WHEN DANGER STRIKES--

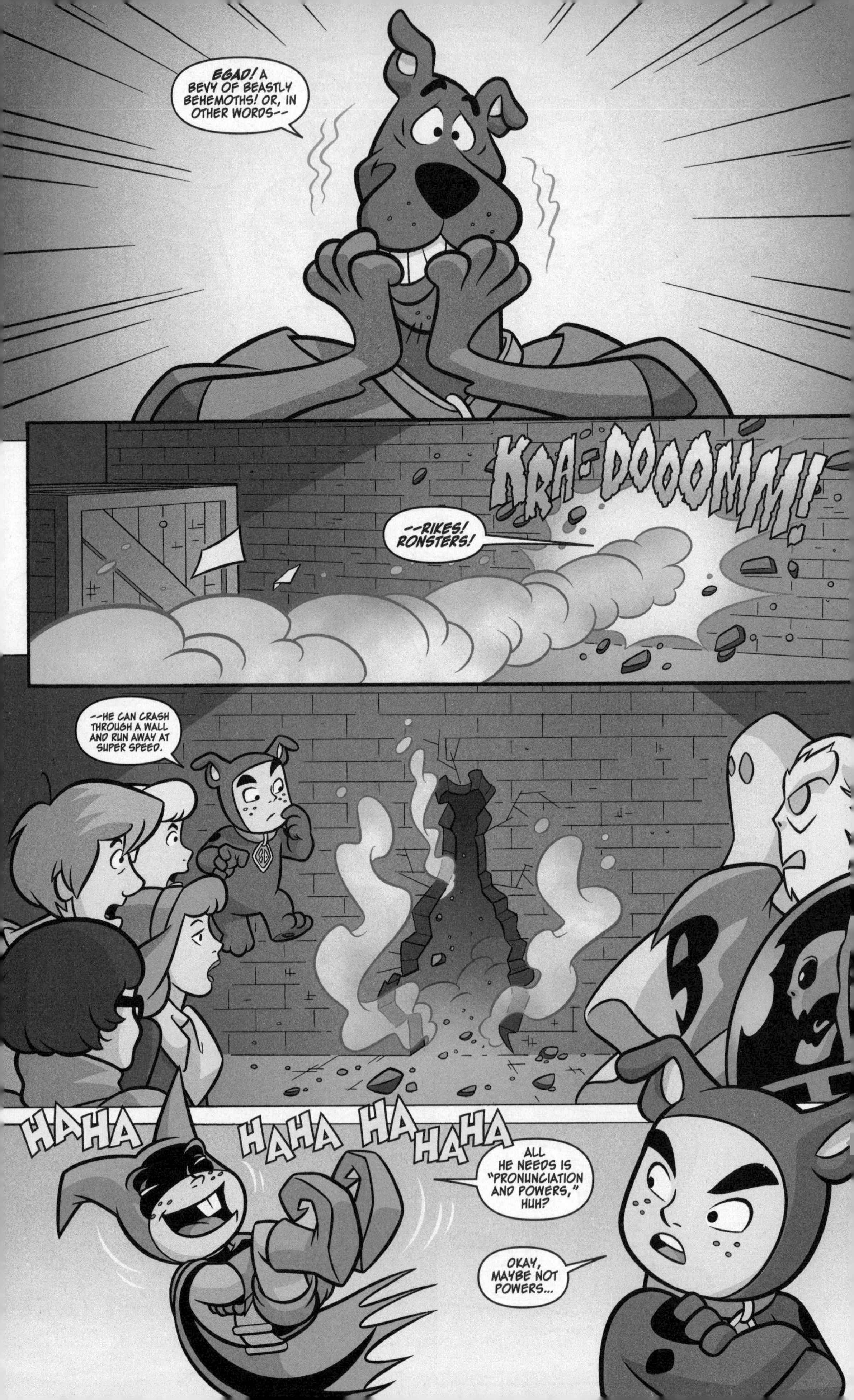
EGAD! A BEVY OF BEASTLY BEHEMOTHS! OR, IN OTHER WORDS--
KRA-DOOOMM!
--RIKES! RONSTERS!
--HE CAN CRASH THROUGH A WALL AND RUN AWAY AT SUPER SPEED.
HAHA HAHA HAHAHA
ALL HE NEEDS IS "PRONUNCIATION AND POWERS," HUH?
OKAY, MAYBE NOT POWERS...

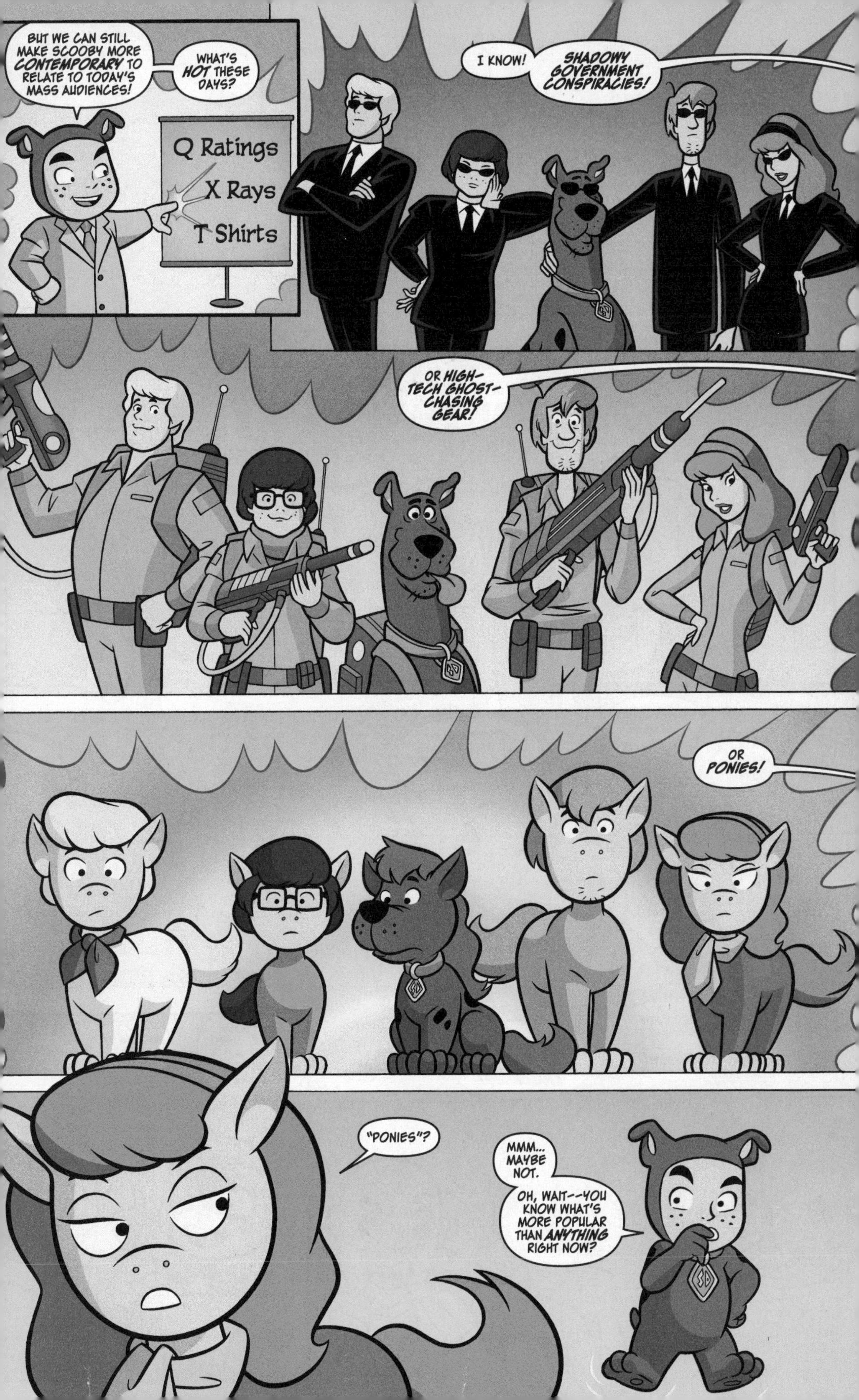
BUT WE CAN STILL MAKE SCOOBY MORE CONTEMPORARY TO RELATE TO TODAY'S MASS AUDIENCES!
WHAT'S HOT THESE DAYS?
Q Ratings
X Rays
T Shirts
I KNOW!
SHADOWY GOVERNMENT CONSPIRACIES!
OR HIGH-TECH GHOST-CHASING GEAR!
OR PONIES!
"PONIES"?
MMM... MAYBE NOT.
OH, WAIT--YOU KNOW WHAT'S MORE POPULAR THAN ANYTHING RIGHT NOW?

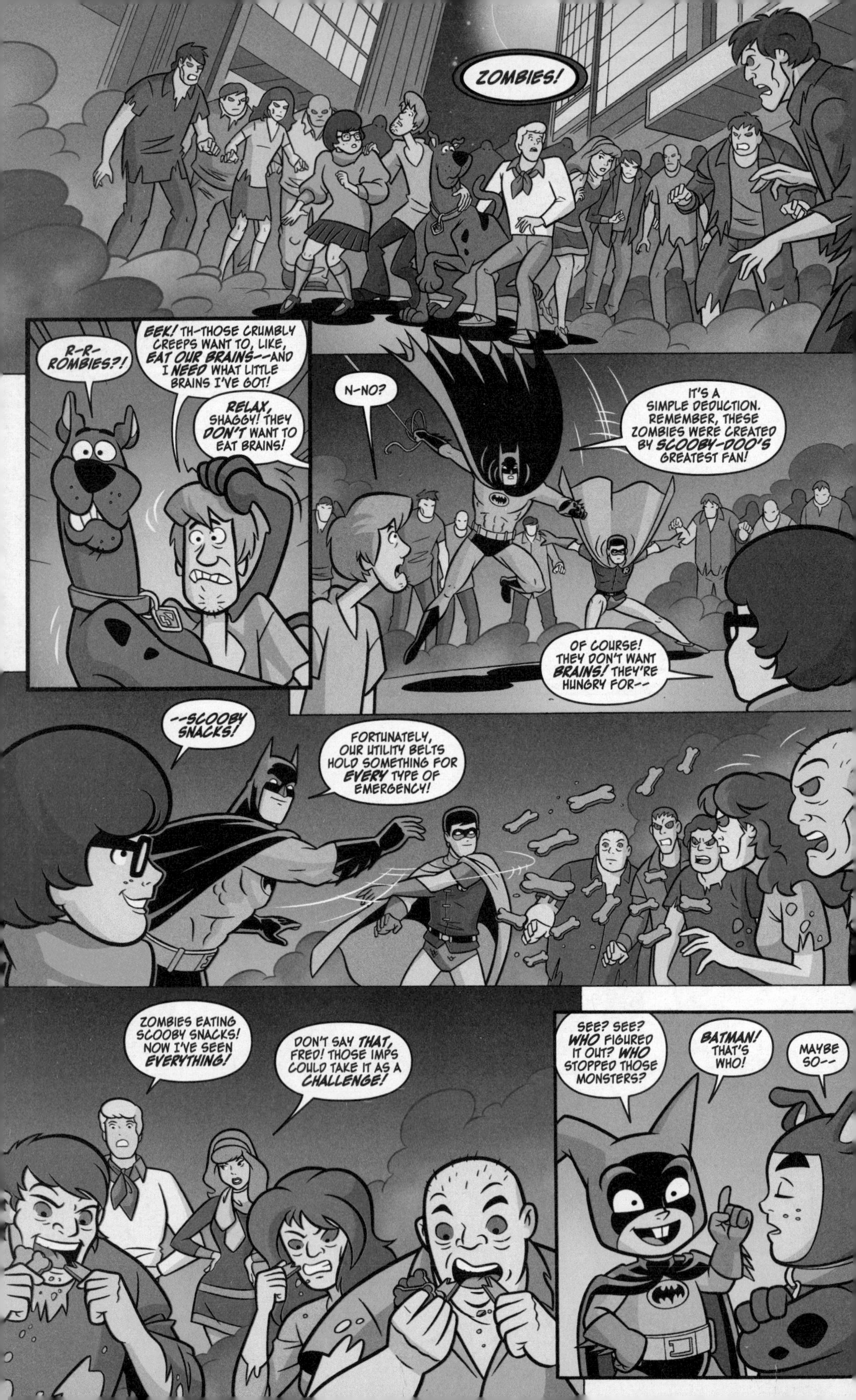
ZOMBIES!
R-R-ROMBIES?!
EEK! TH-THOSE CRUMBLY CREEPS WANT TO, LIKE, EAT OUR BRAINS--AND I NEED WHAT LITTLE BRAINS I'VE GOT!
RELAX, SHAGGY! THEY DON'T WANT TO EAT BRAINS!
N-NO?
IT'S A SIMPLE DEDUCTION. REMEMBER, THESE ZOMBIES WERE CREATED BY SCOOBY-DOO'S GREATEST FAN!
OF COURSE! THEY DON'T WANT BRAINS! THEY'RE HUNGRY FOR--
--SCOOBY SNACKS!
FORTUNATELY, OUR UTILITY BELTS HOLD SOMETHING FOR EVERY TYPE OF EMERGENCY!
ZOMBIES EATING SCOOBY SNACKS! NOW I'VE SEEN EVERYTHING!
DON'T SAY THAT, FRED! THOSE IMPS COULD TAKE IT AS A CHALLENGE!
SEE? SEE? WHO FIGURED IT OUT? WHO STOPPED THOSE MONSTERS?
BATMAN! THAT'S WHO!
MAYBE SO--

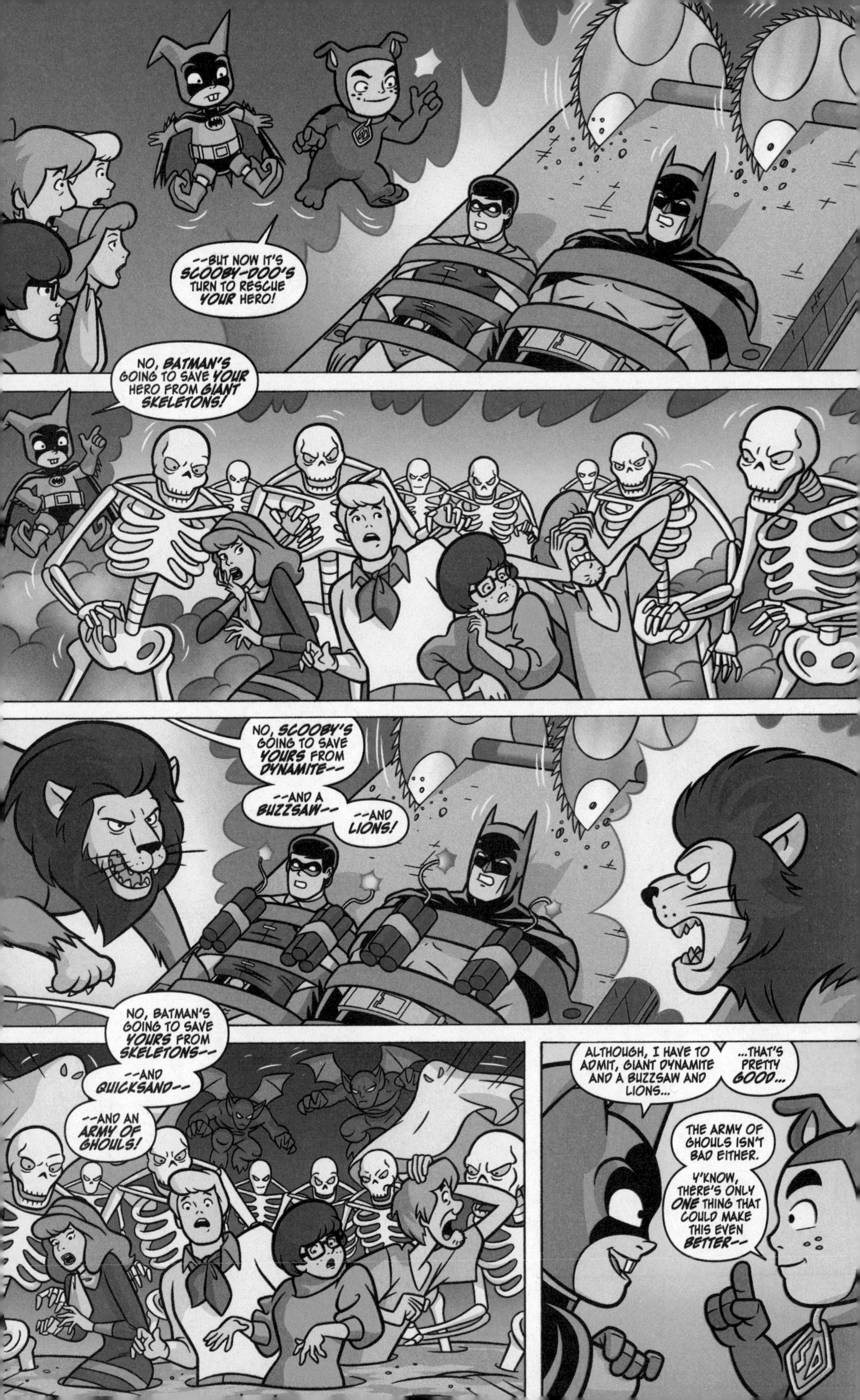
--BUT NOW IT'S SCOOBY-DOO'S TURN TO RESCUE YOUR HERO!
NO, BATMAN'S GOING TO SAVE YOUR HERO FROM GIANT SKELETONS!
NO, SCOOBY'S GOING TO SAVE YOURS FROM DYNAMITE--
--AND A BUZZSAW--
--AND LIONS!
NO, BATMAN'S GOING TO SAVE YOURS FROM SKELETONS--
--AND QUICKSAND--
--AND AN ARMY OF GHOULS!
ALTHOUGH, I HAVE TO ADMIT, GIANT DYNAMITE AND A BUZZSAW AND LIONS...
...THAT'S PRETTY GOOD...
THE ARMY OF GHOULS ISN'T BAD EITHER.
Y'KNOW, THERE'S ONLY ONE THING THAT COULD MAKE THIS EVEN BETTER--

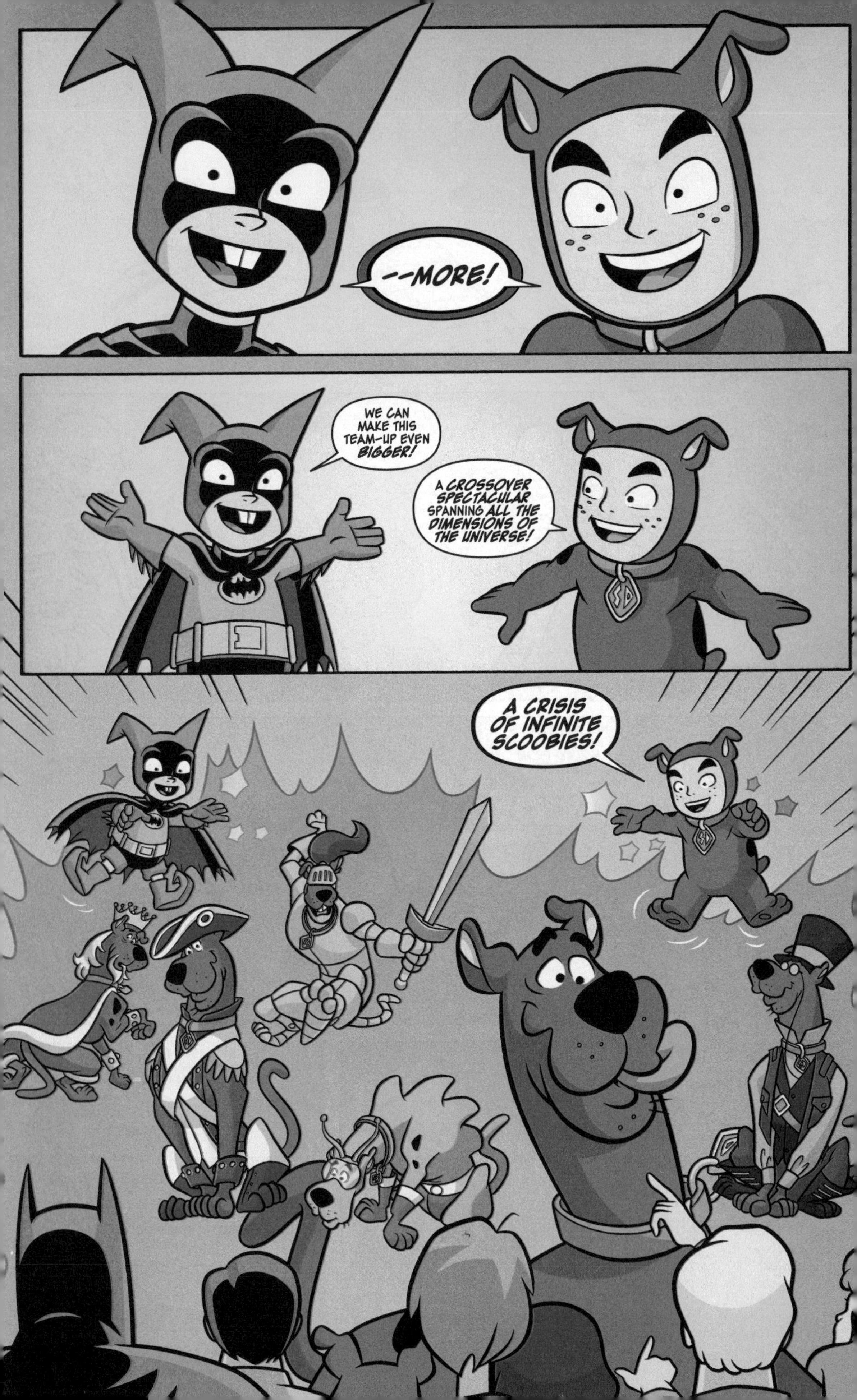
--MORE!
WE CAN MAKE THIS TEAM-UP EVEN BIGGER!
A CROSSOVER SPECTACULAR SPANNING ALL THE DIMENSIONS OF THE UNIVERSE!
A CRISIS OF INFINITE SCOOBIES!

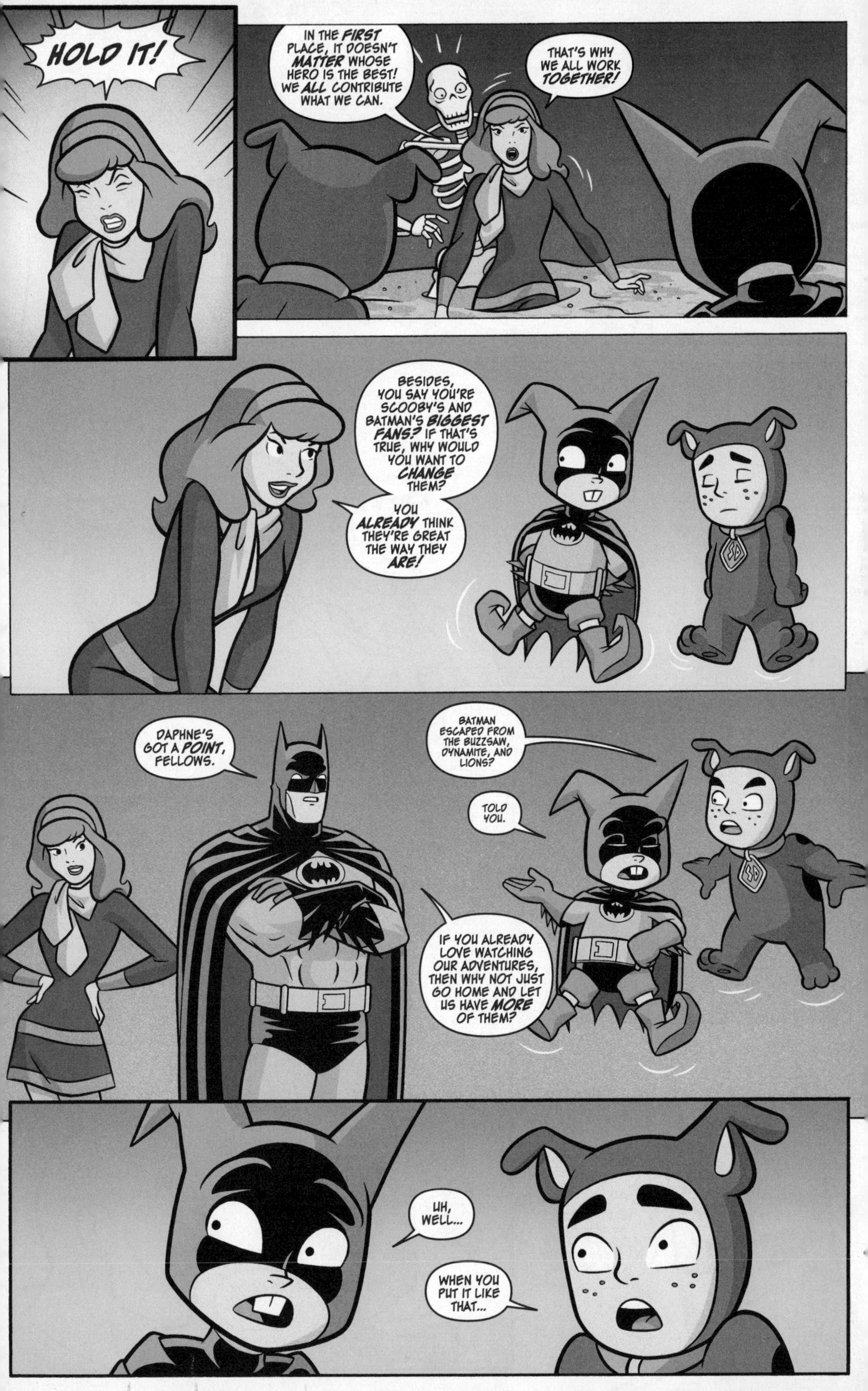
HOLD IT!
IN THE FIRST PLACE, IT DOESN'T MATTER WHOSE HERO IS THE BEST! WE ALL CONTRIBUTE WHAT WE CAN.
THAT'S WHY WE ALL WORK TOGETHER!
BESIDES, YOU SAY YOU'RE SCOOBY'S AND BATMAN'S BIGGEST FANS? IF THAT'S TRUE, WHY WOULD YOU WANT TO CHANGE THEM?
YOU ALREADY THINK THEY'RE GREAT THE WAY THEY ARE!
DAPHNE'S GOT A POINT, FELLOWS.
IF YOU ALREADY LOVE WATCHING OUR ADVENTURES, THEN WHY NOT JUST GO HOME AND LET US HAVE MORE OF THEM?
BATMAN ESCAPED FROM THE BUZZSAW, DYNAMITE, AND LIONS?
TOLD YOU.
UH, WELL...
WHEN YOU PUT IT LIKE THAT...

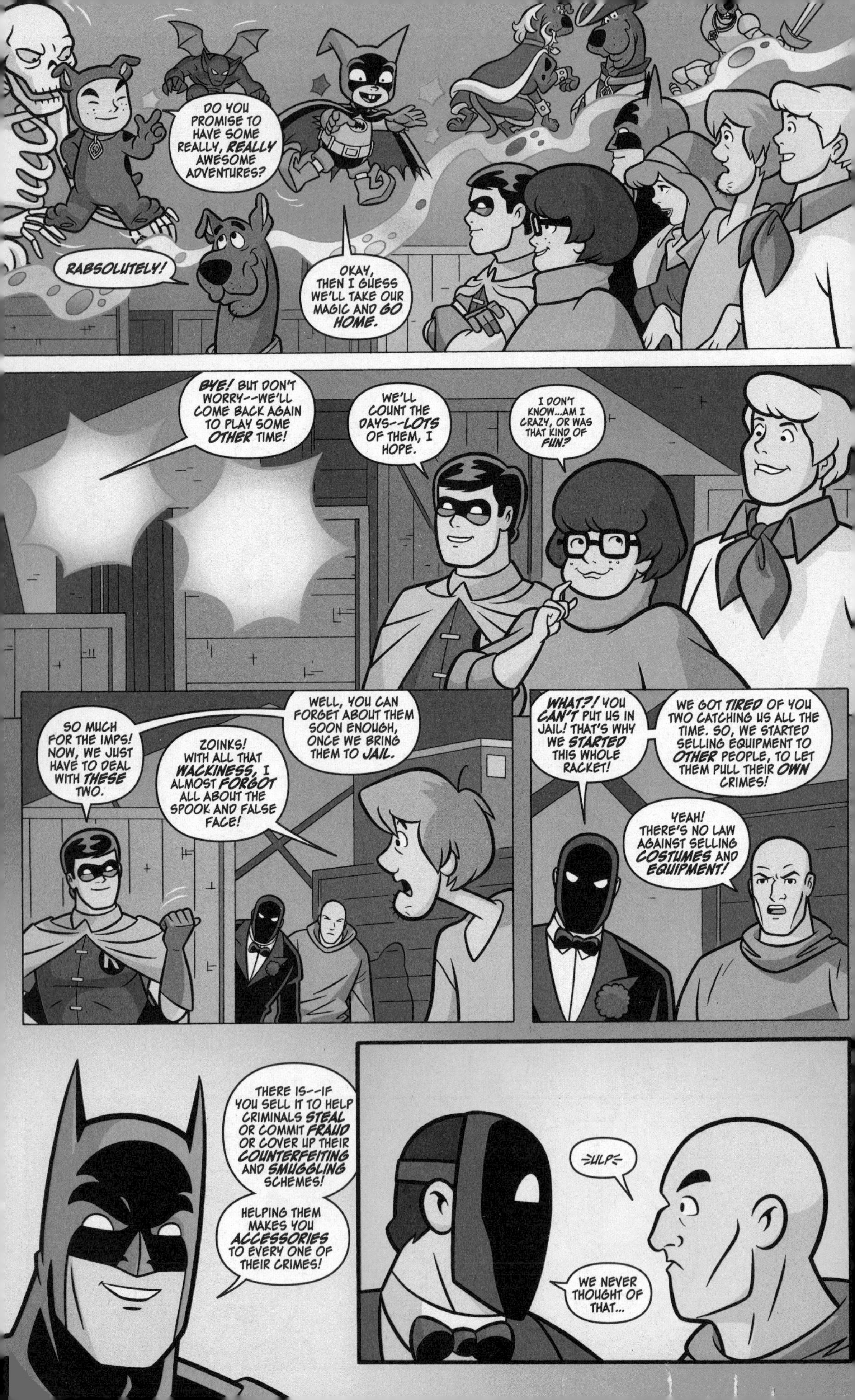
DO YOU PROMISE TO HAVE SOME REALLY, REALLY AWESOME ADVENTURES?
RABSOLUTELY!
OKAY, THEN I GUESS WE'LL TAKE OUR MAGIC AND GO HOME.
BYE! BUT DON'T WORRY--WE'LL COME BACK AGAIN TO PLAY SOME OTHER TIME!
WE'LL COUNT THE DAYS--LOTS OF THEM, I HOPE.
I DON'T KNOW...AM I CRAZY, OR WAS THAT KIND OF FUN?
SO MUCH FOR THE IMPS! NOW, WE JUST HAVE TO DEAL WITH THESE TWO.
WELL, YOU CAN FORGET ABOUT THEM SOON ENOUGH, ONCE WE BRING THEM TO JAIL.
ZOINKS! WITH ALL THAT WACKINESS, I ALMOST FORGOT ALL ABOUT THE SPOOK AND FALSE FACE!
WHAT?! YOU CAN'T PUT US IN JAIL! THAT'S WHY WE STARTED THIS WHOLE RACKET!
WE GOT TIRED OF YOU TWO CATCHING US ALL THE TIME. SO, WE STARTED SELLING EQUIPMENT TO OTHER PEOPLE, TO LET THEM PULL THEIR OWN CRIMES!
YEAH! THERE'S NO LAW AGAINST SELLING COSTUMES AND EQUIPMENT!
THERE IS--IF YOU SELL IT TO HELP CRIMINALS STEAL OR COMMIT FRAUD OR COVER UP THEIR COUNTERFEITING AND SMUGGLING SCHEMES!
HELPING THEM MAKES YOU ACCESSORIES TO EVERY ONE OF THEIR CRIMES!
=ULP=
WE NEVER THOUGHT OF THAT...

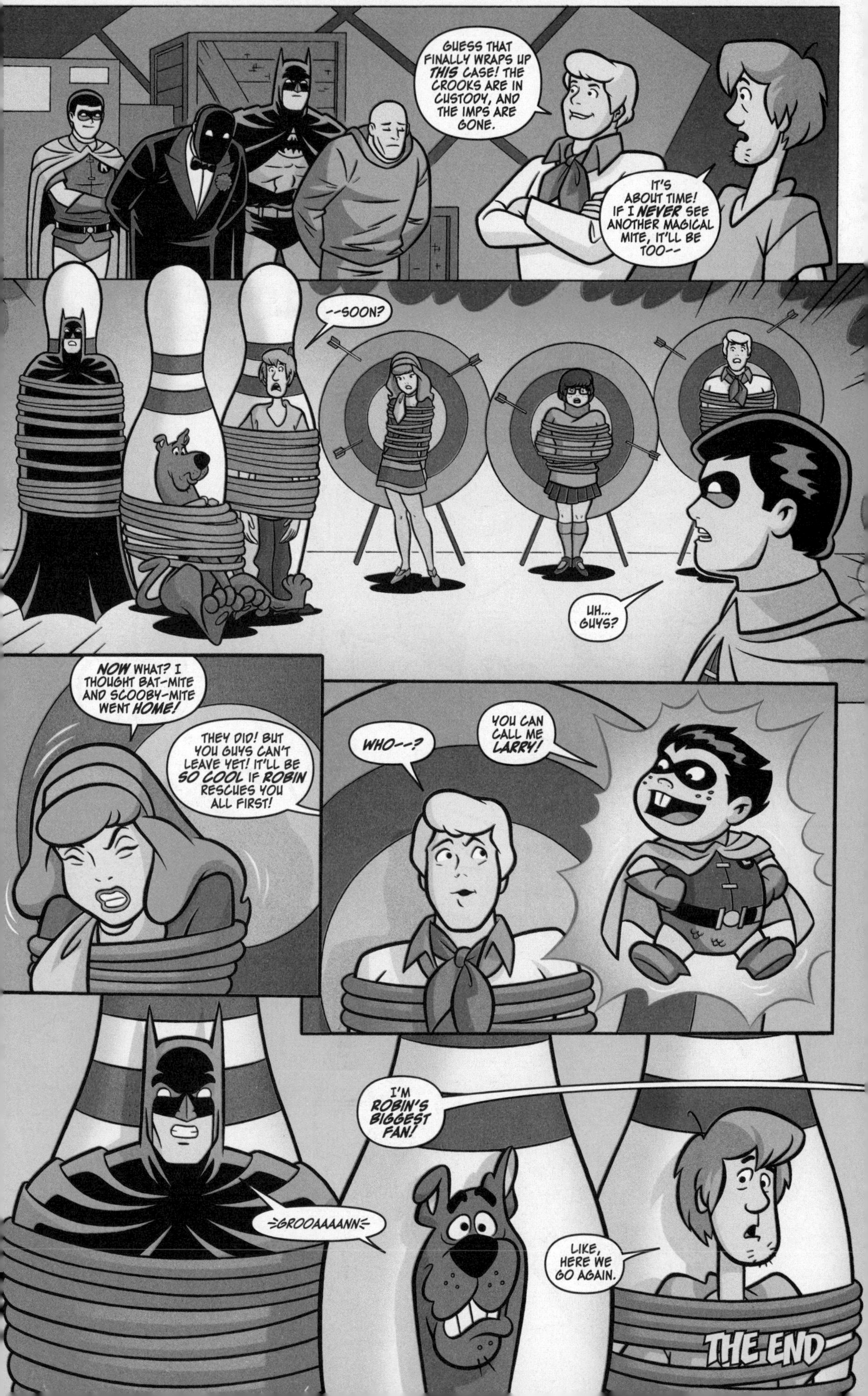
GUESS THAT FINALLY WRAPS UP THIS CASE! THE CROOKS ARE IN CUSTODY, AND THE IMPS ARE GONE.
IT'S ABOUT TIME! IF I NEVER SEE ANOTHER MAGICAL MITE, IT'LL BE TOO--
--SOON?
UH... GUYS?
NOW WHAT? I THOUGHT BAT-MITE AND SCOOBY-MITE WENT HOME!
THEY DID! BUT YOU GUYS CAN'T LEAVE YET! IT'LL BE SO COOL IF ROBIN RESCUES YOU ALL FIRST!
WHO--?
YOU CAN CALL ME LARRY!
I'M ROBIN'S BIGGEST FAN!
=GROOAAAANN=
LIKE, HERE WE GO AGAIN.
THE END

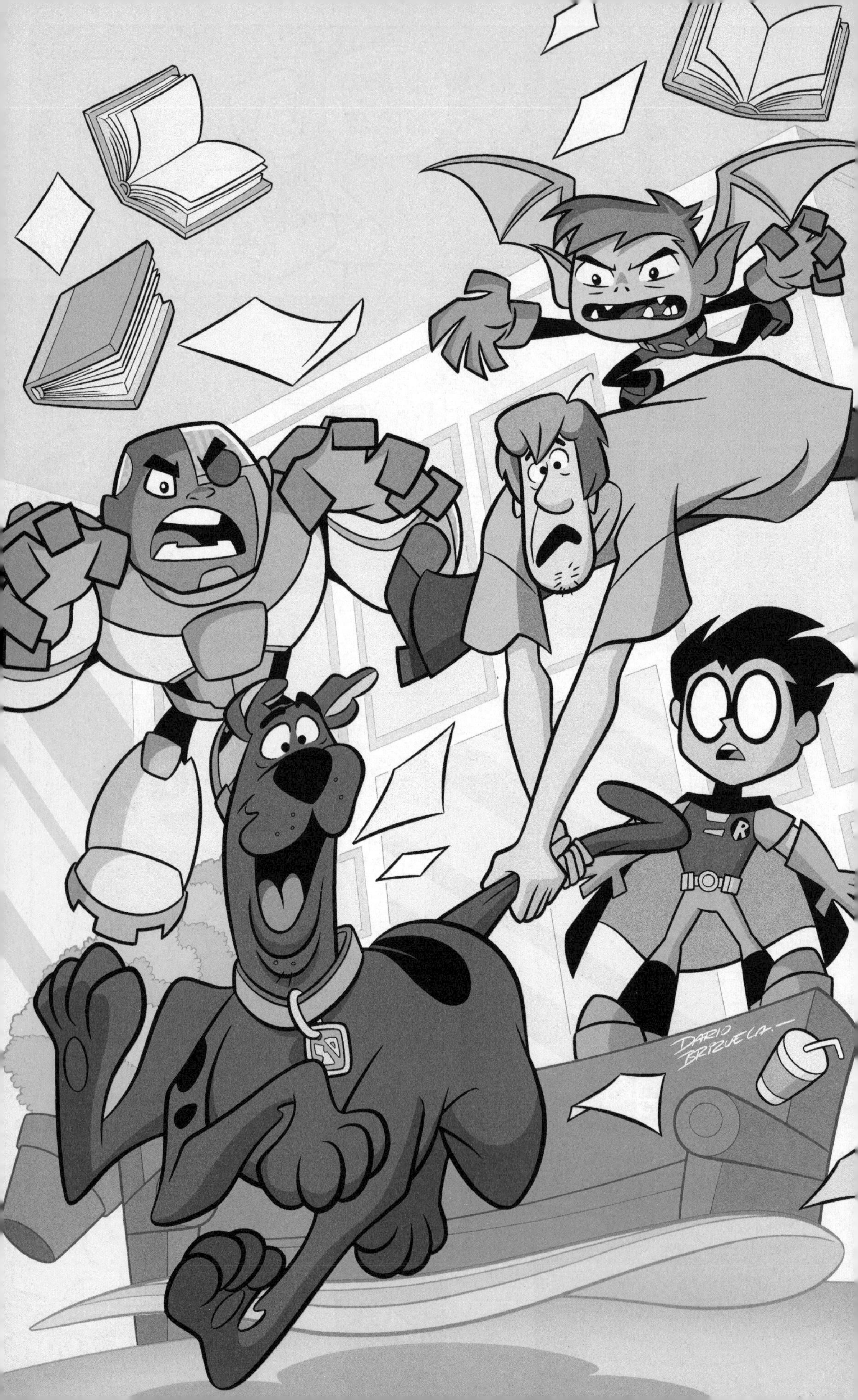
DARIO BRIZUELA

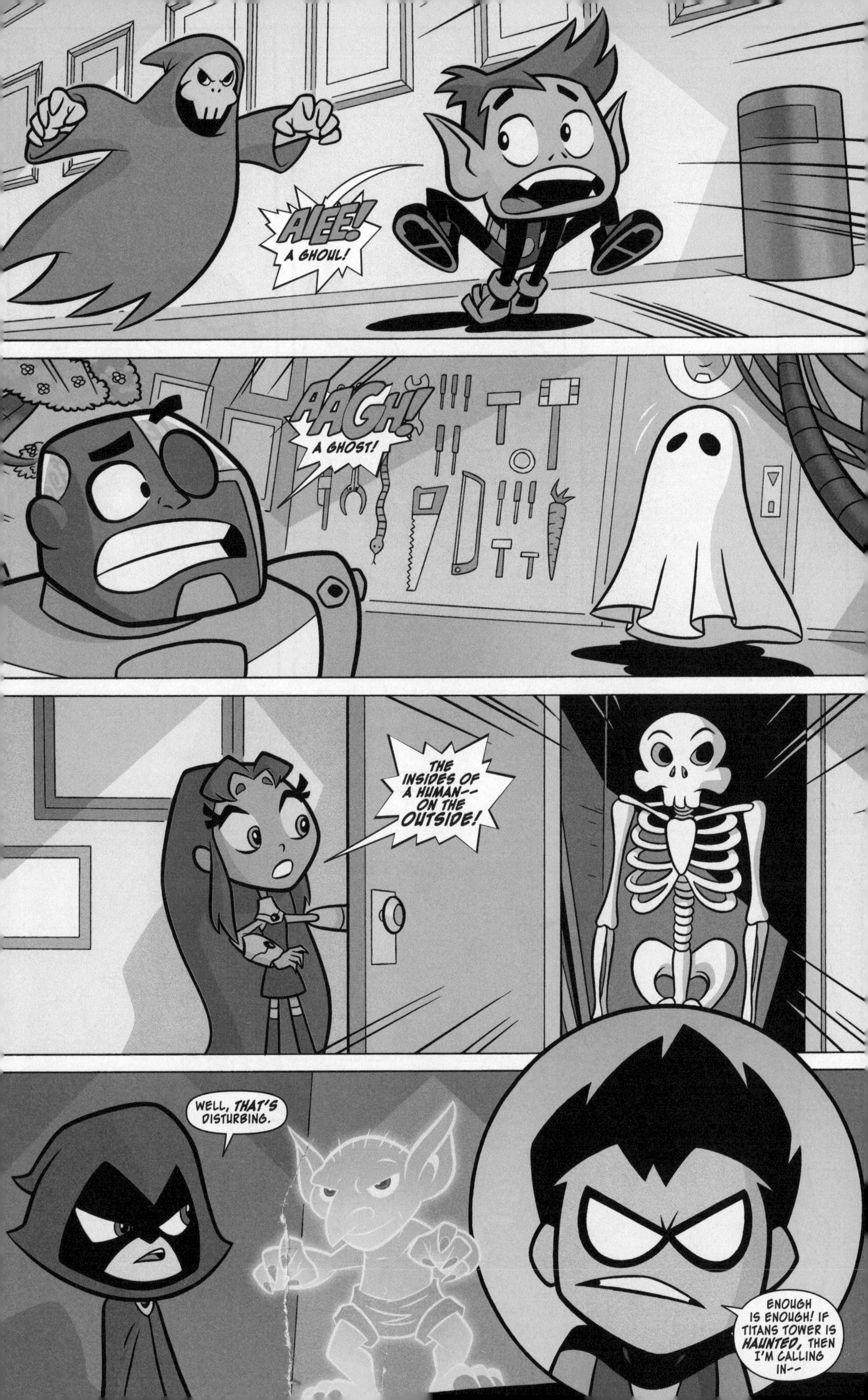
AIEE! A GHOUL!
AAGH! A GHOST!
THE INSIDES OF A HUMAN-- ON THE OUTSIDE!
WELL, THAT'S DISTURBING.
ENOUGH IS ENOUGH! IF TITANS TOWER IS HAUNTED, THEN I'M CALLING IN--

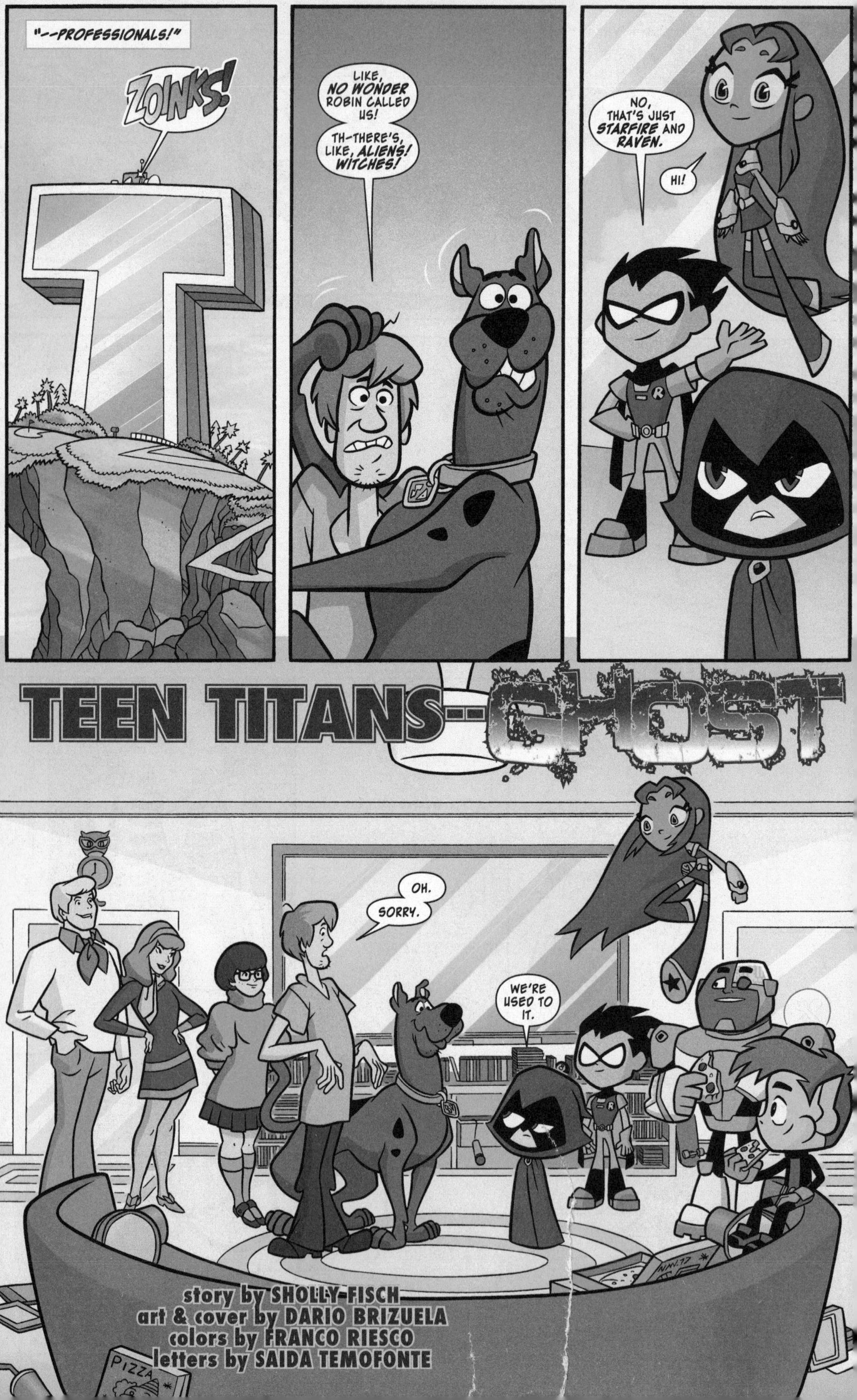
"--PROFESSIONALS!"
ZOINKS!
LIKE, NO WONDER ROBIN CALLED US!
TH-THERE'S, LIKE, ALIENS! WITCHES!
NO, THAT'S JUST STARFIRE AND RAVEN.
HI!
TEEN TITANS--GHOST
OH.
SORRY.
WE'RE USED TO IT.
story by SHOLLY FISCH
art & cover by DARIO BRIZUELA
colors by FRANCO RIESCO
letters by SAIDA TEMOFONTE
PIZZA

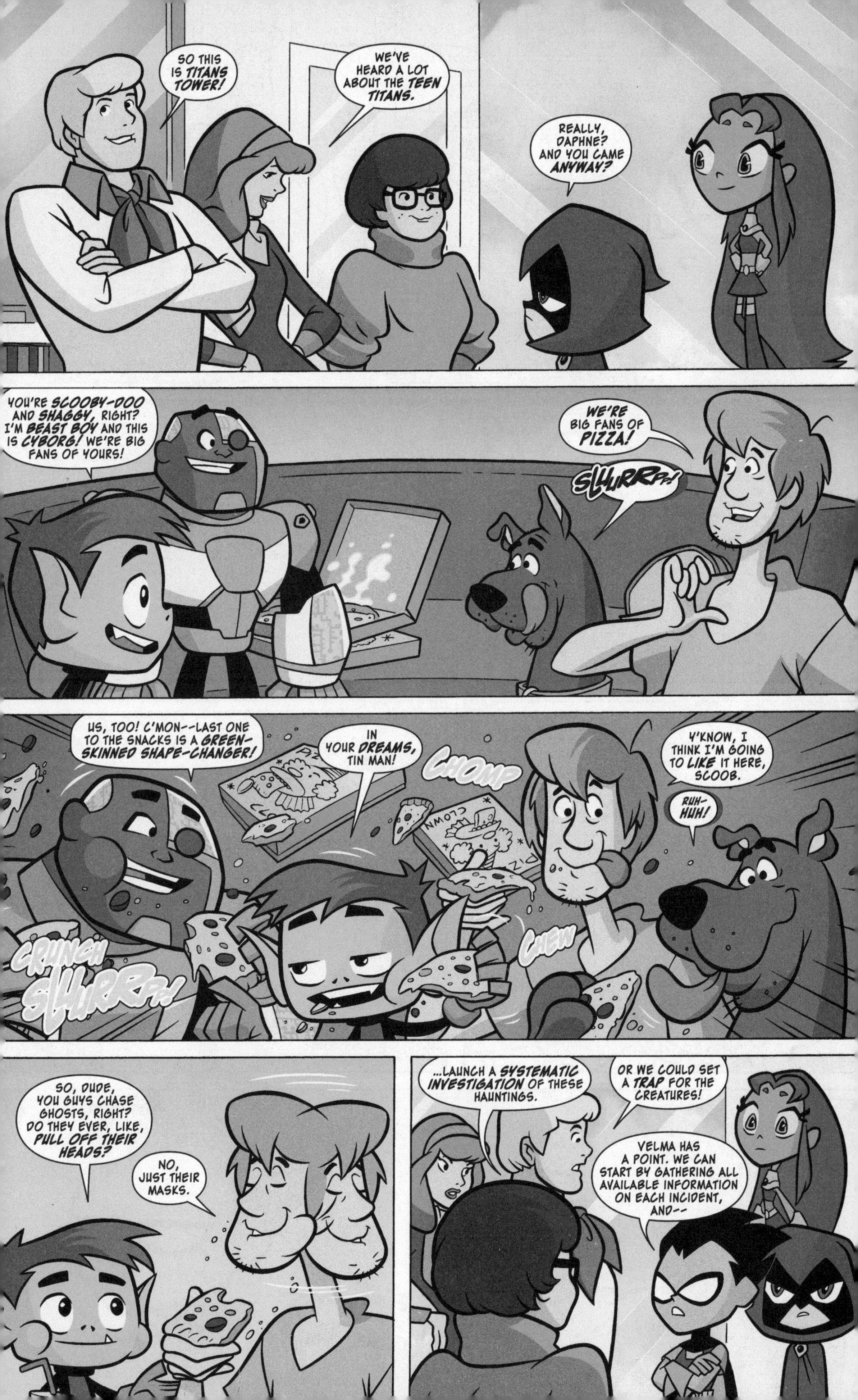
SO THIS IS TITANS TOWER!
WE'VE HEARD A LOT ABOUT THE TEEN TITANS.
REALLY, DAPHNE? AND YOU CAME ANYWAY?
YOU'RE SCOOBY-DOO AND SHAGGY, RIGHT? I'M BEAST BOY AND THIS IS CYBORG! WE'RE BIG FANS OF YOURS!
WE'RE BIG FANS OF PIZZA!
SLUURRPP!
US, TOO! C'MON--LAST ONE TO THE SNACKS IS A GREEN-SKINNED SHAPE-CHANGER!
IN YOUR DREAMS, TIN MAN!
CHOMP
Y'KNOW, I THINK I'M GOING TO LIKE IT HERE, SCOOB.
RUH-HUH!
CLOWN
CRUNCH
SLUURRPP!
CHEW
SO, DUDE, YOU GUYS CHASE GHOSTS, RIGHT? DO THEY EVER, LIKE, PULL OFF THEIR HEADS?
NO, JUST THEIR MASKS.
...LAUNCH A SYSTEMATIC INVESTIGATION OF THESE HAUNTINGS.
OR WE COULD SET A TRAP FOR THE CREATURES!
VELMA HAS A POINT. WE CAN START BY GATHERING ALL AVAILABLE INFORMATION ON EACH INCIDENT, AND--

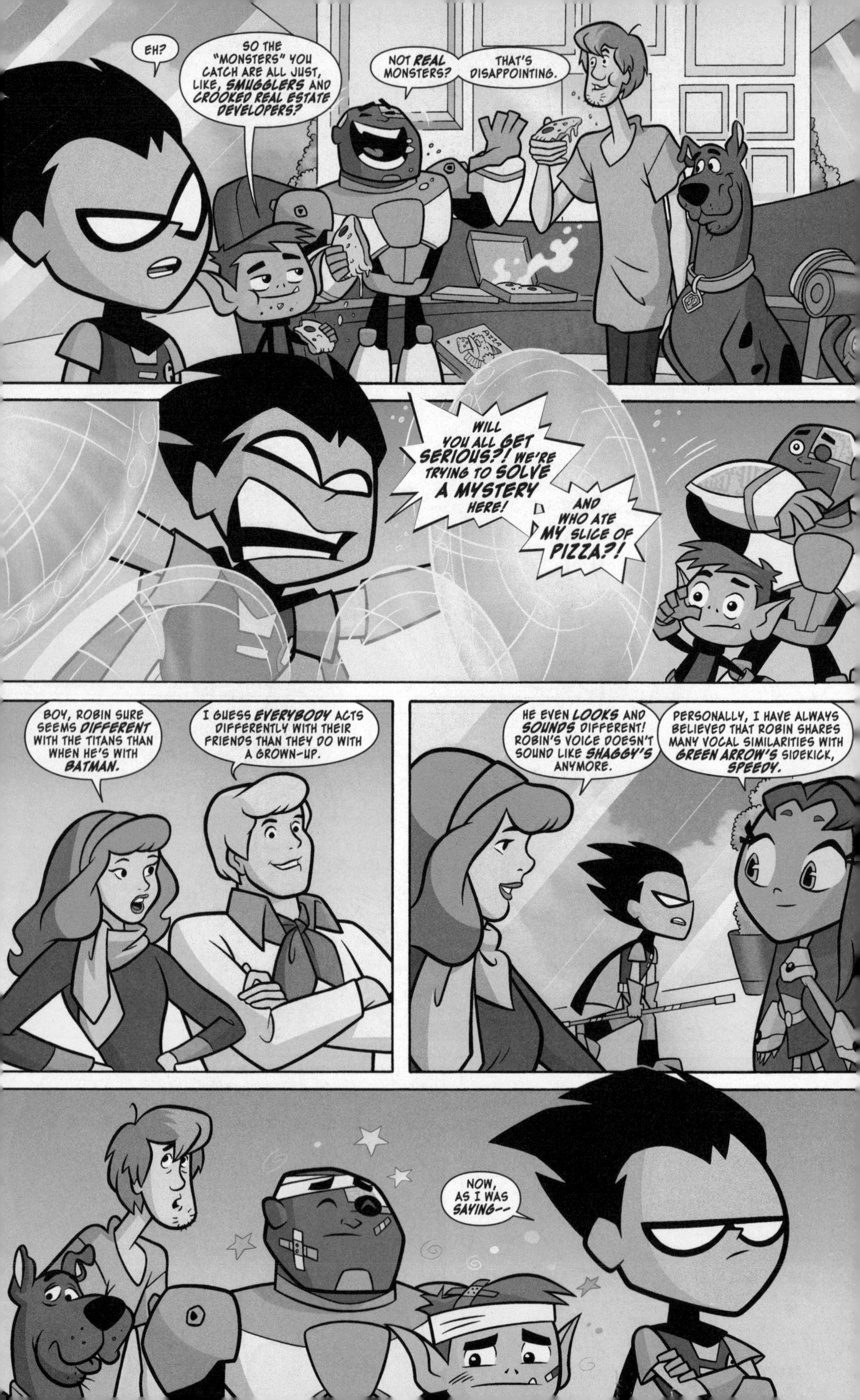
EH?
SO THE "MONSTERS" YOU CATCH ARE ALL JUST, LIKE, SMUGGLERS AND CROOKED REAL ESTATE DEVELOPERS?
NOT REAL MONSTERS?
THAT'S DISAPPOINTING.
PIZZA
WILL YOU ALL GET SERIOUS?! WE'RE TRYING TO SOLVE A MYSTERY HERE!
AND WHO ATE MY SLICE OF PIZZA?!
BOY, ROBIN SURE SEEMS DIFFERENT WITH THE TITANS THAN WHEN HE'S WITH BATMAN.
I GUESS EVERYBODY ACTS DIFFERENTLY WITH THEIR FRIENDS THAN THEY DO WITH A GROWN-UP.
HE EVEN LOOKS AND SOUNDS DIFFERENT! ROBIN'S VOICE DOESN'T SOUND LIKE SHAGGY'S ANYMORE.
PERSONALLY, I HAVE ALWAYS BELIEVED THAT ROBIN SHARES MANY VOCAL SIMILARITIES WITH GREEN ARROW'S SIDEKICK, SPEEDY.
NOW, AS I WAS SAYING--

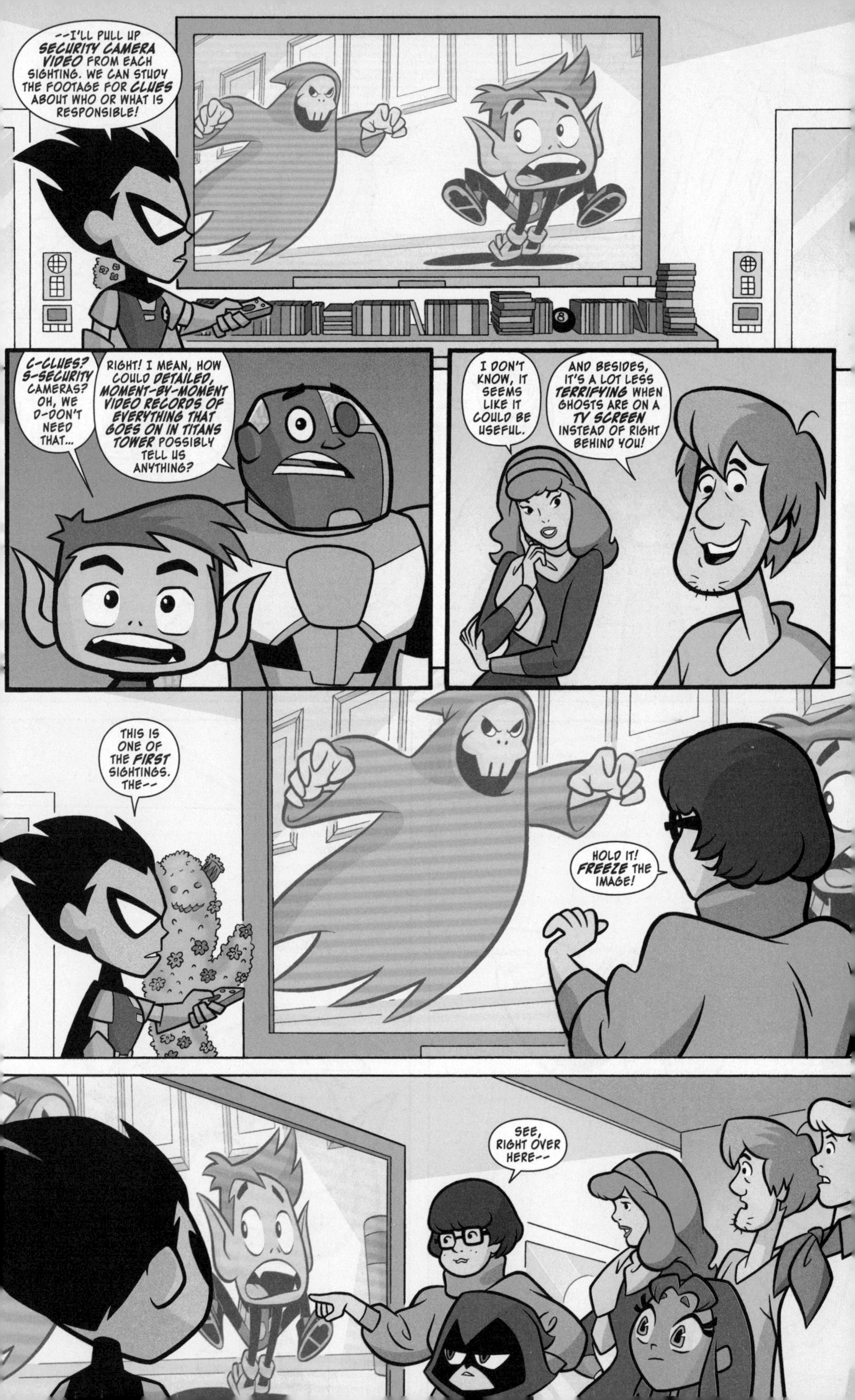
--I'LL PULL UP SECURITY CAMERA VIDEO FROM EACH SIGHTING. WE CAN STUDY THE FOOTAGE FOR CLUES ABOUT WHO OR WHAT IS RESPONSIBLE!
C-CLUES? S-SECURITY CAMERAS? OH, WE D-DON'T NEED THAT...
RIGHT! I MEAN, HOW COULD DETAILED, MOMENT-BY-MOMENT VIDEO RECORDS OF EVERYTHING THAT GOES ON IN TITANS TOWER POSSIBLY TELL US ANYTHING?
I DON'T KNOW, IT SEEMS LIKE IT COULD BE USEFUL.
AND BESIDES, IT'S A LOT LESS TERRIFYING WHEN GHOSTS ARE ON A TV SCREEN INSTEAD OF RIGHT BEHIND YOU!
THIS IS ONE OF THE FIRST SIGHTINGS. THE--
HOLD IT! FREEZE THE IMAGE!
SEE, RIGHT OVER HERE--

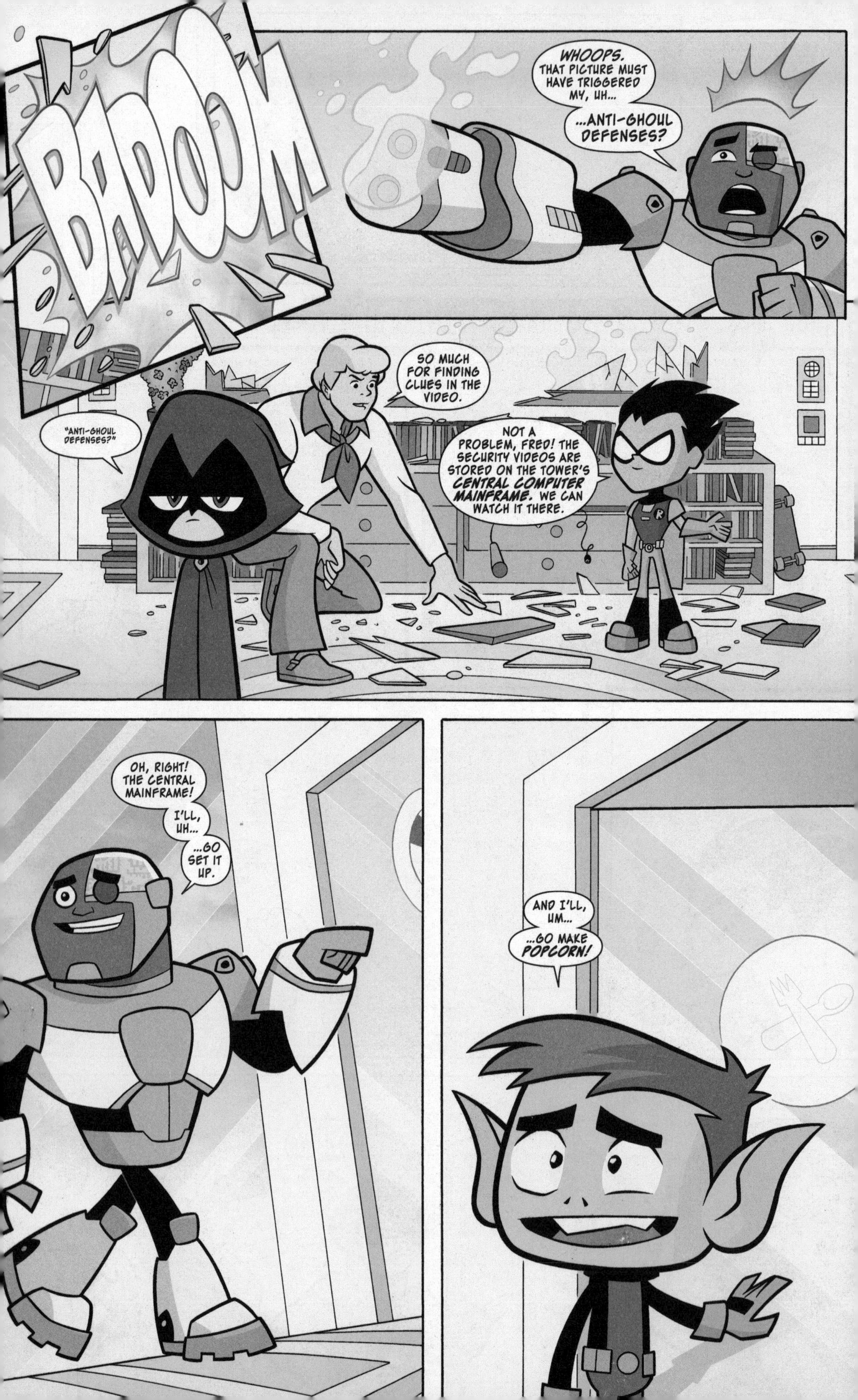
BADOOM
WHOOPS. THAT PICTURE MUST HAVE TRIGGERED MY, UH...
...ANTI-GHOUL DEFENSES?
"ANTI-GHOUL DEFENSES?"
SO MUCH FOR FINDING CLUES IN THE VIDEO.
NOT A PROBLEM, FRED! THE SECURITY VIDEOS ARE STORED ON THE TOWER'S CENTRAL COMPUTER MAINFRAME. WE CAN WATCH IT THERE.
OH, RIGHT! THE CENTRAL MAINFRAME!
I'LL, UH...
...GO SET IT UP.
AND I'LL, UM...
...GO MAKE POPCORN!

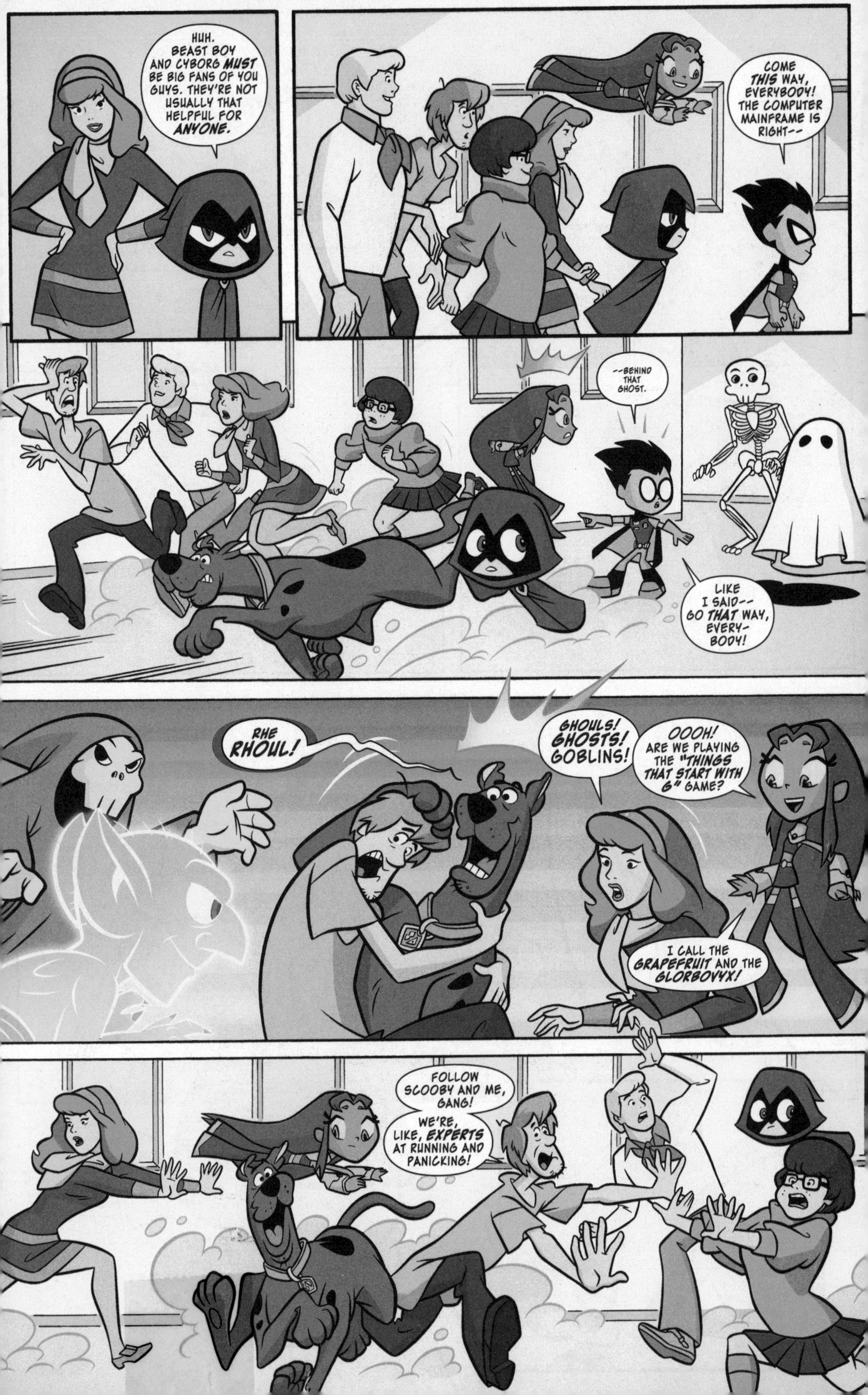
HUH. BEAST BOY AND CYBORG MUST BE BIG FANS OF YOU GUYS. THEY'RE NOT USUALLY THAT HELPFUL FOR ANYONE.
COME THIS WAY, EVERYBODY! THE COMPUTER MAINFRAME IS RIGHT--
--BEHIND THAT GHOST.
LIKE I SAID-- GO THAT WAY, EVERY-BODY!
RHE RHOUL!
GHOULS! GHOSTS! GOBLINS!
OOOH! ARE WE PLAYING THE "THINGS THAT START WITH G" GAME?
I CALL THE GRAPEFRUIT AND THE GLORBOVYX!
FOLLOW SCOOBY AND ME, GANG!
WE'RE, LIKE, EXPERTS AT RUNNING AND PANICKING!

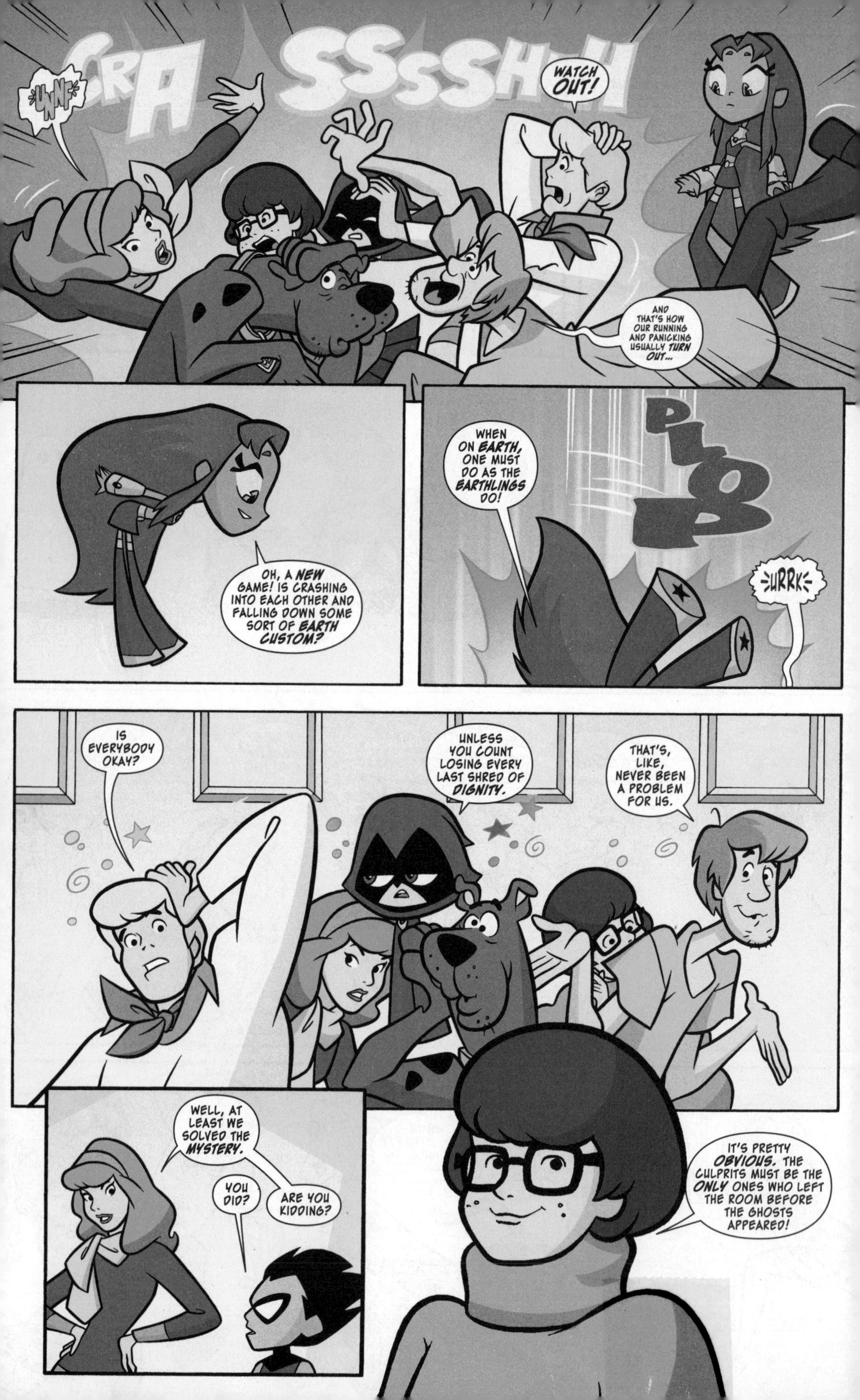

CRASSSSHH
UNNF
WATCH OUT!
AND THAT'S HOW OUR RUNNING AND PANICKING USUALLY TURN OUT...
OH, A NEW GAME! IS CRASHING INTO EACH OTHER AND FALLING DOWN SOME SORT OF EARTH CUSTOM?
WHEN ON EARTH, ONE MUST DO AS THE EARTHLINGS DO!
PLOP
URRK
IS EVERYBODY OKAY?
UNLESS YOU COUNT LOSING EVERY LAST SHRED OF DIGNITY.
THAT'S, LIKE, NEVER BEEN A PROBLEM FOR US.
WELL, AT LEAST WE SOLVED THE MYSTERY.
YOU DID?
ARE YOU KIDDING?
IT'S PRETTY OBVIOUS. THE CULPRITS MUST BE THE ONLY ONES WHO LEFT THE ROOM BEFORE THE GHOSTS APPEARED!

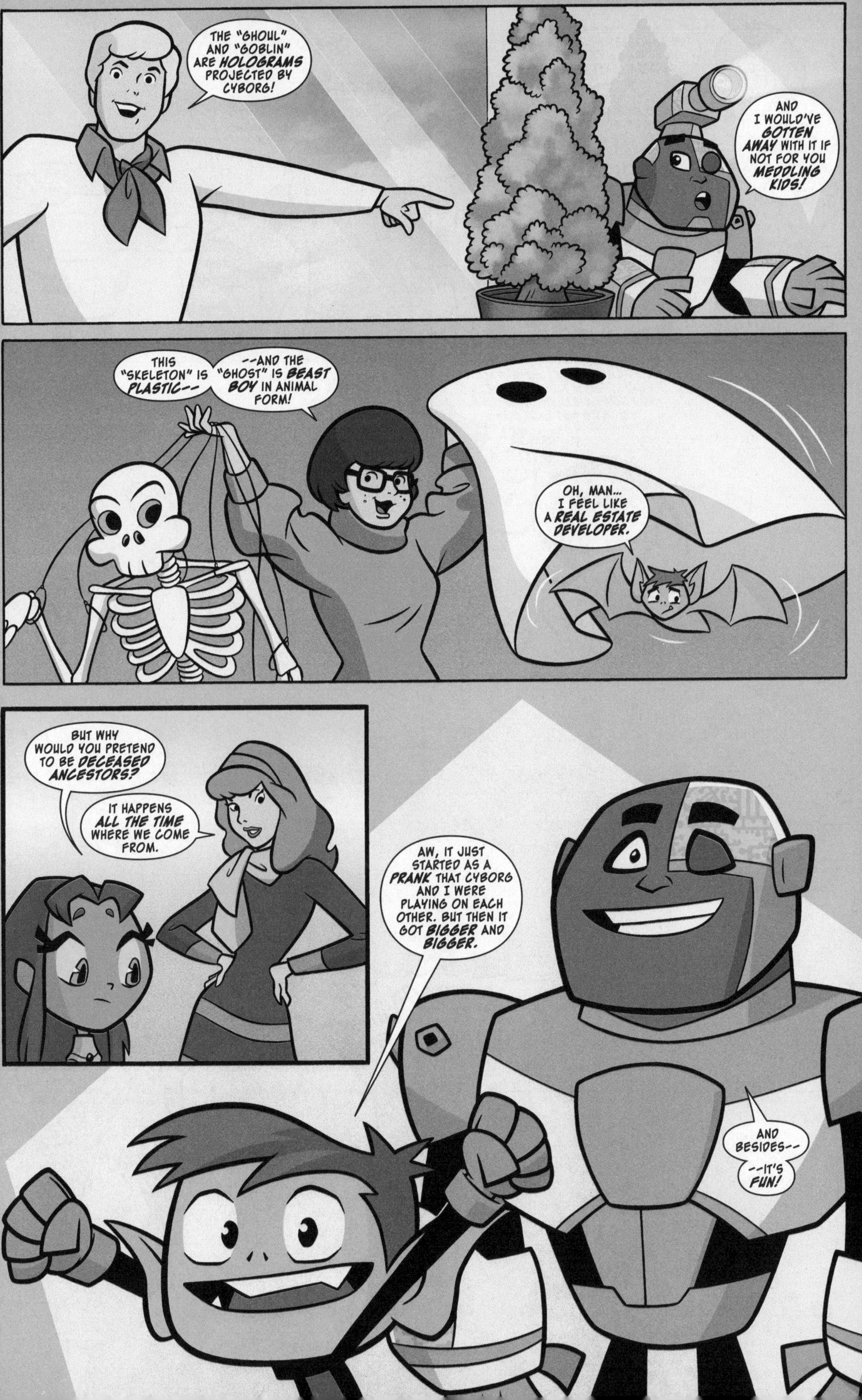
THE "GHOUL" AND "GOBLIN" ARE HOLOGRAMS PROJECTED BY CYBORG!
AND I WOULD'VE GOTTEN AWAY WITH IT IF NOT FOR YOU MEDDLING KIDS!
THIS "SKELETON" IS PLASTIC--
--AND THE "GHOST" IS BEAST BOY IN ANIMAL FORM!
OH, MAN... I FEEL LIKE A REAL ESTATE DEVELOPER.
BUT WHY WOULD YOU PRETEND TO BE DECEASED ANCESTORS?
IT HAPPENS ALL THE TIME WHERE WE COME FROM.
AW, IT JUST STARTED AS A PRANK THAT CYBORG AND I WERE PLAYING ON EACH OTHER. BUT THEN IT GOT BIGGER AND BIGGER.
AND BESIDES--
--IT'S FUN!

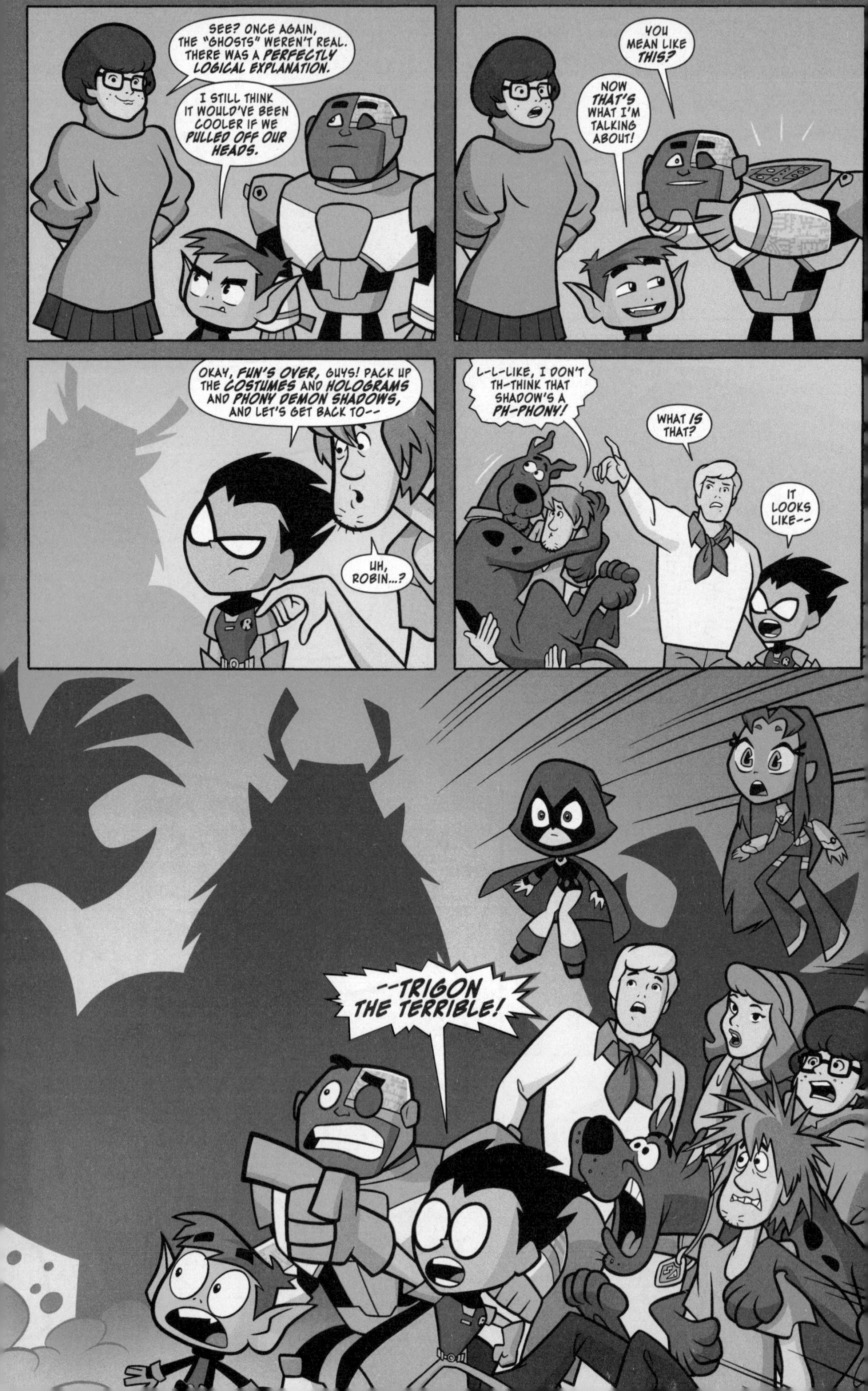

SEE? ONCE AGAIN, THE "GHOSTS" WEREN'T REAL. THERE WAS A PERFECTLY LOGICAL EXPLANATION.
I STILL THINK IT WOULD'VE BEEN COOLER IF WE PULLED OFF OUR HEADS.
YOU MEAN LIKE THIS?
NOW THAT'S WHAT I'M TALKING ABOUT!
OKAY, FUN'S OVER, GUYS! PACK UP THE COSTUMES AND HOLOGRAMS AND PHONY DEMON SHADOWS, AND LET'S GET BACK TO--
UH, ROBIN...?
L-L-LIKE, I DON'T TH-THINK THAT SHADOW'S A PH-PHONY!
WHAT IS THAT?
IT LOOKS LIKE--
--TRIGON THE TERRIBLE!

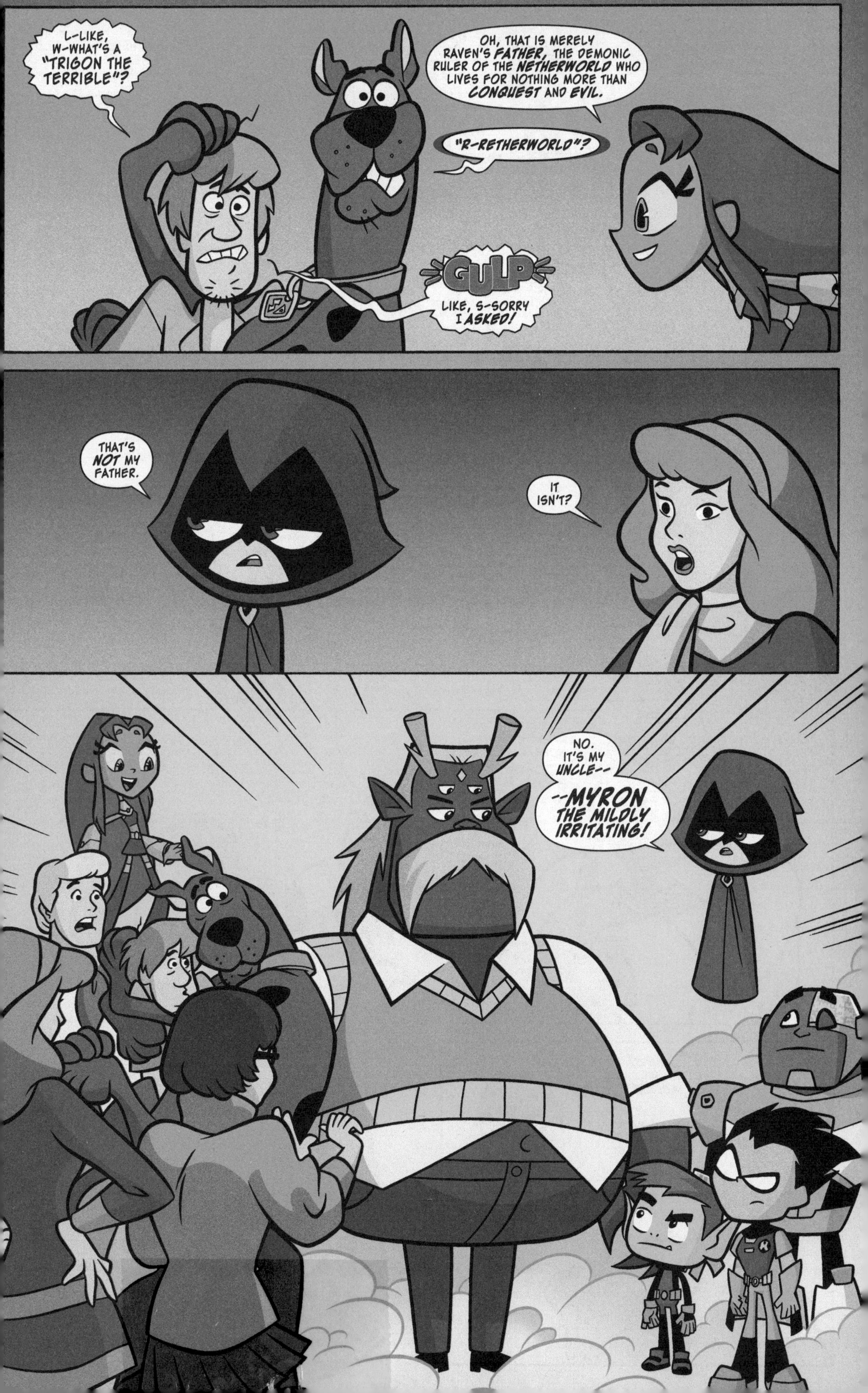
L-LIKE, W-WHAT'S A "TRIGON THE TERRIBLE"?
OH, THAT IS MERELY RAVEN'S FATHER, THE DEMONIC RULER OF THE NETHERWORLD WHO LIVES FOR NOTHING MORE THAN CONQUEST AND EVIL.
"R-RETHERWORLD"?
GULP
LIKE, S-SORRY I ASKED!
THAT'S NOT MY FATHER.
IT ISN'T?
NO. IT'S MY UNCLE--
--MYRON THE MILDLY IRRITATING!

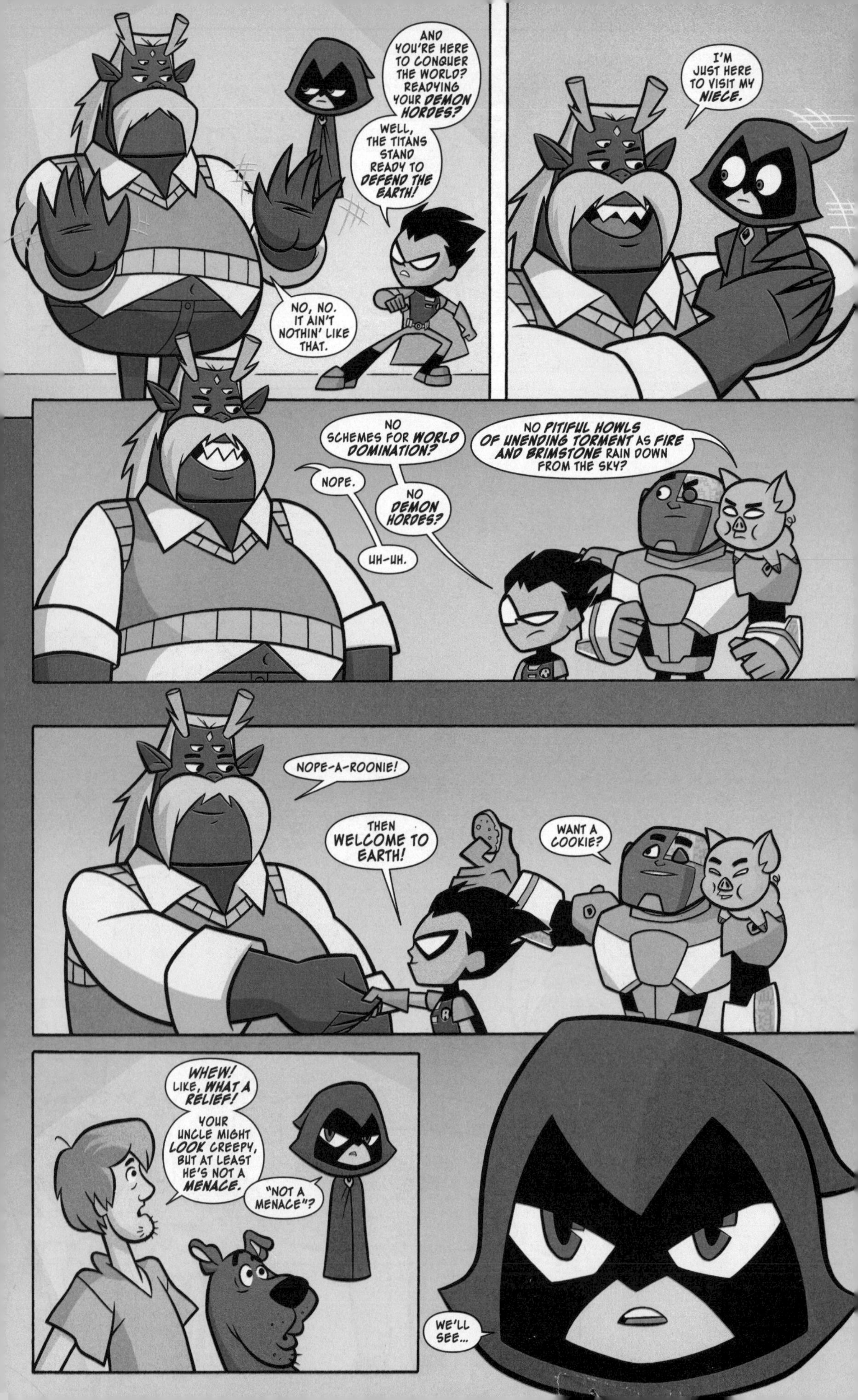

AND YOU'RE HERE TO CONQUER THE WORLD? READYING YOUR DEMON HORDES?
WELL, THE TITANS STAND READY TO DEFEND THE EARTH!
NO, NO. IT AIN'T NOTHIN' LIKE THAT.
I'M JUST HERE TO VISIT MY NIECE.
NO SCHEMES FOR WORLD DOMINATION?
NOPE.
NO DEMON HORDES?
UH-UH.
NO PITIFUL HOWLS OF UNENDING TORMENT AS FIRE AND BRIMSTONE RAIN DOWN FROM THE SKY?
NOPE-A-ROONIE!
THEN WELCOME TO EARTH!
WANT A COOKIE?
WHEW! LIKE, WHAT A RELIEF!
YOUR UNCLE MIGHT LOOK CREEPY, BUT AT LEAST HE'S NOT A MENACE.
"NOT A MENACE"?
WE'LL SEE...

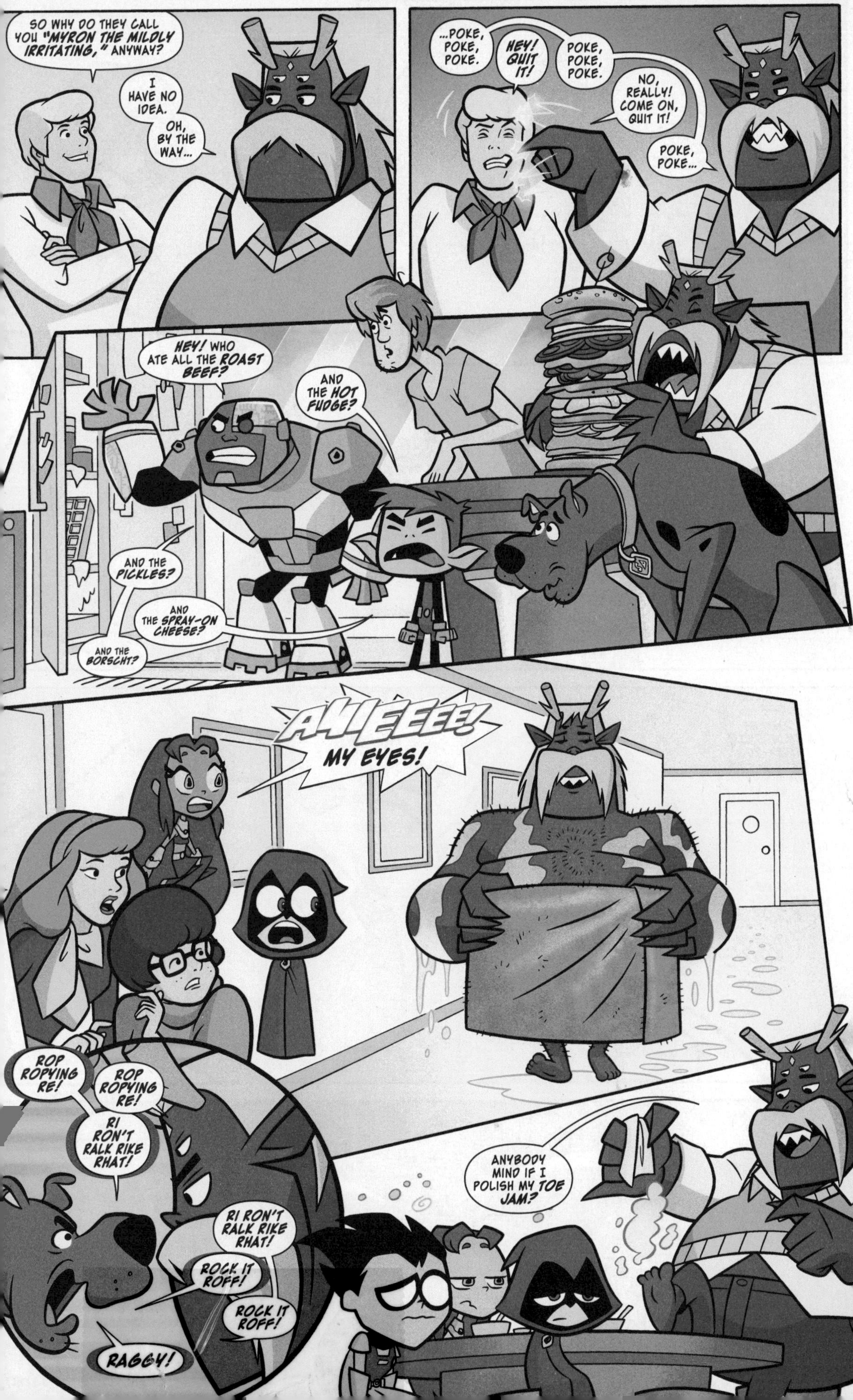

SO WHY DO THEY CALL YOU "MYRON THE MILDLY IRRITATING," ANYWAY?
I HAVE NO IDEA.
OH, BY THE WAY...
...POKE, POKE, POKE.
HEY! QUIT IT!
POKE, POKE, POKE.
NO, REALLY! COME ON, QUIT IT!
POKE, POKE...
HEY! WHO ATE ALL THE ROAST BEEF?
AND THE HOT FUDGE?
AND THE PICKLES?
AND THE SPRAY-ON CHEESE?
AND THE BORSCHT?
AWEEEE! MY EYES!
ROP ROPYING RE!
ROP ROPYING RE!
RI RON'T RALK RIKE RHAT!
ANYBODY MIND IF I POLISH MY TOE JAM?
RI RON'T RALK RIKE RHAT!
ROCK IT ROFF!
ROCK IT ROFF!
RAGGY!

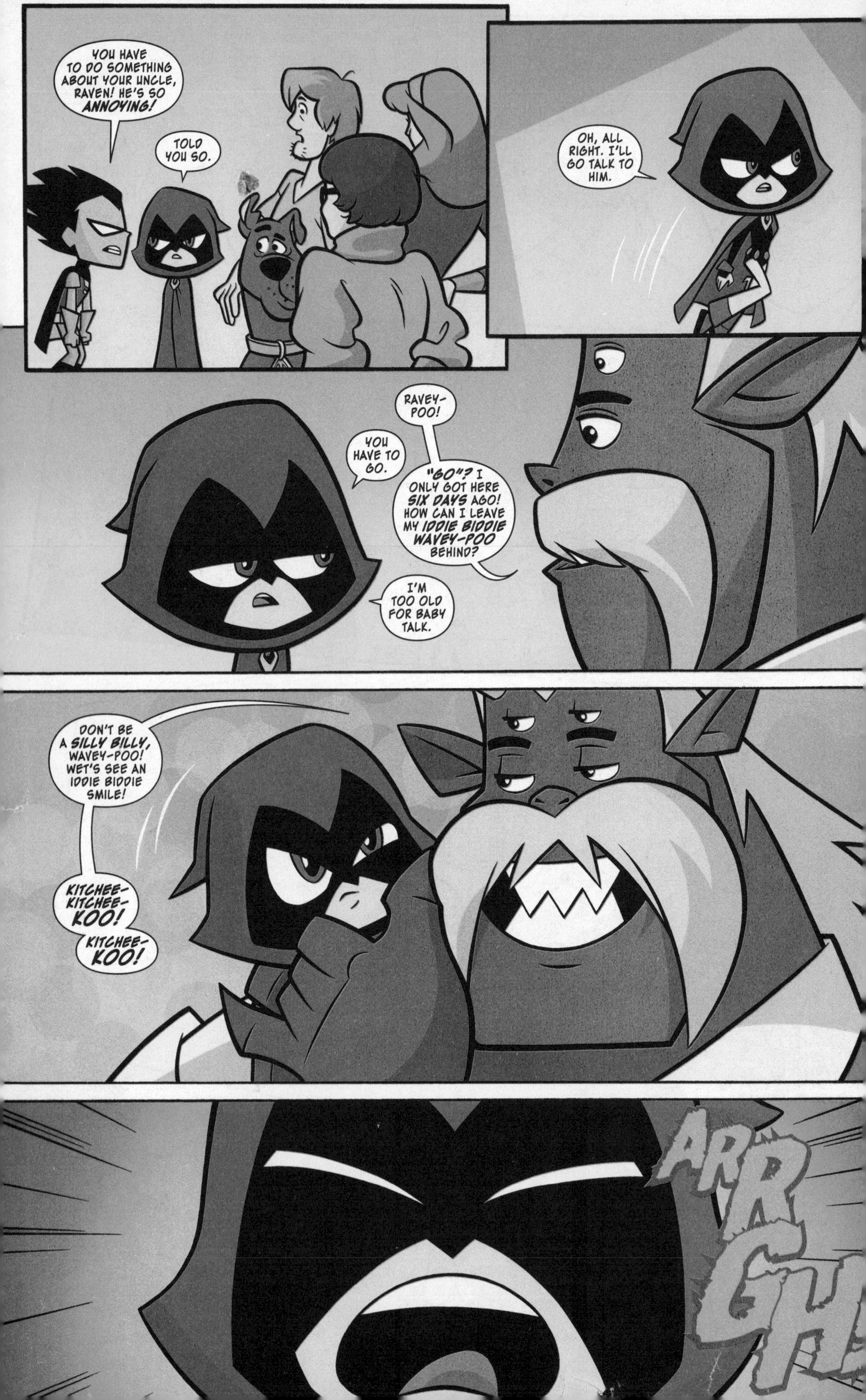
YOU HAVE TO DO SOMETHING ABOUT YOUR UNCLE, RAVEN! HE'S SO ANNOYING!
TOLD YOU SO.
OH, ALL RIGHT. I'LL GO TALK TO HIM.
RAVEY-POO!
YOU HAVE TO GO.
"GO"? I ONLY GOT HERE SIX DAYS AGO! HOW CAN I LEAVE MY IDDIE BIDDIE WAVEY-POO BEHIND?
I'M TOO OLD FOR BABY TALK.
DON'T BE A SILLY BILLY, WAVEY-POO! WET'S SEE AN IDDIE BIDDIE SMILE!
KITCHEE-KITCHEE-KOO!
KITCHEE-KOO!
ARRGH

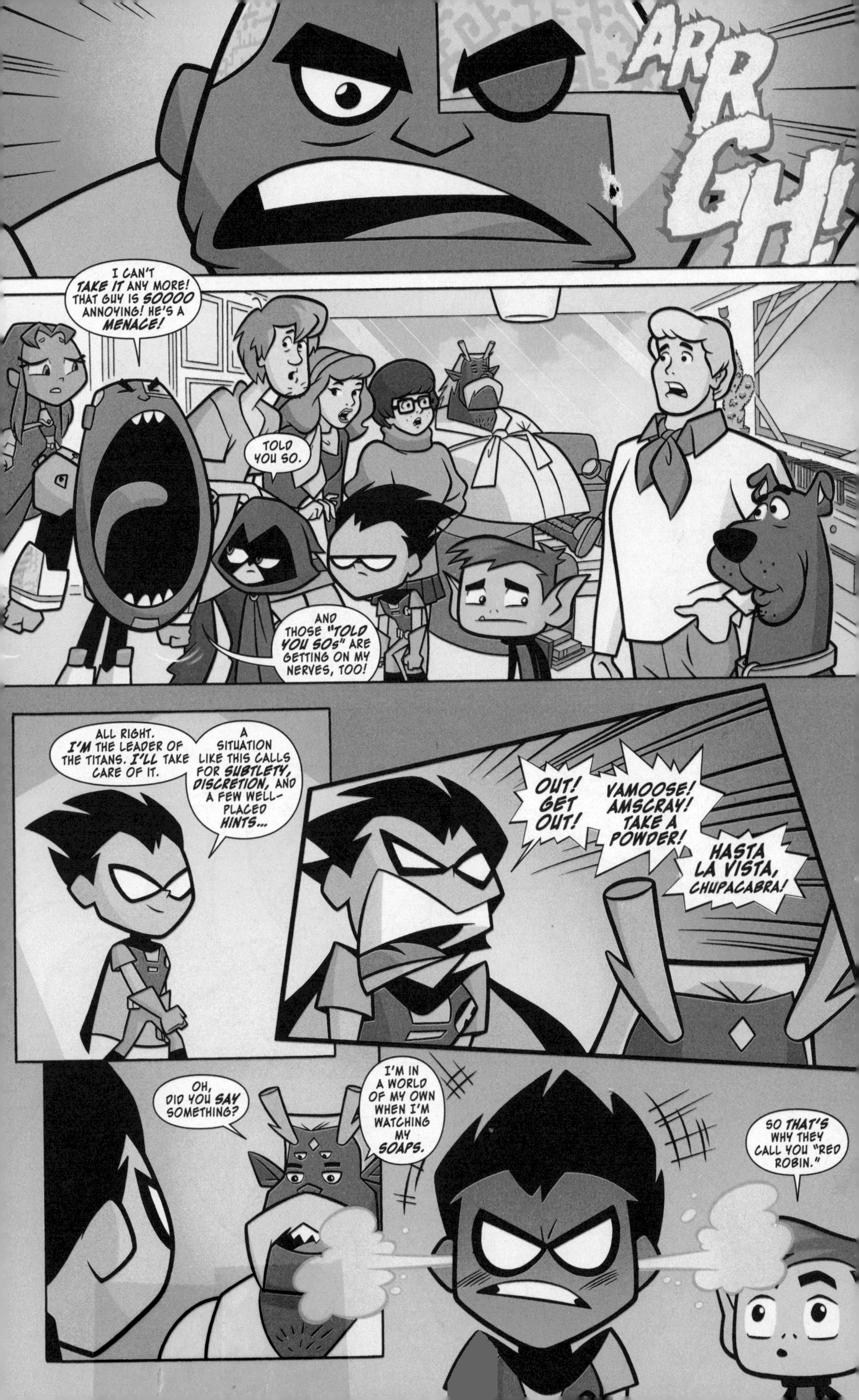
ARRGH!
I CAN'T TAKE IT ANY MORE! THAT GUY IS SOOOO ANNOYING! HE'S A MENACE!
TOLD YOU SO.
AND THOSE "TOLD YOU SOs" ARE GETTING ON MY NERVES, TOO!
ALL RIGHT. I'M THE LEADER OF THE TITANS. I'LL TAKE CARE OF IT.
A SITUATION LIKE THIS CALLS FOR SUBTLETY, DISCRETION, AND A FEW WELL-PLACED HINTS...
OUT! GET OUT!
VAMOOSE! AMSCRAY! TAKE A POWDER!
HASTA LA VISTA, CHUPACABRA!
OH, DID YOU SAY SOMETHING?
I'M IN A WORLD OF MY OWN WHEN I'M WATCHING MY SOAPS.
SO THAT'S WHY THEY CALL YOU "RED ROBIN."

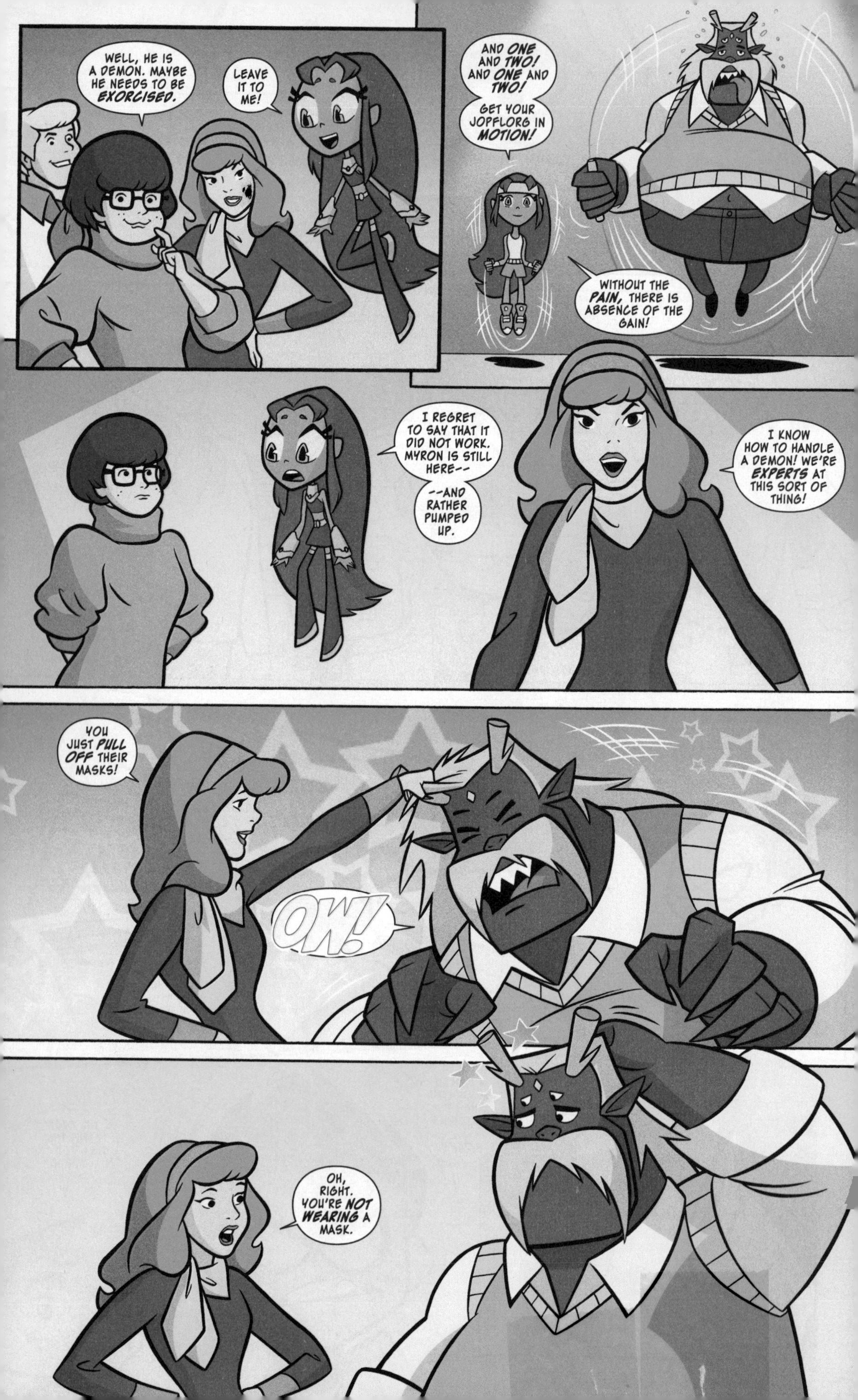
WELL, HE IS A DEMON. MAYBE HE NEEDS TO BE EXORCISED.
LEAVE IT TO ME!
AND ONE AND TWO! AND ONE AND TWO!
GET YOUR JOPFLORG IN MOTION!
WITHOUT THE PAIN, THERE IS ABSENCE OF THE GAIN!
I REGRET TO SAY THAT IT DID NOT WORK. MYRON IS STILL HERE--
--AND RATHER PUMPED UP.
I KNOW HOW TO HANDLE A DEMON! WE'RE EXPERTS AT THIS SORT OF THING!
YOU JUST PULL OFF THEIR MASKS!
OW!
OH, RIGHT. YOU'RE NOT WEARING A MASK.

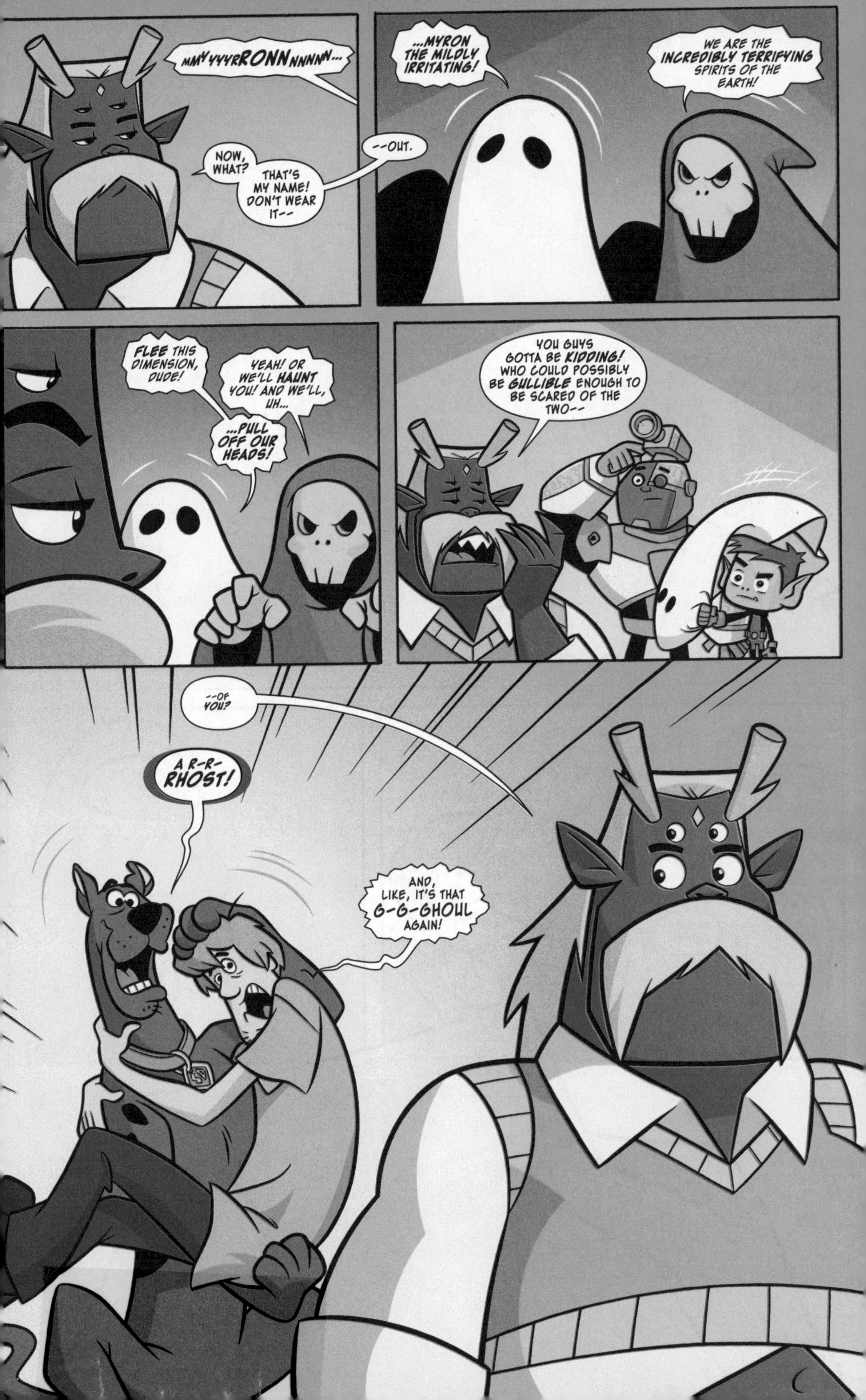

MMYYYYRRONNNNNNN...
NOW, WHAT?
THAT'S MY NAME! DON'T WEAR IT--
--OUT.
...MYRON THE MILDLY IRRITATING!
WE ARE THE INCREDIBLY TERRIFYING SPIRITS OF THE EARTH!
FLEE THIS DIMENSION, DUDE!
YEAH! OR WE'LL HAUNT YOU! AND WE'LL, UH...
...PULL OFF OUR HEADS!
YOU GUYS GOTTA BE KIDDING! WHO COULD POSSIBLY BE GULLIBLE ENOUGH TO BE SCARED OF THE TWO--
--OF YOU?
A R-R-RHOST!
AND, LIKE, IT'S THAT G-G-GHOUL AGAIN!

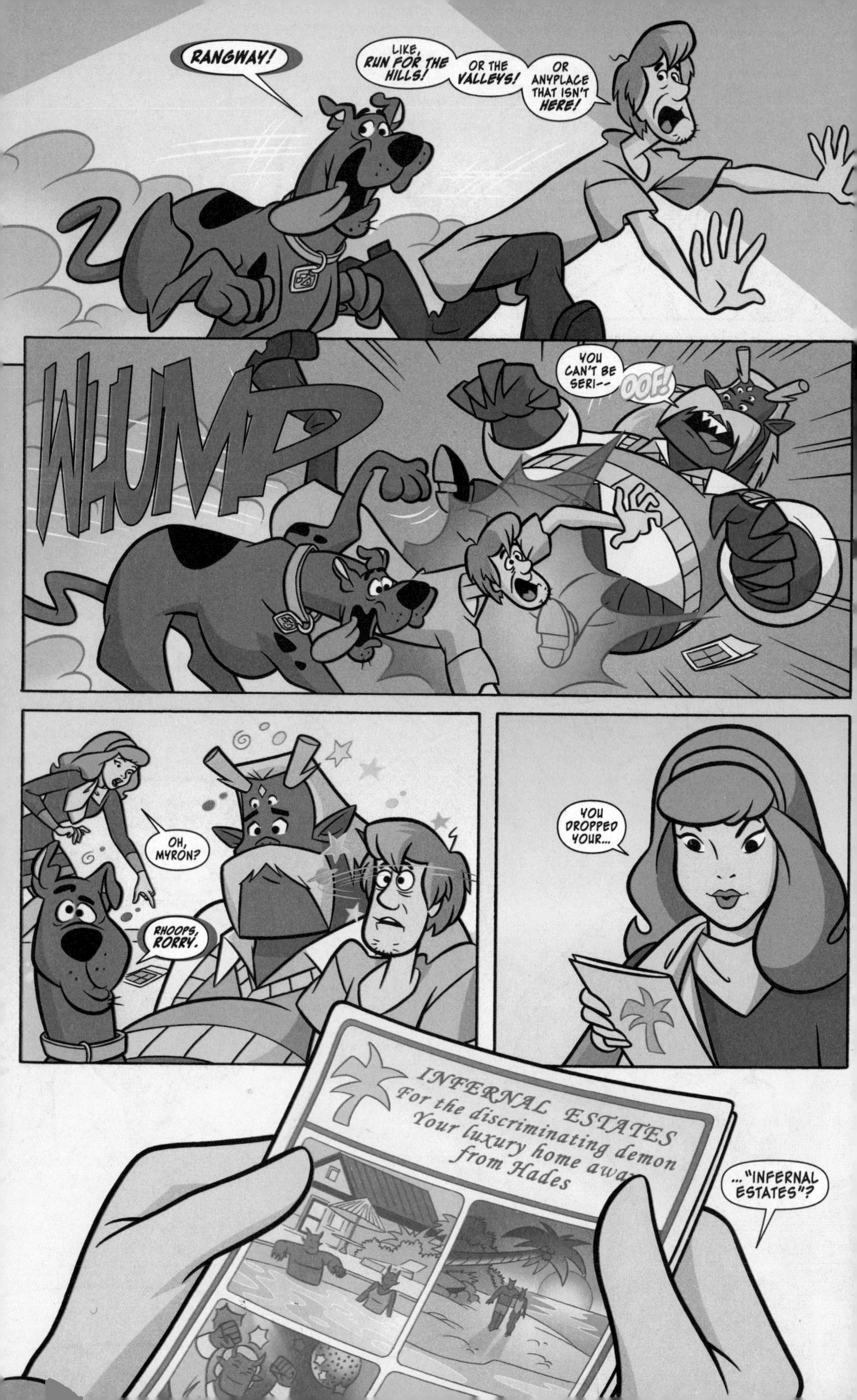
RANGWAY!
LIKE, RUN FOR THE HILLS!
OR THE VALLEYS!
OR ANYPLACE THAT ISN'T HERE!
WHUMP
YOU CAN'T BE SERI--
OOF!
OH, MYRON?
RHOOPS, RORRY.
YOU DROPPED YOUR...
INFERNAL ESTATES
For the discriminating demon
Your luxury home away
from Hades
..."INFERNAL ESTATES"?

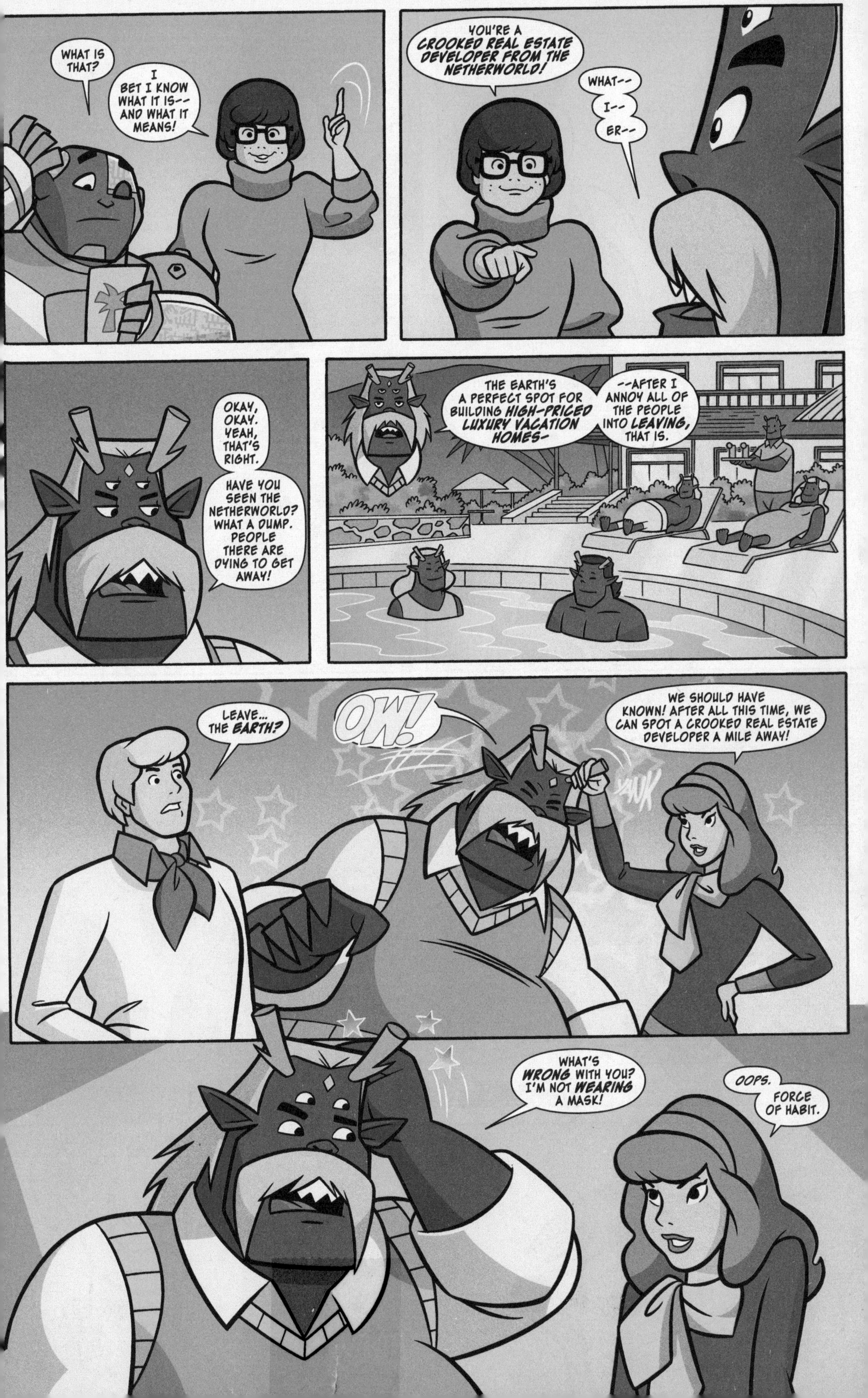
WHAT IS THAT?
I BET I KNOW WHAT IT IS-- AND WHAT IT MEANS!
YOU'RE A CROOKED REAL ESTATE DEVELOPER FROM THE NETHERWORLD!
WHAT--
I--
ER--
OKAY, OKAY. YEAH, THAT'S RIGHT.
HAVE YOU SEEN THE NETHERWORLD? WHAT A DUMP. PEOPLE THERE ARE DYING TO GET AWAY!
THE EARTH'S A PERFECT SPOT FOR BUILDING HIGH-PRICED LUXURY VACATION HOMES-
--AFTER I ANNOY ALL OF THE PEOPLE INTO LEAVING, THAT IS.
LEAVE... THE EARTH?
OW!
YANK
WE SHOULD HAVE KNOWN! AFTER ALL THIS TIME, WE CAN SPOT A CROOKED REAL ESTATE DEVELOPER A MILE AWAY!
WHAT'S WRONG WITH YOU? I'M NOT WEARING A MASK!
OOPS.
FORCE OF HABIT.

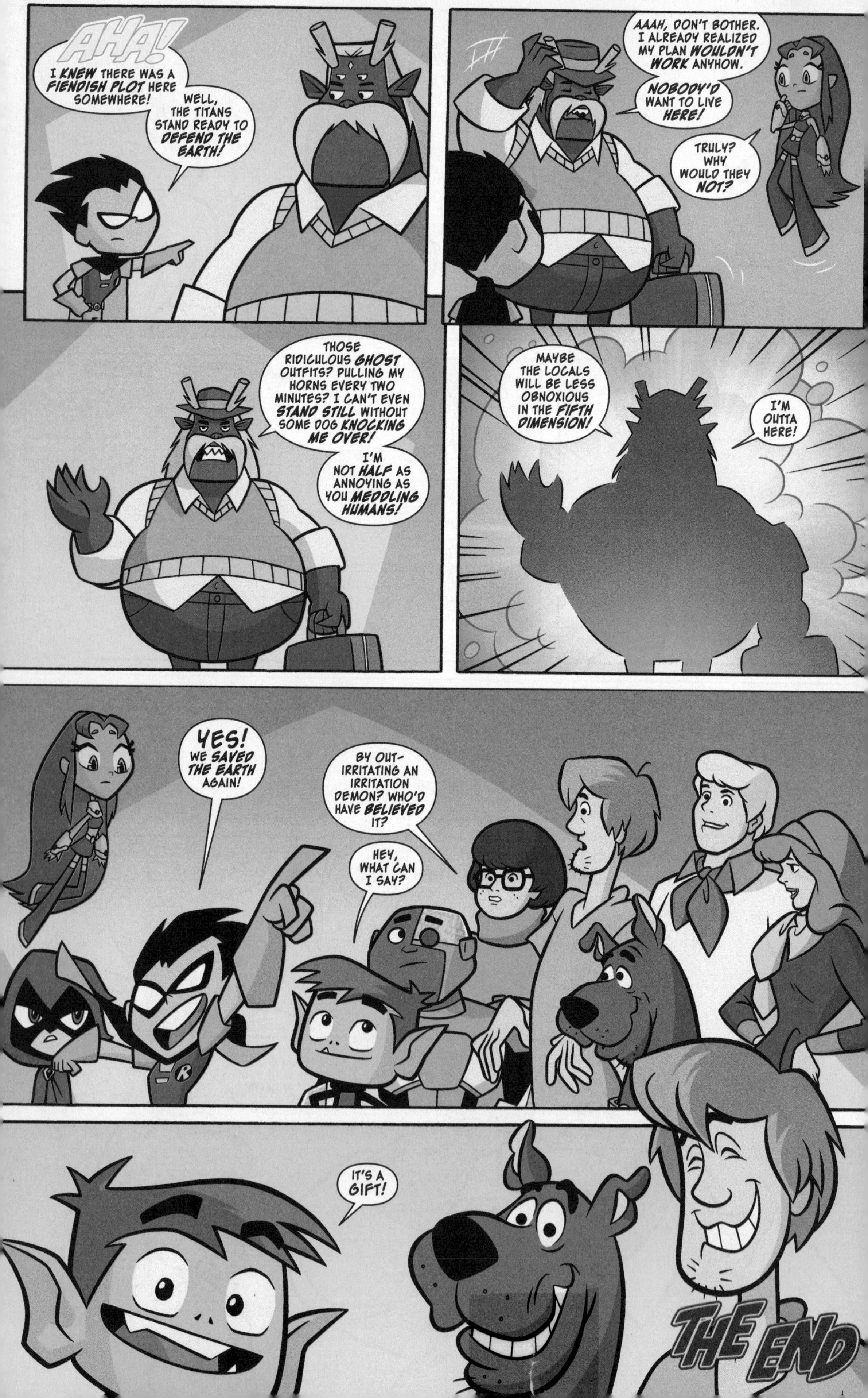
AHA!
I KNEW THERE WAS A FIENDISH PLOT HERE SOMEWHERE!
WELL, THE TITANS STAND READY TO DEFEND THE EARTH!
AAAH, DON'T BOTHER. I ALREADY REALIZED MY PLAN WOULDN'T WORK ANYHOW.
NOBODY'D WANT TO LIVE HERE!
TRULY? WHY WOULD THEY NOT?
THOSE RIDICULOUS GHOST OUTFITS? PULLING MY HORNS EVERY TWO MINUTES? I CAN'T EVEN STAND STILL WITHOUT SOME DOG KNOCKING ME OVER!
I'M NOT HALF AS ANNOYING AS YOU MEDDLING HUMANS!
MAYBE THE LOCALS WILL BE LESS OBNOXIOUS IN THE FIFTH DIMENSION!
I'M OUTTA HERE!
YES! WE SAVED THE EARTH AGAIN!
BY OUT-IRRITATING AN IRRITATION DEMON? WHO'D HAVE BELIEVED IT?
HEY, WHAT CAN I SAY?
IT'S A GIFT!
THE END

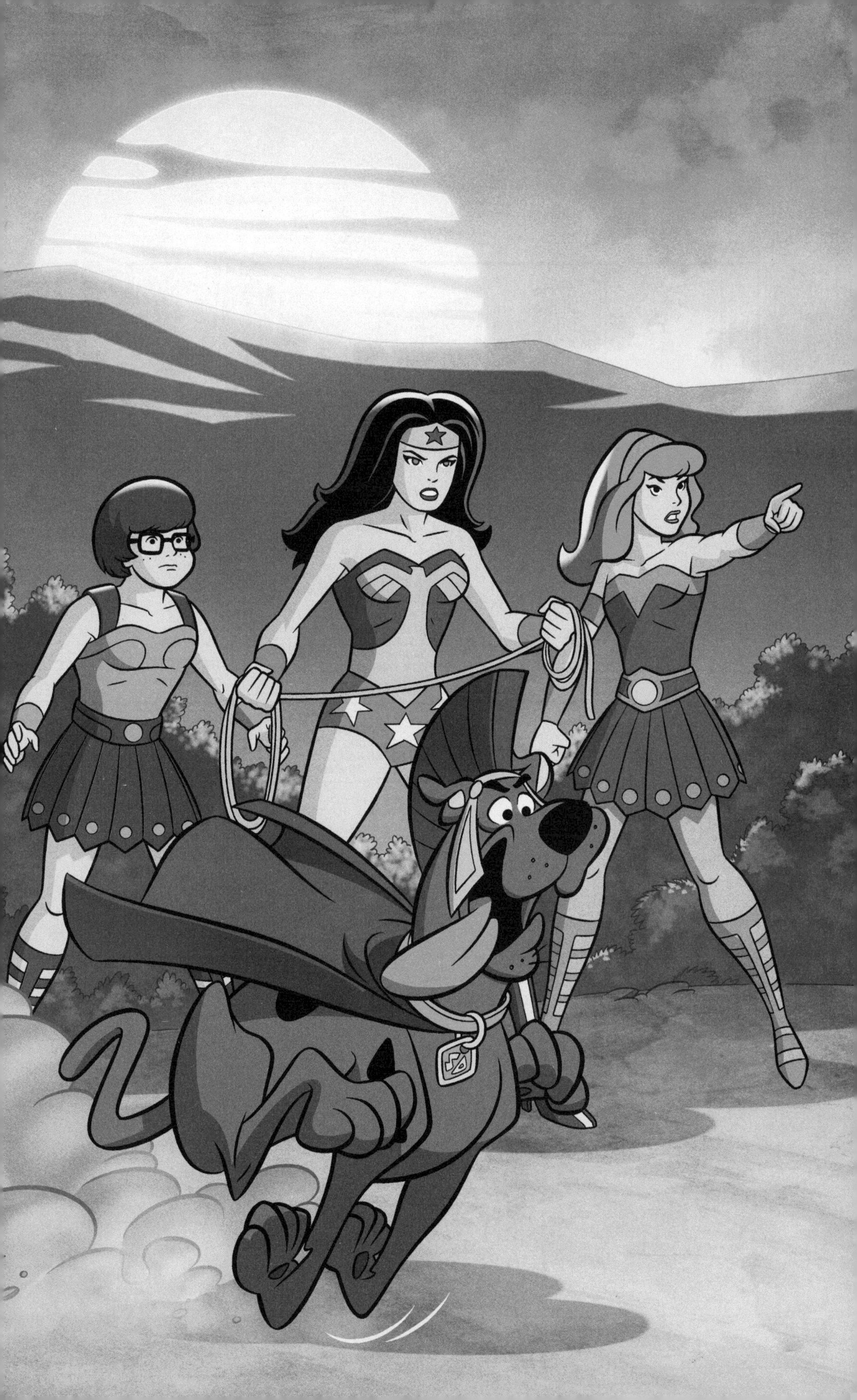

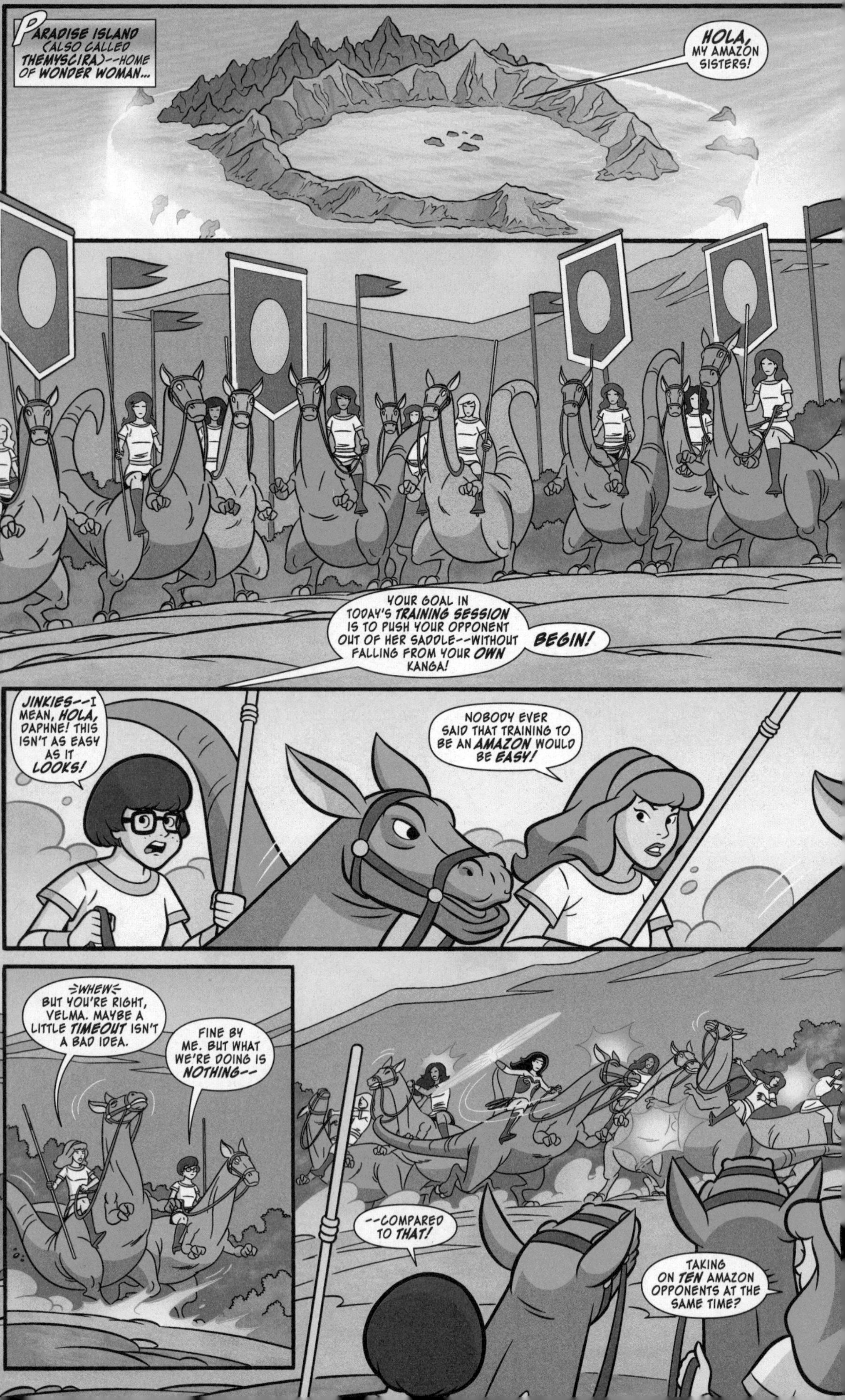
PARADISE ISLAND (ALSO CALLED THEMYSCIRA)--HOME OF WONDER WOMAN...
HOLA, MY AMAZON SISTERS!
YOUR GOAL IN TODAY'S TRAINING SESSION IS TO PUSH YOUR OPPONENT OUT OF HER SADDLE--WITHOUT FALLING FROM YOUR OWN KANGA!
BEGIN!
JINKIES--I MEAN, HOLA, DAPHNE! THIS ISN'T AS EASY AS IT LOOKS!
NOBODY EVER SAID THAT TRAINING TO BE AN AMAZON WOULD BE EASY!
=WHEW= BUT YOU'RE RIGHT, VELMA. MAYBE A LITTLE TIMEOUT ISN'T A BAD IDEA.
FINE BY ME. BUT WHAT WE'RE DOING IS NOTHING--
--COMPARED TO THAT!
TAKING ON TEN AMAZON OPPONENTS AT THE SAME TIME?

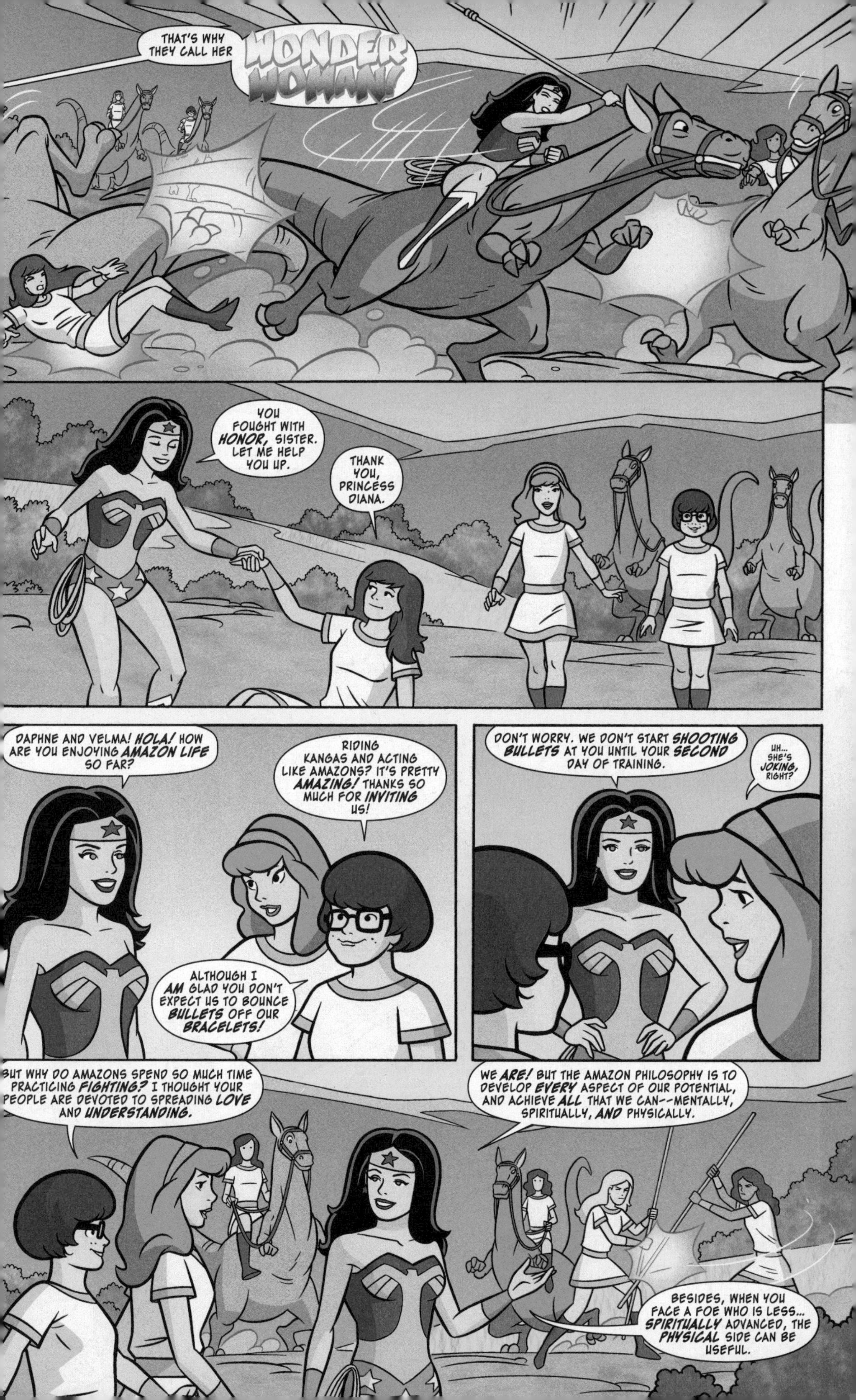
THAT'S WHY THEY CALL HER
WONDER WOMAN!
YOU FOUGHT WITH HONOR, SISTER. LET ME HELP YOU UP.
THANK YOU, PRINCESS DIANA.
DAPHNE AND VELMA! HOLA! HOW ARE YOU ENJOYING AMAZON LIFE SO FAR?
RIDING KANGAS AND ACTING LIKE AMAZONS? IT'S PRETTY AMAZING! THANKS SO MUCH FOR INVITING US!
ALTHOUGH I AM GLAD YOU DON'T EXPECT US TO BOUNCE BULLETS OFF OUR BRACELETS!
DON'T WORRY. WE DON'T START SHOOTING BULLETS AT YOU UNTIL YOUR SECOND DAY OF TRAINING.
UH... SHE'S JOKING, RIGHT?
BUT WHY DO AMAZONS SPEND SO MUCH TIME PRACTICING FIGHTING? I THOUGHT YOUR PEOPLE ARE DEVOTED TO SPREADING LOVE AND UNDERSTANDING.
WE ARE! BUT THE AMAZON PHILOSOPHY IS TO DEVELOP EVERY ASPECT OF OUR POTENTIAL, AND ACHIEVE ALL THAT WE CAN--MENTALLY, SPIRITUALLY, AND PHYSICALLY.
BESIDES, WHEN YOU FACE A FOE WHO IS LESS... SPIRITUALLY ADVANCED, THE PHYSICAL SIDE CAN BE USEFUL.

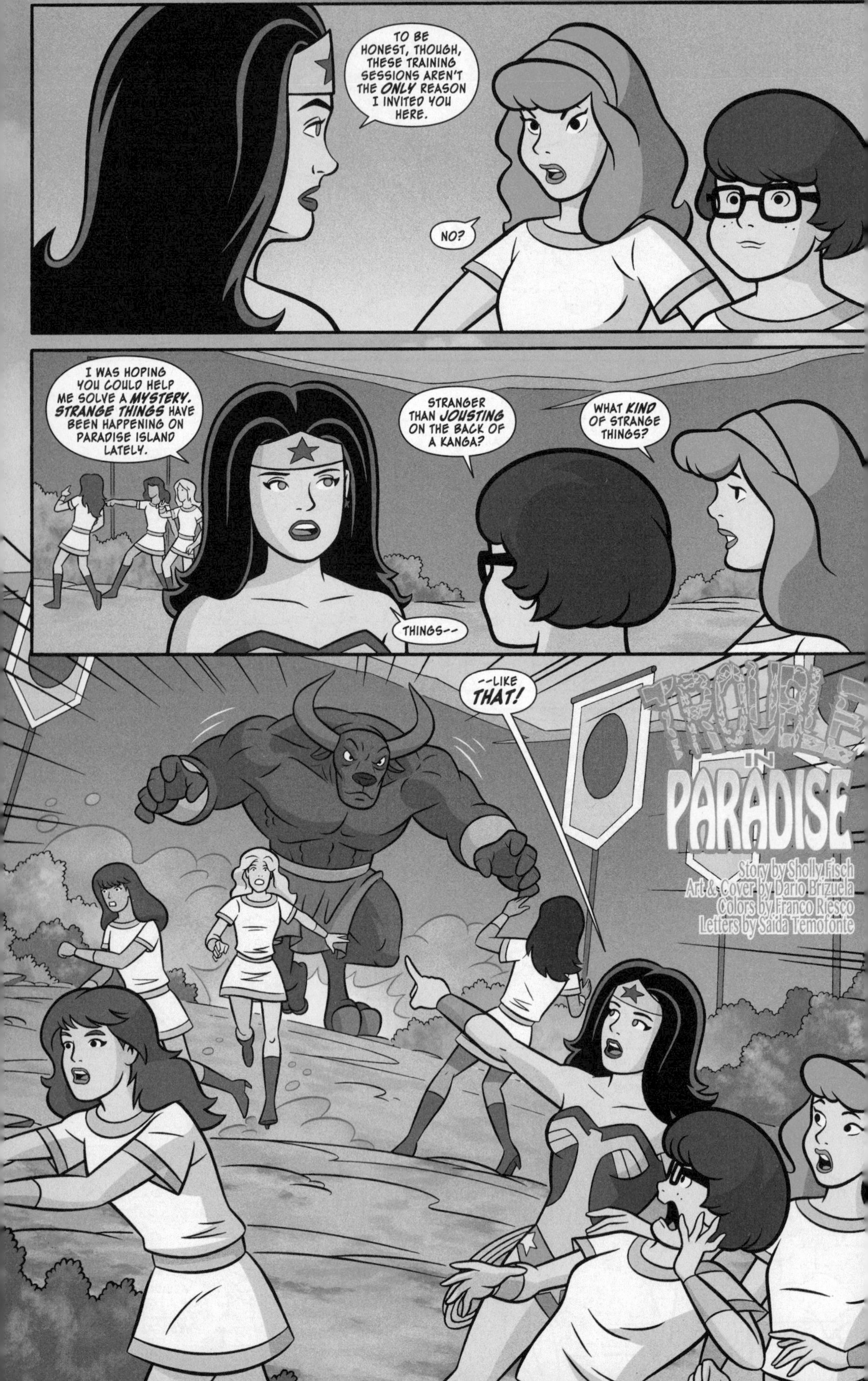

TO BE HONEST, THOUGH, THESE TRAINING SESSIONS AREN'T THE *ONLY* REASON I INVITED YOU HERE.
NO?
I WAS HOPING YOU COULD HELP ME SOLVE A *MYSTERY*. *STRANGE THINGS* HAVE BEEN HAPPENING ON PARADISE ISLAND LATELY.
STRANGER THAN *JOUSTING* ON THE BACK OF A KANGA?
WHAT *KIND* OF STRANGE THINGS?
THINGS--
--LIKE *THAT!*
TROUBLE IN PARADISE
Story by Sholly Fisch
Art & Cover by Dario Brizuela
Colors by Franco Riesco
Letters by Saida Temofonte

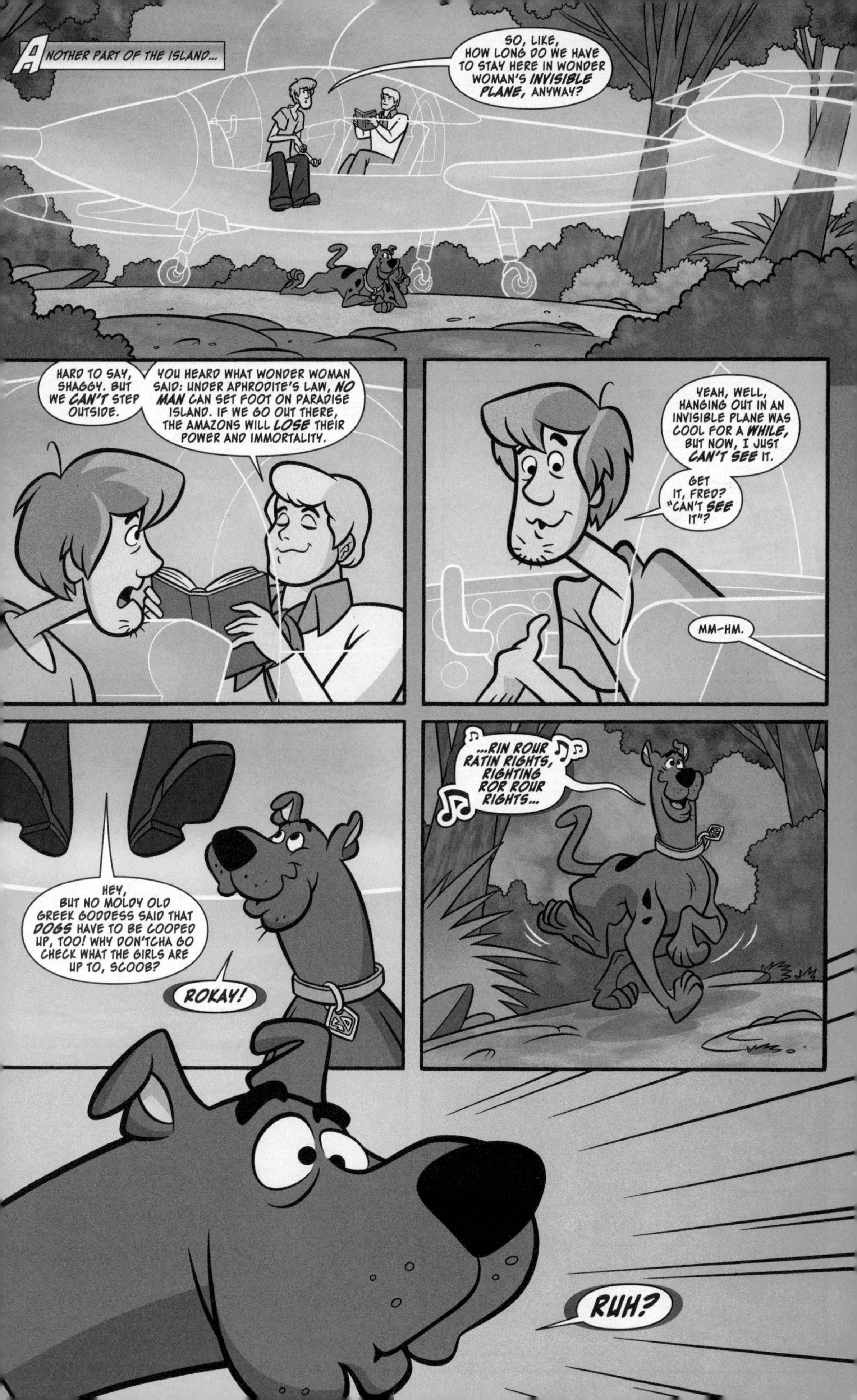
ANOTHER PART OF THE ISLAND...
SO, LIKE, HOW LONG DO WE HAVE TO STAY HERE IN WONDER WOMAN'S INVISIBLE PLANE, ANYWAY?
HARD TO SAY, SHAGGY. BUT WE CAN'T STEP OUTSIDE.
YOU HEARD WHAT WONDER WOMAN SAID: UNDER APHRODITE'S LAW, NO MAN CAN SET FOOT ON PARADISE ISLAND. IF WE GO OUT THERE, THE AMAZONS WILL LOSE THEIR POWER AND IMMORTALITY.
YEAH, WELL, HANGING OUT IN AN INVISIBLE PLANE WAS COOL FOR A WHILE, BUT NOW, I JUST CAN'T SEE IT.
GET IT, FRED? "CAN'T SEE IT"?
MM-HM.
HEY, BUT NO MOLDY OLD GREEK GODDESS SAID THAT DOGS HAVE TO BE COOPED UP, TOO! WHY DON'TCHA GO CHECK WHAT THE GIRLS ARE UP TO, SCOOB?
ROKAY!
...RIN ROUR RATIN RIGHTS, RIGHTING ROR ROUR RIGHTS...
RUH?

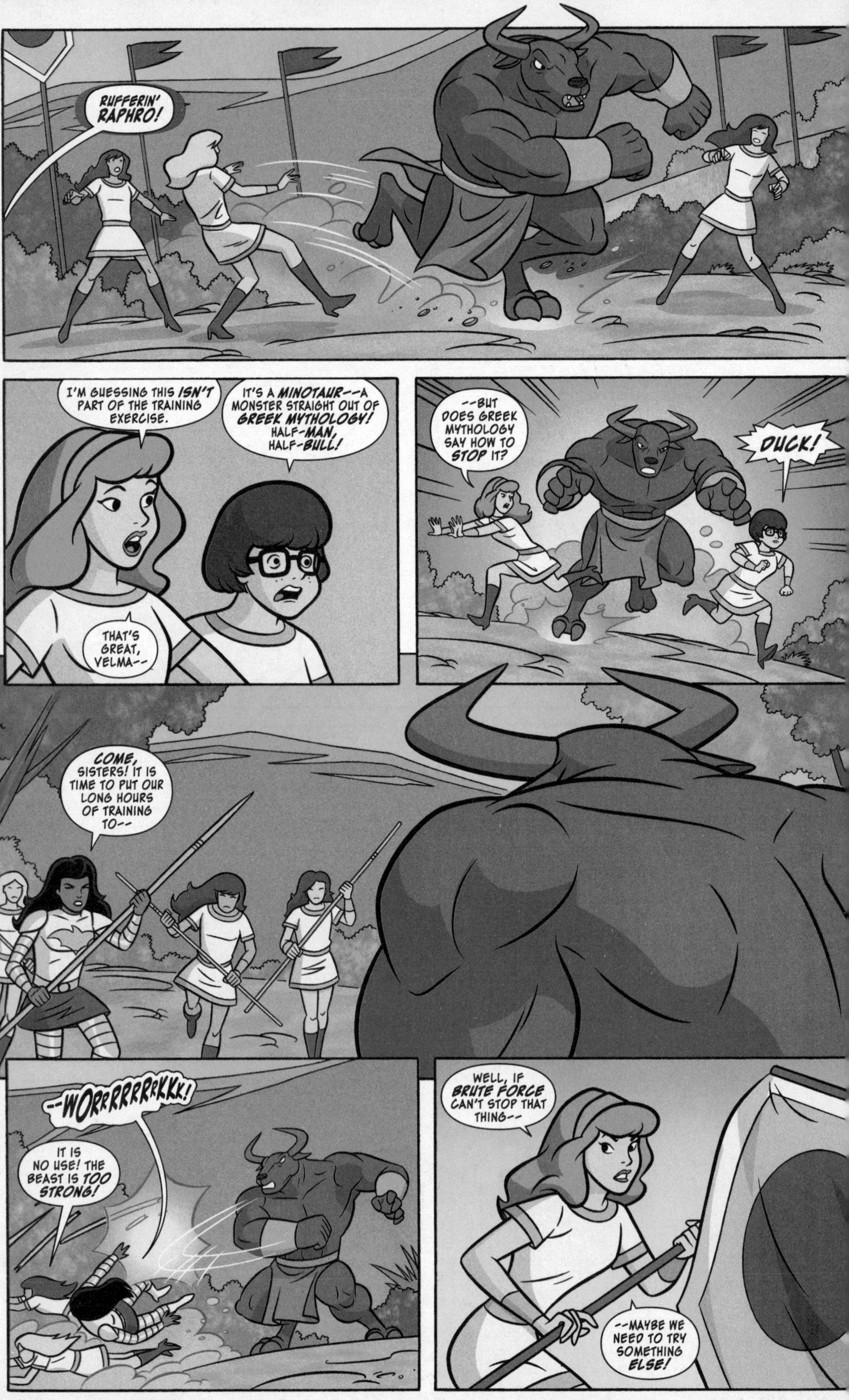
RUFFERIN' RAPHRO!
I'M GUESSING THIS ISN'T PART OF THE TRAINING EXERCISE.
IT'S A MINOTAUR--A MONSTER STRAIGHT OUT OF GREEK MYTHOLOGY! HALF-MAN, HALF-BULL!
THAT'S GREAT, VELMA--
--BUT DOES GREEK MYTHOLOGY SAY HOW TO STOP IT?
DUCK!
COME, SISTERS! IT IS TIME TO PUT OUR LONG HOURS OF TRAINING TO--
--WORRRRRRKKK!
IT IS NO USE! THE BEAST IS TOO STRONG!
WELL, IF BRUTE FORCE CAN'T STOP THAT THING--
--MAYBE WE NEED TO TRY SOMETHING ELSE!

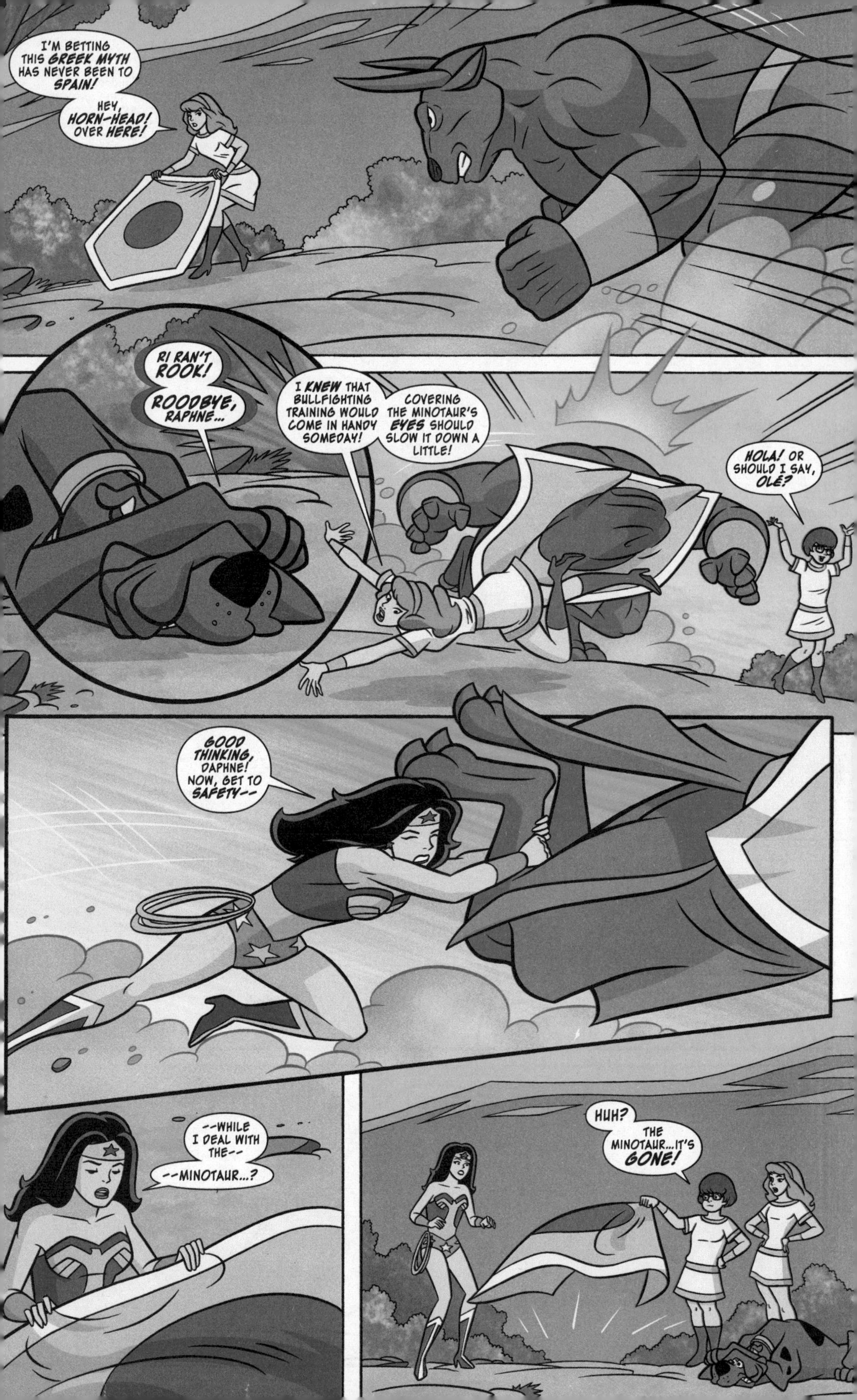
I'M BETTING THIS GREEK MYTH HAS NEVER BEEN TO SPAIN!
HEY, HORN-HEAD! OVER HERE!
RI RAN'T ROOK!
ROODBYE, RAPHNE...
I KNEW THAT BULLFIGHTING TRAINING WOULD COME IN HANDY SOMEDAY!
COVERING THE MINOTAUR'S EYES SHOULD SLOW IT DOWN A LITTLE!
HOLA! OR SHOULD I SAY, OLÉ?
GOOD THINKING, DAPHNE! NOW, GET TO SAFETY--
--WHILE I DEAL WITH THE--
--MINOTAUR...?
HUH?
THE MINOTAUR...IT'S GONE!

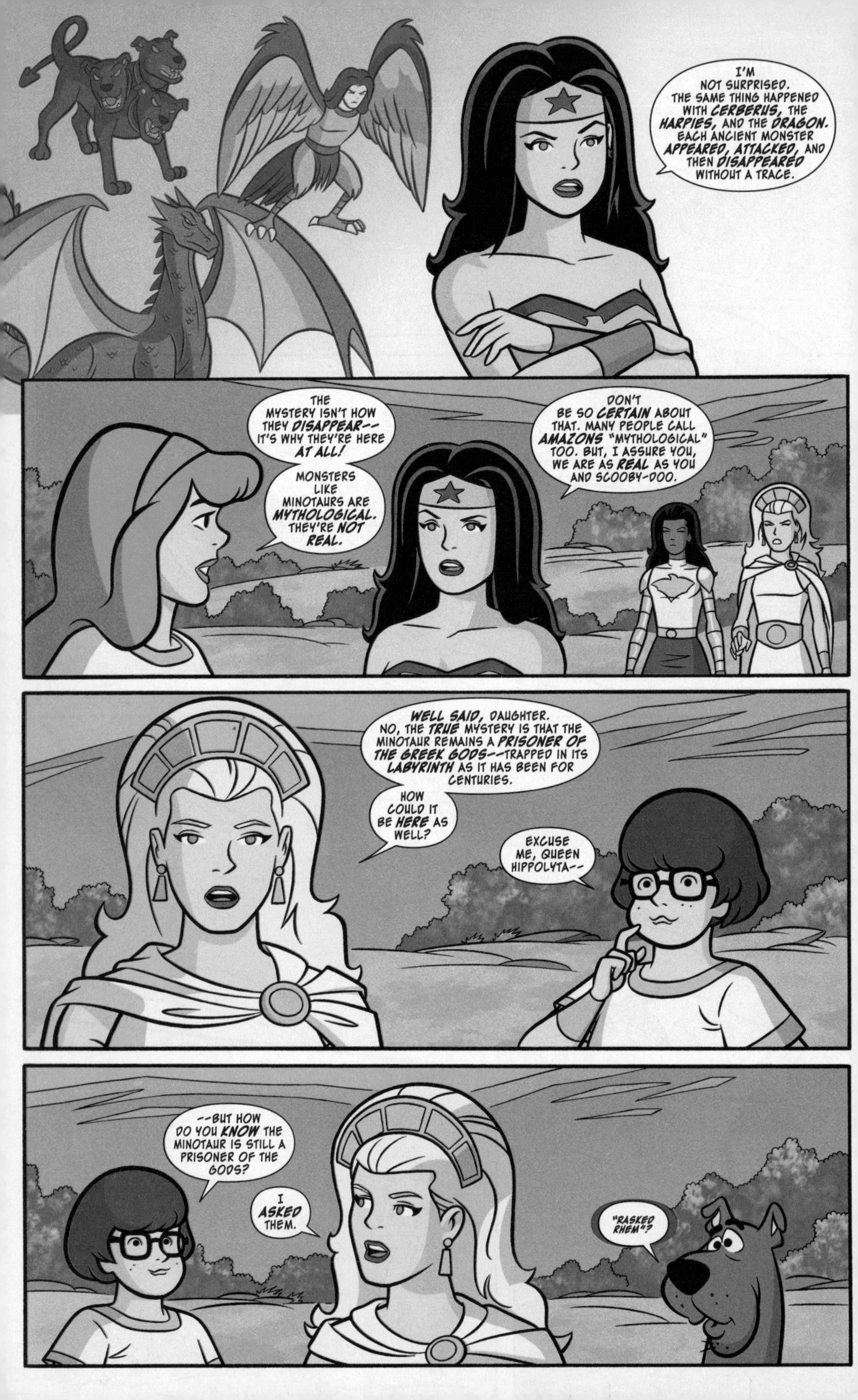

I'M NOT SURPRISED. THE SAME THING HAPPENED WITH CERBERUS, THE HARPIES, AND THE DRAGON. EACH ANCIENT MONSTER APPEARED, ATTACKED, AND THEN DISAPPEARED WITHOUT A TRACE.
THE MYSTERY ISN'T HOW THEY DISAPPEAR-- IT'S WHY THEY'RE HERE AT ALL!
MONSTERS LIKE MINOTAURS ARE MYTHOLOGICAL. THEY'RE NOT REAL.
DON'T BE SO CERTAIN ABOUT THAT. MANY PEOPLE CALL AMAZONS "MYTHOLOGICAL" TOO. BUT, I ASSURE YOU, WE ARE AS REAL AS YOU AND SCOOBY-DOO.
WELL SAID, DAUGHTER. NO, THE TRUE MYSTERY IS THAT THE MINOTAUR REMAINS A PRISONER OF THE GREEK GODS--TRAPPED IN ITS LABYRINTH AS IT HAS BEEN FOR CENTURIES.
HOW COULD IT BE HERE AS WELL?
EXCUSE ME, QUEEN HIPPOLYTA--
--BUT HOW DO YOU KNOW THE MINOTAUR IS STILL A PRISONER OF THE GODS?
I ASKED THEM.
"RASKED RHEM"?

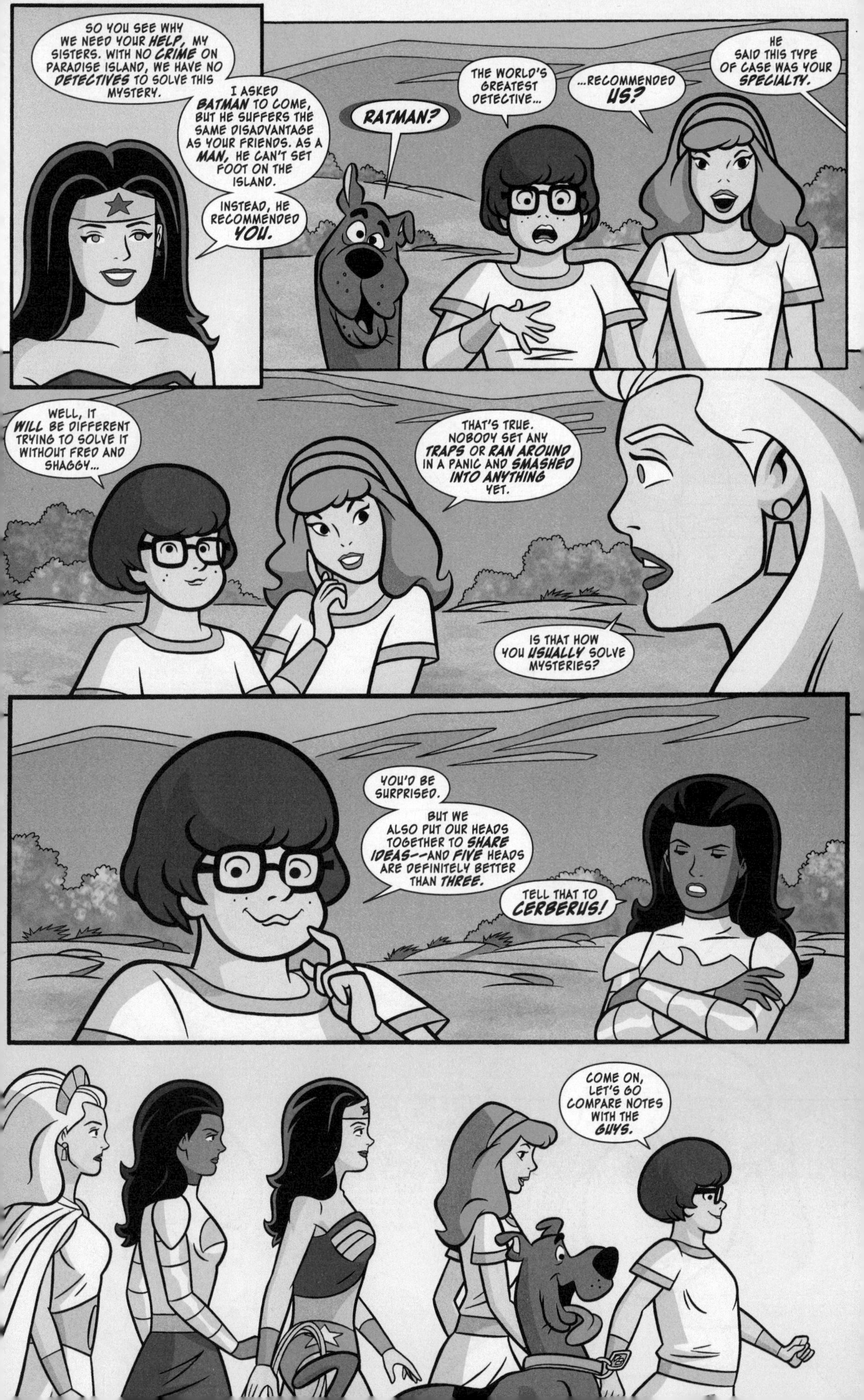
SO YOU SEE WHY WE NEED YOUR HELP, MY SISTERS. WITH NO CRIME ON PARADISE ISLAND, WE HAVE NO DETECTIVES TO SOLVE THIS MYSTERY.
I ASKED BATMAN TO COME, BUT HE SUFFERS THE SAME DISADVANTAGE AS YOUR FRIENDS. AS A MAN, HE CAN'T SET FOOT ON THE ISLAND.
INSTEAD, HE RECOMMENDED YOU.
RATMAN?
THE WORLD'S GREATEST DETECTIVE...
...RECOMMENDED US?
HE SAID THIS TYPE OF CASE WAS YOUR SPECIALTY.
WELL, IT WILL BE DIFFERENT TRYING TO SOLVE IT WITHOUT FRED AND SHAGGY...
THAT'S TRUE. NOBODY SET ANY TRAPS OR RAN AROUND IN A PANIC AND SMASHED INTO ANYTHING YET.
IS THAT HOW YOU USUALLY SOLVE MYSTERIES?
YOU'D BE SURPRISED.
BUT WE ALSO PUT OUR HEADS TOGETHER TO SHARE IDEAS--AND FIVE HEADS ARE DEFINITELY BETTER THAN THREE.
TELL THAT TO CERBERUS!
COME ON, LET'S GO COMPARE NOTES WITH THE GUYS.

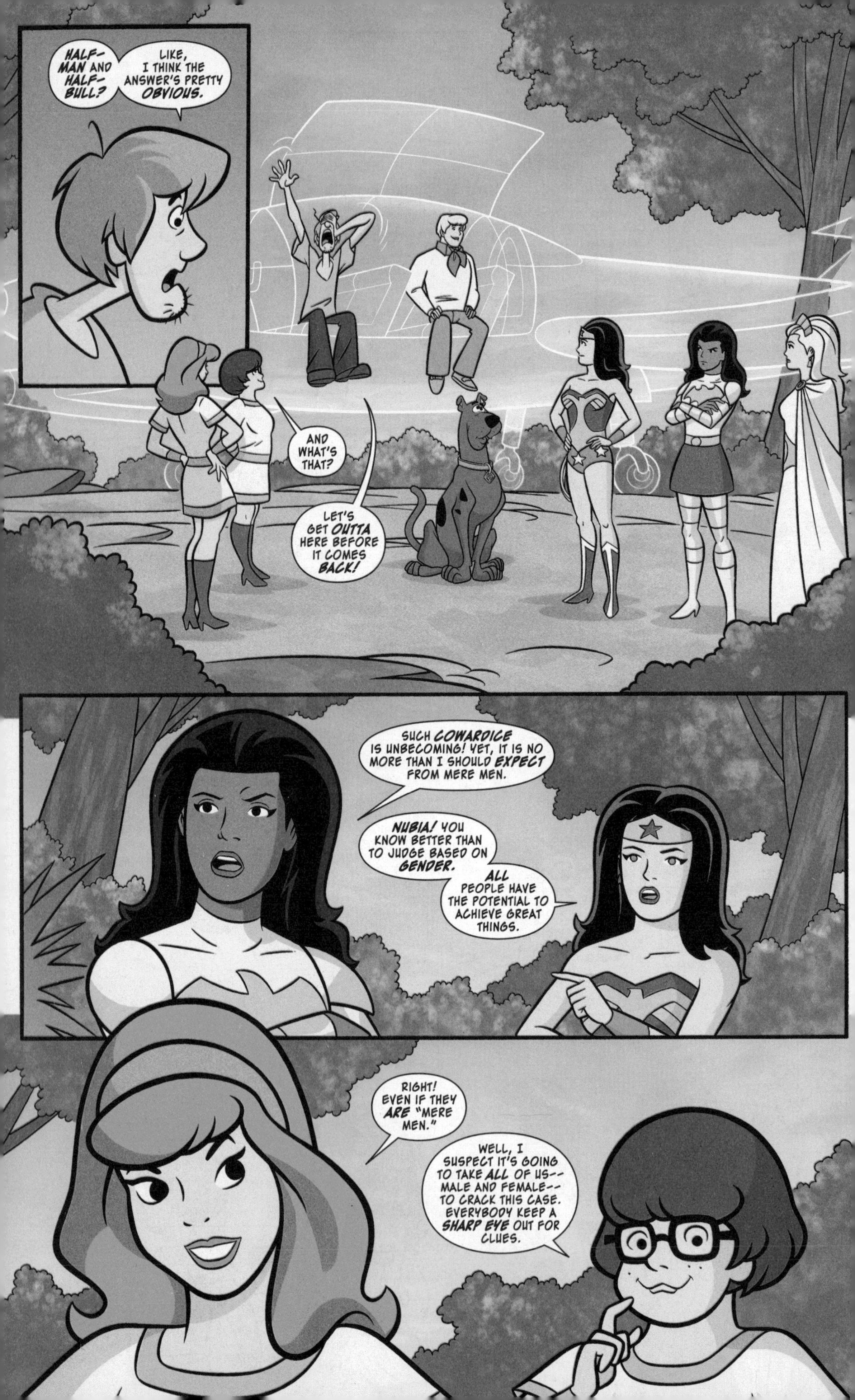

HALF-MAN AND HALF-BULL?
LIKE, I THINK THE ANSWER'S PRETTY OBVIOUS.
AND WHAT'S THAT?
LET'S GET OUTTA HERE BEFORE IT COMES BACK!
SUCH COWARDICE IS UNBECOMING! YET, IT IS NO MORE THAN I SHOULD EXPECT FROM MERE MEN.
NUBIA! YOU KNOW BETTER THAN TO JUDGE BASED ON GENDER.
ALL PEOPLE HAVE THE POTENTIAL TO ACHIEVE GREAT THINGS.
RIGHT! EVEN IF THEY ARE "MERE MEN."
WELL, I SUSPECT IT'S GOING TO TAKE ALL OF US--MALE AND FEMALE--TO CRACK THIS CASE. EVERYBODY KEEP A SHARP EYE OUT FOR CLUES.

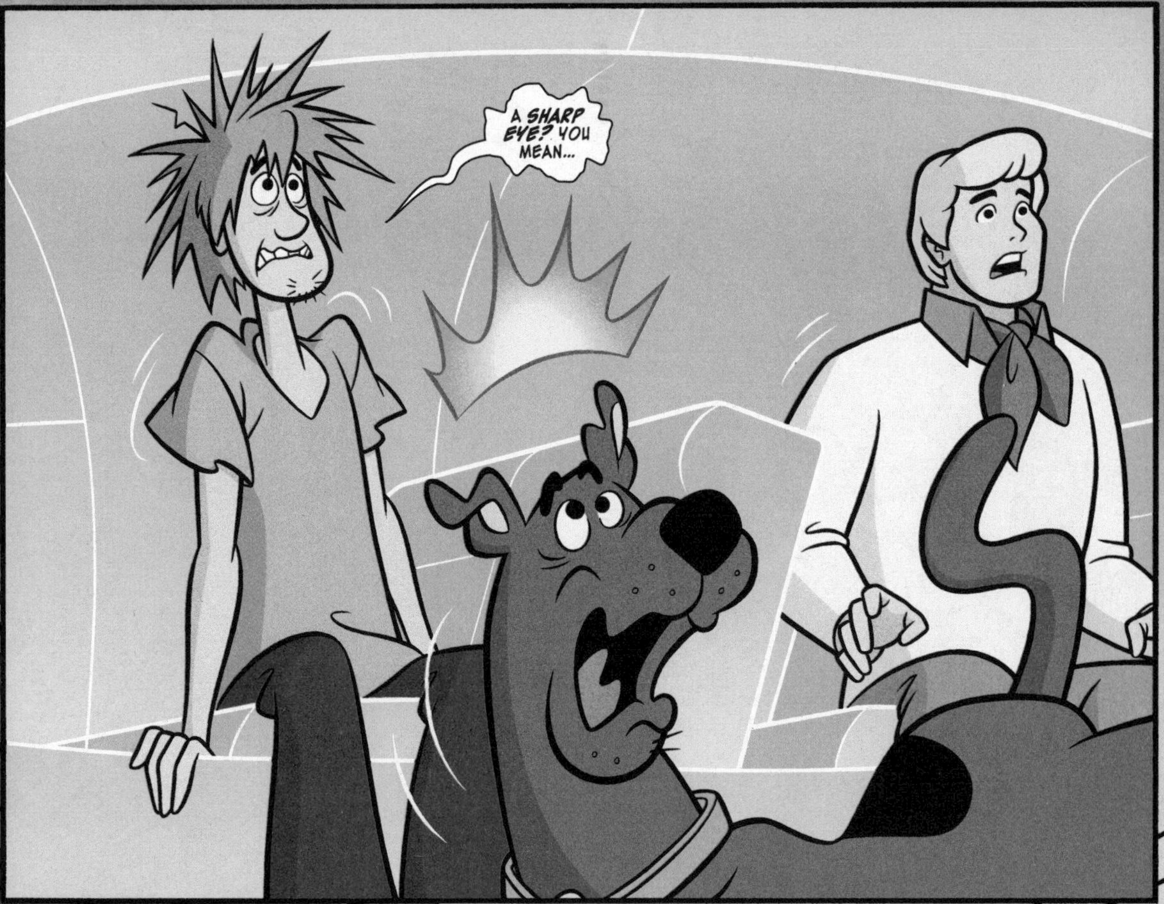
A SHARP EYE? YOU MEAN...

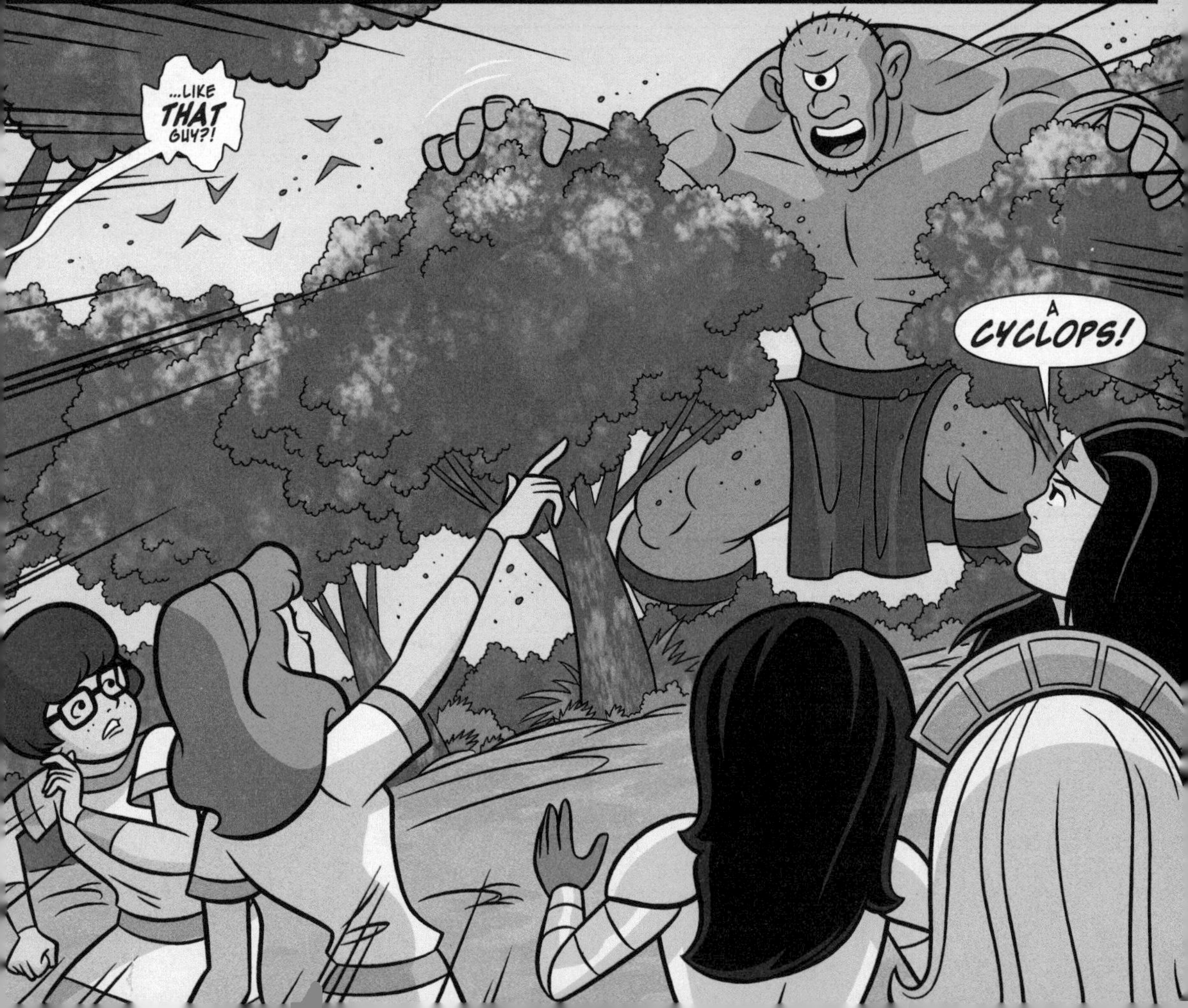
...LIKE THAT GUY?!
A CYCLOPS!

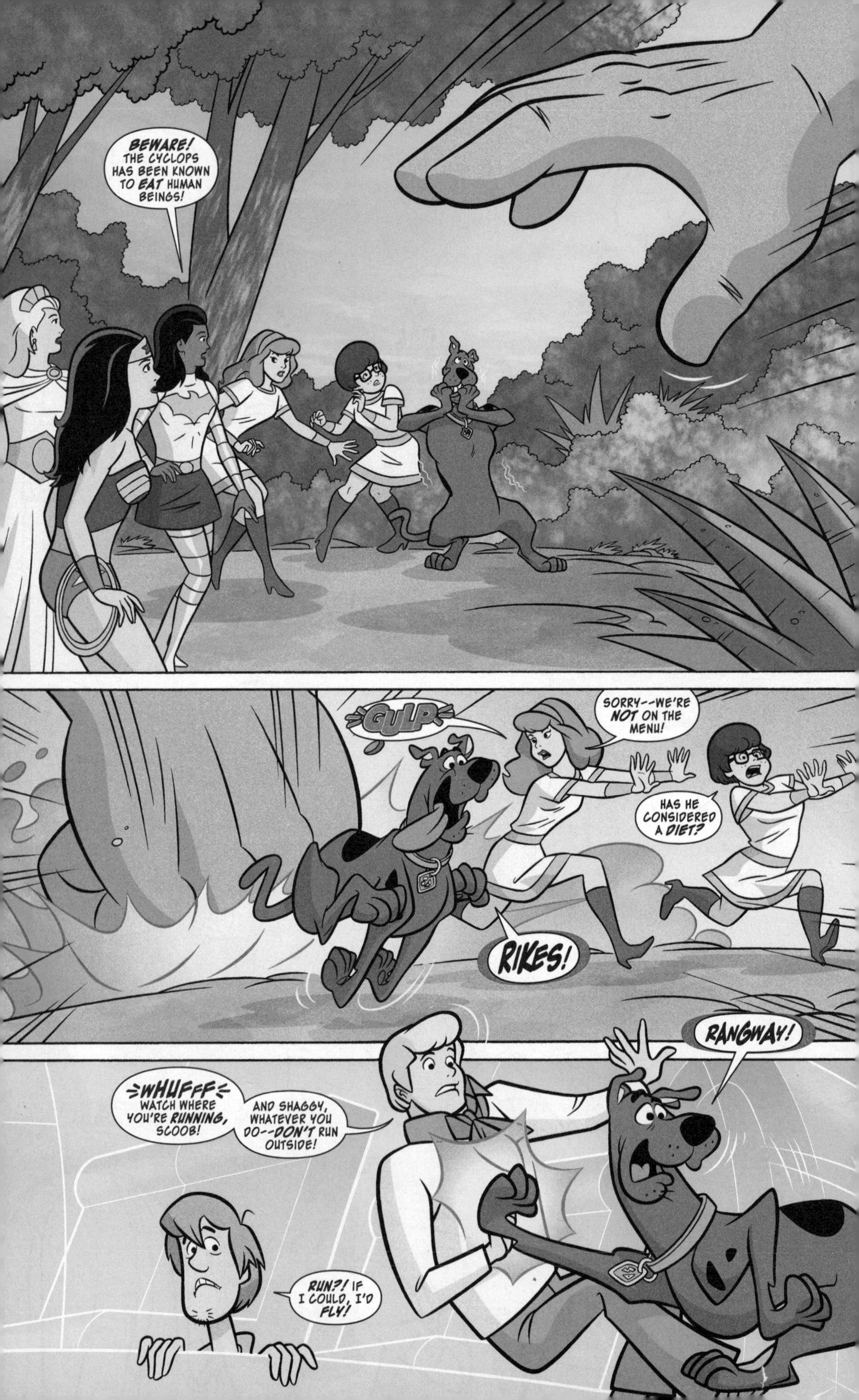
BEWARE! THE CYCLOPS HAS BEEN KNOWN TO EAT HUMAN BEINGS!
GULP
SORRY--WE'RE NOT ON THE MENU!
HAS HE CONSIDERED A DIET?
RIKES!
RANGWAY!
WHUFFF WATCH WHERE YOU'RE RUNNING, SCOOB!
AND SHAGGY, WHATEVER YOU DO--DON'T RUN OUTSIDE!
RUN?! IF I COULD, I'D FLY!

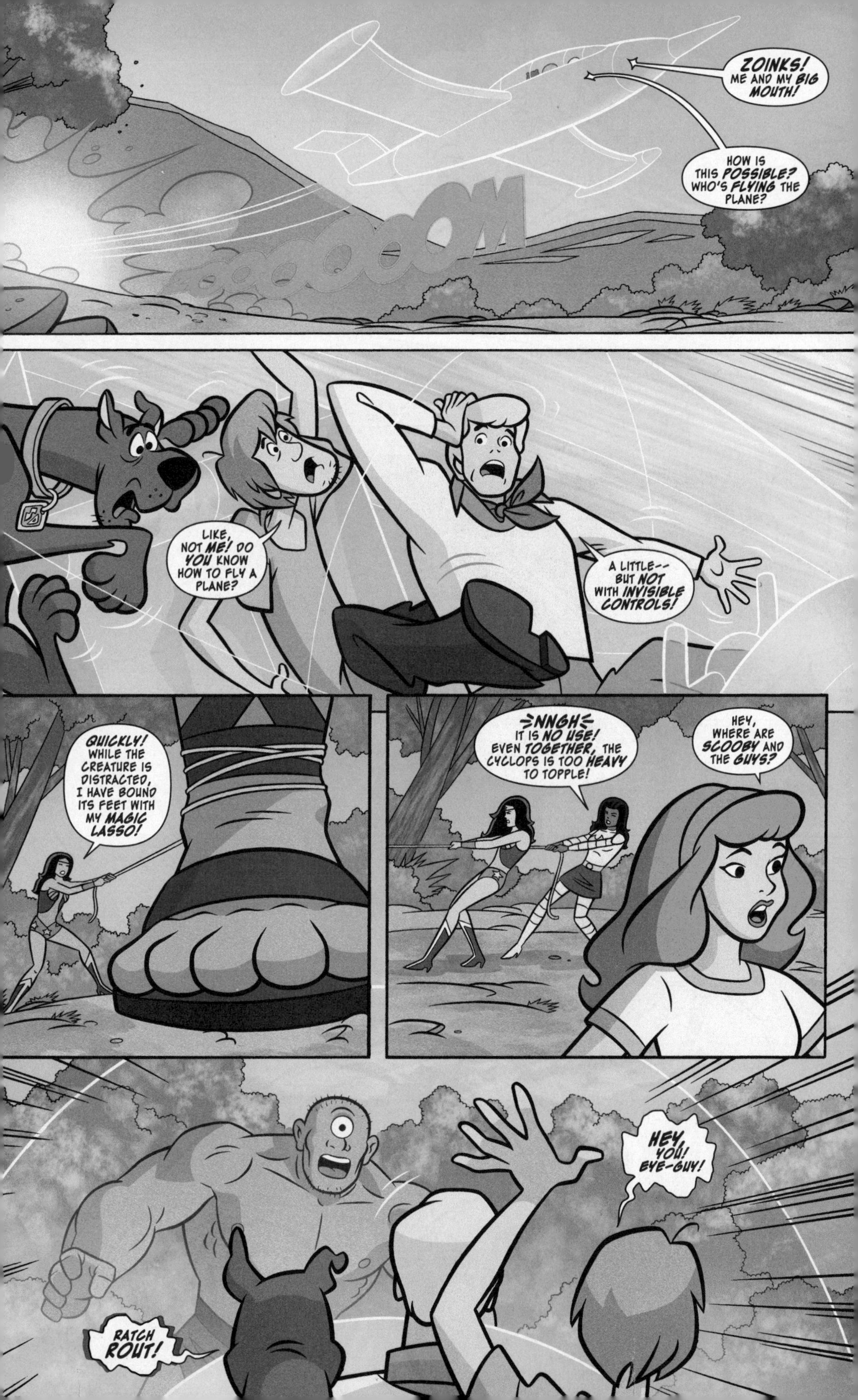
ZOINKS! ME AND MY BIG MOUTH!
HOW IS THIS POSSIBLE? WHO'S FLYING THE PLANE?
BOOOOOOM
LIKE, NOT ME! DO YOU KNOW HOW TO FLY A PLANE?
A LITTLE-- BUT NOT WITH INVISIBLE CONTROLS!
QUICKLY! WHILE THE CREATURE IS DISTRACTED, I HAVE BOUND ITS FEET WITH MY MAGIC LASSO!
NNGH IT IS NO USE! EVEN TOGETHER, THE CYCLOPS IS TOO HEAVY TO TOPPLE!
HEY, WHERE ARE SCOOBY AND THE GUYS?
HEY, YOU! EYE-GUY!
RATCH ROUT!

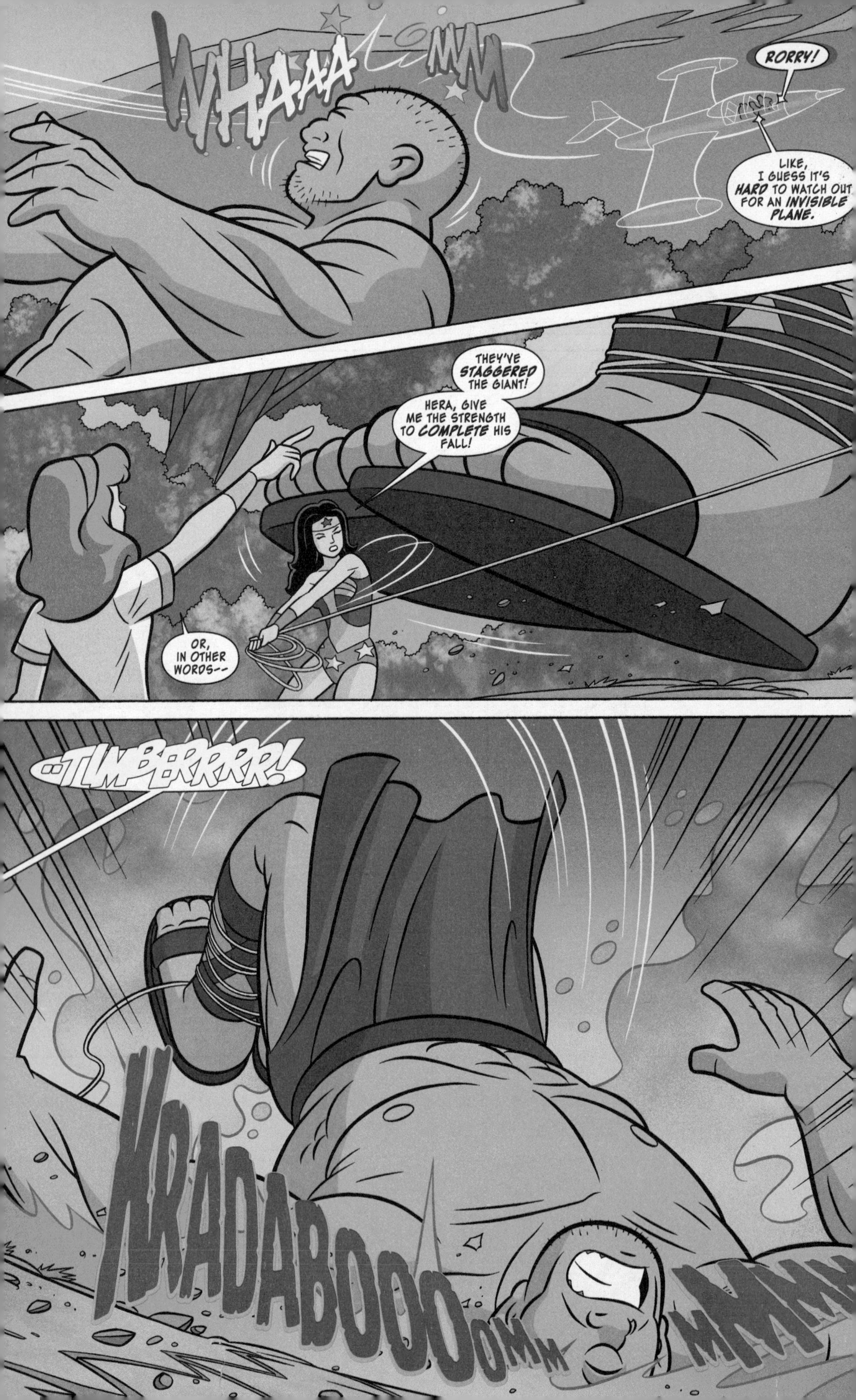
WHAAA MMM
RORRY!
LIKE, I GUESS IT'S HARD TO WATCH OUT FOR AN INVISIBLE PLANE.
THEY'VE STAGGERED THE GIANT!
HERA, GIVE ME THE STRENGTH TO COMPLETE HIS FALL!
OR, IN OTHER WORDS--
--TIMBERRRRR!
KRADABOOOOMMM MMM

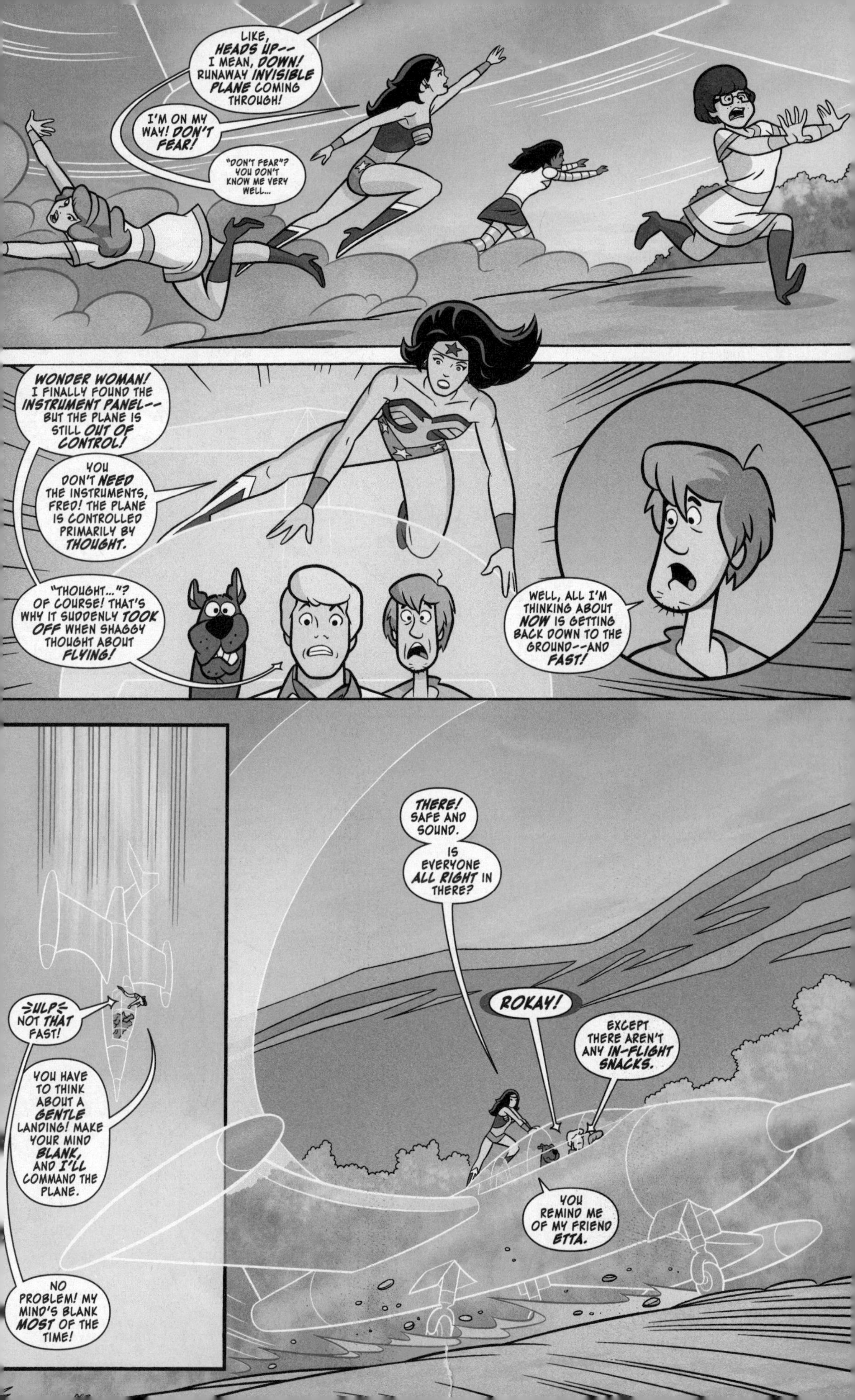
LIKE, HEADS UP-- I MEAN, DOWN! RUNAWAY INVISIBLE PLANE COMING THROUGH!
I'M ON MY WAY! DON'T FEAR!
"DON'T FEAR"? YOU DON'T KNOW ME VERY WELL...
WONDER WOMAN! I FINALLY FOUND THE INSTRUMENT PANEL-- BUT THE PLANE IS STILL OUT OF CONTROL!
YOU DON'T NEED THE INSTRUMENTS, FRED! THE PLANE IS CONTROLLED PRIMARILY BY THOUGHT.
"THOUGHT..."? OF COURSE! THAT'S WHY IT SUDDENLY TOOK OFF WHEN SHAGGY THOUGHT ABOUT FLYING!
WELL, ALL I'M THINKING ABOUT NOW IS GETTING BACK DOWN TO THE GROUND--AND FAST!
=ULP= NOT THAT FAST!
YOU HAVE TO THINK ABOUT A GENTLE LANDING! MAKE YOUR MIND BLANK, AND I'LL COMMAND THE PLANE.
NO PROBLEM! MY MIND'S BLANK MOST OF THE TIME!
THERE! SAFE AND SOUND.
IS EVERYONE ALL RIGHT IN THERE?
ROKAY!
EXCEPT THERE AREN'T ANY IN-FLIGHT SNACKS.
YOU REMIND ME OF MY FRIEND ETTA.

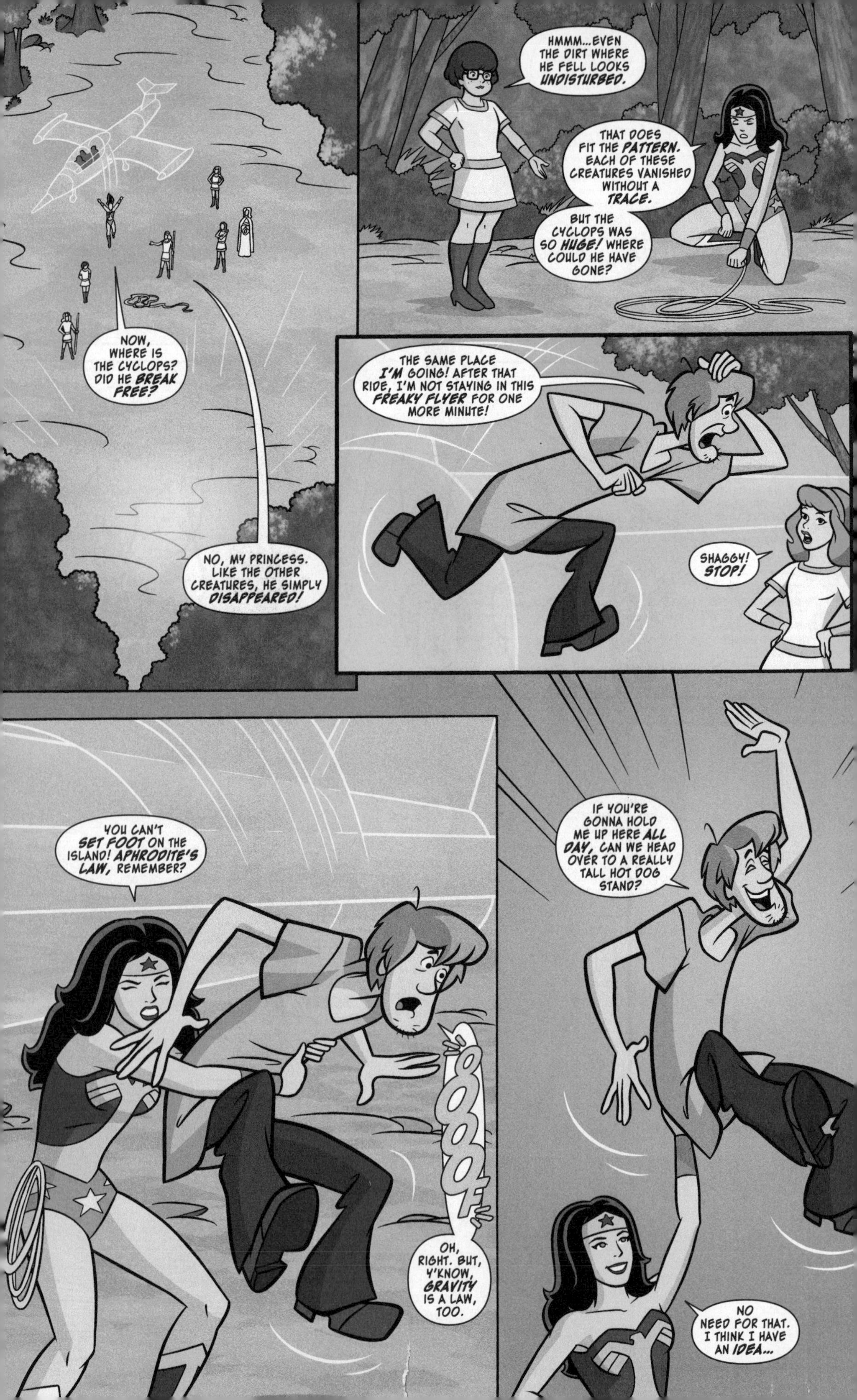
NOW, WHERE IS THE CYCLOPS? DID HE BREAK FREE?
NO, MY PRINCESS. LIKE THE OTHER CREATURES, HE SIMPLY DISAPPEARED!
HMMM...EVEN THE DIRT WHERE HE FELL LOOKS UNDISTURBED.
THAT DOES FIT THE PATTERN. EACH OF THESE CREATURES VANISHED WITHOUT A TRACE.
BUT THE CYCLOPS WAS SO HUGE! WHERE COULD HE HAVE GONE?
THE SAME PLACE I'M GOING! AFTER THAT RIDE, I'M NOT STAYING IN THIS FREAKY FLYER FOR ONE MORE MINUTE!
SHAGGY! STOP!
YOU CAN'T SET FOOT ON THE ISLAND! APHRODITE'S LAW, REMEMBER?
OOOOF!
OH, RIGHT. BUT, Y'KNOW, GRAVITY IS A LAW, TOO.
IF YOU'RE GONNA HOLD ME UP HERE ALL DAY, CAN WE HEAD OVER TO A REALLY TALL HOT DOG STAND?
NO NEED FOR THAT. I THINK I HAVE AN IDEA...

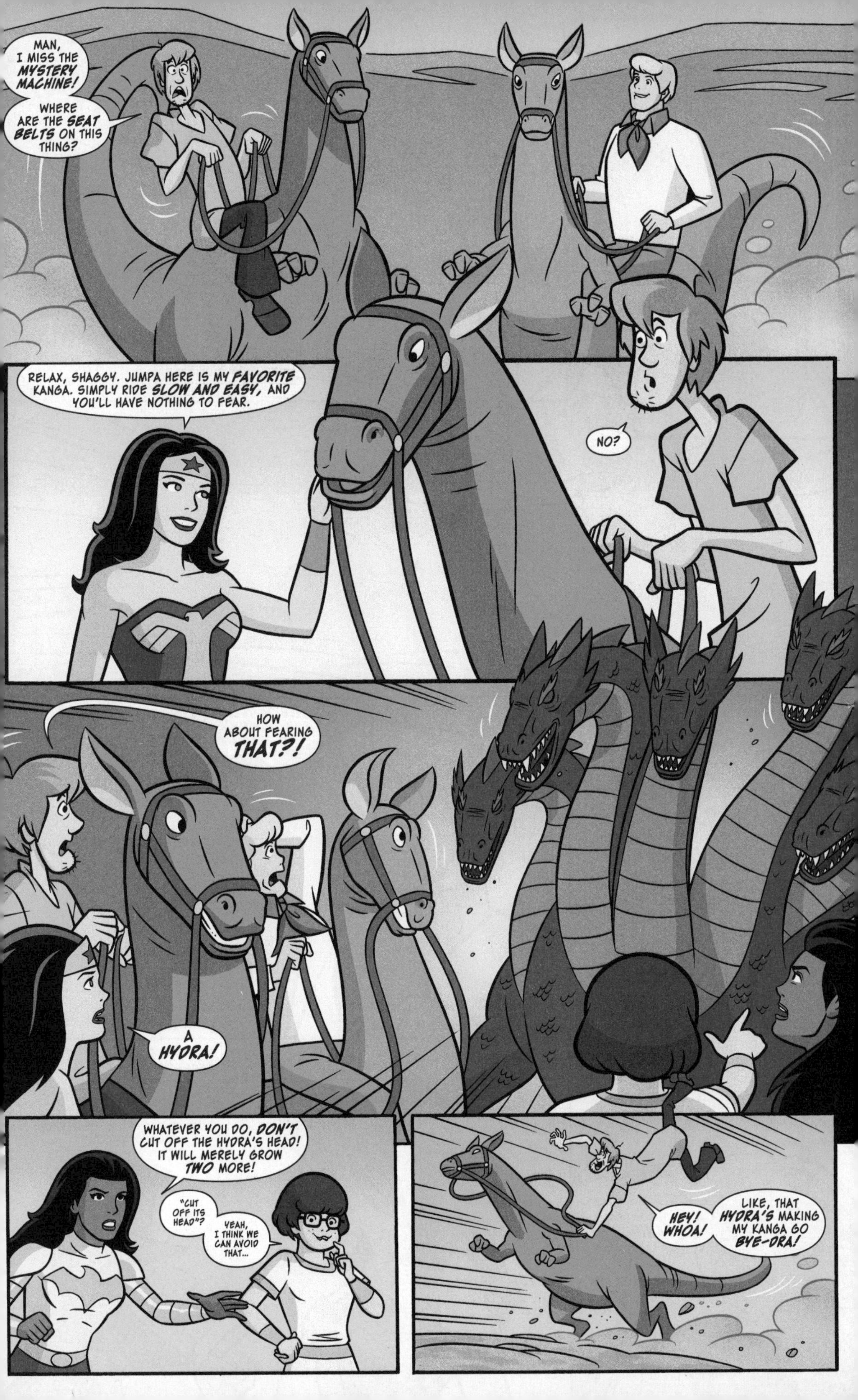
MAN, I MISS THE MYSTERY MACHINE!
WHERE ARE THE SEAT BELTS ON THIS THING?
RELAX, SHAGGY. JUMPA HERE IS MY FAVORITE KANGA. SIMPLY RIDE SLOW AND EASY, AND YOU'LL HAVE NOTHING TO FEAR.
NO?
HOW ABOUT FEARING THAT?!
A HYDRA!
WHATEVER YOU DO, DON'T CUT OFF THE HYDRA'S HEAD! IT WILL MERELY GROW TWO MORE!
"CUT OFF ITS HEAD"?
YEAH, I THINK WE CAN AVOID THAT...
HEY! WHOA!
LIKE, THAT HYDRA'S MAKING MY KANGA GO BYE-DRA!

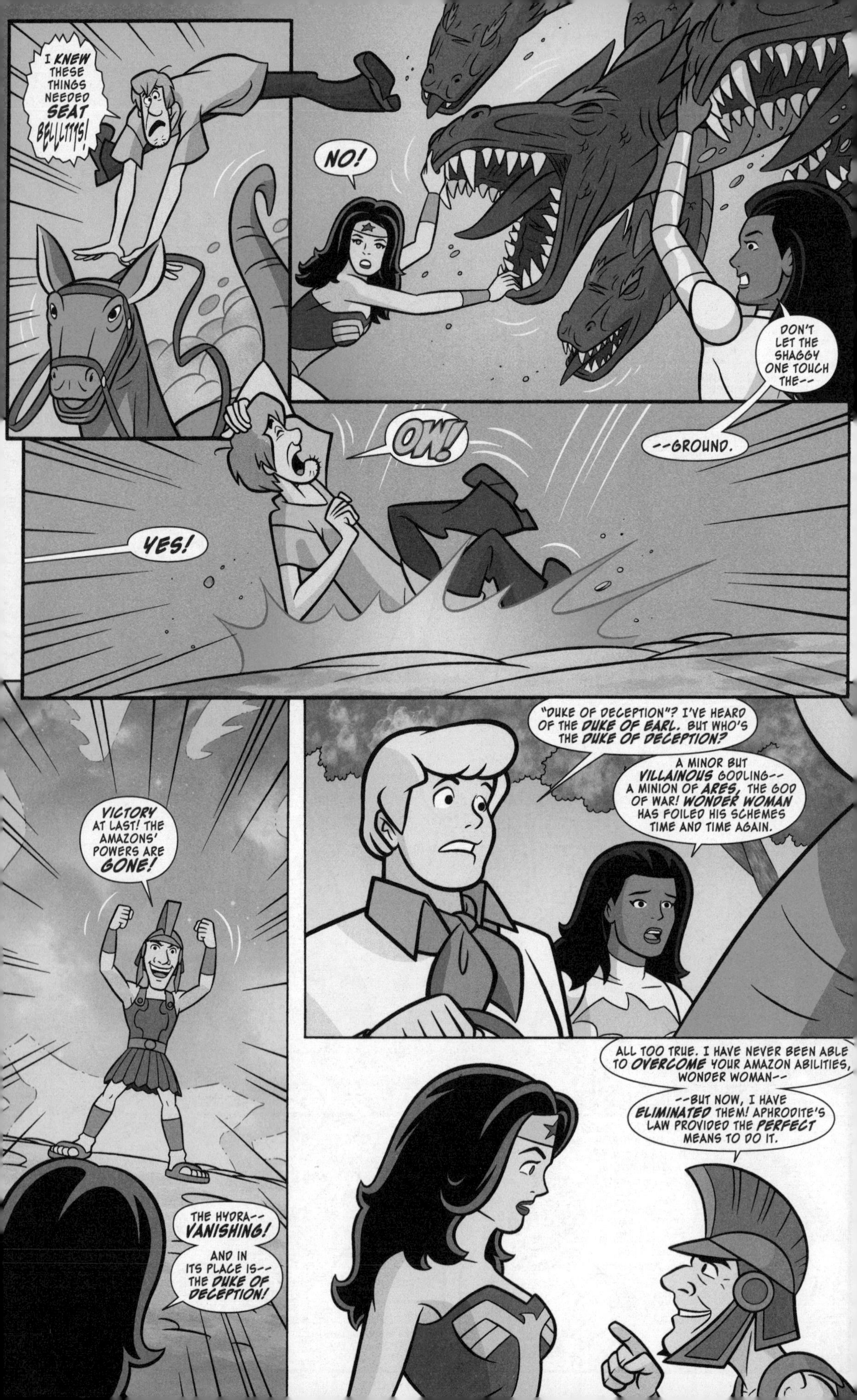
I KNEW THESE THINGS NEEDED SEAT BELLLTTS!
NO!
DON'T LET THE SHAGGY ONE TOUCH THE--
--GROUND.
OW!
YES!
VICTORY AT LAST! THE AMAZONS' POWERS ARE GONE!
THE HYDRA--VANISHING!
AND IN ITS PLACE IS--THE DUKE OF DECEPTION!
"DUKE OF DECEPTION"? I'VE HEARD OF THE DUKE OF EARL. BUT WHO'S THE DUKE OF DECEPTION?
A MINOR BUT VILLAINOUS GODLING--A MINION OF ARES, THE GOD OF WAR! WONDER WOMAN HAS FOILED HIS SCHEMES TIME AND TIME AGAIN.
ALL TOO TRUE. I HAVE NEVER BEEN ABLE TO OVERCOME YOUR AMAZON ABILITIES, WONDER WOMAN--
--BUT NOW, I HAVE ELIMINATED THEM! APHRODITE'S LAW PROVIDED THE PERFECT MEANS TO DO IT.

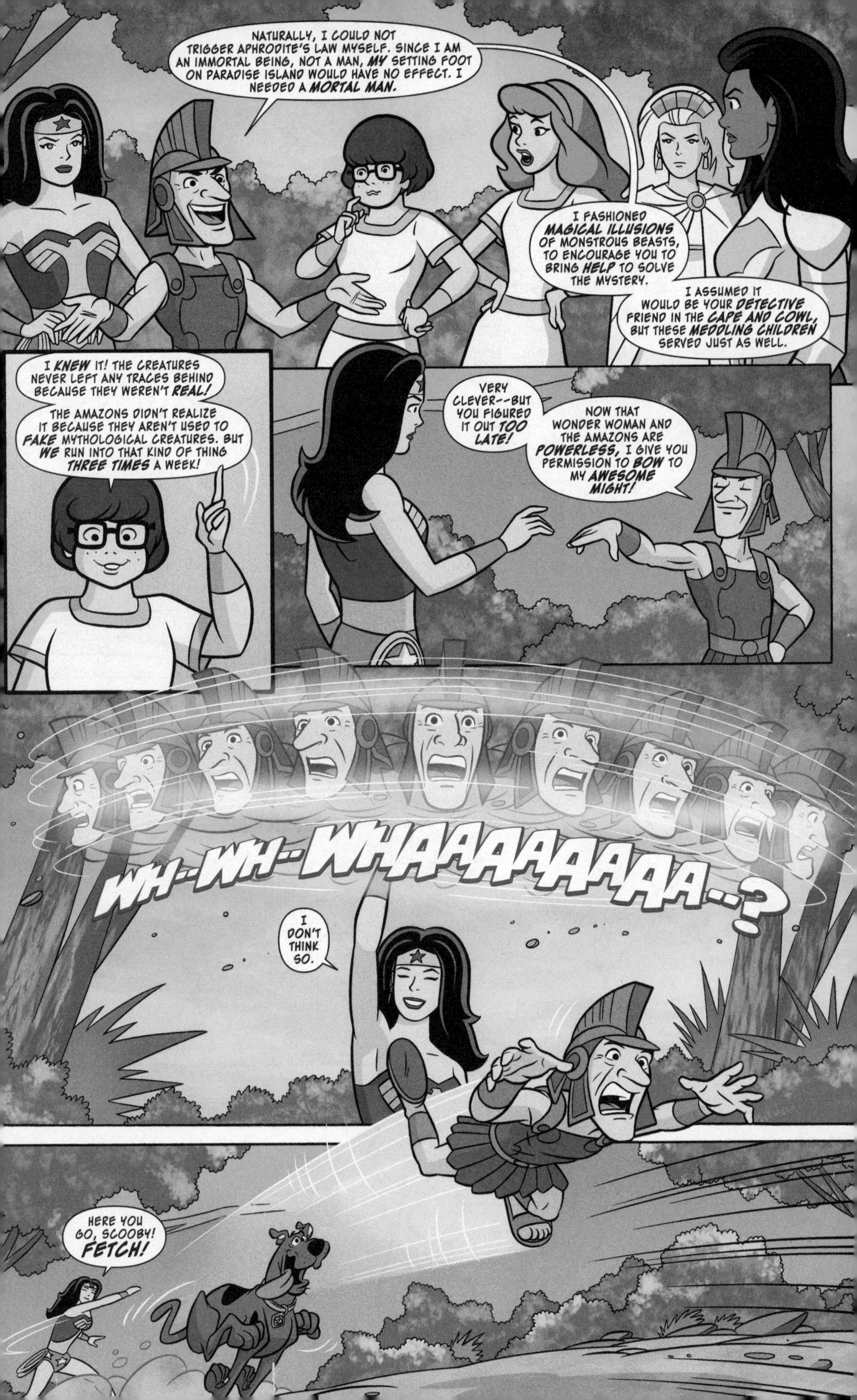
NATURALLY, I COULD NOT TRIGGER APHRODITE'S LAW MYSELF. SINCE I AM AN IMMORTAL BEING, NOT A MAN, MY SETTING FOOT ON PARADISE ISLAND WOULD HAVE NO EFFECT. I NEEDED A MORTAL MAN.
I FASHIONED MAGICAL ILLUSIONS OF MONSTROUS BEASTS, TO ENCOURAGE YOU TO BRING HELP TO SOLVE THE MYSTERY.
I ASSUMED IT WOULD BE YOUR DETECTIVE FRIEND IN THE CAPE AND COWL, BUT THESE MEDDLING CHILDREN SERVED JUST AS WELL.
I KNEW IT! THE CREATURES NEVER LEFT ANY TRACES BEHIND BECAUSE THEY WEREN'T REAL!
THE AMAZONS DIDN'T REALIZE IT BECAUSE THEY AREN'T USED TO FAKE MYTHOLOGICAL CREATURES. BUT WE RUN INTO THAT KIND OF THING THREE TIMES A WEEK!
VERY CLEVER--BUT YOU FIGURED IT OUT TOO LATE!
NOW THAT WONDER WOMAN AND THE AMAZONS ARE POWERLESS, I GIVE YOU PERMISSION TO BOW TO MY AWESOME MIGHT!
WH-WH-WHAAAAAAAAA..?
I DON'T THINK SO.
HERE YOU GO, SCOOBY! FETCH!

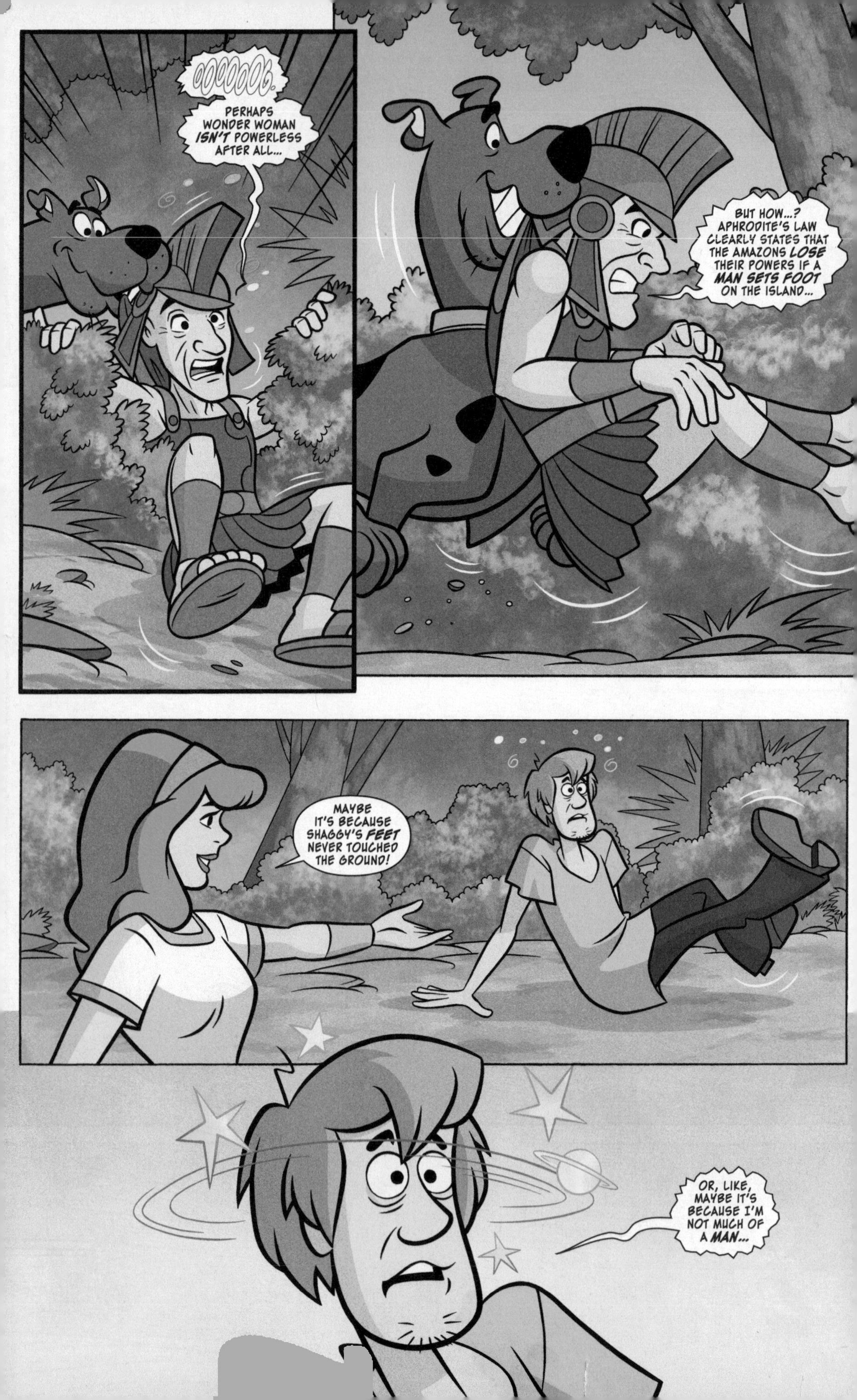
OOOOOOG
PERHAPS WONDER WOMAN ISN'T POWERLESS AFTER ALL...
BUT HOW...? APHRODITE'S LAW CLEARLY STATES THAT THE AMAZONS LOSE THEIR POWERS IF A MAN SETS FOOT ON THE ISLAND...
MAYBE IT'S BECAUSE SHAGGY'S FEET NEVER TOUCHED THE GROUND!
OR, LIKE, MAYBE IT'S BECAUSE I'M NOT MUCH OF A MAN...

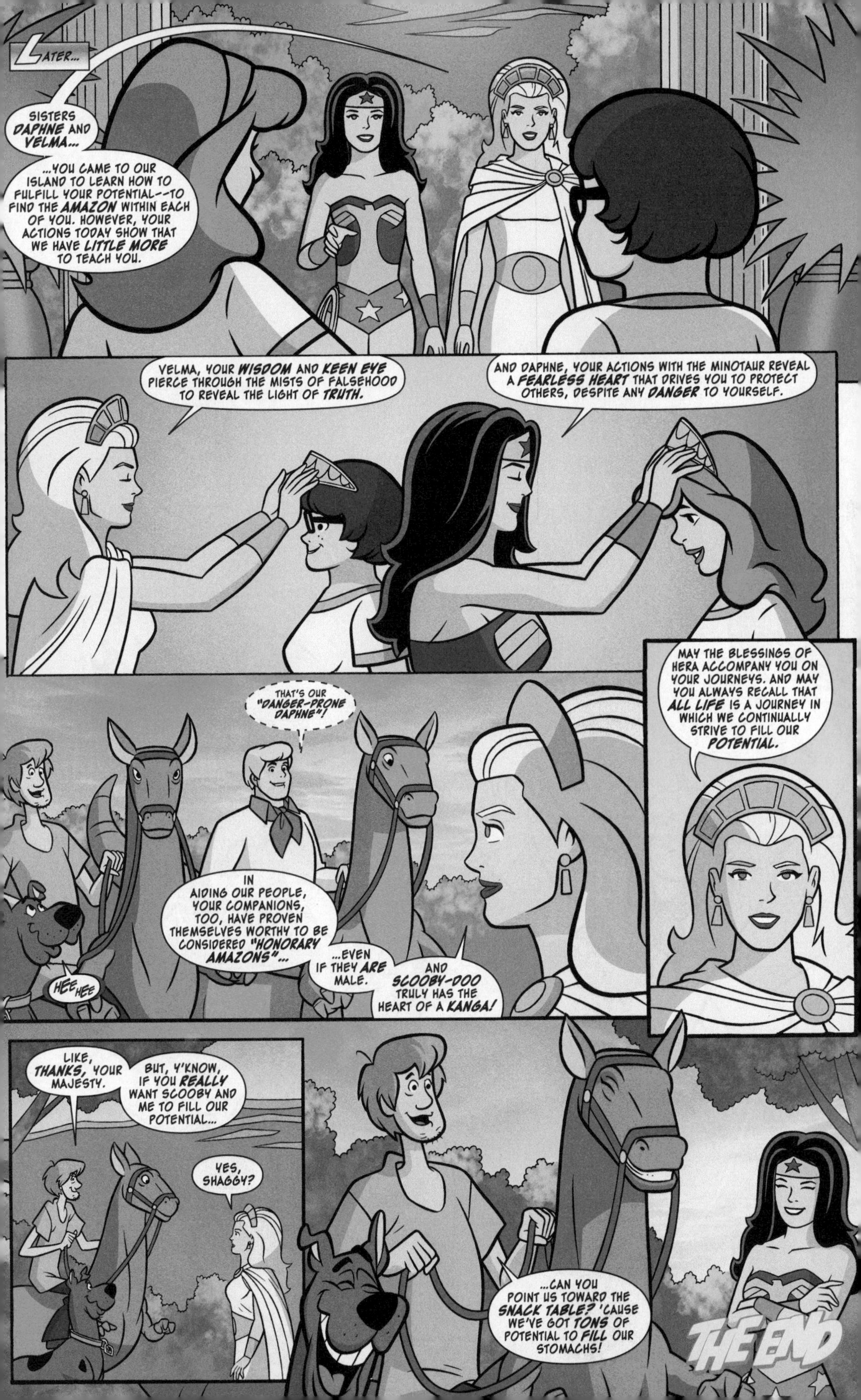
LATER...
SISTERS DAPHNE AND VELMA...
...YOU CAME TO OUR ISLAND TO LEARN HOW TO FULFILL YOUR POTENTIAL--TO FIND THE AMAZON WITHIN EACH OF YOU. HOWEVER, YOUR ACTIONS TODAY SHOW THAT WE HAVE LITTLE MORE TO TEACH YOU.
VELMA, YOUR WISDOM AND KEEN EYE PIERCE THROUGH THE MISTS OF FALSEHOOD TO REVEAL THE LIGHT OF TRUTH.
AND DAPHNE, YOUR ACTIONS WITH THE MINOTAUR REVEAL A FEARLESS HEART THAT DRIVES YOU TO PROTECT OTHERS, DESPITE ANY DANGER TO YOURSELF.
THAT'S OUR "DANGER-PRONE DAPHNE"!
IN AIDING OUR PEOPLE, YOUR COMPANIONS, TOO, HAVE PROVEN THEMSELVES WORTHY TO BE CONSIDERED "HONORARY AMAZONS"...
HEE HEE
...EVEN IF THEY ARE MALE.
AND SCOOBY-DOO TRULY HAS THE HEART OF A KANGA!
MAY THE BLESSINGS OF HERA ACCOMPANY YOU ON YOUR JOURNEYS. AND MAY YOU ALWAYS RECALL THAT ALL LIFE IS A JOURNEY IN WHICH WE CONTINUALLY STRIVE TO FILL OUR POTENTIAL.
LIKE, THANKS, YOUR MAJESTY.
BUT, Y'KNOW, IF YOU REALLY WANT SCOOBY AND ME TO FILL OUR POTENTIAL...
YES, SHAGGY?
...CAN YOU POINT US TOWARD THE SNACK TABLE? 'CAUSE WE'VE GOT TONS OF POTENTIAL TO FILL OUR STOMACHS!
THE END

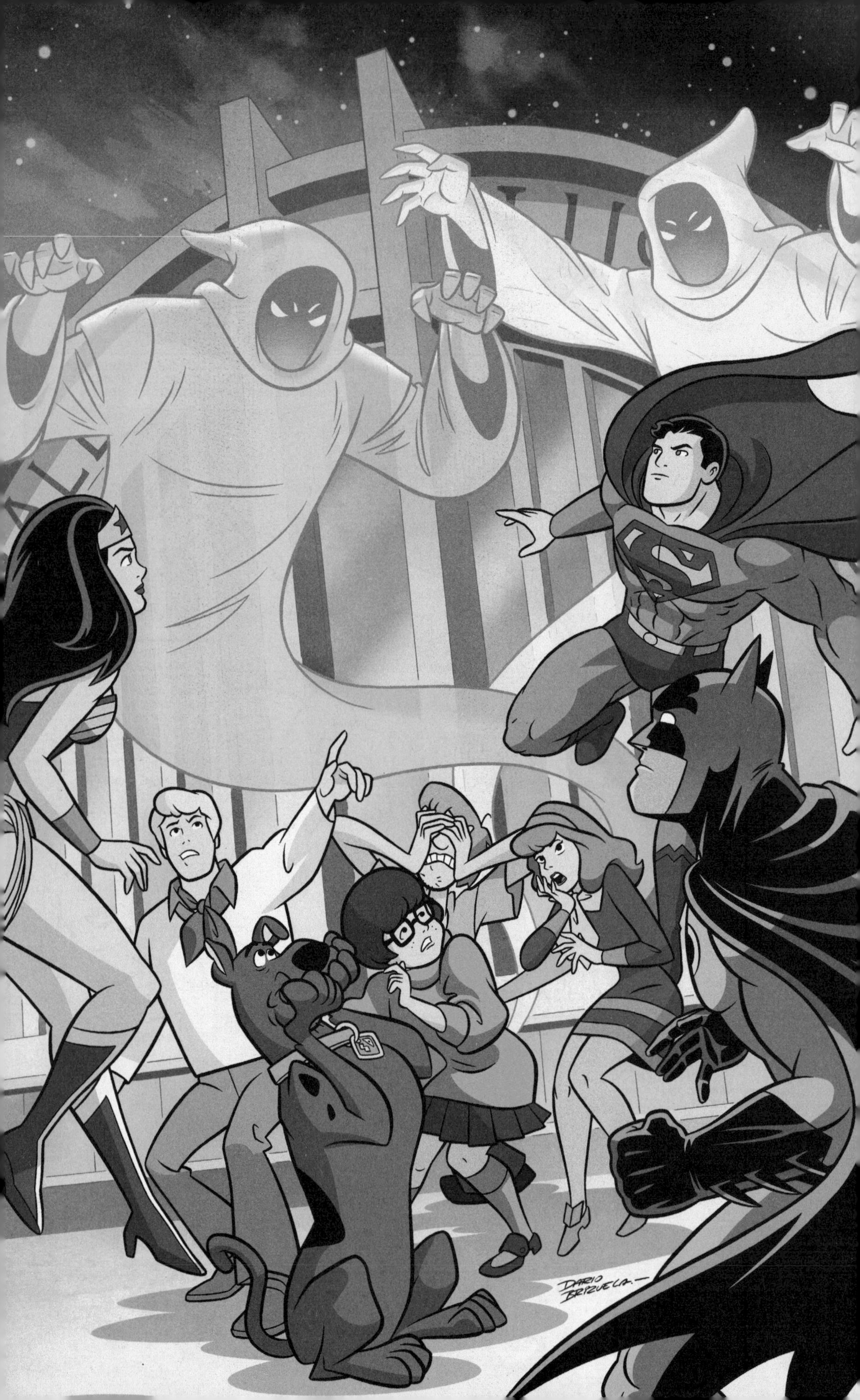
DARIO BRIZUELA

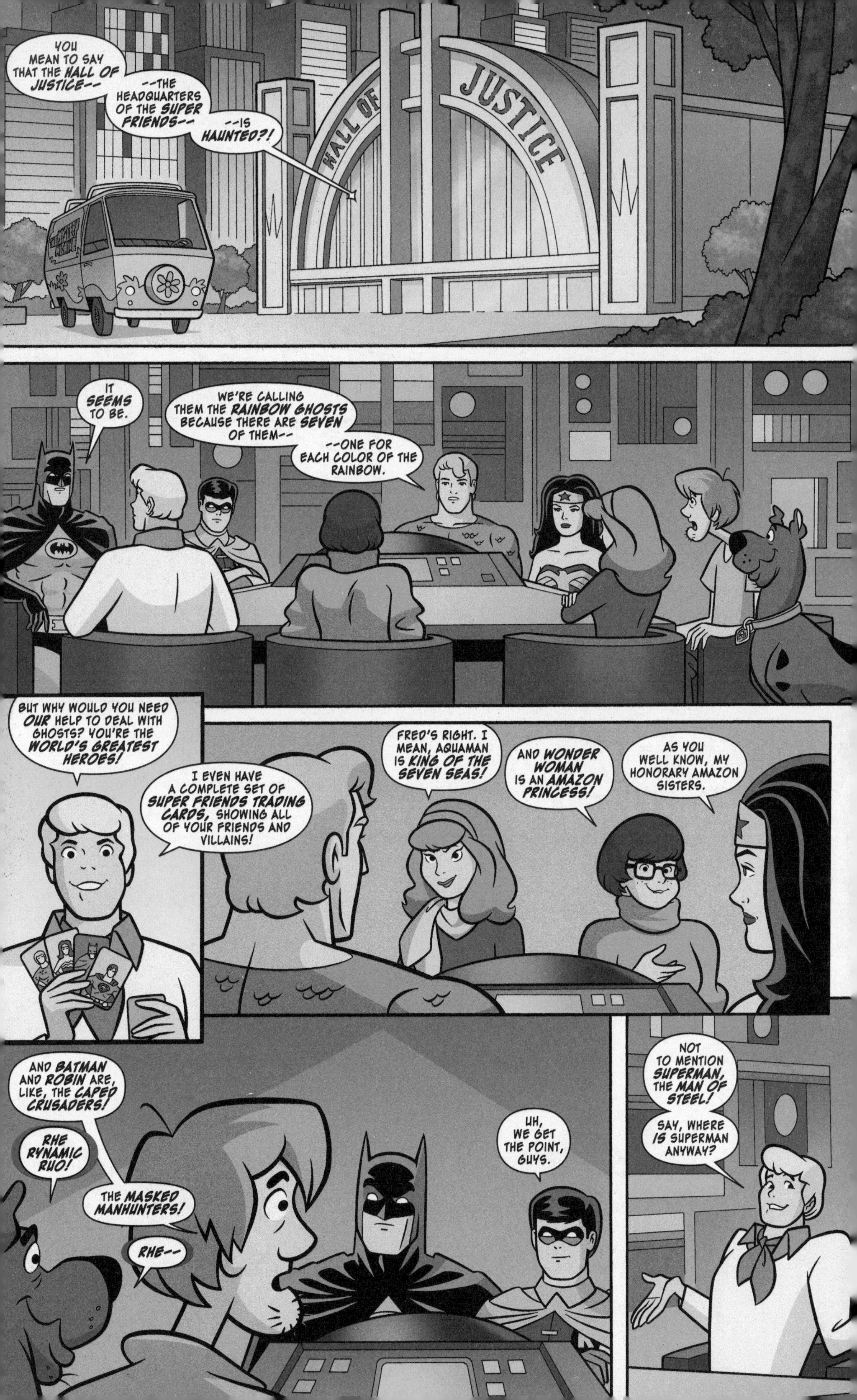

YOU MEAN TO SAY THAT THE HALL OF JUSTICE--
--THE HEADQUARTERS OF THE SUPER FRIENDS--
--IS HAUNTED?!
HALL OF JUSTICE
IT SEEMS TO BE.
WE'RE CALLING THEM THE RAINBOW GHOSTS BECAUSE THERE ARE SEVEN OF THEM--
--ONE FOR EACH COLOR OF THE RAINBOW.
BUT WHY WOULD YOU NEED OUR HELP TO DEAL WITH GHOSTS? YOU'RE THE WORLD'S GREATEST HEROES!
I EVEN HAVE A COMPLETE SET OF SUPER FRIENDS TRADING CARDS, SHOWING ALL OF YOUR FRIENDS AND VILLAINS!
FRED'S RIGHT. I MEAN, AQUAMAN IS KING OF THE SEVEN SEAS!
AND WONDER WOMAN IS AN AMAZON PRINCESS!
AS YOU WELL KNOW, MY HONORARY AMAZON SISTERS.
AND BATMAN AND ROBIN ARE, LIKE, THE CAPED CRUSADERS!
RHE RYNAMIC RUO!
THE MASKED MANHUNTERS!
RHE--
UH, WE GET THE POINT, GUYS.
NOT TO MENTION SUPERMAN, THE MAN OF STEEL!
SAY, WHERE IS SUPERMAN ANYWAY?

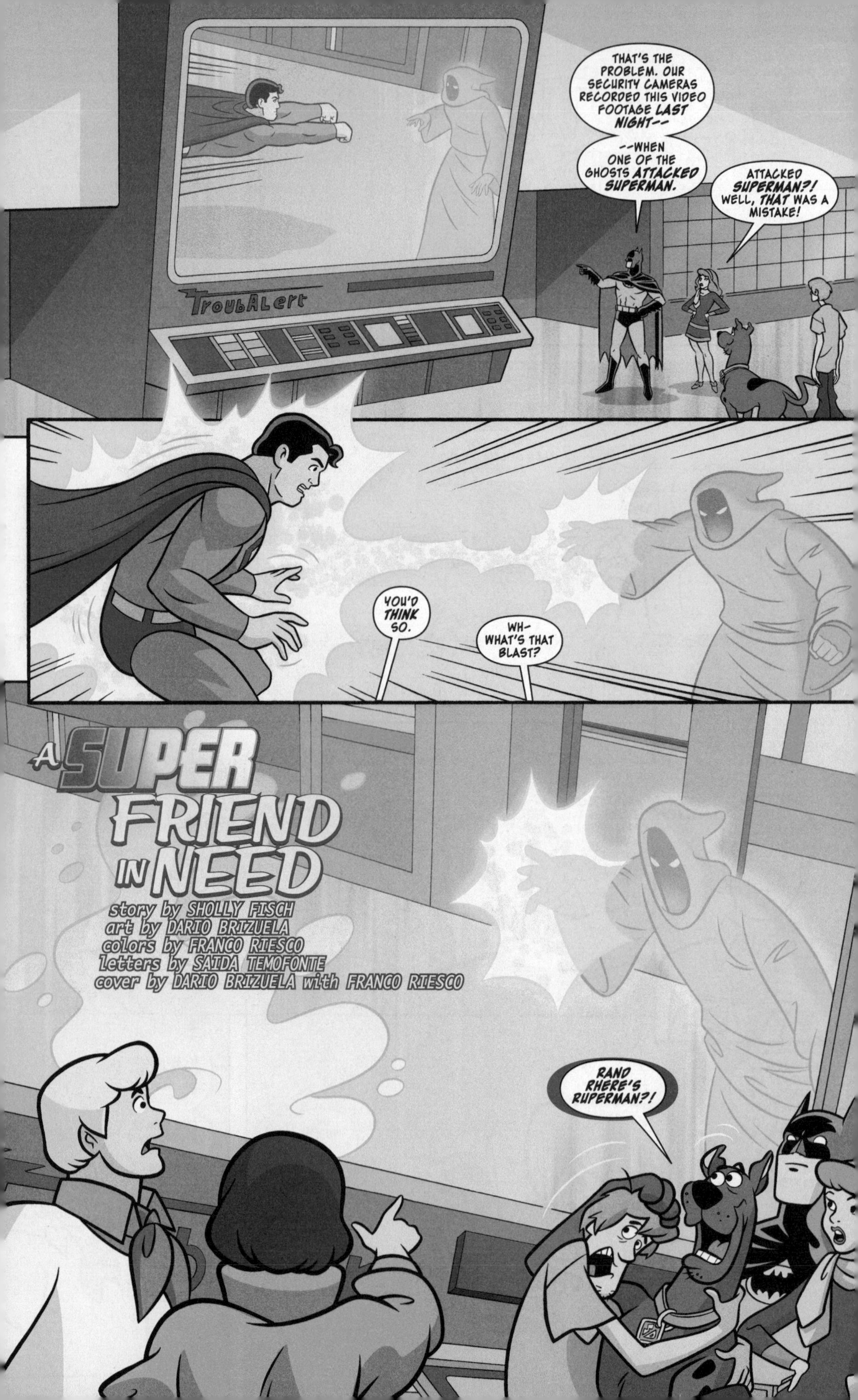
TroubAlert
THAT'S THE PROBLEM. OUR SECURITY CAMERAS RECORDED THIS VIDEO FOOTAGE LAST NIGHT--
--WHEN ONE OF THE GHOSTS ATTACKED SUPERMAN.
ATTACKED SUPERMAN?! WELL, THAT WAS A MISTAKE!
YOU'D THINK SO.
WH- WHAT'S THAT BLAST?
A SUPER FRIEND IN NEED
story by SHOLLY FISCH
art by DARIO BRIZUELA
colors by FRANCO RIESCO
letters by SAIDA TEMOFONTE
cover by DARIO BRIZUELA with FRANCO RIESCO
RAND RHERE'S RUPERMAN?!

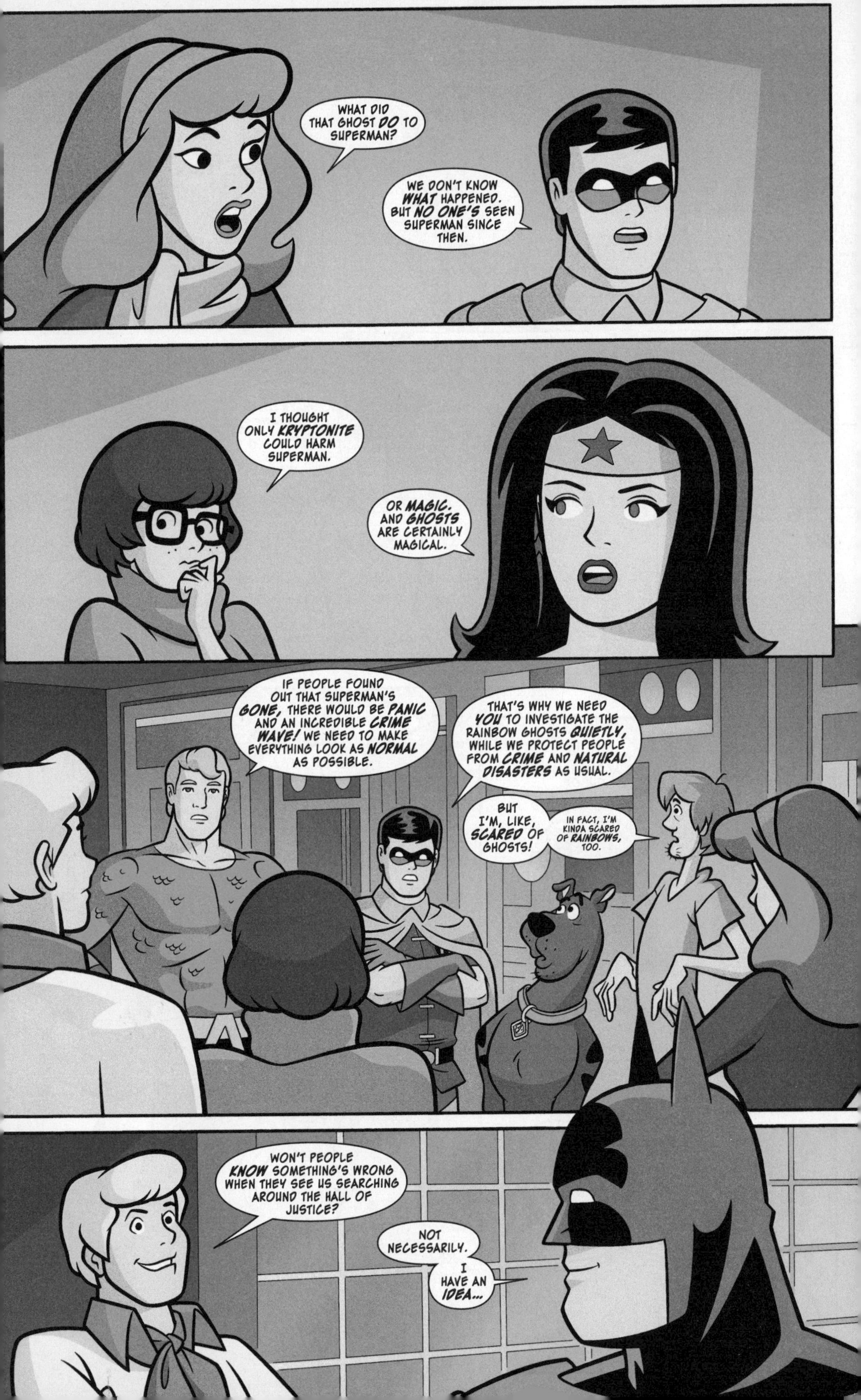
WHAT DID THAT GHOST DO TO SUPERMAN?
WE DON'T KNOW WHAT HAPPENED. BUT NO ONE'S SEEN SUPERMAN SINCE THEN.
I THOUGHT ONLY KRYPTONITE COULD HARM SUPERMAN.
OR MAGIC. AND GHOSTS ARE CERTAINLY MAGICAL.
IF PEOPLE FOUND OUT THAT SUPERMAN'S GONE, THERE WOULD BE PANIC AND AN INCREDIBLE CRIME WAVE! WE NEED TO MAKE EVERYTHING LOOK AS NORMAL AS POSSIBLE.
THAT'S WHY WE NEED YOU TO INVESTIGATE THE RAINBOW GHOSTS QUIETLY, WHILE WE PROTECT PEOPLE FROM CRIME AND NATURAL DISASTERS AS USUAL.
BUT I'M, LIKE, SCARED OF GHOSTS!
IN FACT, I'M KINDA SCARED OF RAINBOWS, TOO.
WON'T PEOPLE KNOW SOMETHING'S WRONG WHEN THEY SEE US SEARCHING AROUND THE HALL OF JUSTICE?
NOT NECESSARILY.
I HAVE AN IDEA...

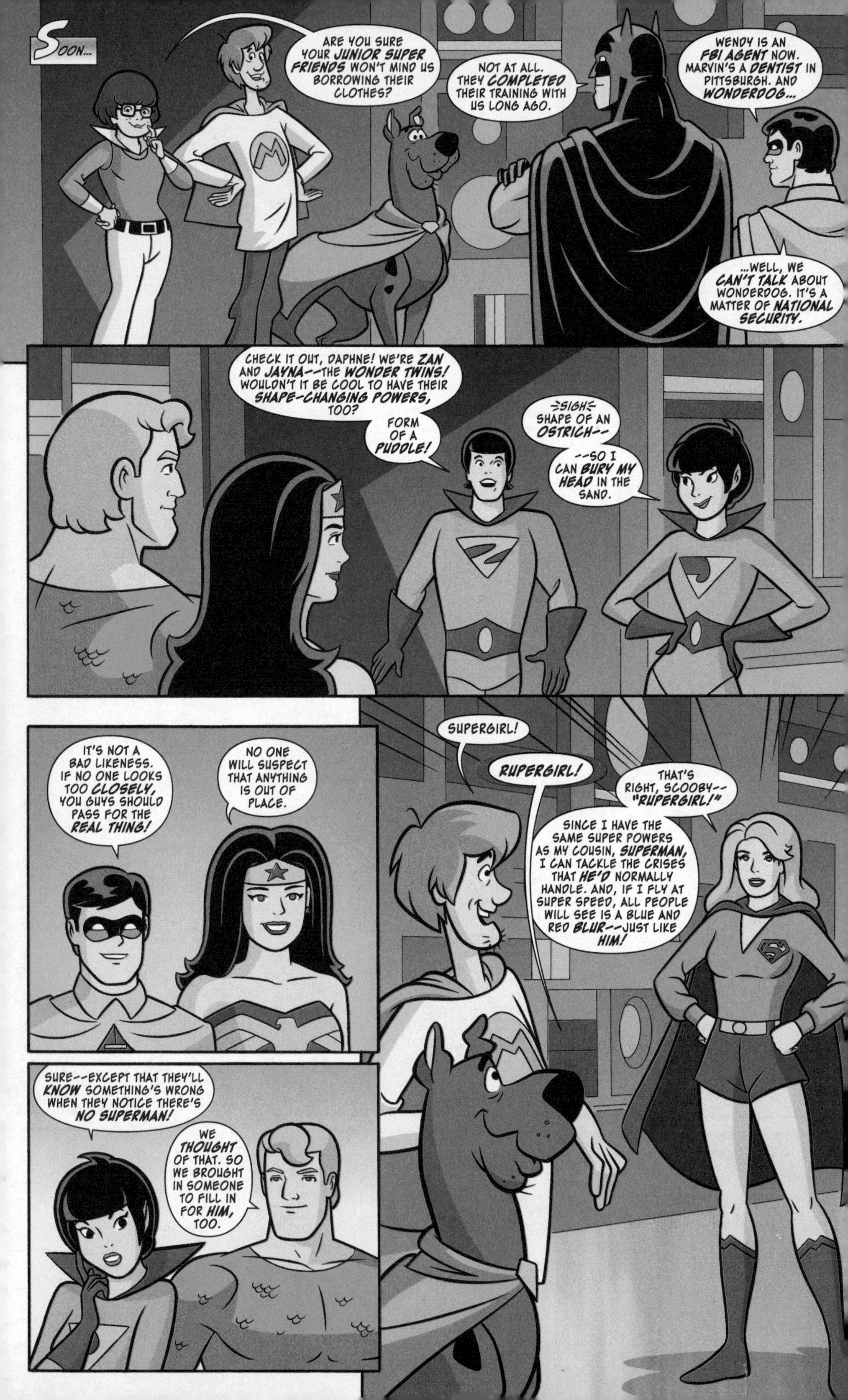
SOON...
ARE YOU SURE YOUR JUNIOR SUPER FRIENDS WON'T MIND US BORROWING THEIR CLOTHES?
NOT AT ALL. THEY COMPLETED THEIR TRAINING WITH US LONG AGO.
WENDY IS AN FBI AGENT NOW. MARVIN'S A DENTIST IN PITTSBURGH. AND WONDERDOG...
...WELL, WE CAN'T TALK ABOUT WONDERDOG. IT'S A MATTER OF NATIONAL SECURITY.
CHECK IT OUT, DAPHNE! WE'RE ZAN AND JAYNA--THE WONDER TWINS! WOULDN'T IT BE COOL TO HAVE THEIR SHAPE-CHANGING POWERS, TOO?
FORM OF A PUDDLE!
SIGH SHAPE OF AN OSTRICH--
--SO I CAN BURY MY HEAD IN THE SAND.
IT'S NOT A BAD LIKENESS. IF NO ONE LOOKS TOO CLOSELY, YOU GUYS SHOULD PASS FOR THE REAL THING!
NO ONE WILL SUSPECT THAT ANYTHING IS OUT OF PLACE.
SURE--EXCEPT THAT THEY'LL KNOW SOMETHING'S WRONG WHEN THEY NOTICE THERE'S NO SUPERMAN!
WE THOUGHT OF THAT. SO WE BROUGHT IN SOMEONE TO FILL IN FOR HIM, TOO.
SUPERGIRL!
RUPERGIRL!
THAT'S RIGHT, SCOOBY--"RUPERGIRL!"
SINCE I HAVE THE SAME SUPER POWERS AS MY COUSIN, SUPERMAN, I CAN TACKLE THE CRISES THAT HE'D NORMALLY HANDLE. AND, IF I FLY AT SUPER SPEED, ALL PEOPLE WILL SEE IS A BLUE AND RED BLUR--JUST LIKE HIM!

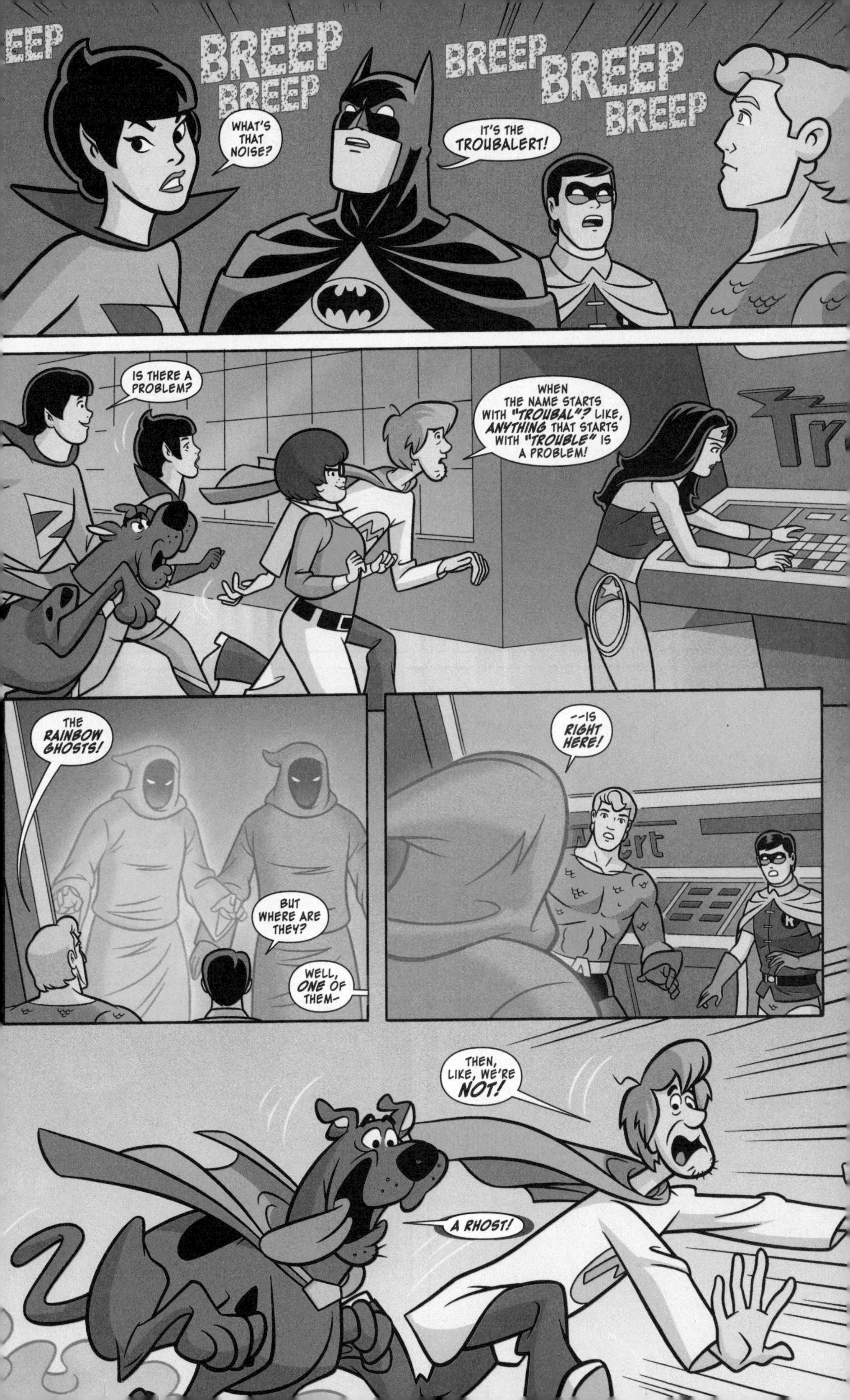
EEP
BREEP
BREEP
WHAT'S THAT NOISE?
BREEP BREEP
BREEP
IT'S THE TROUBALERT!
IS THERE A PROBLEM?
WHEN THE NAME STARTS WITH "TROUBAL"? LIKE, ANYTHING THAT STARTS WITH "TROUBLE" IS A PROBLEM!
THE RAINBOW GHOSTS!
BUT WHERE ARE THEY?
WELL, ONE OF THEM-
--IS RIGHT HERE!
THEN, LIKE, WE'RE NOT!
A RHOST!

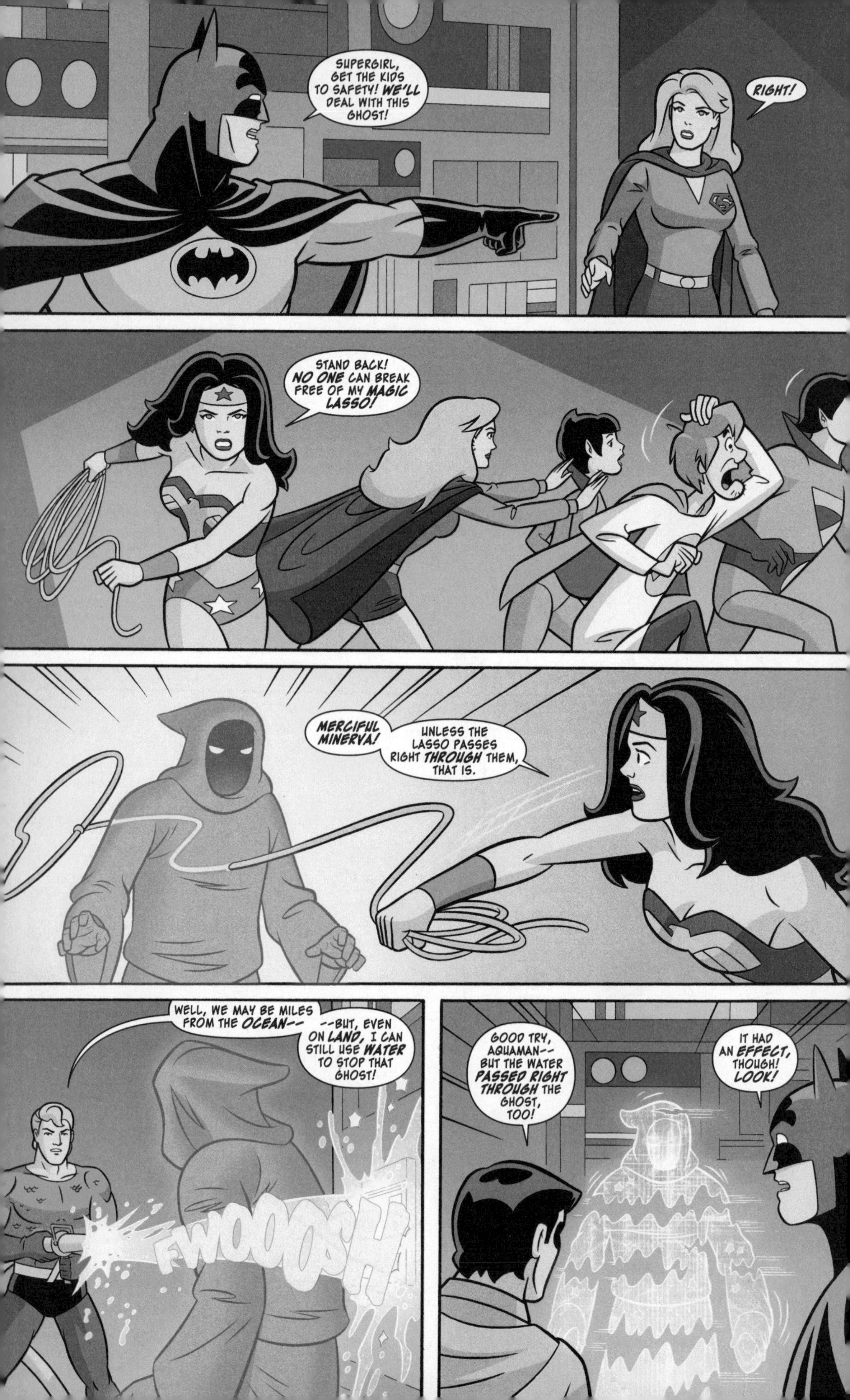
SUPERGIRL, GET THE KIDS TO SAFETY! WE'LL DEAL WITH THIS GHOST!
RIGHT!
STAND BACK! NO ONE CAN BREAK FREE OF MY MAGIC LASSO!
MERCIFUL MINERVA!
UNLESS THE LASSO PASSES RIGHT THROUGH THEM, THAT IS.
WELL, WE MAY BE MILES FROM THE OCEAN--
--BUT, EVEN ON LAND, I CAN STILL USE WATER TO STOP THAT GHOST!
FWOOOSH!
GOOD TRY, AQUAMAN--BUT THE WATER PASSED RIGHT THROUGH THE GHOST, TOO!
IT HAD AN EFFECT, THOUGH! LOOK!

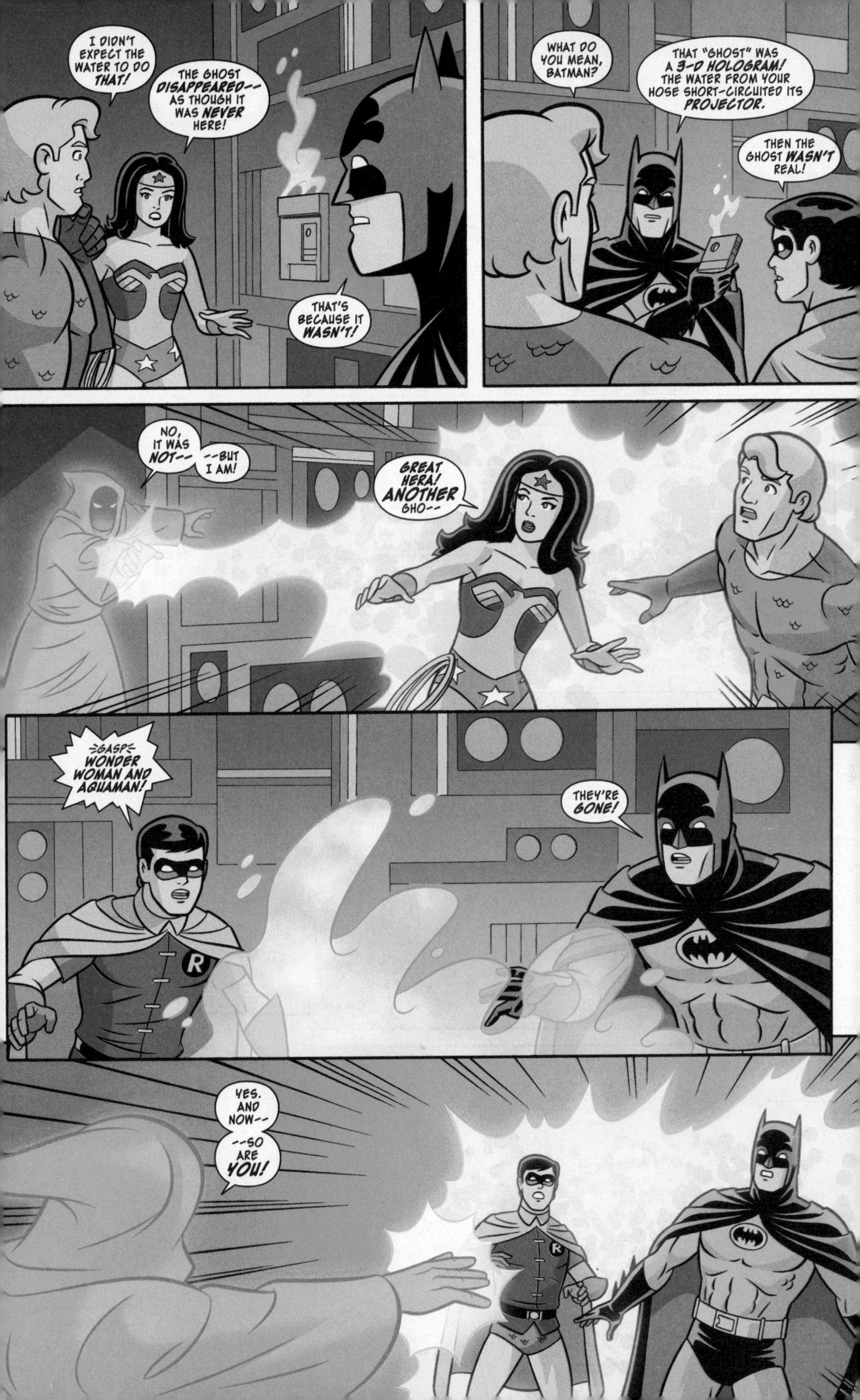
I DIDN'T EXPECT THE WATER TO DO THAT!
THE GHOST DISAPPEARED-- AS THOUGH IT WAS NEVER HERE!
THAT'S BECAUSE IT WASN'T!
WHAT DO YOU MEAN, BATMAN?
THAT "GHOST" WAS A 3-D HOLOGRAM! THE WATER FROM YOUR HOSE SHORT-CIRCUITED ITS PROJECTOR.
THEN THE GHOST WASN'T REAL!
NO, IT WAS NOT--
--BUT I AM!
GREAT HERA! ANOTHER GHO--
GASP WONDER WOMAN AND AQUAMAN!
THEY'RE GONE!
YES. AND NOW--
--SO ARE YOU!

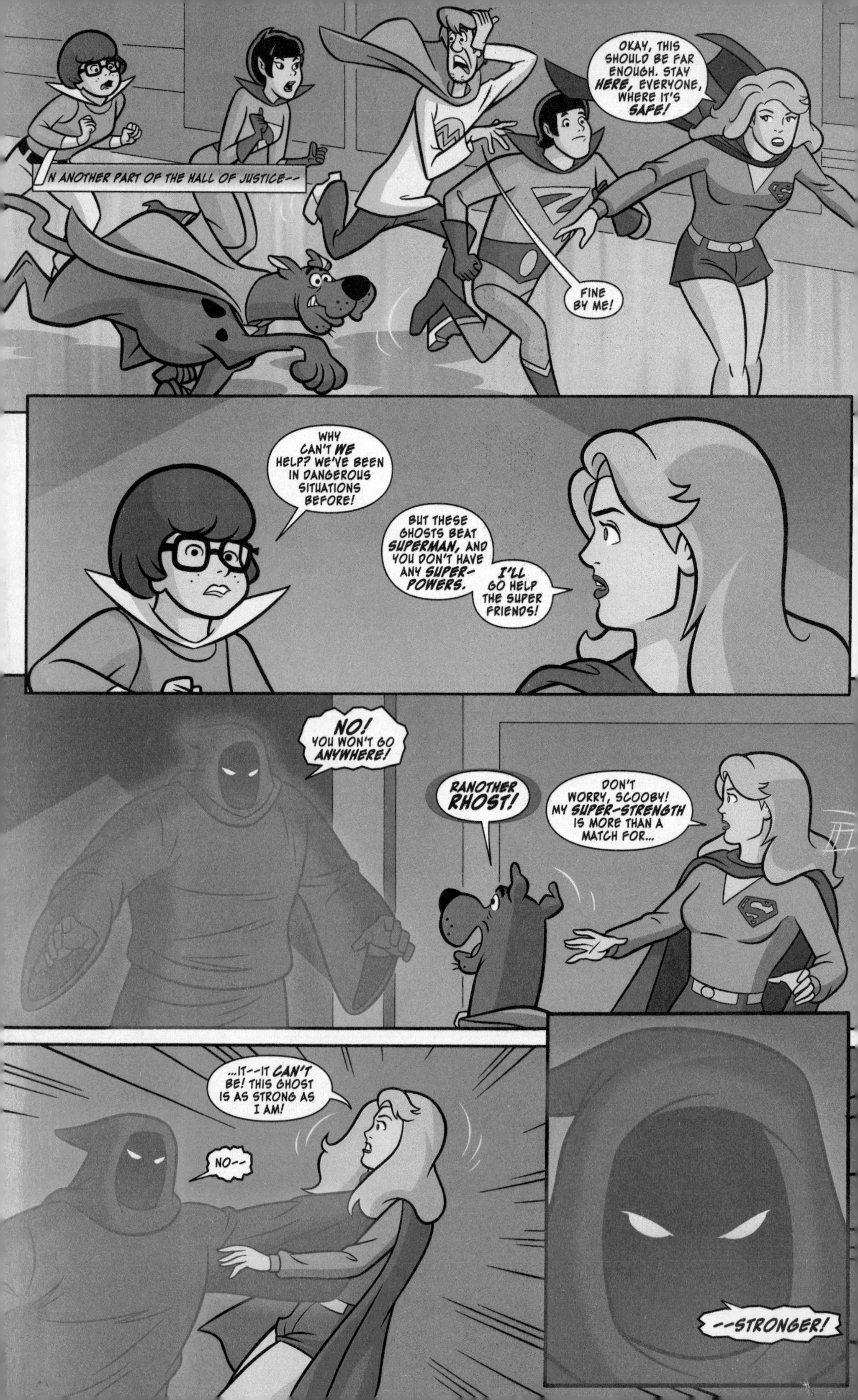

N ANOTHER PART OF THE HALL OF JUSTICE--
OKAY, THIS SHOULD BE FAR ENOUGH. STAY HERE, EVERYONE, WHERE IT'S SAFE!
FINE BY ME!
WHY CAN'T WE HELP? WE'VE BEEN IN DANGEROUS SITUATIONS BEFORE!
BUT THESE GHOSTS BEAT SUPERMAN, AND YOU DON'T HAVE ANY SUPER-POWERS.
I'LL GO HELP THE SUPER FRIENDS!
NO! YOU WON'T GO ANYWHERE!
RANOTHER RHOST!
DON'T WORRY, SCOOBY! MY SUPER-STRENGTH IS MORE THAN A MATCH FOR...
...IT--IT CAN'T BE! THIS GHOST IS AS STRONG AS I AM!
NO--
--STRONGER!

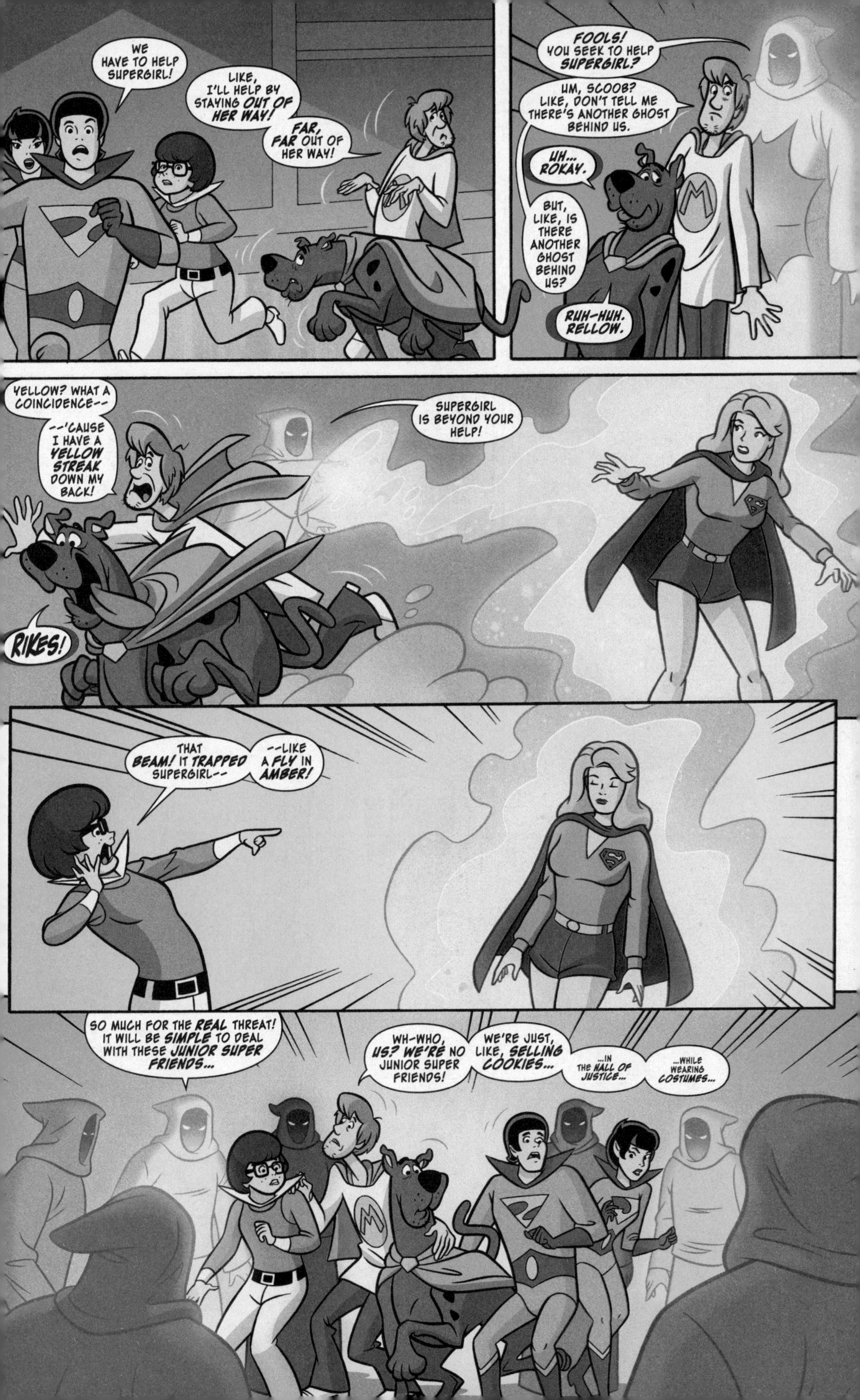
WE HAVE TO HELP SUPERGIRL!
LIKE, I'LL HELP BY STAYING OUT OF HER WAY!
FAR, FAR OUT OF HER WAY!
FOOLS! YOU SEEK TO HELP SUPERGIRL?
UM, SCOOB? LIKE, DON'T TELL ME THERE'S ANOTHER GHOST BEHIND US.
UH... ROKAY.
BUT, LIKE, IS THERE ANOTHER GHOST BEHIND US?
RUH-HUH. RELLOW.
YELLOW? WHAT A COINCIDENCE--
--'CAUSE I HAVE A YELLOW STREAK DOWN MY BACK!
SUPERGIRL IS BEYOND YOUR HELP!
RIKES!
THAT BEAM! IT TRAPPED SUPERGIRL--
--LIKE A FLY IN AMBER!
SO MUCH FOR THE REAL THREAT! IT WILL BE SIMPLE TO DEAL WITH THESE JUNIOR SUPER FRIENDS...
WH-WHO, US? WE'RE NO JUNIOR SUPER FRIENDS!
WE'RE JUST, LIKE, SELLING COOKIES...
...IN THE HALL OF JUSTICE...
...WHILE WEARING COSTUMES...

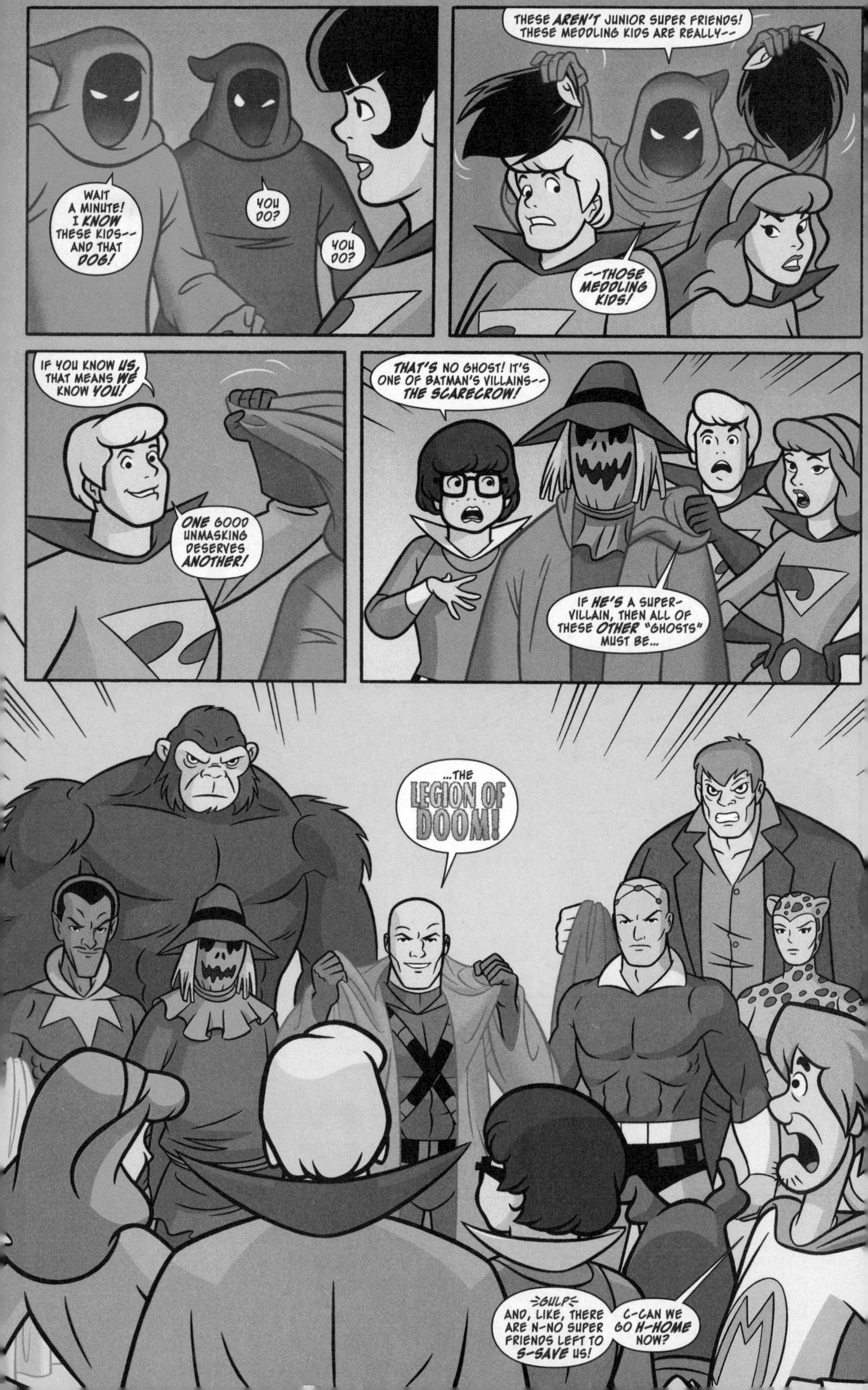

WAIT A MINUTE! I KNOW THESE KIDS-- AND THAT DOG!
YOU DO?
YOU DO?
THESE AREN'T JUNIOR SUPER FRIENDS! THESE MEDDLING KIDS ARE REALLY--
--THOSE MEDDLING KIDS!
IF YOU KNOW US, THAT MEANS WE KNOW YOU!
ONE GOOD UNMASKING DESERVES ANOTHER!
THAT'S NO GHOST! IT'S ONE OF BATMAN'S VILLAINS-- THE SCARECROW!
IF HE'S A SUPER-VILLAIN, THEN ALL OF THESE OTHER "GHOSTS" MUST BE...
...THE LEGION OF DOOM!
=GULP= AND, LIKE, THERE ARE N-NO SUPER FRIENDS LEFT TO S-SAVE US!
C-CAN WE GO H-HOME NOW?

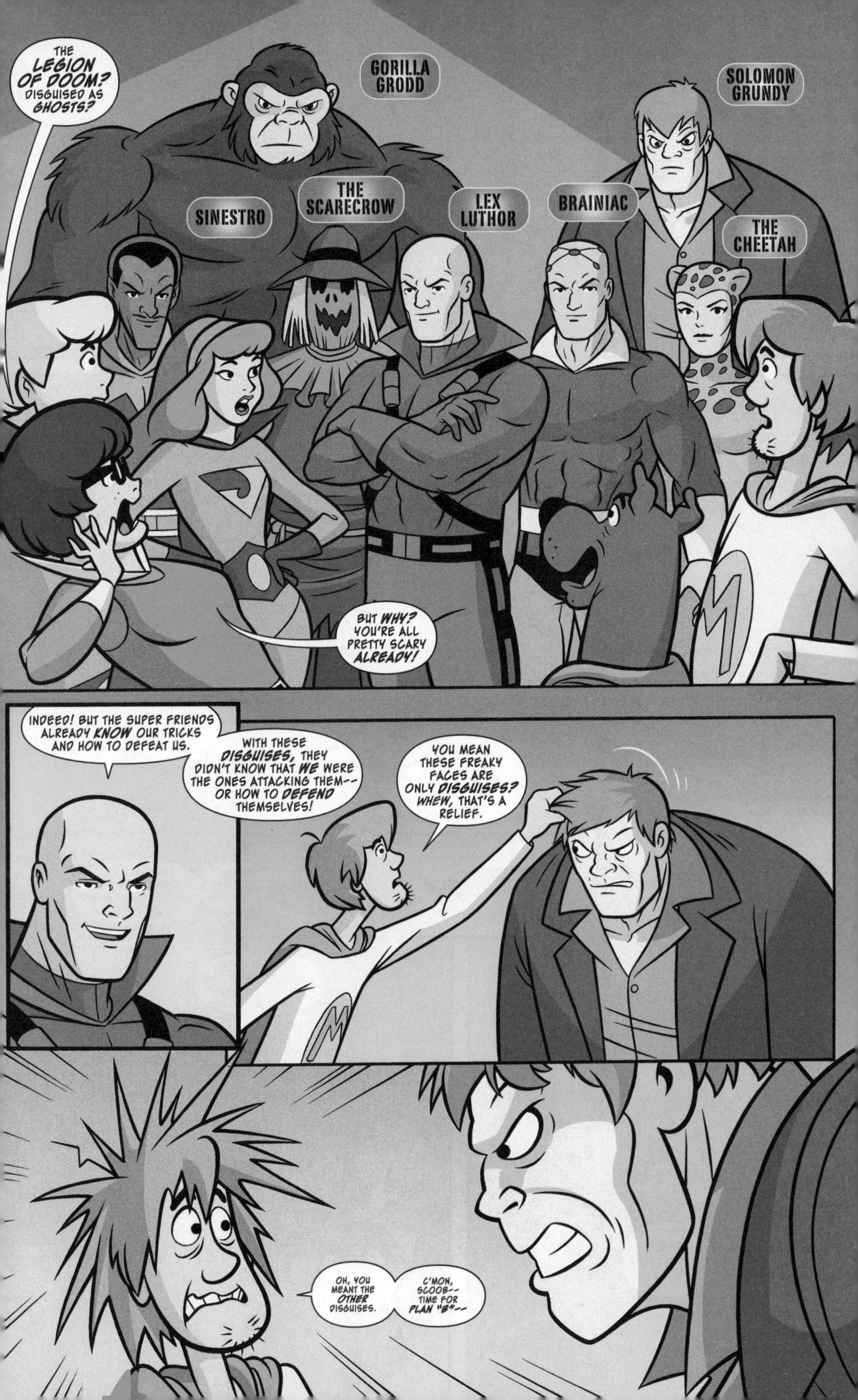
THE LEGION OF DOOM? DISGUISED AS GHOSTS?
GORILLA GRODD
SOLOMON GRUNDY
SINESTRO
THE SCARECROW
LEX LUTHOR
BRAINIAC
THE CHEETAH
BUT WHY? YOU'RE ALL PRETTY SCARY ALREADY!
INDEED! BUT THE SUPER FRIENDS ALREADY KNOW OUR TRICKS AND HOW TO DEFEAT US.
WITH THESE DISGUISES, THEY DIDN'T KNOW THAT WE WERE THE ONES ATTACKING THEM--OR HOW TO DEFEND THEMSELVES!
YOU MEAN THESE FREAKY FACES ARE ONLY DISGUISES? WHEW, THAT'S A RELIEF.
OH, YOU MEANT THE OTHER DISGUISES.
C'MON, SCOOB--TIME FOR PLAN "B"--

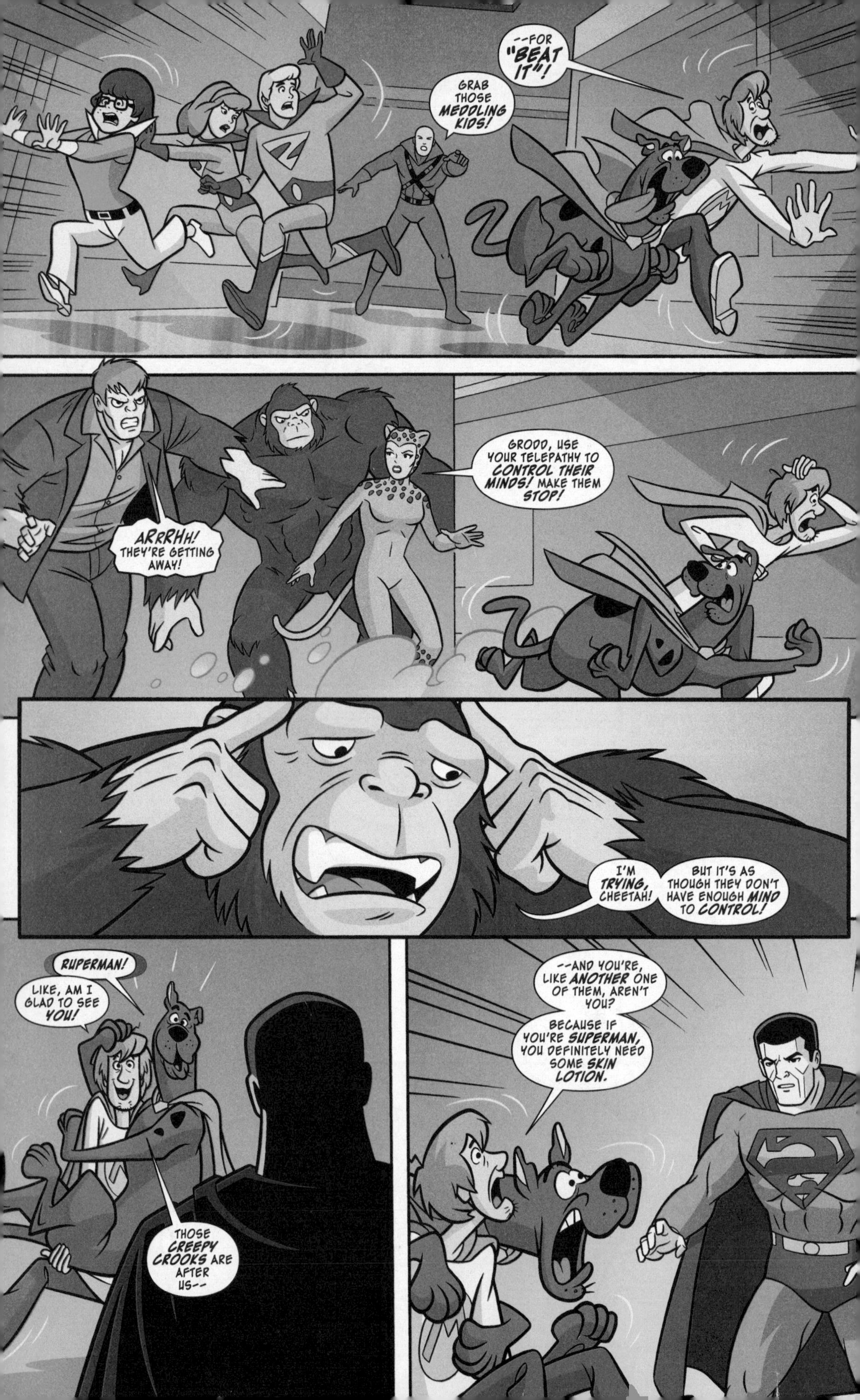
GRAB THOSE MEDDLING KIDS!
--FOR "BEAT IT"!
ARRRHH! THEY'RE GETTING AWAY!
GRODD, USE YOUR TELEPATHY TO CONTROL THEIR MINDS! MAKE THEM STOP!
I'M TRYING, CHEETAH!
BUT IT'S AS THOUGH THEY DON'T HAVE ENOUGH MIND TO CONTROL!
RUPERMAN!
LIKE, AM I GLAD TO SEE YOU!
THOSE CREEPY CROOKS ARE AFTER US--
--AND YOU'RE, LIKE ANOTHER ONE OF THEM, AREN'T YOU?
BECAUSE IF YOU'RE SUPERMAN, YOU DEFINITELY NEED SOME SKIN LOTION.

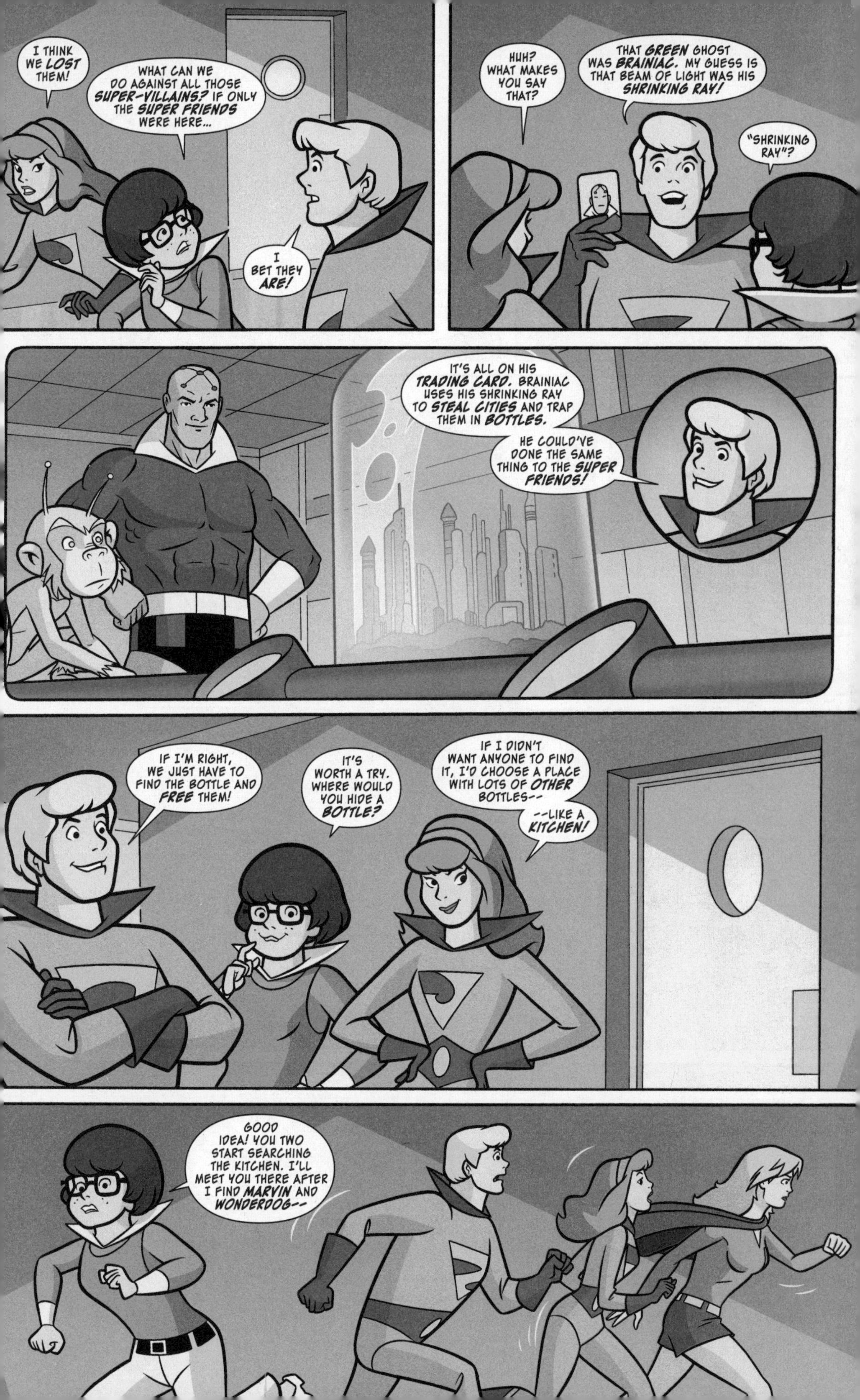
I THINK WE LOST THEM!
WHAT CAN WE DO AGAINST ALL THOSE SUPER-VILLAINS? IF ONLY THE SUPER FRIENDS WERE HERE...
I BET THEY ARE!
HUH? WHAT MAKES YOU SAY THAT?
THAT GREEN GHOST WAS BRAINIAC. MY GUESS IS THAT BEAM OF LIGHT WAS HIS SHRINKING RAY!
"SHRINKING RAY"?
IT'S ALL ON HIS TRADING CARD. BRAINIAC USES HIS SHRINKING RAY TO STEAL CITIES AND TRAP THEM IN BOTTLES.
HE COULD'VE DONE THE SAME THING TO THE SUPER FRIENDS!
IF I'M RIGHT, WE JUST HAVE TO FIND THE BOTTLE AND FREE THEM!
IT'S WORTH A TRY. WHERE WOULD YOU HIDE A BOTTLE?
IF I DIDN'T WANT ANYONE TO FIND IT, I'D CHOOSE A PLACE WITH LOTS OF OTHER BOTTLES--
--LIKE A KITCHEN!
GOOD IDEA! YOU TWO START SEARCHING THE KITCHEN. I'LL MEET YOU THERE AFTER I FIND MARVIN AND WONDERDOG--

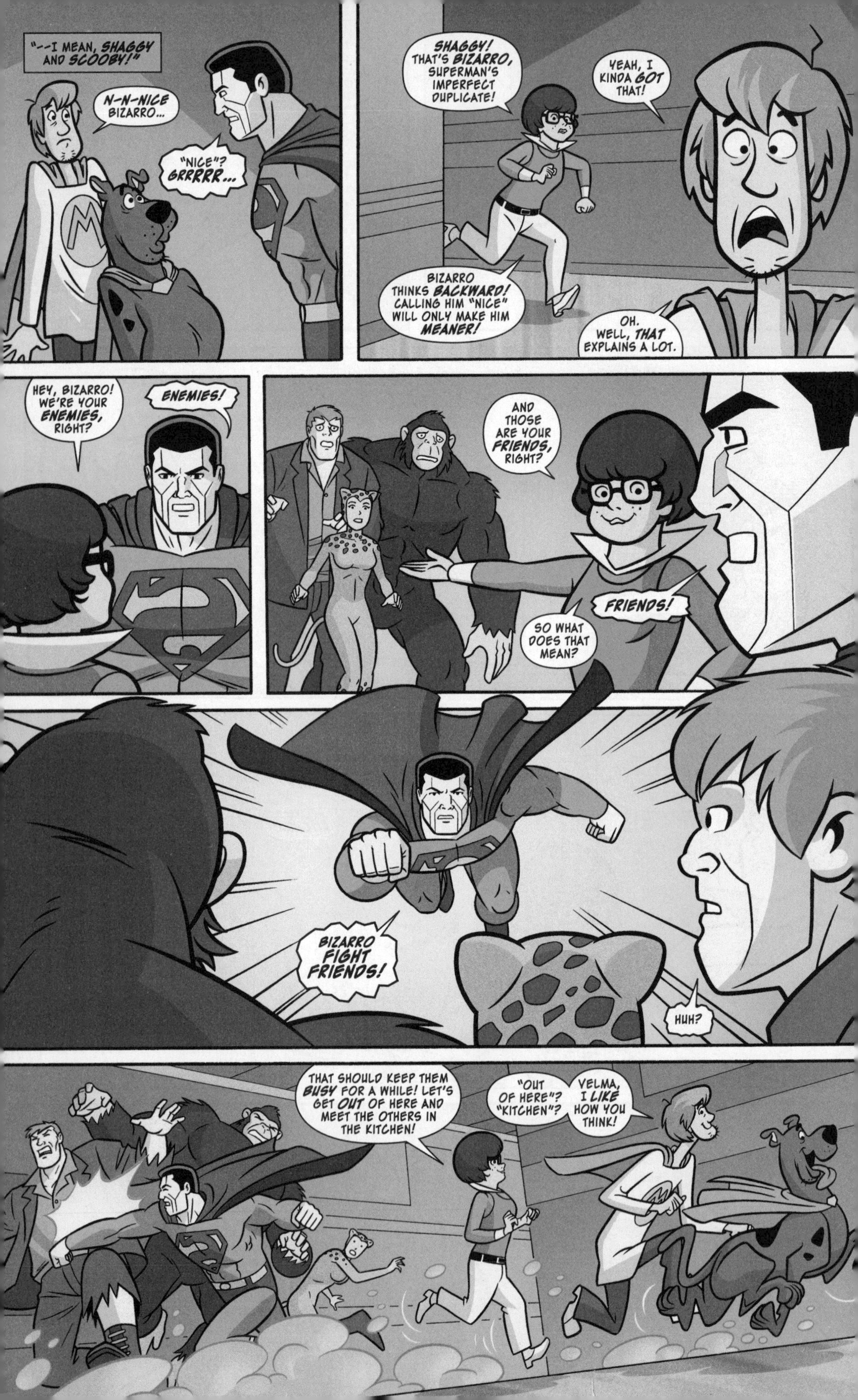
"--I MEAN, SHAGGY AND SCOOBY!"
N-N-NICE BIZARRO...
"NICE"? GRRRRR...
SHAGGY! THAT'S BIZARRO, SUPERMAN'S IMPERFECT DUPLICATE!
YEAH, I KINDA GOT THAT!
BIZARRO THINKS BACKWARD! CALLING HIM "NICE" WILL ONLY MAKE HIM MEANER!
OH. WELL, THAT EXPLAINS A LOT.
HEY, BIZARRO! WE'RE YOUR ENEMIES, RIGHT?
ENEMIES!
AND THOSE ARE YOUR FRIENDS, RIGHT?
FRIENDS!
SO WHAT DOES THAT MEAN?
BIZARRO FIGHT FRIENDS!
HUH?
THAT SHOULD KEEP THEM BUSY FOR A WHILE! LET'S GET OUT OF HERE AND MEET THE OTHERS IN THE KITCHEN!
"OUT OF HERE"? "KITCHEN"?
VELMA, I LIKE HOW YOU THINK!

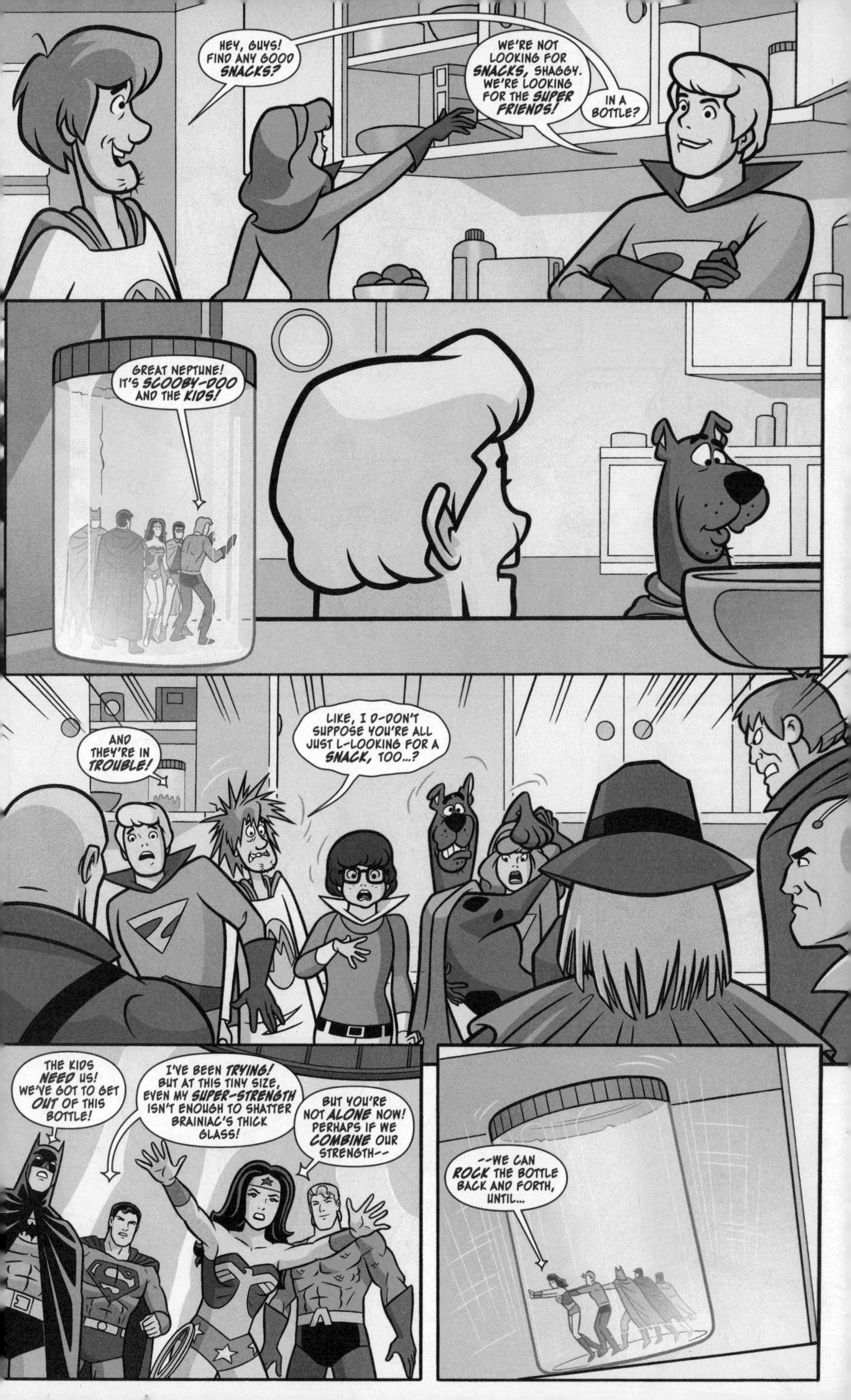
HEY, GUYS! FIND ANY GOOD SNACKS?
WE'RE NOT LOOKING FOR SNACKS, SHAGGY. WE'RE LOOKING FOR THE SUPER FRIENDS!
IN A BOTTLE?
GREAT NEPTUNE! IT'S SCOOBY-DOO AND THE KIDS!
AND THEY'RE IN TROUBLE!
LIKE, I D-DON'T SUPPOSE YOU'RE ALL JUST L-LOOKING FOR A SNACK, TOO...?
THE KIDS NEED US! WE'VE GOT TO GET OUT OF THIS BOTTLE!
I'VE BEEN TRYING! BUT AT THIS TINY SIZE, EVEN MY SUPER-STRENGTH ISN'T ENOUGH TO SHATTER BRAINIAC'S THICK GLASS!
BUT YOU'RE NOT ALONE NOW! PERHAPS IF WE COMBINE OUR STRENGTH--
--WE CAN ROCK THE BOTTLE BACK AND FORTH, UNTIL...

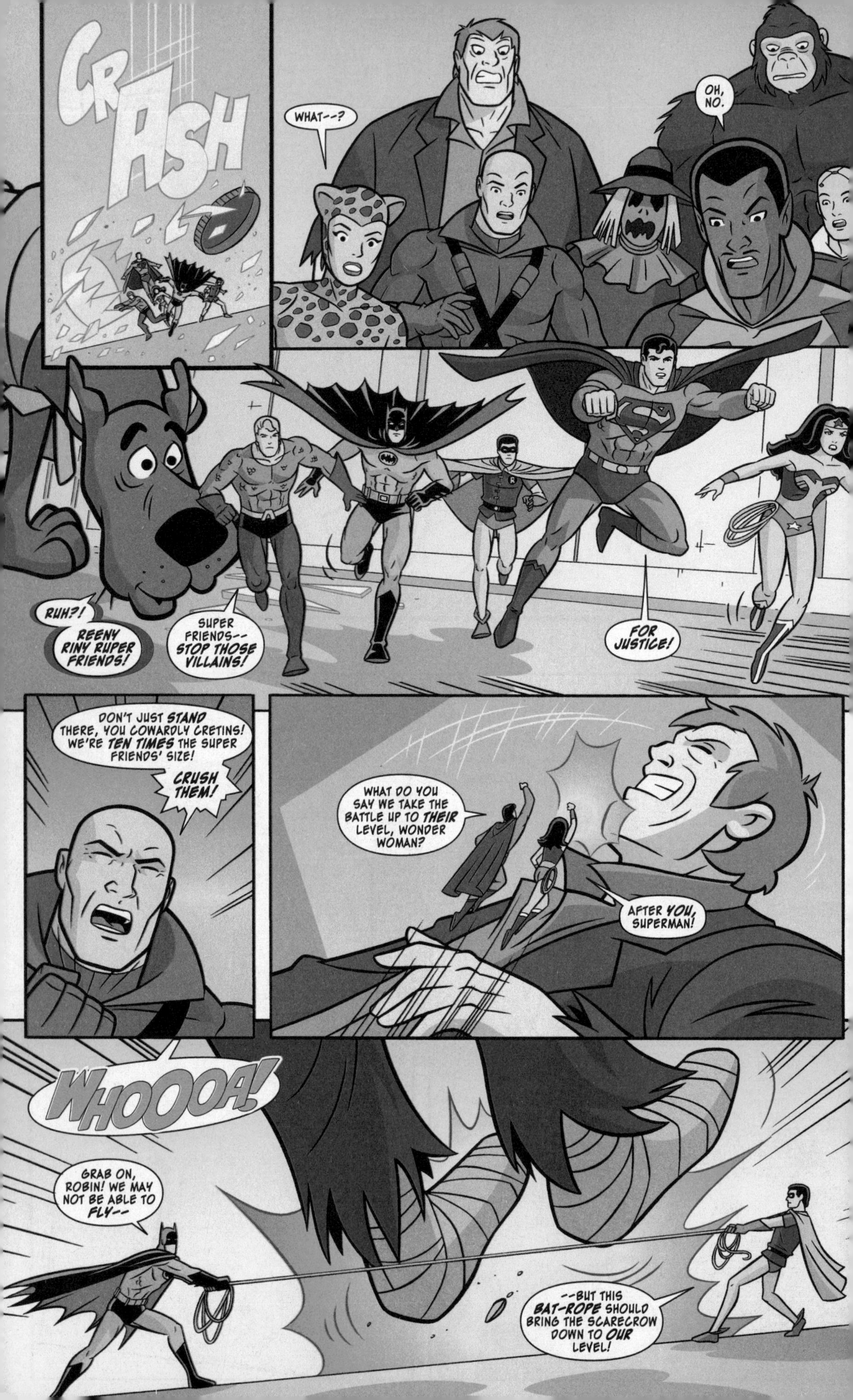
CRASH
WHAT--?
OH, NO.
RUH?! REENY RINY RUPER FRIENDS!
SUPER FRIENDS-- STOP THOSE VILLAINS!
FOR JUSTICE!
DON'T JUST STAND THERE, YOU COWARDLY CRETINS! WE'RE TEN TIMES THE SUPER FRIENDS' SIZE!
CRUSH THEM!
WHAT DO YOU SAY WE TAKE THE BATTLE UP TO THEIR LEVEL, WONDER WOMAN?
AFTER YOU, SUPERMAN!
WHOOOA!
GRAB ON, ROBIN! WE MAY NOT BE ABLE TO FLY--
--BUT THIS BAT-ROPE SHOULD BRING THE SCARECROW DOWN TO OUR LEVEL!

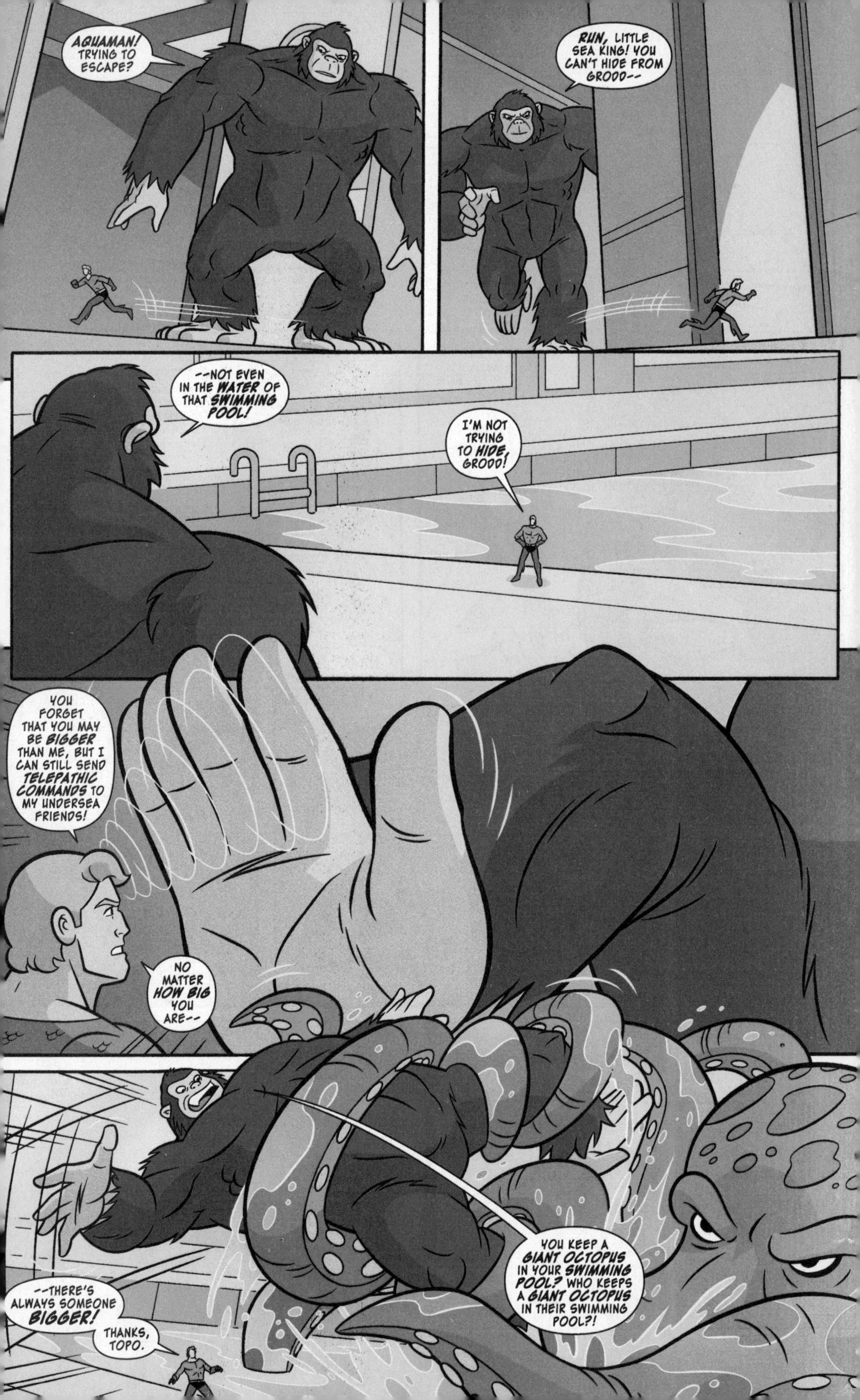
AQUAMAN! TRYING TO ESCAPE?
RUN, LITTLE SEA KING! YOU CAN'T HIDE FROM GRODD--
--NOT EVEN IN THE WATER OF THAT SWIMMING POOL!
I'M NOT TRYING TO HIDE, GRODD!
YOU FORGET THAT YOU MAY BE BIGGER THAN ME, BUT I CAN STILL SEND TELEPATHIC COMMANDS TO MY UNDERSEA FRIENDS!
NO MATTER HOW BIG YOU ARE--
YOU KEEP A GIANT OCTOPUS IN YOUR SWIMMING POOL? WHO KEEPS A GIANT OCTOPUS IN THEIR SWIMMING POOL?!
--THERE'S ALWAYS SOMEONE BIGGER!
THANKS, TOPO.

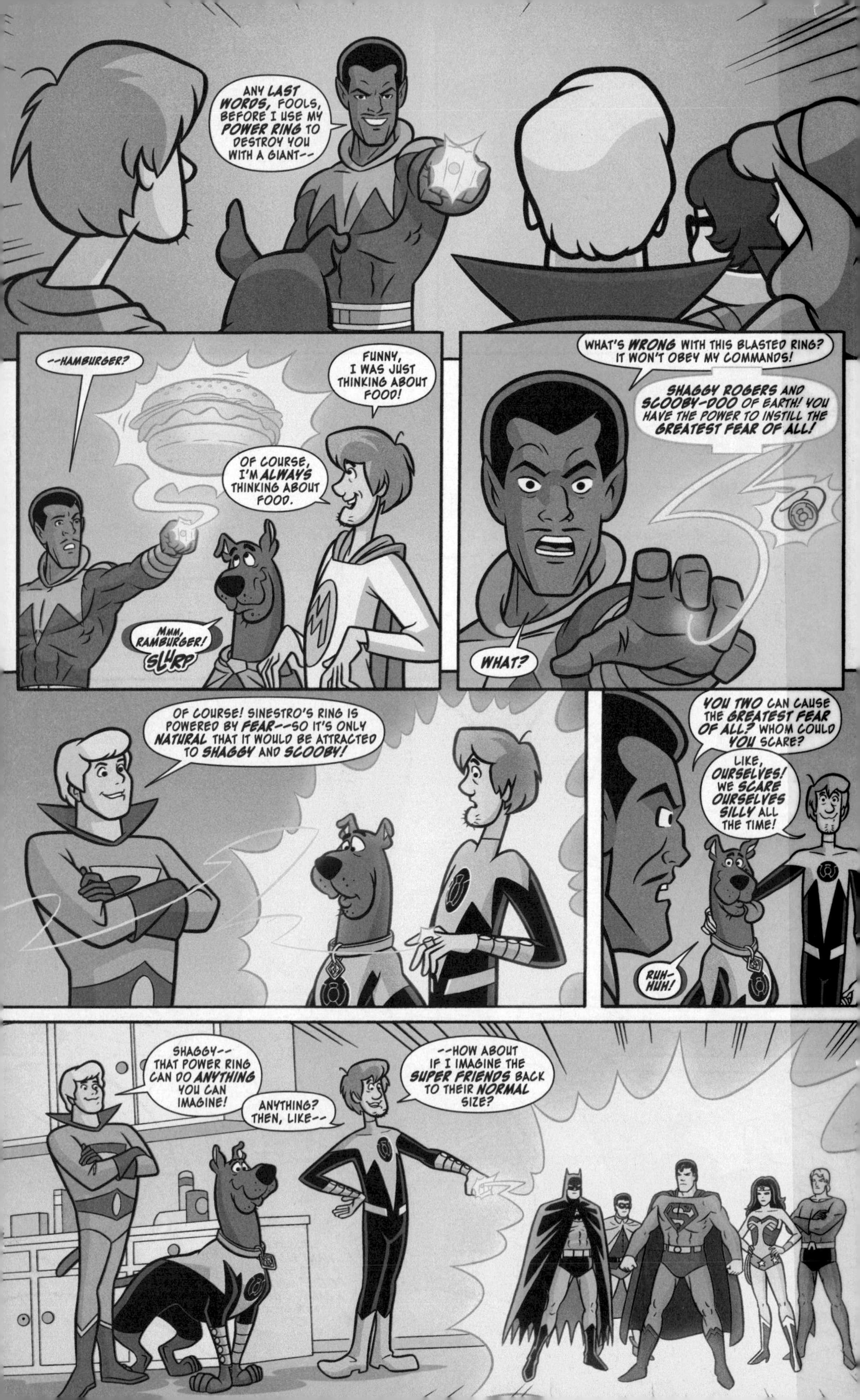
ANY LAST WORDS, FOOLS, BEFORE I USE MY POWER RING TO DESTROY YOU WITH A GIANT--
--HAMBURGER?
FUNNY, I WAS JUST THINKING ABOUT FOOD!
OF COURSE, I'M ALWAYS THINKING ABOUT FOOD.
MMM, RAMBURGER!
SLURP
WHAT'S WRONG WITH THIS BLASTED RING? IT WON'T OBEY MY COMMANDS!
SHAGGY ROGERS AND SCOOBY-DOO OF EARTH! YOU HAVE THE POWER TO INSTILL THE GREATEST FEAR OF ALL!
WHAT?
OF COURSE! SINESTRO'S RING IS POWERED BY FEAR--SO IT'S ONLY NATURAL THAT IT WOULD BE ATTRACTED TO SHAGGY AND SCOOBY!
YOU TWO CAN CAUSE THE GREATEST FEAR OF ALL? WHOM COULD YOU SCARE?
LIKE, OURSELVES! WE SCARE OURSELVES SILLY ALL THE TIME!
RUH-HUH!
SHAGGY--THAT POWER RING CAN DO ANYTHING YOU CAN IMAGINE!
ANYTHING? THEN, LIKE--
--HOW ABOUT IF I IMAGINE THE SUPER FRIENDS BACK TO THEIR NORMAL SIZE?

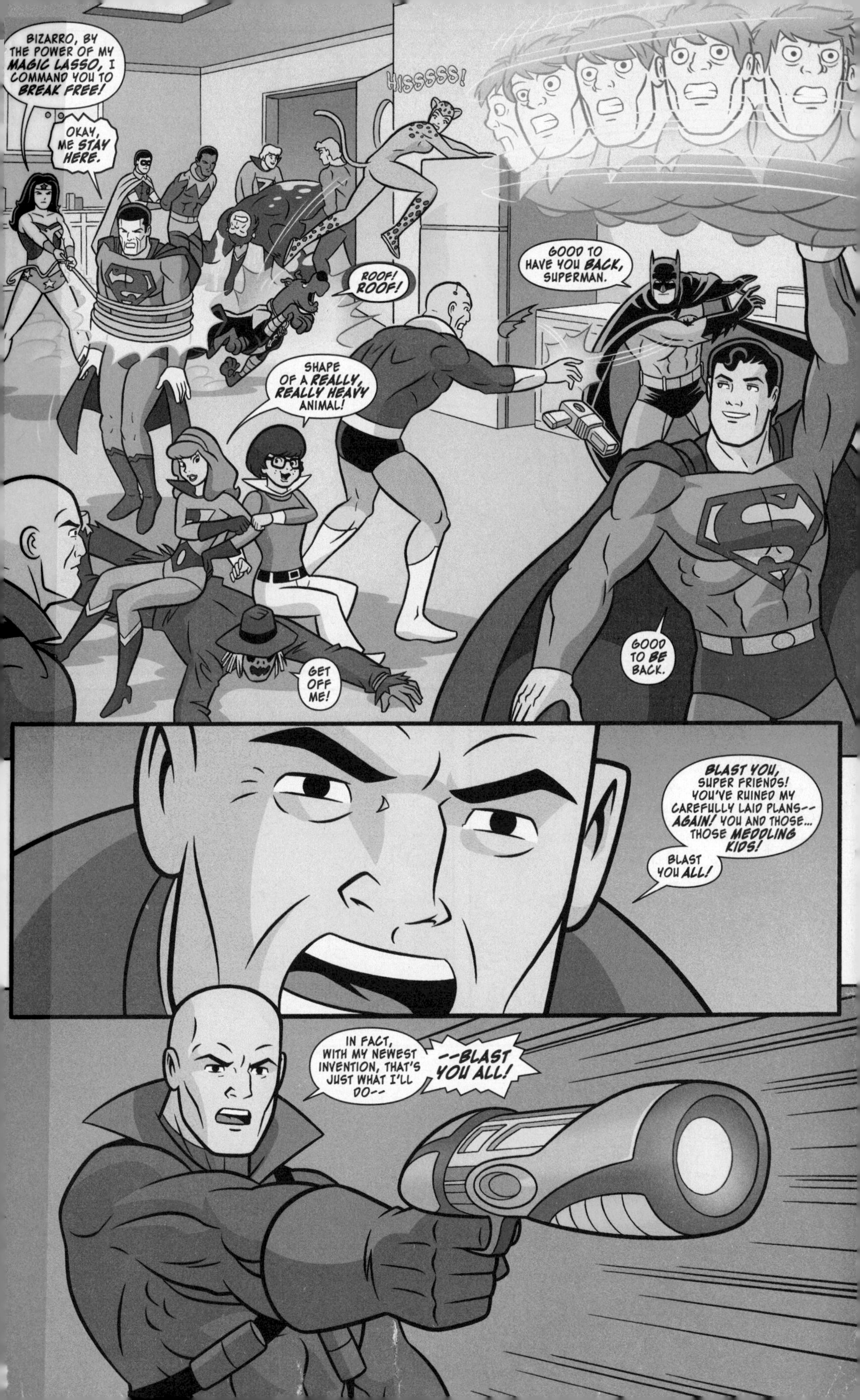
BIZARRO, BY THE POWER OF MY MAGIC LASSO, I COMMAND YOU TO BREAK FREE!
OKAY, ME STAY HERE.
HISSSSS!
ROOF! ROOF!
GOOD TO HAVE YOU BACK, SUPERMAN.
SHAPE OF A REALLY, REALLY HEAVY ANIMAL!
GOOD TO BE BACK.
GET OFF ME!
BLAST YOU, SUPER FRIENDS! YOU'VE RUINED MY CAREFULLY LAID PLANS-- AGAIN! YOU AND THOSE... THOSE MEDDLING KIDS!
BLAST YOU ALL!
IN FACT, WITH MY NEWEST INVENTION, THAT'S JUST WHAT I'LL DO--
--BLAST YOU ALL!

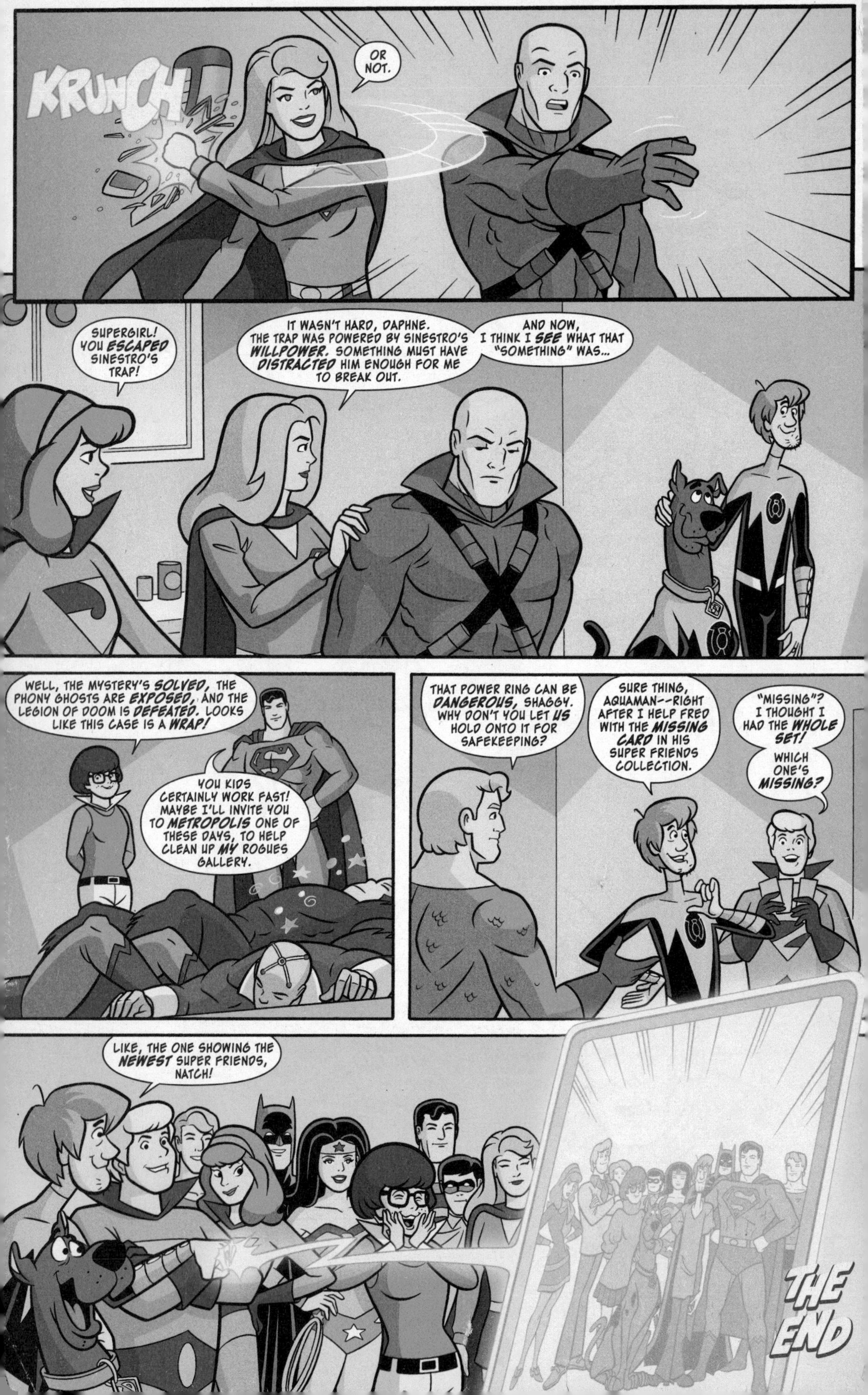
KRUNCH
OR NOT.
SUPERGIRL! YOU ESCAPED SINESTRO'S TRAP!
IT WASN'T HARD, DAPHNE. THE TRAP WAS POWERED BY SINESTRO'S WILLPOWER. SOMETHING MUST HAVE DISTRACTED HIM ENOUGH FOR ME TO BREAK OUT.
AND NOW, I THINK I SEE WHAT THAT "SOMETHING" WAS...
WELL, THE MYSTERY'S SOLVED, THE PHONY GHOSTS ARE EXPOSED, AND THE LEGION OF DOOM IS DEFEATED. LOOKS LIKE THIS CASE IS A WRAP!
YOU KIDS CERTAINLY WORK FAST! MAYBE I'LL INVITE YOU TO METROPOLIS ONE OF THESE DAYS, TO HELP CLEAN UP MY ROGUES GALLERY.
THAT POWER RING CAN BE DANGEROUS, SHAGGY. WHY DON'T YOU LET US HOLD ONTO IT FOR SAFEKEEPING?
SURE THING, AQUAMAN--RIGHT AFTER I HELP FRED WITH THE MISSING CARD IN HIS SUPER FRIENDS COLLECTION.
"MISSING"? I THOUGHT I HAD THE WHOLE SET!
WHICH ONE'S MISSING?
LIKE, THE ONE SHOWING THE NEWEST SUPER FRIENDS, NATCH!
THE END